Books by Jan de Hartog

The Captain   *1966*
The Call of the Sea   *1966*
(INCLUDING *The Lost Sea, The Distant Shore, A Sailor's Life*)
The Hospital   *1964*
The Artist   *1963*
Waters of the New World   *1961*
The Inspector   *1960*
The Spiral Road   *1957*
A Sailor's Life   *1956*
The Little Ark   *1954*
The Distant Shore   *1952*
The Lost Sea   *1951*

Plays

William and Mary   *1963*
The Fourposter   *1951*
Skipper Next to God   *1947*
This Time Tomorrow   *1946*

THE CAPTAIN

THE CAPTAIN

Jan de Hartog

New York *Atheneum* *1966*

Designed by Harry Ford

to Kay and Edgar Seeler of Nantucket Island,

without whose Friendly hospitality

and generous encouragement

this book might never have been written

Note

To those familiar with the Allied Arctic convoys during the Second World War, one episode in this book will present striking similarities to the fate of Convoy PQ 17, which, during its voyage to Murmansk in the summer of 1942, was deserted by its escort and consequently massacred by the German Air Force and U-boat Waffe. The author wishes to state categorically that, although inspired by historical events, this is a work of fiction, and that none of its situations or characters are based on fact, or on the personalities and experiences of real people, alive or dead. Owing to the great number of men involved in the Arctic convoys and the exceptional aspects of that service, some similarities between fact and fiction would seem unavoidable. Where these may occur, they are entirely unintentional and accidental.

A passage from the book STEADY AS YOU GO *is quoted by the kind permission of the author, Bartimeus.*

The stanza on page 389 is quoted from the poem "To an Old Song" by William Edward Hartpole Lecky.

THE CAPTAIN

CHAPTER ONE

I

I found both letters waiting for me among my mail when I came home from Valparaiso, Chile. We had towed there, in four sections, a set of lock gates for a new port the Chilean government was building. It had been a large convoy that had received a lot of publicity even in Holland, where people are blasé when it comes to mammoth towing projects. A fleet of twelve oceangoing tugs had been involved, and I had been convoy commander.

Maybe I owed it to this lofty position, but for once the owners let my tug come home direct, without sending it halfway around the globe to pick up a return tow for Holland. The rest of the convoy were not so fortunate; apart from mine, only two ships were lucky enough to be allowed to turn around and come home without making money for the company on the way. Our last port of call was Punta Arenas in the Straits of Magellan, from where we crossed direct to Rotterdam.

There was quite a lot of mail waiting for me when finally I got to my desk in what my wife calls my "study."

Of course, it isn't; it's the family's general rumpus room when I'm gone, and as I'm gone most of the time, to call it my study is part of the permanent underground campaign she wages to coax me into early retirement or the acceptance of a job ashore. I did not get to my desk immediately; after I had managed to get off the ship, through the customs and out of an invitation for dinner with the owners, there were the rituals of reunion at home: the presents for everybody including the dog, the supper which sent both my wife and my daughter into flusters because something failed to rise, and the "serious" conversation with my son, aged seventeen, about girls.

Then slides were shown of their week at the seaside and of the litter of puppies the dog had had since I left; finally, after everybody else had gone to bed and we had had our private glass of homecoming wine, there was the always surprisingly shy and youthful and passionate love. During its serenely radiant aftermath, an artless, casual voice on my shoulder whispered how glorious it would be once I stayed home for good.

So it was not until the next morning that I finally slit open the first letter of the stack on my desk: the announcement of yet another child born to Heini Rabenschnabel and spouse. The announcement showed a coy drawing of a babe in a mangerlike cradle surrounded by a sunburst, which provoked the irreverent thought that Frau Rabenschnabel seemed to have given birth to Jesus; the legend read: *Hello there! I arrived at dawn on the twelfth of July, happy and rosy, weighing ten pounds, four and a half ounces, and Mutti and Vati have called me Johanna Teresia Anna Marie Klara, Schlumpsi for short, and I cannot wait to come toddling toward you.* Considering that there were now seven (or was it eight?) little Rabenschnabels waiting to come toddling toward me, I did not take the threat too seriously. The whole thing was vaguely depressing; maybe because, on the envelope, sly Heini had managed to include some publicity for his thriving pastry factory, *Rabenschnabel und Söhne, echte Bamberger Kuchen.* I was sent a wooden box containing twenty pounds of those kuchen every Christmas; even the neighbors had of late markedly lost enthusiasm at the receipt of their yearly share of these Teutonic goodies. Each time I thought the appropriate thoughts: how strange life was that to have fished an oil-covered boy out of the icy waters of the Arctic one morning in antiquity should have resulted in a yearly salvo of cookies and a barrage of birth announcements of overweight German babies.

I had already forgotten about Heini when, seven letters down in the stack, I came across its counterpart. At first I had no idea who could be writing to me from a place called Medicine Hat in Alberta, Canada. Then I opened it.

Dear Captain Harinxma, I am the son of Second Lieutenant Richard Tyler, RCNR, who was killed in action on board your vessel in July 1942. I was five months old when he died, so I have no memory of him; all I know of him is by hearsay, mainly from my mother and my grandparents. Mother remarried soon after, and although my stepfather is a wonderful man who has always treated me as if I were his own son, I could not help wondering at times what my own father had really been like. Now that I am a man (teacher at the high school here) and thinking of marriage myself, I feel more than ever the need to know more about my father. Mother, of course, told me all about his heroism, but he has remained, to me, a strangely insubstantial figure. Everybody talks about how courageous he was, and what a wonderful son and husband and father he was; but nobody has ever been able to convey to me a living human being. There seems to be something missing; as you knew him during his last weeks, I thought you might be able to fill in the blanks. I enclose an International Reply Coupon for fifty cents, which should amply cover return postage, should you wish to reply. Hoping to hear from you, yours sincerely, Richard B. Tyler, Jr.

This letter from the baby whose photograph I had been shown twenty-three years before in the chartroom of the old *Isabel Kwel* disturbed me deeply. During the past quarter-century I had often considered writing to Dick Tyler's son off my own bat, only to conclude that I could not do so; now the hour of reckoning had finally come. What should I do? Did I have the right to burden a young mind with the dark and intricate truth of a tormented man's Calvary? Then I realized that "the young man" was older now than his father had been when he died. If anyone should be able to understand Dick Tyler, aged twenty-two, it was Dick Tyler, Jr., aged twenty-four.

I had to think it over. The house was too noisy for anyone to think straight; the only way that I could collect my thoughts was to take out the rowboat to go fishing, as we called it. I never actually fished, I didn't even have a hook to my line; it was just a device to secure peace for an hour or so in the early morning. This was afternoon, so I had to refuse my son, and then I had to refuse the dog; under the pressure of their gloom as they stood staring after me, I turned about and took them both along.

It was the dog who undermined my resolve; I had to take young Martinus because of her. Apart from being fond of dogs in general, I was particularly partial to this one; she was the offspring of the ship's dog of the old *Isabel Kwel*, four generations removed. Four generations of dogs, that was how long ago it was, I thought as I cast off. Antiquity indeed to the seventeen-year-old at the helm.

I looked at him as I rowed. He barely knew me and I

barely knew him, yet there was a bond between us that no words could articulate. It spoke in every gesture, every look, every grin, every silence. Dick Tyler would have made a wonderful father, much better probably than I. What a waste—the lunacy of war.

I did not get the chance to come to a decision that afternoon. Young Martinus and I got to talking, and he told me all about *his* decision, which had sprung up, matured and taken wing while I was gone: he wanted to be a pilot. No, no, not a river pilot, a flyer. What did I think would be the best way for him to go about this: via the Air Force or the training school for commercial pilots of KLM?

While telling him why I favored KLM, I somehow decided to write Dick Tyler's son the truth. It would be quite an undertaking. In order to make him discern the truth behind the distressing facts of his father's last weeks, I would have to tell him a lot about myself. There was no hope of beginning such a project of soul-searching and self-articulation at home; it would have to wait until I was back at sea. I left myself no loophole by acknowledging his letter the following day and promising the full story within the next few months.

My next assignment was Bhatpara on the Hoogly River: a convoy of six tugboats, towing a floating drydock the size of the United Nations building across fifteen thousand miles of open water around the Cape of Good Hope. The maximum speed of the convoy would be three knots, which added up to an ETA of three months after departure. I started writing on the second day out.

2

In the old days, there would have been no question of
the captain of an oceangoing tugboat writing anything
during a voyage except hurried notes in telegraphese in
the ship's log.

Before the war, even the largest tugs carried only a
captain and one mate, who alternated on the bridge, four
hours on, four hours off; now I carry two mates and two
apprentices. I take only one watch every twenty-four
hours; even this is considered overzealous by my staff,
although they are worldly-wise enough not to tell me so
to my face. Social improvements have come so fast since
the war that I am an old-timer at the age of fifty-three;
to have served under pre-war conditions on those spartan
ships makes me a dodo in the eyes of the young, but a
heroic dodo. I know what they are saying about me:
"They don't make 'em like that any more," a compliment
but for the tacit implication, "and they don't need to,
either."

I suppose I had to become a sardonic, tough young
bastard for the sake of mere survival when I was let loose
on the world at the age of eighteen. It was the year 1931,
and it seemed as if I had all the cards stacked against me.
The Great Depression was at its deepest, three quarters
of the Dutch merchant fleet were laid up; to each vessel
in active service, three full complements of officers were
available; even the most modest freighter in those days
counted among its staff several first officers and chief
engineers who served as third and fourth, some even as
apprentices, just to keep from being laid off. So, when I

came out of Naval College with my third officer's ticket in my pocket, there was no hope of finding a post as a mate's apprentice. All I could hope for, if I was lucky, was a job as a messroom boy, cook's assistant or stoker on board any freighter that might be going.

It was the commander of the Naval College himself who broke the news. He was typical of the school, hidebound, tradition-ridden and as remote from the reality of the world as a monk. Yet he was a decent man and, for some reason, he seemed to be concerned about me. Maybe it was my background that appealed to a romantic streak in his character: my father had been chief officer of a large freighter of the Rotterdam-Lloyd Line when he died. Occasionally their ships were used to transport Moslem pilgrims from the Dutch East Indies to Jidda, the harbor of Mecca on the Red Sea; on one of those hadji trips, as they were known, the overcrowded ship had been struck by an epidemic of the plague and he had fallen victim to it. I had barely known him; I was three years old when it happened. My mother, who had to survive on a small pension, set her mind on turning me into a worthy replacement for her late hero. It was decided that I was to become a sailor even before I knew what the word meant. She worked all her life at grueling, degrading jobs, without even the most humble luxuries that would have lent some grace to her existence, only to see me through Naval College. Her pride and single-mindedness in making her son into a ship's officer must have looked touching to people like the commander; I suppose I must have been the only one in a position to know that her determination gradually became an obsession, almost a form of insanity. I loved her dearly, but to me she was not a normal human being. But then, maybe, no mother is, to her own son.

The commander, when he told me in his office on that

last day of school that all I could hope for was a menial position on board some tramp freighter, was aware of what this would mean to my mother. The standard pep talk—that times were sure to change, and that to serve as a mess boy would enable me at least to collect sea days toward my second officer's ticket—was sure to fall on deaf ears as far as she was concerned. While he was telling me all this, I sat there wondering what the real reason was for his calling me in, and then he told me. There was a chance for me to ship out as a mate's apprentice, but not on a freighter—on an oceangoing tugboat. He happened to know that there was one such post available and he was sure that he could arrange for me to be accepted for it. I began to thank him profusely because I assumed that this was what he was after; he remained oddly unaffected by my gratitude, it even seemed to embarrass him. Then he told me that before I took on this position I had to realize one thing clearly: once I decided to throw in my lot with the oceangoing tugboat business, it was a decision for life. I could not hope to move back from deep-sea towing into the Merchant Marine, not as an officer, for although this was highly unfair and a thorn in the side of everyone in Holland who cared about the sea and ships, the law was that sea days acquired on oceangoing tugboats were not valid for the examinations for deck officer in the Merchant Marine.

It was the first time I had heard about this law; at that moment, its full implication did not penetrate to me. I remember his telling me that the law had been the result of political lobbying some ten years before, when shipping had been booming and companies had vied with one another trying to buy deck officers and engine-room personnel away from the oceangoing tugboat companies, as obviously they were highly experienced and versatile sailors. Of the two deep-sea towing firms then in existence, one had countered the wooing away of its personnel by increasing its salaries, whereas the other, older and more experienced, had managed to get this dirty law passed, which chained oceangoing tugboat officers to the deep-sea towing business for life and thus put them at the mercy of one company, for of the two large firms only the more experienced one had survived: Kwel's International Tugboat Company. The commander felt it his duty to warn me that it was an "old-fashioned company" that liked to "keep its people in their places."

As I said, much of this did not register at the time. Only later did I realize that, while he had obviously felt he should acquaint me with the opportunity of shipping out as a mate's apprentice, the commander had tried to warn me not to accept the post unless I felt that it would be too hard on my mother for me to sail as a messroom boy, even though any reasonable person would realize that it was only temporary: the Depression could not last forever.

So I became mate's apprentice to Captain Bosman of the oceangoing tugboat *Cornelia Kwel*, an undistinguished master of an undistinguished ship. To me, however, preconditioned as I was by the national legend that labeled the deep-sea towing business "Holland's Glory," he embodied my boyhood dreams. The Dutch had a virtual monopoly on deep-sea towing; the individual captains were nationally famous men, their names known to every boy in Holland. All large convoys were covered extensively by the press and followed with great interest by the Dutch; I knew that my mother, for one, would be mightily pleased to see her son join the gallery of national heroes, be it, for the time being, only potentially.

I was lucky that for my first voyage I hit upon a man as unrepresentative of the species as Captain Bosman. He was a pedestrian personality compared with the flamboyant prima donnas that normally commanded Dutch oceangoing tugboats, but he was a man of culture and consideration. He must have been a frustrated teacher, for during that long voyage around the Cape of Good Hope to the Dutch East Indies, crawling along at three miles an hour with a dredge in tow, he stimulated me to go on studying. He unlocked for me the mysteries of navigation, which thus far had remained largely abstract, by making the phases of the celestial ephemeris seem as simple as the works of his alarm clock, which he seemed to prefer to the sacred chronometer. He also gave me useful hints as to behavior once I found myself a captain faced with my first command. He must have taken a fancy to me, or maybe I was just a new and unjaundiced ear into which he could vent his pent-up, peevish disapproval of the theatrical extroverts who were his colleagues. According to him, none of those hams had received any education beyond elementary school, for the examination for the Master's ticket of an oceangoing tugboat consisted mainly of shouting: whoever could yell the commands connected with emergencies the loudest was sure to pass. Of course, half of the explanation was that the majority of them were the sons of skippers of tugboats or dredges or barges, or of the weavers of the primeval willow mats that formed the foundation for Holland's dikes, who lived, an amphibious tribe, in the tidal forest of the delta of the Rhine. Captain Bosman himself was the son of the verger of the largest Calvinist church in Amsterdam, which, compared to those mudlarks, made him a scion of an intellectual aristocracy. He was, I suppose, one of those unfortunate creatures who will forever be unhappy because they consider themselves just a little too good for their jobs; some of his intellectual snobbery, I'm afraid, rubbed off on me.

I am not sure that I have ever managed to free myself from it entirely.

Captain Knol of the *Amanda Kwel*, my next superior, was one of the real heroes of Holland's Glory. After many famous voyages and spectacular salvages, he had entered the ranks of the demigods whose names were household words to the Dutch. He had so far not been honored by having a cigar named after him, as had the legendary Bokke Loppersum, but on the teen-age stock exchange his photograph was at par with that of Captain Koen Parmentier, famous flyer, winner of the Melbourne Race, and worth two of the German Kaiser, exiled in Holland. Photographs of Captain Knol looking stern and determined were occasionally seen in shopwindows to enliven the dreariness of a pyramid of butter or a display of underwear; to be appointed his junior mate was quite an honor.

I cannot adequately describe my disillusion once I became familiar with this august hero. He was no doubt a master craftsman and a stickler for tidiness, but he could barely write, never read a word, not even the newspaper, left all ciphering in connection with navigation to me; his only activity in the solitary splendor of his cabin seemed to be the giving of loud, ringing belches at all hours of day or night, which became more startling to the watch on the bridge as the tow entered the tropics and he took to leaving his portholes open. It was small wonder that he had digestive troubles; everybody on board had. Food on Kwel's International Tugboat Company was little better than fodder. Conditions in general were archaic; officers and crew were housed in medieval discomfort and treated by the company the way a medieval baron would treat his serfs. Nobody talked about "the company"—only about "Mr. Kwel." It was a one-man business, run in a completely tyrannical fashion; as far as Mr. Kwel was concerned, the industrial revolution had never taken place.

I suppose that modern psychology would have a few things to say about it, but the fact remains that after a few years in Mr. Kwel's chain gang I had turned from an undistinguished though pleasant pupil of Amsterdam's Naval College into a tough, sardonic junior mate, as cool as they come, with only one all-consuming passion: a virulent hatred for Mr. Kwel and all he stood for. On the surface, he stood for capitalist exploitation of captive labor; I suppose that in my subconscious, however, he became identified with other things besides: with the fact that I had been groomed for a sailor's life without having been consulted; with the fact that my father, by dying young, had deserted me and left me to the care of a doting but more and more disturbed, lonely woman; with the Depression itself, felt as an injustice by all the young men of my generation, who found themselves faced with its overwhelming odds at the beginning of their careers. In this instance Mr. Kwel even took on the guilt of God.

As I could not discuss any of this with anyone, after I had left Captain Bosman's ship, I took to keeping a diary. This resulted in my delighted discovery of an unsuspected talent; I cannot remember when the idea first occurred to me, but at a given moment I saw clearly what I should do: write a book on the tugboat business to denounce the law on the sea days and the tyrant Mr. Kwel. From that moment on, I had a secret dream: to find a job ashore, a sinecure that would enable me to devote the larger part of my working day to my apostolic writing. I spent hours daydreaming of this, mainly during night watches on the bridge, although I knew full well that for me to leave the sea before I had even become a mate would break my mother's heart.

It remained my futile, secret dream for the next few

years. The emergence of a man called Hitler improved world business and cured the stock market of its lingering malaise by starting the arms race; I got my Master's ticket for oceangoing tugboats, but promotion still seemed far away. I was told via the grapevine that I was in line to be appointed mate to the great Captain Loppersum of the new flagship of the fleet, the *Isabel Kwel*, a veritable dinosaur among tugboats, which was about to be launched after a period of gestation amounting to several years. She had been designed by Mr. Kwel himself and could be described as a floating engine surrounded by fuel tanks, with the crew's and the staff's quarters tucked away in corners as an afterthought; as a result, her action radius exceeded that of any existing tugboat in the world. The fact that she could roam the oceans at will for a virtually unlimited time, combined with her gigantic strength, her water cannons capable of extinguishing full-scale fires at sea, her pumps of sufficient capacity to keep afloat vessels which normally would have had to be abandoned, made her a robber baron's dream ship. The genius of her creator was best expressed, however, in the fact that the state had footed half of the bill for her construction, in exchange for the privilege of welding two sets of trolley rails on her aft deck and cutting two gates in her stern coaming so she could double as a mine layer in time of war. It had been an astute exploitation, on Mr. Kwel's part, of the rising international tension: this way, his argument had been, the state could acquire a full-fledged mine layer at half price and wouldn't even be saddled with the cost of her upkeep until the outbreak of hostilities.

The chance to serve as Captain Loppersum's mate was tempting. He was the unofficial Admiral of the Dutch tugboat fleet, a Friesian of gigantic stature and gargantuan appetites, ideal foil for newspaper cartoonists with his wide-set eyes, high cheekbones and Viking's beard. He was a great sailor and internationally acknowledged as such; I had no idea why I, of all people, should be singled out to be appointed mate in his shadow on board Mr. Kwel's pet tugboat. I asked the chief accountant when I came to collect my wages for the voyage we had just finished; he was pompously reticent, reminded me that there were many rumors without substance in circulation; when I had turned to go, he added, "However, I wouldn't be surprised if it were true. I think I'm justified in saying that Mr. Kwel has had his eye on you for some time."

"Don't be silly," I said, irreverently. "He's never set eyes on me and I've never set eyes on him."

The accountant smiled smugly. "Mr. Kwel has other sources of information, young man, and I'll thank you to remember that the whole thing is speculation anyhow."

Speculation or no, I was indeed appointed first officer on board the *Isabel Kwel* at the end of my next voyage; to turn it down gave me a deep unexpected satisfaction. I turned it down because, in the meantime, something had happened that, although it came as an emotional shock to me, suddenly set me free. While I was at sea, nine thousand miles away, my mother had died, officially of a stroke but in reality because she was simply worn out after a hard, lonely life of ruthless self-sacrifice. I had to put her affairs in order; only while doing so did it dawn on me that there was no need for me to postpone the realization of my secret dream any longer. I found that I had never quite realized to what extent it had been she who had kept me a prisoner on Mr. Kwel's chain gang; now that there was no one left on earth to be fooled with the importance of my seagoing position, I applied for a job ashore. I received an invitation the following day to go and see the Harbor Master of Amsterdam; I went to see him, and when I left his office half an hour later, I had been made "Nautical Adviser to the Chamber of Commerce for Amsterdam Harbor." The title was impressive; in practice, what the job amounted to was skipper of a sight-seeing launch, operated by the city, which took foreign dignitaries on junkets and visiting businessmen for a tour of the harbor. It seemed the ideal sinecure for a budding writer, but the salary was proportionate. Even if I were to live as economically as possible, it was not enough; so, to supplement it, I accepted a secondary job: "winter mate" on the inactive list of Kwel's International Tugboat Company. This meant that I had to be available during the storm season to serve on any salvage tug that might have to turn around for another sortie on coming home from a rescue job. Theoretically, a relief crew was put on in that case to give the permanent one a rest; in practice, the permanent crew always voted to stay on board, even if they had not slept for forty-eight hours, the reason being that crews of salvage tugs shared in the profits should a vessel in distress be picked up. I received ten guilders a month for this; on the strength of that princely sum, I moved into a huge town-operated boardinghouse for blue-collar bachelors called "The Proud Workers' Home." It seemed the ideal impersonal lodging for a man waiting for inspiration, but I was destined never to put pen to paper. Within a week of my moving into this melancholy beehive of lonely men on the dole, I fell in love.

The girl's name was Sophie and she was an assistant librarian attached to the Zoo. I met her in a secondhand bookshop where we were both browsing; I happened to collide with her as I came strolling around a set of bookshelves absent-mindedly, reading Proust. I apologized, incoherent and blushing, for the impact had been most pleasurable. She was rather plump, with a large mouth,

huge eyes and a bosom that no man could possibly over-
look. Her hair was dark and shiny and she wore it in heavy
braids; her voice as she said "Oh! I'm so sorry" was
intriguingly husky. In short: love at first sight.

On board the oceangoing tugboats, my life had been
perforce ascetic; I had, despite my sardonic swagger, remained innocent and inexperienced to an almost embarrassing degree. To an intellectual snob, the sexual escapades
of tugboat crews on distant shores were bovine bangings
in a barnyard; for me, the stopovers had turned out to be
far too short for human courtship, let alone intellectual
wooing.

I proceeded to woo Sophie most intellectually. We went
through endless conversational sessions in the perpetual
dusk of the saurian pavilion in the Zoo, where ultimately,
forced almost by exhaustion, we ended up in an embrace
on an iron bench under the prehistoric gaze of a glassy-
eyed iguana. After that first reckless lunge, I felt suddenly
overcome by a craving for walks; we walked for hours
along the river, watching the barges and the clouds collide
in the mirror of the water, until, again forced by exhaustion, we keeled over in the reeds. After this, I took her to
concerts, where she sat swooning with heaving breast under the thunderous titillations of Stravinsky's "Sacre du
printemps," which sounded to me like a chief engineer
whistling *La Traviata* over the sucking kisses of well-oiled
pistons. We had expensive, minutely proportioned meals
in a café called The Prince of Budapest, where gipsies
who had fled from the Nazis used their violins for the
musical rape of dining Dutch hausfraus. They would
crowd the strapless Sophie so closely with their quavering,
sobbing violins that I felt like spitting into the orifices of
their instruments or sticking my fork among the strings.
It took a long time before she finally fell under the on-

slaught of motionless kisses, endless walks, Stravinsky and the gipsies' fiddles. In retrospect, I feel the deepest admiration for her, for to have a deep-sea tugboat officer of Arabian pretensions and kindergarten experience for a lover without limiting him to one cataclysmic encounter means that a woman must be either truly in love or of a most understanding disposition, the more so as I was certainly not in love with anyone except with the debonair, masterful, impetuous lover I discovered myself to be. Sophie turned out to be the ideal partner for a clumsy, inhibited lout; the moment my lips touched hers, she went totally limp in my arms to a point where I had to take care that I did not try to sneak a kiss in public. Under those conditions, even Leporello would have succumbed to the delusion that he was Don Juan.

But our bliss was short-lived. Under the pretext of wanting to give me a taste of the family life which I had never known, she inveigled me into accompanying her home and meeting her parents. They were a charming, rather overwhelming Jewish couple who, once they got over the shock of their daughter bringing home a goy, smothered me with premature parental love. I was treated to delicious dishes, hand-knitted sweaters, jars of exotic, highly spiced goodies to take with me to The Proud Workers' Home; when Sophie started to talk marriage, I realized that the whole thing had been part of a well-conceived, carefully prepared plot. I responded with a sense of outrage and betrayal; I had never stopped to ask myself whether Sophie was in love with me or just having wonderful fun, as I was; for the sake of expediency, I had vaguely assumed the latter. Now my nonchalance caught up with me, and I suddenly realized that I was in mortal danger. I had not the slightest intention of marrying anybody; if there was one overriding passion in my life, it was for emotional and financial independence. After having spent my days in bondage, first to my mother and later to Mr. Kwel, I was not about to exchange my new-found freedom for another ball and chain, however precious the metal. But my resolve was all in the mind; instead of telling her so and breaking off our relationship then and there, I remained noncommittal whenever matrimony was mentioned, while continuing to stuff myself with the fruit of Paradise. One evening, as I arrived for my weekly helping of home life, I found the parents in a solemn mood. Sophie was sent out to get something from the delicatessen store around the corner; when I offered to go myself, it was obvious that I was upsetting a stratagem. After she had left, her father told me that because of the recent pogroms in Hitler Germany, his wife and he had decided to accept an invitation from his brother to go to the United States. They wanted to take Sophie with them, but she had refused, obviously because of me. They would desist from trying to persuade her further if we could see our way to getting married before they left; otherwise they would have to insist that she go with them. I suddenly felt cornered, trapped; my reaction was so violent that it surprised even me. I don't quite know what I said, but the gist of it was obvious. I left before Sophie came back, on the pretext that I had to think it over.

That night I wrote a long letter which I tore up three times; it ended as a short letter in which I said that I felt times were too uncertain and my own future too insecure to make marriage at this point anything but irresponsible. I strongly advised them to take Sophie with them to the United States. I even managed to make it sound like a sacrifice.

In a sense, it was. I knew I would miss her horribly, but, at the same time, I could not bear the idea that she

would pass up a chance to go to the United States for my
sake, for it would mean another claim upon me, another
chip chiseled away from the newly acquired rock of my
independence. They left and she stayed behind. I did not
see her for a few weeks, then we met again, supposedly
by chance. Like most love affairs among the young, it was
all very messy, full of momentous decisions clumsily
broken, grand gestures ending in a sheepish scratching of
the head. It did not penetrate to me at the time that she
had actually put her life in danger in order to stay near me;
in those days, the German threat was not taken seriously,
at least not by the Dutch. We had remained neutral in the
last war and had culled a neat profit from it. If war were to
break out, we were sure it would be the same way again,
and as to Sophie running any danger should the Germans
invade, it seemed less real as a threat than the danger of
her being struck by lightning. I remember thinking smugly
that her parents fleeing from their imaginary danger might
well be on their way to an appointment in Samarra.

We carried on as before, but marriage was no longer
mentioned between us. In a sense, this studious avoidance
of the subject exerted more pressure than its frequent mention before had done; I might have succumbed after all
if events had not decided our future for us. In September
1939, when Germany invaded Poland, the Dutch Army
and Navy were mobilized. As a "winter mate," I had to
report for wartime duty on tugboats in the naval station
of Den Helder, a harbor in the north of Holland far from
Amsterdam. Before either of us had realized the magnitude
of the calamity in which we were involved, I sank back
on the seat of a third-class compartment in the train for
Den Helder after a heart-rending farewell on the platform, limp with passion, despair and relief.

3

In Den Helder, I found waiting for me a complete crew, most of whom had not set foot on a tugboat for years either, some of them never. We were directed to man the oceangoing tugboat *Constance Kwel* while waiting for our captain to arrive. The red-faced sergeant of the administration, who barked that order at us from behind a desk covered with telephones, a typewriter and a thermos flask, went redder when I remarked that the *Constance* had been lost in a shipwreck off the Friesian Islands a year and a half before. He bellowed that that was none of my damn business—if the books said there was an oceangoing tugboat called the *Constance Kwel,* then there *was* an oceangoing tugboat called the *Constance Kwel.* Until the vessel was located, we were billeted in the attic of a school.

We lived in that attic, sleeping in straw, swapping stories, playing gin rummy, getting fleas and growing beards, for three weeks. The whole thing was a lark; our chief engineer was a boy of twenty-one who had never handled a diesel engine of more than sixty-five horsepower; the captain had either left Holland or was a completely mythological character in the books of the Royal Dutch Navy, so I was promoted by the sergeant in charge of impostors to Master of the oceangoing tugboat *Constance Kwel.* After those first three weeks of total idleness, we received some haphazard training; we made a couple of sorties on an old harbor tug called the *Deborah Kwel* while her permanent crew was on week-end leave. I cannot say that I was very successful in my efforts to play at tugboats again; I ran her aground several times and managed to dent her icebreaker bow while docking her at the Navy pier. It was a shame the way I handled that ship; old salts stood ashore shaking their heads, disgusted. But I didn't care a damn; if the Navy did not like what I was doing, let them send me home. I must confess that I felt a sneaking satisfaction in thus defiling Holland's Glory; at last, after a lifetime of serfdom, I was getting some of my own back.

Then came May 10, 1940: the German invasion, the cruel bombing of defenseless Rotterdam by the Luftwaffe, the German parachutists dropped behind the lines. I was put on extra duty as a sentry outside the Naval Yard with orders to admit no one who could not repeat the phrase "Scheve Scheveningse Schoenen" with the rasping "ch" that makes Dutch less a language than a means to wear off one's tonsils without surgery. The whole of our war lasted only four days; then the Queen fled to England with her cabinet on a destroyer, and the Netherlands Armed Forces capitulated to the invader. But those four days had sufficed for Mr. Kwel to spirit all his tugboats, large and small, out of the Dutch ports and across to England, towing strings of barges as they went.

He also managed to alert his relief crews and to provide transport for them; they were not forced to go, only given the opportunity to escape the enemy and serve their country on harbor and deep-sea tugboats at a reduced wage, based on the salaries for Naval ratings. I wasn't too impressed by the threat of being overwhelmed by the enemy; chances were that the Germans would leave me be, whereas the British were sure to send me into action. And if they didn't, Mr. Kwel would. So, I had no other reason for enlisting than a general urge to escape, not so much from the prison of an occupied country as from the corner into which I had painted myself with regard to Sophie. I loved her desperately, of course; but I needed time to think, and freedom to think without the unblinking gaze of her grave, patient eyes upon me.

So, on the night of the fourteenth, as the German regiments were tramping into the outskirts of Den Helder, I found myself headed out to sea on the old *Deborah Kwel*, bound for Greenock, Scotland, towing seven canal barges with whole tribes of Dutch watermen and their families on board, who seemed to have no idea how lucky they were that the weather was so balmy and still and the night so dark. The darkness of the Dutch coastline, I suddenly realized, meant that all lighthouses and beacons had been extinguished; this gave me, for the first time, a sense of tragedy. Oddly, my first thought was not for Sophie but for Captain Bosman; I wondered if he had been in Holland when it happened and, if so, whether he had made it. I had not thought of him for years; yet there I stood, watching the dark coast of Holland dissolve in the night, thinking about him and the old *Cornelia Kwel* with deep concern.

He had made it, all right. When we arrived in Greenock we found it full of Dutch tugs; obviously, Kwel's entire fleet had been concentrated here. The *Cornelia* was the first I spotted as we docked; she did not look a day older, plump and graceless and spotless as ever; Captain Bosman was notorious as the only skipper in the fleet who painted even the tires hanging over his sides for barges to slam against. I found him on the quayside, smoking his pipe, hands clasped behind his back. He did not seem surprised to see me, nor particularly elated. He just nodded in response to my ebullient greeting; then he said, without taking his pipe out of his mouth, "Well! Quite a jamboree, it seems."

Remembering how he had told me, one night on the bridge in the Indian Ocean, about being caught by the

First World War in Hamburg with his pants down, I ventured, "Must be funny to go through all this for a second time, sir?"

He thought that over for a moment or two, then he took his pipe out of his mouth, said, "No. It's funnier the first time," and knocked the dottle out of his pipe on the heel of his boot.

These were the last words we exchanged; I never saw him again. Three months later, the *Cornelia Kwel* was reported missing in action.

My mate, two engineers and I exchanged the straw in the attic of a Dutch school for squeaking beds in a rundown hotel on the Clyde, hastily requisitioned as a billet for allied naval officers. We were promoted, together with a surprising number of compatriots in the same position as we, to lieutenants in the Navy Reserve and given uniforms with two wavy gold rings on the sleeves. We were told we were headed for the rank of lieutenant commander, two and a half wavy rings, two months later; after two days, we were given a ship to play with. She was an old harbor tugboat called *Blazer* with a freshly painted Navy number on her bow, a magic rune intended to transform her from a peaceable domestic plodder into a man-of-war. It was a case of the new clothes of the Emperor; old *Blazer*, instantly rechristened "*Blazes*," could never be made to look like a warship. Her silhouette was the very image of harmless humility, her fraying walrus mustache gave her the bovine benevolence of a sea cow with an insatiable appetite for weeds.

As it turned out, she was a training vessel for ocean-going tugboat officers and crews. The British had a sharp idea that the gallant allies who had come over without a ship of their own badly needed training. Old "*Blazes*" was ideal for the purpose; she was indestructible. Every day at daybreak she set out for the Firth of Clyde, her bridge swarming with would-be mates and captains, her aft deck alive with amateurs being taught how to lay mines and catapult depth charges. On her foredeck loitered the gun crews, waiting their turn to be instructed in the use of pom-pom and Oerlikon. The food was plentiful; on board old *"Blazes"* we had our first encounter with Spam, powdered eggs and the only green vegetable England grew throughout the war, Brussels sprouts. It was a carefree time; we began by adopting the British Navy slang and playing at tugboat captains, whom they referred to as "tug drivers." We took to eating our meals with one hand in our laps, to dancing the Lambeth Walk in the local social center, to standing automatically in line for everything and to calling one another "old chap." Only occasionally did we ask ourselves what else we were being trained for.

It did not take long before our destination was revealed. On the Western Approaches a regular salvage service under British command had been started, called OTWA for Oceangoing Tugboats Western Approaches. A vast number of tugs, mostly elderly harbor craft, were concentrated in ports on the west coast waiting for reports from the Fleet Air Arm that a freighter or a tanker had dropped out of convoy after being disabled by enemy action. These ships which failed to sink were called "lame ducks," and it was OTWA's job to bring them in. As one of our Navy instructors put it, "You chaps are going to be, one might say, the stretcher-bearers of the ocean."

The prospect attracted me. Maybe it was the tugboat sailor's normal attitude; I did not feel like firing guns or hurling depth charges to destroy ships, I would much rather salvage them. The prospect of joining OTWA was so attractive that I longed to end my training; we had been given to understand by the British that many Dutch tugboats had joined OTWA, most of them with young crews and young captains. We felt fortunate to become part of it at this early stage.

But a few days before we were due to travel to West-port, a large harbor on the west coast of England where OTWA headquarters was situated, I was called in to see our chief training officer, a charming, boyish commander of the British Navy, to whom we all had taken an instant liking. He had nurtured that empathy during our training period to the point where he could have made us feel fortunate had we been selected for the exciting duty of marching ahead of tanks to explode landmines. Although he must have known what our life expectancy was in the suicide brigade called OTWA, I am sure he did not fool us cynically; he seemed genuinely fond of us. It is a peculiarly English inconsistency that does not seem to bother them in the slightest, but even to make some mystical sense to their green and pleasant souls. The reasoning behind it seems to be that if a man has to go, he might as well go gracefully and, if possible, in high spirits.

I turned up for my appointment with some eagerness, expecting another of those personal sessions from which, on previous occasions, I had come away feeling on top of the world, absolutely raring to throw myself at the U-boats and the Luftwaffe, unarmed but for an antiquated pom-pom gun, like the Spitfire pilots of the Battle of Britain whose infectious motto was "Death, where is thy stingalingaling?"

The commander received me with a surprising lack of his usual outgoing boyishness. When I was ushered in by the strutting robot of a foot-stamping rating, he did not rise behind his desk and come to meet me to shake me warmly by the hand, as was his custom, though he was never quite able to hide the fact that handshaking was a foreign custom he had only recently acquired. This time, he remained seated behind his desk, indicated a chair and said, "Sit down, Captain. I think you and I had better have a little chat, hadn't we?"

I must have looked at him with genuine innocence, for when I answered "What do you mean, sir? What's up?" he seemed to unbend somewhat.

He gave me a scrutinizing look. "You mean to say you don't know?"

I had no idea what he was talking about; all I could guess was that it must have something to do with my training. "Know what?" I asked.

"Well," he said, obviously puzzled, "maybe I had better let this speak for itself, then," and he handed me a letter.

It was from the Admiralty, informing the Commander of Training, OTWA, that the trainee Harinxma, Martinus (Netherlands) was removed from his class at the request of his government and should report to Dutch Shipping, Room 505, Bel Air House, London W.1., at 0915 next Monday. It was signed, illegibly, by a Rear Admiral Graham Fosdyn-Tick, Bart., RN.

I looked at him in amazement; his frown relented somewhat, but his boyish blue eyes went on probing mine. "You mean to say that you didn't know about this?" he asked.

"I have no idea what it's about," I answered. "Have you?"

"Not the foggiest. I suppose your people want you for some other duty. Any idea which?"

I shrugged my shoulders. "What do they mean by 'Dutch Shipping,' sir?"

"Not the foggiest." He put his feet on his desk, which seemed to indicate he accepted my innocence. "Some civilian outfit, I'd say. I've been unable to find mention of it in our List of Services. Were you a professional tugboat man?"

"Indeed, sir," I confessed, without enthusiasm. "I left active service some time ago with the rank of mate; and apart from some ritual messing around with an old tug in the harbor of Den Helder, I haven't had any practice since."

"You mean to say you do not intend to make that your profession after the end of hostilities?"

"Not if I can help it!" I must have said it with feeling, for he raised his eyebrows, and his face relaxed in a smile.

"Well, old boy, maybe you can duck this one; but you had better go and find out what it's all about. Should you see a chance, I trust you'll wangle out of it. I have had my eye on you from the word go to build up the spirit of this OTWA thing, the 'esprit de corps' as the Frogs put it; and I must confess it came as a bit of a blow when I received this, er, thing this morning. I had the impression that you rather looked forward to OTWA."

"Oh, I do, sir, I do," I hastened to assure him. "Believe me, sir, I ask for nothing better than to proceed as planned. I promise you that if I can, I'll be back on the next train. Is Transport making out my ticket? Let's ask them to make it a return."

He got up behind his desk and came around and pumped my hand in that peculiar self-conscious way, the Raj adapting to the natives. He even went so far as to pat my shoulder and say, "All right, old boy, all right. Sorry if I suspected you of some unsavory double-dealing for a moment. On second thought, I don't think this is too serious; I may even be in a position where I can help you next Monday by jotting a line or two to H.M.S. *Spartacus* asking them to bring it home to your people that we are in desperate need of you ourselves. How would that be?"

H.M.S. *Spartacus*, I knew, was our regional headquarters. "I wish you'd do that, sir," I answered sincerely. "Believe me, to be drafted back into the civilian towing business is the last thing I want."

"All right, all right," he said with a few more pats on my shoulder that made me feel rather like a horse, as they suggested he was pacifying a large and emotional specimen of another species. "You go and see your people as ordered, and tell them just that, there's a good chap. I, for my part, will do whatever I can to support your request to, er, what was it? Dutch Shipping, quite. So long, now. Ta-ta." He shepherded me out of his office and then called his orderly with a voice that was a great deal less charming but that somehow suggested a return to his own family.

I left with the feeling that everything was settled to the satisfaction of both of us.

CHAPTER TWO

I

When I emerged from King's Cross Station, one sunny morning in June, London was under air attack. There was an acrid stench of smoke and cordite in the air, and the choking dryness of dust; fire engines were clanging in nearby streets, smoke hung in dark, writhing clouds low in the bright blue sky. Airplane engines droned dully in the distance, with the occasional high, whining snarl of a banking fighter plane; an alert was in operation, but no one seemed to take any notice of it. People trooped out of the station as if oblivious of the staccato stutter of ack-ack guns in the park, the shuddering thuds of distant explosions, the tremors to which the very soil seemed to be prone. That sky, those stoic people plodding about their business with sullen disdain for the calamity in which they and their city were involved, created an atmosphere of unreality; my instinctive reaction, after the first stomach-clutching spasm of panic, was the thought that I had nothing to do with this, for it was not my quarrel, and a pleasant sense of not belonging came over me, which seemed to impart a mystic immunity.

31

Even so, I hurried back into the safety of an underground station and set out by Tube for the address given to me, watching on the way with incredulous astonishment the spectacle of an entire city disappearing underground and taking up residence in the shelter of its subway stations. Every platform was lined with triple tiers of bunks; families camped like nomads among their possessions. It was the first time that the reality of war was brought home to me. It left me feeling lonely, and homesick for Sophie.

When I finally arrived in front of Bel Air House, I thought there must have been a mistake; it turned out to be a block of flats, a most unlikely place for the head office of "Dutch Shipping." As just at that moment sirens started to yowl again for another alert, I went inside anyhow. A hall porter who sat behind a little desk with candles in the lobby, looking worried, directed me to the basement and a door numbered 505. I had no idea as yet whom I was supposed to meet there, but at that moment curiosity was not uppermost in my mind. Whoever it was, I was delighted that he had had the good sense to set up shop in the basement.

It took me some time to find the door. The basement was as crowded as the subway stations had been. Obviously, most of the families living in the building had decided to take shelter down below. There were many children, and virtually all the adults were women, many of them in housecoats and slippers, carrying cats or cages with budgerigars. In addition to this homely gear, several of them wore steel helmets at feminine angles and every one carried a gas mask slung around her shoulders. The atmosphere was jolly; it gave the scene a Mardi Gras aspect that, for some reason, made a direct hit on this particular building appear unlikely. I suppose I was witness to the emergence of the spirit of London that finally won out.

When finally I knocked at door number 505, the racket of voices, miaows, parrot shrieks and distant rumbling thunder had grown to such volume that it took a while before there was any response to my knocking. Finally the door was opened from the inside by a frightened, starkly made-up young woman in a sky-blue twin set, tweed skirt and high-heeled shoes, standing in what seemed to be a cloakroom with a desk in it.

"Yes?" she asked with a voice genteel with terror.

"Good morning," I said. "My name is Harinxma. I was due to report here half an hour ago. I'm sorry I'm a little late, but there's a bit of a commotion outside, as you may have noticed." I went in for this long quasi-British speech to put her at her ease, but discovered that I was overcome by a compulsive urge for brainless chatter.

"Oh, yes." She swallowed. "Of course. Would you like to go straight in? Mr. Kwel is expecting you."

"Mr. Who?" I asked.

"Mr. Kwel, sir," she repeated, a little hysterically. "Maybe I had better announce you first." She gave me a smile that must have meant to be secretarial and efficient but made her look as if she were about to burst into tears. She hastily turned around and knocked on a door among the coats; a man's voice answered, "Come in."

She stuck her head in and muttered something, then turned around and held the door open for me. As I passed her on my way in, I was struck by her stupendous B.O.

I found myself in a small bed-sitting room with a make-shift desk and a row of old cardboard files on the bed. Behind the desk a thin man rose to greet me, a surprisingly young man in a gray business suit, his hair plastered to his narrow skull, his eyes gray and expressionless, his mouth functional. I looked around, expecting to see someone else; during all those years of sensuously nurtured hatred, I had

had what I imagined to be a clear picture of Mr. Kwel in my mind: old, grizzled, leonine, with a thick nose marbled by varicose veins, shaggy eyebrows and fierce, piercing eyes. I knew this probably was a biased picture, but never in all my days at sea would I have imagined the tyrant of Holland's Glory to be this vague, vacant bank manager, so conservatively dressed, purse-mouthed and precise.

It was distaste at first sight, but nothing like the caldron of inner turmoil I had expected to result from my first confrontation with the bogeyman of my life. This was not a man anyone could hate, for he seemed completely impersonal; if anything, he inspired the thought that he was sitting in for someone else, and I felt impatient to get past him at the real adversary.

But there was no one else in the room. Incredible as it seemed, this was he. This rubber-stamp functionary, with his tiny tie pin and prissy gray suit, his manicured hands and signet ring, was the sobering reality behind the demon of my subconscious, the lecherous god of evil of my fantasies, snorting fire, slavering blood. When he spoke, the whole thing became grotesque; his voice was high and rather effeminate, with a wince of whining gentility to it, like that of his secretary. My distaste turned into disgust. I felt like walking out without a word, but when he gestured at a chair, I sat down meekly and made small conversation about the mess outside and the marvel that, despite everything, the trains ran on time. While he sat there, sizing me up, I took in the homely little room with its sofa full of files, its litho of Dürer's praying hands and a reproduction of van Gogh's bridge at Arles; in the corner was a cretonne curtain, hiding a bathroom or a kitchenette. There was something about the room that seemed to bring about a sense of security; only when the thin gray man behind the desk got down to business did I realize it wasn't the room, it was he.

He leafed through a file on his desk, brought out a sheaf of papers and said, "Harinxma, I have arranged for your release from the training program in Greenock because you can render a better service to the war effort in another capacity." I was about to settle into the role of respectful listener to that kind of talk when he threw me by flashing a smile, startling and totally mirthless. "This, of course," he added, "is what I told the British."

I said, uncertainly, "I see."

"I see no point in letting my officers, trained experts every one of them in a highly specialized trade, be squandered on some suicidal scheme concocted by some amateurs on a basis of unlimited manpower. We did not coach you from scratch to send you out to be slaughtered on an irresponsible mission, as these OTWA people would. I am here to see to it that when the war is over, Holland will still have some boats and some men left to pick up deep-sea towing where we were forced to leave it when this started."

He had said it quite calmly and matter-of-factly, but I sensed beneath his unemotional exterior a burning anger, a steely resolve. It began to appear less ludicrous that this should be the notorious Mr. Kwel, last of the slave owners. Outside, the bombs seemed to be dropping closer; the hubbub in the passage had died down; the lamp overhead started to clatter as the shudders that shook the building increased in intensity. But there was that curious feeling of security he exuded by his total unconcern for the calamity in which we were all involved. As he went on talking, he opened a drawer and produced a candle which he proceeded to light with a gold cigarette lighter from a waistcoat pocket.

"As you know, we managed to salvage most of our

fleet in the nick of time. We also managed to salvage almost all our officers and crews. So we are setting out with a fighting chance. But we'll need all our wits about us, for make no mistake: this is going to be a long war."

As if God had been waiting respectfully for him to finish lighting his candle, the lights went out the moment the wick caught fire. He paid no attention to it, but calmly went on talking, putting the candle in a holder and the cigarette lighter back in his pocket. "Our large craft have all been dispatched by now on distant projects, well out of range," he continued. "Our medium craft, however, have been requisitioned for coastal duty around the British Isles. It is dangerous work, and we must expect heavy casualties. But it is my conviction that a great deal less should be blamed on brute force and bad luck in this war than people are doing. I am convinced that, with a superb craftsman for a captain and a highly trained crew of experts, a tugboat stands a much better chance than when it is manned by schoolboys and commanded by an amateur, as will be the case in this abortion called OTWA."

The door opened without warning and the secretary with the B.O. appeared ghostlike in the candlelight. Her eyes were round with terror; she stood there as if she were six years old and afraid of thunder.

"Mr. Kwel, sir," she said in a high, tense voice, "the lights went out."

"I know, Miss Crumb," he replied, irritably. "I suggest you follow suit and light your candle. Now, may we have privacy, please?"

"Yes, sir," she quavered. "Yes, Mr. Kwel. Yes, sir . . . " But she made no move; she looked at him pleadingly, hitching up that smile which made her look as if she were about to burst into tears; then there was a colossal crash overhead; from the passage came a multiple squeal of feminine voices.

"Close the door please, Miss Crumb," Mr. Kwel said calmly.

"Yessir," she whispered, but she did not obey. Her eyes roved in abject terror around the safe little room where we calm, self-confident men sat chatting in total security. Out of an animal urge for survival, she clutched at our presence by saying, "I don't think I'd like to . . . to light my candle, sir, if you don't mind. . . . Beg pardon, sir, but I would . . . I would like to sit in the kitchenette over there, if that's all right with you, sir. . . . I–I'll close the curtain, for . . . I want you to be private. . . ."

What she said was sensible enough, but it sounded as if she offered herself to him totally, in abject surrender, to save her naked life. I felt a sudden sympathy for her; I would have liked to take her in my arms, B.O. and all, and make love to her in that dark little room with the miaows and the brainless parrot shrieks in the background. She and I belonged to the same world, the world of the slaves, pawns on the chessboard of the mighty.

"All right, Miss Crumb," Mr. Kwel said. "Close the door, and you can go and sit in the kitchen."

She obeyed and tiptoed toward the cretonne curtain in the corner.

Then I heard him say, "It has been arranged with the Dutch government that you shall be reassigned to Kwel's International Tugboat Company with the rank of Master. I am appointing you for service as a relief captain on our coastal craft until such date as you shall be assigned a ship of your own."

I forgot about Miss Crumb and stared at him incredulously. Heaven knew that I didn't exactly underestimate myself, but even I knew that I was not ready for a command, not at this point. He must be out of his mind.

If he was, he didn't look it. He picked up some sheets from his desk and shoved them across to me, saying, "Here is the agreement in quadruplicate; sign where it says 'Employee.' Here is your first assignment sheet: you'll take over the *Anna Kwel* for one voyage only, South Shields to Tilbury round trip. Outward bound, you'll have thirteen barges in tow. You know the ship?"

I did. One of the worst and oldest: two funnels, steam engine, no guts left and an all-pervading stench of toadstools. "I do, sir," I said.

"It will be up to you how you tow those barges: as one unit, in tandem, or in single file. As a matter of fact, virtually everything will be left to your discretion on these runs. You'll be able to operate with a minimum of interference from the head office." Again he flashed me one of those disturbing, mirthless smiles. "All I ask is one thing: bring her back. With each ship we lose, we are edged further out of the deep-sea towing business. If we lose enough of them, Holland will never be able to recover her present position after the war. By signing this agreement, you accept a share of the responsibility for the future. Have you got a pen on you?"

I hadn't; he produced a gold one from another waistcoat pocket. I knew that it was ludicrous, that I had no business signing on as a Master at this stage, that he had hypnotized himself into believing that I was a "superb craftsman" who would help him to keep his boats out of the hands of those irresponsible British and safe from the guns of those ludicrous Germans. It was odd, however: I could not bring myself to attribute his determination to shabby greed alone; there was more to him than just a ruthless merchant. But perhaps I was just kidding myself, to make my subservience seem less dismal as I meekly signed myself back into slavery with the pen of my massa.

As I sat writing my name in quadruplicate, somebody in the passage opened the outer door and called in a jolly female tennis voice, "Okay, chaps! All clear! We've done it again!" Then the door was slammed shut.

Mr. Kwel, who had been watching me as I signed, ignored the interruption. "All right," he said, "that's that. Now let me give you the things you'll need. First, here is a book of transport vouchers; I have presigned them, all you need do is fill in your station of departure and your destination. Here is a check made out to Hope Brothers which will cover the cost of your uniform, two shirts, three pairs of socks, two sets of underwear and one pair of shoes, for you'll have to hand back what you are wearing at present to the British Navy. You will also need a duffel bag; all of this you can get at Hope Brothers. The address is here. Here is a copy of your Master's Certificate, duly legalized. I would advise you to keep it in a safe place, but in any case the original is in our files. Here is a new Netherlands passport, all prepared except for your signature; you'll have to sign these application forms for it, which my office has already filled out on your behalf. The photograph is on the young side, it dates from the time you were, I believe, mate's apprentice to Captain Bosman."

I was duly impressed by this virtuoso display of efficiency. The photograph looked hilarious: a fat boy with a peaked cap on the top of his head, his cheeks blown out, his eyes wide, as if he had been startled with his mouth full. It brought home to whom it might concern that I was very young to be a captain, and that my experience could best be described as limited. I suddenly got cold feet; this was crazy. I could not seriously think of going to Hope Brothers, having myself fitted out with long drawers, socks and a captain's uniform, and climbing the bridge of the *Anna Kwel* in South Shields. She might be ancient and fusty, but she was still a formidable vessel, a whale shark compared to the sea cow, old *"Blazes."* I suddenly felt an overwhelming homesickness for the commander, my friends in Greenock. H.M.S. *Blazer* seemed a rapidly receding vision of youth and sunlight and happiness; the oceangoing tugboat *Anna Kwel* loomed on the horizon as a monster of ill-omen, a black slaver manned with dour old professionals who would welcome their new captain like a pack of foxes a fat duckling. I knew that it amounted to rebellion, but I blurted out, "Frankly, sir, I don't think I'm qualified. I mean . . ."

He flashed that thin, aseptic smile at me again, then he said, "You'll be all right. If you feel insecure, you may find it helpful to grow a mustache. Now, how about signing these passport applications? Your train leaves at six o'clock from King's Cross, if it's still standing, and you still have quite a day ahead of you."

While I sat reading through the application forms for the passport already issued by the obedient government-in-exile, I became conscious of a secretive strangling noise behind me. It came from the kitchenette; it must be Miss Crumb, throwing up discreetly in the sink. Shortly afterward there was the drumming sound of tap water turned on, so the water supply still worked in London.

As I rose to leave, he stretched out his hand; I pressed it gingerly.

"Goodbye, Captain, and good luck. Glad to have you with us."

"Goodbye, sir." I hesitated for a moment, there had been something else I wanted to say, something essential; but I could not remember it. On my way to the door, I wondered whether I should say goodbye to Miss Crumb, now hidden behind the cretonne curtain, or allow her to return from the bank of the River Styx at her ease. I already had my hand on the doorknob when I remembered the important thing I should have said.

"How about the British, sir? I'll have to inform the commander in Greenock—"

"Don't worry, Harinxma," he said, back behind his desk. "That has been done."

As I crossed the dark little hall and groped for the front door, I reflected that it would have been nice if he could have seen his way to being a little more gracious about the fact that the outcome of our meeting had been a foregone conclusion; but maybe he had wanted to rub it in, in case his serf might be getting ideas.

The corridor outside was still crowded with women, children and their pets; elderly men in shiny new blue overalls, wearing steel helmets with the letter W painted on them and carrying lanterns, moved among them. "All right, ladies and gentlemen!" they were calling. "Let's get a move on! Let's all get back to our flatlets now! You'll probably find some glass damage, but there has been no direct hit on this building and we'll see to it that you are boarded up as soon as possible. Now let's get moving, please; come on, let's move along now . . ."

I worked my way through the throng; as I emerged from the lobby, which looked gay and festive with many candles, I found chaos outside. The street, covered with rubble and broken glass, was blocked by deserted automobiles, standing crazily about like cars abandoned in a blizzard. I smelled that acrid stench again of smoke and cordite; there were fires all along the street, the façades of gutted buildings crumbled with sudden, heart-stopping rumblings. To walk down that street was like walking along the edge of a frozen pond; the shattered glass crunched underfoot like thin ice.

I managed to get a taxi a few streets away and told the driver to take me to Hope Brothers; he received the order with pleased surprise, as if he had been longing to go there. Once under way, he opened the glass partition that separated us and started to tell me what had happened to him in broad Cockney, which amounted to a foreign language. But all that was expected of me, as it turned out, was an occasional "Fancy that."

He kept it up for the rest of the drive, and it was a long one. It looked as if Hope Brothers were protected by a veritable Maginot Line of rubble. We had to turn around four times because the road was blocked; a heavy pall of black smoke hung over East London, where the docks lay. This much I understood from his long monologue: the waterfront had copped it worst; old 'itler was after them petrol tanks and power stations, but 'ad I 'eard that gunboat on the river? That 'ad really given 'im what for.

When finally he managed to reach Hope Brothers, we had made a virtual tour of the City. He refused a tip, saying, "No, guv'nor. You just pay what it says on the meter. If I'd been able to get straight through, it would have only been 'arf that much." So we parted with a handshake that suddenly made him self-conscious; I had forgotten it was a foreign custom.

Inside Hope Brothers, even the First World War had not yet started. It may have been somewhat darker in there than usual, as the shopwindows had been boarded up; but the electricity worked in this neighborhood, crystal chandeliers shed an Edwardian light. The collars of the assistants seemed to be higher than those in the outside world; the dummies modeling tartan dressing gowns and short khaki raincoats with bowler hats all wore mustaches, which reminded me that I was supposed to grow one myself. When

I finally stood scrutinizing my reflection, clad in what seemed to be an embarrassingly narrow-hipped and slope-shouldered uniform with a peaked cap of astonishing width, I had to admit that Mr. Kwel's advice had been sound; in that outfit I didn't look a day older than nineteen.

The captain's rings were sewn onto my uniform while I tried on shirts, socks, ballroom shoes and combination BVD's that my Edwardian Virgil assured me were "absolutely standard." When the jacket came back, I saw I had been given the British Merchant Navy's version of a Master's rings: four stripes and diamond. They did not go all the way around the sleeve, but covered only the outside half. "Wartime restrictions, you know," my mentor explained. I also got a duffel bag there, a complete set of toilet articles, a shoeshine kit, a greatcoat with captain's shoulder tabs and a terrycloth bathrobe that managed to look military. When, eventually, I stood looking worriedly at my old uniform with the two wavy Navy rings, the assistant read my thoughts; or maybe, with Mr. Kwel's uncanny efficiency, he had been briefed beforehand.

"Just leave these togs with us, Captain," he said. "We'll dispatch them back to Central Depot for you. We have all the details."

It came as a shock, on leaving the timeless world of Hope Brothers, to find the ravaged city outside.

2

I spent the rest of the day trying to get to King's Cross Station. Twice I had to dodge into a bomb shelter with an oddly lackadaisical crowd; I listened to stories of narrow escapes told by overbearing middle-aged ladies, a type fate seemed to have singled out for me. I had my face licked by a dog while listening to the story of its mistress' being hunted by the Luftwaffe; I was handed tea by lady volunteers and managed to have my pocket picked. When I finally reached King's Cross Station, all I possessed besides my duffel bag were the coins in my pocket, my passport and the book of transport vouchers. I tried to remember what my wallet had contained and ended by wondering what a thief in burning London would do with a Dutch Master's Certificate for oceangoing tugboats and a sheet with instructions, headed *"Anna Kwel,"* starting with the words, "You will find her lying behind the bar in South Shields." I did not bother to envisage what he would do with five pounds, ten shillings.

I was saluted with markedly more deference by the controlling sergeant at the gate than I had been when I had checked out of the station as a lieutenant that morning. Maybe it had something to do with the fact that, as a captain, I was supposed to travel first-class. The train seemed to be about to leave on schedule; it was made up of carriage after carriage full of schoolchildren with labels attached to their coats, twittering like birds. I finally found an empty first-class compartment; when I opened it, it welcomed me with a smell of peace. It seemed as if the war had not yet penetrated there; its red plush seats and Victorian antimacassars, freshly laundered, seemed to be waiting for the usual occupants, bankers and members of Parliament hiding behind *The Times*, not a Dutch tug driver lugging a duffel bag.

As the train pulled out of the station into the night, the air-raid sirens were wailing once more. I lowered the window in one of the doors and watched the fantastic spectacle of London under attack, seen from a box in a cinema before the sound had been turned on. The noise of the train clanking and squealing drowned out the rumble of the guns and the thudding of distant detonations; searchlight beams groped blindly about the sky; the graceful garlands of multicolored tracer bullets rose and drooped among them, flak shells exploded like fireworks. But the most poignant thing that came toward me from the night, and that has haunted me ever since although I did not realize its impact at the time, was the smell of London during the blitz: an oddly Levantine smell, like the Mediterranean off Cyprus in summer, when the wind from parched Turkish hills wafts out to sea the neutral, unsensuous scent of ancient dust.

As the train entered the blacked-out countryside, I shut the window, sat down in the corner, and saw my reflection floating along, faint and ghostly, in the night outside. I gazed at my double and wondered how long it would take to grow a mustache. Where were all those little children going, with their labels and their school uniforms? I wondered how Sophie was, and was taken unawares by the wave of homesickness that swamped me at the thought of her. It was clear now that her parents had been right: of course we should have married. How different my life would have been if only we had! It did not occur to me that I was at last in a position where I could indulge in these thoughts with impunity; between me and her now stood the German Wehrmacht, to protect me against myself. Instead of sorting out the events of the day as I had planned to do, I spent the first part of the journey daydreaming about the life Sophie and I could have had, and would have the moment the war was over.

Halfway through the night, the compartment became very hot and I took off some of my captain's disguise because I began to perspire profusely. In shirt sleeves, tie loose, hair tousled, I watched a gray day break over a dreary landscape of slag heaps, factories and rows of uniform drab little red houses, all belching smoke. I had to change trains in a vast anonymous station; from a newspaper displayed outside a station kiosk I discovered it to be Newcastle-on-Tyne. I had an hour to spare before the train left for South Shields; I did not feel like going out into the town, for I had little money to spend if I wanted any breakfast and a taxi to take me to the ship. I hung idly around the stationer's kiosk, in which an elderly woman in a flowered dress was rummaging, turning around in the small space like a dog preparing to lie down. When she finally had taken up position and peered out at the world, which was I, I asked her, mainly because our eyes met, whether she had anything to read other than newspapers and magazines. She frowned in thought; then she answered, smiling, with a broad North Country accent, "Oh, you'll be meaning books! Yes, Captain, I may have just what you want."

She turned around; then she turned back, beaming, and showed me her secret cache of culture: *Point Counter Point* by Aldous Huxley, in two volumes, a pocket edition that looked the worse for wear. She glanced up and down the platform, secretively, and her voice went down to a conspiratorial whisper when she said, "I can let you have this at a good price, Captain! It's a German edition. It's in English, all right, but printed by the Jerries. . . . Maybe they'll have me up for selling it and if you'd been a naval person I wouldn't have offered it to you, but considering that you're one of the boys . . ." It was the first time that I became aware of the peculiar preference the Tyneside English seemed to have for the Merchant Marine during the war.

When I did not jump at her offer, because I was mentally counting my change to see if I could afford it, she hid the guilty books and continued, somewhat dourly, "Then, of course, there are *these* . . ." These turned out to be a Woolworth edition of *The Cricket on the Hearth* and a flashy-looking brochure entitled *Geordies and Huns—Stirring Stories of Contributions to Victory Made by Sons of the Tyne.*

"How much is the Huxley?" I asked.

She relaxed with a smile; she had judged me right. "Oh, I don't know," she said. "I can't ask you what it says on the cover. How about a shilling for the two of them?"

It was a bargain that an intellectual snob could not pass up. "I'll take it," I said, and put two sixpences on the stack of newspapers in her window.

"Just a tick," she said. "I'd better wrap them up, it's kind of black market, isn't it?"

She wrapped them in a page of last Sunday's *News of the World;* when I came away, I carried a parcel more conspicuous than books, displaying the headline, "Grave Allegations Against Scoutmaster." When, in the end, I settled down once again in splendid isolation in a first-class compartment of the train to South Shields, I read about the scoutmaster. I did not really know why I had bought those books; when I sat staring out of the window at more rows of drab little houses, slag heaps, factory chimneys and, far away, the russet sheen of distant moors, I finally confessed to myself how apprehensive I was of my impending confrontation with the crew of one of the oldest, most experienced deep-sea tugboats in the world. For some reason, I had bought the books under the pressure of that apprehension.

In South Shields I took a taxi to where the old *Anna Kwel* lay moored. Her tattered Dutch flag and the familiar emblem on her two grimy stacks caused an unexpected twinge of recognition, like homecoming. She could, as she lay there, be nothing but Dutch; they did not build ships like that anywhere else in the world. They did not make crews like that anywhere else either, I reflected as I saw them on the aft deck, pretending not to have been waiting to see who had been foisted upon them as captain by the head office. They looked surly and tough, typical of the oceangoing tugs in their obvious distaste for uniform, their passion to express individual independence in beards, bowler hats, lumbermen's jackets and balaklavas with tassels. Like old hoboes picked off a freight train attending a line-up, they stood staring and spitting at the shore.

They must have spotted me long before they let on; they looked away studiously as I teetered toward the ship in my ballroom pumps, across the cobbles and crane rails, duffel bag on my shoulder. I imagined I saw a twinge of alarm cross the hirsute face of an old man standing outside the galley at the sight of the baby-faced rookie in a brand-new uniform. It suddenly occurred to me that the personality of the skipper must be even more important to a crew during a war than in peacetime. Now that U-boats, torpedo planes, dive bombers and strafing aircraft had been added to the list of risks of coastal traffic after all beacons had been removed and all lighthouses extinguished, they were literally at the mercy of the experience and quick-wittedness of their captain. I felt for a moment like walking straight past them onto the next ship: a homely Danish coaster which seemed more likely to be waiting for a stumbling, gauche youth in a brand-new captain's uniform. In an unnerving moment of identification, I saw myself approaching through their eyes; I concluded that, were I the mate on board that ship, my heart would now sink into my shoes.

When I finally stood poised on the edge of the quayside, an obscenely fat character with plastered-down hair parted in the middle, like a member of a barbershop quartet, emerged from the galley, carrying a pail of potato peelings. His grimy T-shirt, barred with horizontal red stripes like a mid-channel buoy, was strained by his breasts; his eight-months-pregnant belly was underslung by the belt of a blood-smeared apron; a pair of steel-rimmed spectacles, one arm of its frame tucked down his cleavage, dangled on his chest. He was about to dump the peelings over the rail when he looked up at me, squinting against the sun, and asked, in a surprising falsetto, "Anything I can do for you, boy?"

It was the moment of truth. For a second, we stood staring at each other, speechless; then I said, "You can catch this," and threw my duffel bag at him.

I don't know what prompted me to do it; I had expected it as little as he. The piece of luggage sailing down at him caught him off balance; but with a surprising agility for such an obese body he managed to catch it without letting go of his pail. He glowered at me, but the alter ego which had thrown the bag against my will said, "Take that to my cabin, will you?" Then I looked around at the charcoal burners, still eyeing me motionlessly but with dumb thoughts of violence now muddying the cold indifference of their stares, and asked, "Well? Is any of you characters going to give me a hand to get on board?" Had anyone had the effrontery to address me like that, I would have turned away and let him drop dead. For a second, it looked as if I had screwed up this assignment from the word go; then the hirsute old man came slowly toward me on thumping clogs and stretched out a huge hand. "What do you expect me to do?" I asked. "Jump? Come here. I'll step on your shoulder."

Never, not in my wildest dreams, would I have thought myself capable of such a callous command. I might as well have asked him to prostrate himself for me so I could wipe my boots on his jersey. But, unbelievably, he lowered his hand obediently, turned around, proffering his shoulder, and braced himself at the rail. I put my right foot on his shoulder and jumped onto the deck with a jaunty bounce that gave my youth away.

The cook, still clutching my duffel bag, his pail with peelings poised on the rail, gaped at me.

"Good morning," I said. "My name is Harinxma. Has my cabin been cleared?"

"Y-yes, C-captain," the old man whom I had used as a stepladder stammered. "I c-cleaned it m-myself. The agent t-told us . . ."

"All right," I said. "How about taking me there?"

"Yes, sure," the cook replied, with a servility that filled me with disgust for myself as well as for him. "Here," he said to the old man, "hold this," and he handed him the pail. He heaved my duffel bag onto his shoulders. "This way, Captain," and he turned away. My alter ego asked the old man in passing, "You the bosun?"

"Y-yes, C-captain, sir . . ." he answered, another serf.

"All right. We'll leave at slack tide."

This was the only order I had worked out beforehand while gazing at the grimy Tyneside from the train. He only had a choice of two replies; he could either answer, "But, Captain, high tide is not till midnight!" or "Yes, sir."

He chose the first. "Beg p-pardon, C-captain," he stammered, "high t-tide won't b-be until s-sundown, and what with all the l-lights g-gone . . ."

I eyed him coldly and said, as to an apprentice, "Since when do we tow a string of barges with the tide, bosun?"

This rash remark, made uniquely for its theatrical impact, meant that I had now committed myself as to how I would handle my first tow even before seeing it. Had he said, "Yes, sir," I would have postponed my decision as to how to handle it until I had seen what it was made up of, like any sane man. Only if it consisted of Dutch barges or Thames barges where leeboards were involved would one arrange a tow in a single file, as to lash these alongside one another in tandem might damage them; towing in a single file must be done against the tide, when the current enables the tugboat to maintain steerage while actually lying at a dead stop. The sudden look of bafflement and respect on the face of the old bosun was gratifying; I had been in the business long enough to know that this piece of gossip would work its way around the ship in record time: "Hey, that new Old Man certainly knows his stuff! He may look like a schoolboy, but he's a tugboat man all right! Who the hell is he? Harinxma? Any of you ever heard that name before?"

I doubted it, but, if I was lucky, someone would pretend he had, just to seem important.

As I followed the cook up the bridge steps, past the wireless cubicle and the engine-room skylight, I sniffed a faint autumnal scent. I had not been mistaken about the old *Anna Kwel;* the smell of toadstools was discernible, despite those of used steam and of the acid in the batteries stored in the louvered box between her stacks. Before I followed the cook through the door to the captain's cabin, I glanced at the bridge. The engine-room telegraph had not been polished, the bridge itself looked grimy with dirt, and grit seeped from the sandbags that barricaded the wheelhouse against shrapnel and machine-gun fire.

The cabin was an exact replica of the scores of tugboat captains' cabins I had known. Dark mahogany paneling and white gloss paint; a narrow bunk on the left with drawers underneath; to the right a wardrobe with small mahogany desk attached, its chair secured to the floor by a length of chain; between the head of the bunk and the washstand opposite, the communicating door to the chartroom. The size of the cabin was that of a single sleeper on board an overnight train.

"Thanks, Cook," I said, looking around. "You can go ahead and put my things away." At that, I opened the door to the chartroom and stepped over the high threshold into the cubicle next door. It had been an unusual request to make to a cook; who did I think I was, to use him as a valet? But I could not help myself; I had been completely taken over by that alter ego. The cook seemed too abashed to assert himself. God only knew how long my luck would last.

The chartroom was standard too: chart rack on the ceiling, chart table to the right with drawers underneath, to the left an oilskin locker, a leatherette sofa and a tall set of drawers reaching to the ceiling for files, the ship's papers and the captain's booze. No chair here, just a stool, also chained to the floor. The two compasses, protractor and parallel ruler on the chart table looked old and worn; the ship's sextant was so ancient that its silver scale had been worn down to brass; the chronometer ticking breathlessly in its padded box looked like an antique. The *Anna Kwel* was a shabby ship, not even a packhorse: an old mule, sexless and featureless; about all she was good for now was to be turned into dogfood. To send men to sea in a worn-out vessel like this summed up Mr. Kwel's mentality. Much as I might pride myself on my intellectual independence, I was again a slave among slaves, trusty in the prison of Holland's Glory. The chartroom was even more depressing than the cabin; I turned around and opened the communicating door again and saw the pregnant cook standing beside my bunk, steel-rimmed spectacles on the tip of his nose, peering at the two volumes of Huxley. As I appeared in the doorway, he hastily dropped them, tucked his glasses back in his décolletage and continued to dig my clothes out of the duffel bag.

"Have you had any breakfast, Captain?" he asked, ingratiatingly.

"No," I answered. "If you still have something going, bring it to the chartroom."

I turned away again, without waiting for his reply. This time I left the door open. I pulled the stool from underneath the chart table, took *Brown's Nautical Almanac* and the *Coast Pilot* from the shelf overhead and started to leaf through them. I realized now what had prompted me to buy the Huxley books—I was eager to establish an identity, create an image, however incongruous. I was such a completely unknown entity to the crew, and my exterior was so unprepossessing, that the sooner they could refer to me as a "character" the better. If I played this right, some mythomaniac among them was bound to exclaim at a given moment, "Wait a minute! I know who he is! The Bookworm!"—or The Doc or The Professor. "Don't you know? Surely you've heard of him? No? Well, *I* have! Oh boy, *have* I! He's a real bastard, he is, but as for the job, he knows his stuff, all right. Of course! Good old Bookworm, why didn't I recognize him straight off?"

The moment they gave me a nickname, I would be accepted. In my effort to achieve this, I overacted shamelessly, but the crew seemed oddly eager to act their part in the mystification. First, as I sat there leafing through the *Almanac*, there was a knock at the door. I called, "Yes?"

A middle-aged man with a haggard face in which no illusions were left stuck his head in. He was wearing a shabby peaked cap with the emblem of Kwel's International; he must be the mate—the chief or the second engineer would have looked paler and turned up in overalls.

"Yes, Mate?" I said.

He looked at me without expression, a moment of tacit scrutiny without illusion, then he asked, "Do you want me to put Williams on watch with that boil in his neck or don't you?"

For a split second, realizing that he was calling my bluff, I felt the beginning of a panic; then suddenly, out of the past, came the laconic voice of Captain Bosman telling his apprentice underneath the Byzantine extravagance of the tropical night, "Once you're a captain, it's a good idea to give serial numbers to the questions they throw at you and to reply 'yes' to the odd ones and 'no' to the even ones. For, you see, by the time they get to you, they have weighed the pros and cons to a standstill in their own minds. . . ."

So I replied, "Yes," without batting an eyelid.

The mate continued to scrutinize me for a moment, in motionless silence, then he said, "Okay. Prins is the name."

"Glad to know you, Prins," I said calmly, despite a sudden fit of palpitations. "Mine is Harinxma. I'll take the first watch, but I'd like you to be on the bridge. All right?"

"Anything you say," the melancholy mate said, cheerlessly. "You're the boss." With that, he withdrew his head and closed the door.

As if he had been standing in the wings, waiting for his cue, the cook appeared in the communicating doorway, carrying a tray.

"Your breakfast, Captain," he said.

"Thank you."

He put down a grimy plate with an inch-thick sandwich and a mug of the strong ship's tea that probably accounts for most sea captains' ulcers. "About our stores, Captain,

I have that offer for stewed pears in heavy syrup, by the barrel, at a discount. Do you want me to take it or don't you?"

This being question number two, an even one, I answered promptly, "No."

He stood for a moment at a loss as to how to take this extraordinary self-confidence, then he said, almost reverently, "Very good, Captain, sir. Thank you, Captain. Yes, sir," and he backed out.

The moment he had stepped over the threshold onto the boatdeck, his slippers clattered off at a run, like castanets; obviously he could not wait to report to his anxious audience in the galley.

I needed a moment to recover from my own audacity, eyes closed, thinking with gratitude of Captain Bosman; then I picked up the limp, bulging sandwich with both hands and looked at it, undelighted. It was a cheese sandwich: one thin slice of processed cheese between two greasy layers of margarine twice its thickness, on gray, tasteless bread. Whatever changes might have taken place in the world since I had left Kwel's International, its ship's sandwiches had remained the same.

As I sat there, munching, I began to relax a little and was overcome by a feeling of loneliness. I was no longer afraid that I would bungle the job; I began to believe that Mr. Kwel had indeed known what he was doing when he picked me for a relief captain. With a little luck, I would be able to meet most situations, even the surprising ones, with a modicum of self-confidence, as long as I remembered what Captain Bosman would have done. It was not fear of the job that gave me this growing sense of despondency; it was the homelessness, the sense of belonging nowhere: temporary captain, living out of his duffel bag in other men's cabins for one trip at a time. It seemed a dismal prospect; I had no means of knowing that it was the normal feeling of every new captain, young or old, whether of a transatlantic liner or a trawler on the Grand Banks. It was my first taste of being a Master after God, the loneliest job in the world.

3

My self-confidence lasted until late that afternoon, when we cast off to move upstream and pick up our tow for Tilbury. I had shot my bolt when I announced that I would tow it in single file against the current, so I had to leave at low tide. It was a gray windless day with low-hanging cloud; darkness would fall soon with that sky. I had no idea what type of barges to expect; as we steamed upriver toward the terminal where we were to pick them up, I gradually came to feel certain that the lot of them would be standard hundred-foot lighters which any tugboat captain would have lashed together, four abreast, and pushed out to sea regardless of the tide. The traffic in the mouth of the Tyne was heavy; immediately beyond the outer buoy lay the minefields; there was not much room to play with for a long, sluggish string of barges. The sooner I disentangled myself from the traffic of freighters, tankers and fishermen coming and going, the better it would be.

My luck held out; when I swung the *Anna Kwel* around in the current at the terminal, I saw moored to the dock a motley batch of small craft, most of them Dutch canal barges with leeboards. And as if that were not enough, I even discovered the long low alligator-like silhouette of a Thames barge among them, at least a hundred years old, with leeboards like the wings of a prehistoric saurian. I could have come to no other decision in this case than to tow these craft in single file, against the current, even if I had spent hours plotting the tow on paper. Old *Anna* handled surprisingly well, considering her size; I knew at once that she would not give me any trouble. One thing I had learned all right, during my year as the skipper of a harbor launch, and that was how to handle a vessel. I felt confident I would be able to thread a needle with this one.

We tied up alongside the Thames barge; I stepped over to have a look at the ships and to decide on their sequence in the tow. On board the Dutch barges I was welcomed with the proud surliness typical of the waterman; they had all crossed the North Sea during that one day in May when the Germans had been approaching the coast, a beautiful day, warm, calm and hazy. They had puttered across the glassy sea with their small auxiliary engines in complete safety; but although the east coast of England was safer for small craft than the west coast of Holland, they could not possibly operate in the coastal trade under their own power; they had to be towed. Their crews were mostly made up of man and wife, and, expert as the Dutch bargees might be at handling their craft, they had no notion of navigation. To let them blunder about in the narrow channels through the minefields up and down the coast of England in fog and rain and at dead of night would mean they would finish by blowing themselves up. As it was, those channels, though swept continuously by the Royal Navy, were beset by drifting mines.

I had no experience of the coastal run; I had no idea what I was in for. I did not realize, that day, that most of those taciturn bargees and their stolid wives were doomed to fall under the murderous cannon and machine-gun fire of German raiders. Tows like this one, ponderously crawling along the narrow lanes of the mine-swept channels, were perfect game for the young hunters of the Luftwaffe, and although the wheelhouses of the barges were protected by sandbags, they were pathetically vulnerable. Most of them had too few watertight bulkheads anyhow, and all of them were so shallow that a direct hit of cannonshell would slam straight through their cargo and through their bottoms. Out of the hundreds of Dutch canal barges that had scurried across the hazy North Sea that day in May 1940, only a handful returned home after the war.

When I began to sort them out that afternoon, I found that they were just as mulish abroad as they had been at home. They argued about their place in the tow; all of them wanted to be the last in line, so as to save strain on their bollards; all of them dug in their heels when they were told to stop procrastinating and obey orders. The crew of the *Anna Kwel* followed my floundering tour of the barges with fascination. The taciturn mate sat smoking a pipe on the aft deck, calmly watching the young upstart getting snarled up in a monumental snafu.

When at last I had managed to make up the tow, almost two hours had been squandered in endless deliberations. The sky was getting lower; the smell of fog was in the air and, as far as I was concerned, the smell of fear. My self-confidence was almost gone by the time we finally set out: thirteen surly barges in single file connected by shortened hawsers. The hawsers would be played out to their full length only after we had rounded the outer buoy and made the sharp starboard turn into the channel between the minefields. The tide was running fast and strong, traffic was heavy; I had to nose my way into midstream with such caution that we made little headway. The run from the terminal to the outer buoy was about five miles; at the speed I was going, I would barely make it before the tide turned. And I had better, for to be forced to stop or even slow down while running downstream with a string of craft like these, without power of their own and no steerage to speak of, meant they would crowd in on me from behind. To have a tow pile up on my stern would be an unpropitious beginning, to say the least.

I paced the bridge with a nonchalance that would not have deceived a child. I knew that everybody on board the tug realized the potentialities of the situation. If they were praying, they probably prayed that I might find myself trussed by a knot of rudderless barges, drifting helplessly toward the minefields. The mate, on the bridge as I had so high-handedly requested, stood smoking his pipe in the lee of the wheelhouse with an air of complacency.

We already had the jetties of South Shields harbor entrance in sight when suddenly fog descended over us. It blotted out the world so thoroughly that I could barely discern the first barge of the tow astern. There was nothing for it; I had to stop. I rang the engine down to Dead Slow and ordered the bosun to shoot the lead, not to find out the depth of the river but to check on our ground speed. We were still going too fast; I called the engine room through the speaking tube on the bridge, and when a raucous voice answered, "Yeah," I told him to take back the revolutions until we were barely ticking over. The mate, meanwhile, went on quietly smoking his pipe by the wheelhouse, enjoying himself. The ship seemed to be very quiet all at once; so quiet that the sound of footsteps behind me made me whip around. I saw a tall thin character with a big nose and small eyes amble onto the bridge with an expression of anticipation, as if he had been called out to see the nudes.

"Who are you?" I asked, sharply.

"Stutter, Hendrik W., radio officer. At your service, Admiral," the character said with a poker face. "Do you mind if I stay to look?"

"Look at what?"

"The corrida," he answered, with unnerving candor. "I am an aficionado. What I love about bullfights is the moment of truth."

"Fancy that," I said, icily; but it was no longer my self-confident, level-headed alter ego who spoke. It was my true self, the reckless boy in a jam, trying to bluff his way out, with a cracked voice, the fear of death closing the door on his composure.

We crawled on at a snail's pace for what seemed an eternity. The mate made our foghorn bray every two minutes, provoking the deep hoarse roar of freighters, the snarl of tugboats, the high idiotic whooping of a siren, the breathy goatlike "Maa-aa" of a hand-operated Norwegian horn. From all directions a whole fleet seemed to be converging on us and yet I saw nothing, nothing at all, not a buoy, not a shadow, not a ship; it was as if some vindictive deity had blinded me with a swirling cloud, peopled with the pot-bellied, bird-beaked, surrealist monsters of the paintings by Hieronymus Bosch. I stood there, clutching the rail, trying to calm down the trembling of my calves and the banging of my heart. Any moment now, the tide would turn and we would start to drift sideways into the traffic lane or into the minefields out there in the fog.

And then, without warning, the way it had come down, the fog lifted. I discovered we had remained in the same place: the pierheads well in sight, the houses of South Shields blinking wetly in a pale diffused sunlight, the channel crowded with craft, all stopped, some of them crosswise in the slack tide. My tow was in fairly good shape, only the last two units had begun to drift out; I had to get out of there fast. It would be a matter of minutes before the tide turned; because of the delay with the barges at the terminal, I had not studied South Shields Approaches thoroughly enough on the chart. I cursed the war because it had suspended pilot services for small craft; if only I could have handed the responsibility to someone else! But there I was, Master after God of a string of barges half a mile long, about to be turned into a barrier across the channel. I took out the binoculars; they were so moldy that I might as well have gazed through a kaleidoscope, but eventually I discerned the outer buoy. I rang the engine up to full speed; the tow lined up on course; then I nipped into the wheelhouse to take a bearing across the compass of the outer buoy in the distance. I had just lined up when down came the fog again, this time with an acrid stench of factory smoke. I was committed now, I could no longer stop the tow as I had done last time, for the tide was turning, and if I stopped, my barges would soon be all over the place. Theoretically, the solution would have been to swing the whole string of them around 180 degrees and to head back into the current, waiting for the fog to lift, but thirteen barges, even on the short hawser, were too many to swing around in the channel. I had to carry on, putting all my chips on one card: the bearing I had taken on the outer buoy.

There was nothing left for me to do but to pace on the bridge and peer nervously into nothing. I went back into the wheelhouse to check the course again. As I stood staring at the compass, feeling a small rivulet of sweat wriggle down my back, the gleeful radio officer followed me into the wheelhouse and leaned against the wall just inside the door. I felt like yelling at him to get the hell out, but that would have destroyed the image of the calm, self-confident craftsman. After a while, I became too sick with apprehension to be bothered by his presence.

As I stood staring into the emptiness of the fog, listening to the barks, the bellows, the beeps and the bleats of all those ships around me, I had the sudden feeling that I was steering too low. I had no reasonable cause for that suspicion. I could not see a thing out there; for all I knew, the outer buoy might be too far over to starboard by now. But an odd, instinctive restlessness urged me to steer a couple of points higher.

I was so conscious of the fact that I had no concrete observation to justify this impulse that, for a few minutes, I stood there nervously swallowing, trying to hide sick little burps of fear. Then the high, mischievous voice of the wireless operator said, "That old compass is not too reliable, you know. It's kind of sluggish in the northeast quadrant, I understand."

It was so obvious that he intended to rattle me that I suddenly found the strength to say, "Thank you, I wondered about that." I turned to the man at the wheel and said, "Take her up a point."

"Up a point," the calm voice of the helmsman echoed.

"Steady as you go."

"Steady as you go."

We plowed on into the fog at top speed, our foghorn braying with gulps of hot water and a hiss of steam. As the minutes ticked by, everybody on that bridge began to realize that this was serious. The mate still stood in the corner, but his pipe had gone out and I could sense his apprehension. The wireless operator stood quite still, staring fixedly ahead into the fog. We must have left the pierheads behind us by now, but I could not see a thing. We were in the open, and if we missed that outer buoy we would find ourselves in the minefields within a matter of minutes. I cursed myself for having given in to that impulse to steer higher; why in the name of God hadn't I stuck to my observation and trusted the accuracy of my eye rather

than some somnambulistic prompting? I saw the torso of
a seaman in a duffel coat and a balaklava emerge on the
fo'c'sle, peering into the fog. Of course, I should have
ordered a lookout! How damn stupid, why had I forgotten? The foredeck of the tug was so short that it did not
make too much difference, but even so I should have
thought of it. I suddenly realized that I had done everything wrong. I had, from the word go, guilelessly stumbled
into one trap after the other until now I was barreling
down at a speed of five knots straight for the minefields of
Doggers Bank with a tow of thirteen barges.

I have no idea how long it took; all I remember is that at
the depth of my dejection, when I was about to cover my
face with my hands and to break down sobbing, the voice
of the lookout yelled, surprisingly close, "Thar she is! On
the starboard bow!"

He pointed into the fog. With my heart in my throat, I
gazed into the grayness. Out of that cotton-wool world
emerged a dark bobbing object trailing shrouds of fog,
turning in the swirling tide. It was the outer buoy. If I had
been sailing with full visibility, I would have given it a
wider berth; now I was so stunned by its appearance that
I merely stood there, gaping at it, as it bobbed by. The
swell was not strong enough to operate its bell, it drifted
past silently, ghostlike, was lost in the swirling grayness
astern; then it started to ring out as the wash of the tugboat
rocked it.

I stood there, stunned by the realization that I had been
saved by outrageous luck. I had to do something now,
give my next order, but I just stood there, speechless, riveted to the spot; then I heard the wireless operator say,
with a sudden sound of sincerity, "Well, I'll be damned!
Neat job, Skipper."

That woke me up. That alter ego took over again and said, "So glad you approve. How about stamping for some coffee?"

"Fair enough," he said. "Will do," and he went out on the boatdeck. It had been exactly the right thing to say; only a skipper who was really experienced in the tugboat business would know that the sole person who could ask for coffee to be brought up was the wireless operator, who did so by stamping on the floor of his cabin, which was right over the galley. In the salvage business, he was not supposed to leave his listening post but to sit there for twenty-four hours a day, earphones on his head, his transmitter at the ready.

Meanwhile, I had subconsciously been listening to the tolling of the buoy each time the wash of a barge rocked it. When I finally said to the helmsman, "All right, bring her over; course south southeast by south," I had counted ten. It meant taking another risk, but not nearly as grave as the one I had taken when I headed full speed into the fog for an invisible buoy four miles away. If I gave my order to swing around too soon, the tail barge would hit the buoy, but I was sure it was the right moment, with that same, strange certainty that had prompted me to change course.

The tow swung around; I went out onto the bridge. Before long, the lookout reported the first marker of the mine-swept channel to starboard. The pregnant cook in the butcher's apron came up with the coffee; I was respectfully served first. As I stood sipping the hot sweet liquid, my eyes filming over with the steam, a voice muttered, "It's lifting again."

It was the mate. His pipe was lit once more. He stood beside me for a little while, stirring his coffee, then he said, "Fog's the very devil on this coast. At every departure, you have to pass your driving test all over again."

I appreciated the gesture, but all I could offer in response was a grunt. I took another sip, and I was sure everybody on that bridge heard my teeth clattering against the mug. It was the reaction. I was trembling so uncontrollably that I had to hold the mug with both hands.

I had no means of knowing that what had happened to me was a manifestation of the sixth sense possessed by every born sailor. You can train a man in navigation, seamanship, celestial observation and the computing of tide, current, speed, wind and drift, and yet he will never be a sailor unless, at the moment of truth when he is forced into a corner from which there is no way out except by instant intuitive action, he unerringly makes the right move.

It took me years to realize this; I certainly had no inkling of it that afternoon when I headed my first tow out to sea as Master, oceangoing tugboats. But, somehow, Mr. Kwel must have known.

CHAPTER THREE

I

As a relief captain, I entered a strange new world, a world without color, with a melancholy all its own.

Maybe it was the time of year: early autumn, when, in the North Sea, all color seems to be drained out of the sky and the water, leaving only shades of gray. The black tug, trailing a string of black barges linked by heavy hawsers drooping into the sea, sailed through a gray, hazy void underneath a gray sky graded in delicate shades. It was either still and empty except for a thin, delicately brushed-in layer of mackerel cloud, or stormy with scudding squalls, racing shadows and distant, slanting patches of rain. But always, port out, starboard home, there was the undulating skyline of the coast of England, black on gray, with occasionally the startling whiteness of chalk cliffs in wintry sunlight, and often the grim black mushroom clouds of burning cities far inland.

In that gray world, there were only a few elemental sounds: steam hissing, the swish of a wave, the screech of a seagull, the mournful tolling of a buoy rocking in the

66

wash. It seemed to have nothing to do with the world of men; it set into relief, with agonizing poignancy, the drabness, the drudgery, the brutishness of war. It provided a backdrop of remote and timeless serenity to the tows of shabby barges, once a family's pride, now paintless and grimy, their decks ingrained with coal dust, their bows buckled and dented, their wheelhouses splintered, untended tears in the tarpaulins on their hatches flapping bleakly in the wind. Most of the barges we towed that fall were Dutch; it seemed unbelievable that some of them dared to hazard outside. But then, they were no longer their own masters; instead they were reduced to pawns at the mercy of bureaucrats in the distant beehives of government offices, who spent their days shuffling bills of lading, swapping names of vessels, shifting tons of cargo and manipulating human fates in a vast, abstract game of Monopoly. Almost every ship in the coastal trade sailed in charter to some government agency or other; there was no escaping the impersonal mechanism of bureaucracy. The crews of the armada of freighters, coasters, lighters, barges, tugs, trawlers and fishing smacks scudding and scurrying, plodding and plunging up and down the British coast were aware that nobody cared a hoot about what they were doing or what happened to them and their ships.

Hardly any of them were armed, not because they were free from enemy attack but because other ships had priority. These were the years of scarcity, when Britain fought the war alone, when freighters were hastily converted into auxiliary warships, when Bofors guns, pom-poms and Oerlikons sprouted on the poops and aft castles of incongruous merchantmen, when anything that would float was drafted to keep up the fleet on which England's life depended.

As far as armaments were concerned, coastal traffic was classed as "non-essential." Not only was it supposed to

have the protection of the R.A.F. and the Fleet Air Arm
but also, even if every single one of its vessels were sunk,
there still was, theoretically, the alternative of transport by
rail or road. So, with dreary, heart-breaking regularity, the
raiders of the Luftwaffe made their routine passes, sinking
barges with cannon fire, machine-gunning wheelhouses and
fo'c'sles, killing and maiming women, children, cooks, captains, deckhands and boys. They sank dignified Protestant
barges with Dutch names like *Isaiah*, *The Four Gospels* and
Roam, I Await Thee. They blew up coasters and ferries
with English names like *Bumblebee*, *Puddletown Martyr*
and *Gracie Fields*. They exploded tankers and tugboats and
welldeck freighters called *Metallurgy V*, *Portland Bill*
and *Maid of Surrey*. And nobody seemed to care about
them, let alone mourn them, least of all the clerk in some
government office who scratched out a name in a ledger,
tore up an index card and filled out a form in quadruplicate
for the Registrar of Births, Deaths and Marriages that
carried the instruction: *If maimed, specify disablement; if
dead, the word "dead" to be filled in.*

Among the myriad nameless, homeless ants, I was, so it
seemed to me, the most homeless, the most expendable.
I did not even have a home address, only "c/o Dutch Shipping, 505 Bel Air House, London W.1." I took over tugboats whose captains were sick or on leave or had died
without replacement. I never stayed on board for more
than a week or so, never had a chance to get to know the
crews, and they never came to know me either, although
some of them pretended they did. It was the familiar defense mechanism of the tugboat crew deprived of their
captain, grasping at a straw of reassurance; via the grapevine of garrulous cooks, I was soon informed that I was
acquiring the reputation of "bringing luck." On every ship
I took over for a few fleeting days and nights I left behind

a number of "intimate friends" who regaled their shipmates, under an oath of secrecy, with titbits of information
I was supposed to have imparted to them. Occasionally, one
of these inventions would get back to me: how I had saved
the *Cornelia Kwel* in a typhoon after Captain Bosman had
been knocked unconscious; how I had determined the
position of a fog-bound tow lost in a minefield by tasting
the sample of the sea bottom brought up by the lead; how
I had smuggled two girls on board in Stockholm before the
war, when runner captain on board the yacht of the Shah
of Persia being towed to the Caspian Sea via Russia, and
kept an orgy going in the Shah's oval bed during the entire
crossing to Leningrad. Some of these stories were as old as
the hills, as for instance the one about tasting the lead,
which I had heard attributed to at least four old tugboat
captains over the years; a few were closer to home, such
as the one that I had deserted a girl back in Holland who
then joined the underground movement and was shot by
the Gestapo, which was why I was so anti-social. Or the
one that I was writing a book about them all, to be published after the war, with everybody's name in it. Yet the
essence of all these fantasies was that I "brought luck."

Actually, they were not far wrong. I had to admit that
I seemed to be leading a charmed life, for during the two
years I trotted up and down the bridle path between John
O'Groats and Land's End with an assortment of unsuit-
able craft, I lost only four vessels of the hundreds I towed
and one man on board my own ship: a stoker who had
come up for a breath of air and proceeded to relieve himself squatting on the stern, a sitting duck for a German
fighter pilot indulging in a run of grouse-shooting before
brunch on a Sunday morning.

But though my reputation as a "character" grew, I,
personally, seemed unable to acquire an identity, perhaps

because of the kind of life I led. There was no place I could come to rest. I lived in other men's cabins, in chartrooms, in sleepers on the Flying Scotsman and dreary rooms in a succession of dreary hotels. In the process, I came to feel very close to Sophie; I even went so far as to send her a fifty-word Red Cross message—the only way of communicating with people in Occupied Europe—in which I wrote that I would remain true to her and that she was in my thoughts every day. But shortly thereafter I had a brief bucolic encounter with a WAAF that had absolutely nothing to do, so it seemed, with the high level on which the souls of Sophie and me communicated, yet for some inexplicable reason I instantly forgot all about her. From a nightly apparition, frolicking uninhibitedly through my adolescent dreams, she burned into a memory that, after a few more rustic romps with members of the female forces, I sometimes stumbled upon with a feeling of embarrassment.

For a while, easy-going promiscuity seemed the answer for everyone concerned. Being Merchant Marine, I was usually scorned by members of the WRNS, who reserved the granting of privileges to officers of the Royal Navy; but WAAFS and ATS, less knowledgeable, saw only a naval officer with four stripes, a wicked eye and a bold manner. But gradually those short encounters became more and more formalized, until they all followed the same impersonal pattern, a sort of sexual morris dance. I reached the ultimate in impersonal formality one night, in some port after some movie, when a young woman, the color of whose uniform I could not even determine because of the blackout, guided me, after the merest of introductions, to a vast warehouse on the edge of some field. I concluded she must be a WAAF, as I discerned the silhouettes of aircraft in the misty darkness beyond the building. She opened the huge door of the hangar in a way that betrayed familiarity; there was a hollow rumbling overhead of well-oiled casters rolling on a rail and the corrugated door slid open. We had been making correct and genteel conversation on our way to our tryst, without even the intimacy of walking arm in arm. I had by then acquired a quasi-Oxford accent and an exaggerated use of service slang, a phase most Allied officers passed through; when she suggested, "Shall we bed down heah? These sacks are quite soft, I believe it's sugah," I answered, "Wizard prang." After some practiced, impersonal manipulations in the dark, there followed the soft tinkle of coins in trousers being lowered, and snappings of elastic indicating the same preparatory measures by my opposite number; then the sudden, stunning shock of total intimacy. For a few seconds, the whole thing seemed desperate and hungry and tender and human, but the detached expertness that had marked our encounter from the beginning brought us swiftly to its technical conclusion. The coins tinkled again and the elastic snapped; then I saluted correctly in the darkness and heard myself say with that ghastly Oxford accent, "I say, thank you very much," and marched off.

Shortly thereafter I received a letter from Sophie's parents in America. Judging by the envelope, it had some trouble finding me, as it was addressed to *Dutch Sailor Martinus Harinxma, Towboats, London.* Among the addresses the Post Office had tried were those of the Salvation Army, the Netherlands Prime Minister and, for some reason known only to the Salvation Army who forwarded it, the Windmill Theatre, a burlesque show on Piccadilly Circus. Finally, it had found its way to Dutch Shipping, 505 Bel Air House, where the efficient Miss Crumb had crossed out the word *Sailor* and written *Captain* over it before forwarding it to the agents in Hull, where it found me. It was a shocking letter, deeply upsetting, full of grotesque accusations and threats, most of them religious and to do with my Life Hereafter. They had received the news, in a relative's letter smuggled out of occupied Europe via Portugal, that Sophie had been picked up in a raid by the Germans and put on transport to Poland. No one knew exactly what that meant at the time, but there were rumors; to her parents, she was about to be murdered, if she hadn't been already, and I was the culprit. I had prevented her leaving with them by my selfish lust, sacrificed the sweetest, kindest child the world had ever known to "a passing infatuation."

Although I shrugged it off and threw the letter out the porthole into the swirling water of the Humber, I was thoroughly rattled. It was bound to haunt me for the rest of my days, and I knew it; its immediate effect was to make me lose interest in "love" in any shape or form. I finally accepted the loneliness of the Master without a ship of his own as a fact of life, and gave up my halfhearted efforts to establish some human contact with the staff and the crew of the ship assigned to me for a spell. I preferred to lie on my bunk, reading, rather than to sit yacking in the messroom in a self-conscious effort to make friends with men I would probably never set eyes on again. Sophie, comfortably stowed away during my waking hours in the compartment labeled *To be dealt with after the war*, broke out of her confinement in my dreams. For months I was beset by subtle variations of the same nightmare, each one ending with the same horrendous climax: she was raped, screaming, struggling, berserk with terror, by a series of faceless, uniformed brutes, while I stood yelling voicelessly in a frenzy of powerless despair on the bank of a river that separated us. The monstrous, incomprehensibly obscene part of that nightmare was that I would wake up, tears streaming down my face, my heart banging wildly, in a state of high sexual excitement. It made me pick up the day with weariness and a sense of unutterable loathing.

I had entered the dark night of the soul, which comes to all men at war, sooner or later, each in his own time. Oddly enough, it made me a better captain. In later years it has occurred to me that, fantastic as it might seem, Mr. Kwel may have been waiting for this to happen. At first I discarded that thought as farfetched, but it kept coming back to me. After all, he knew more about tugboats and the men that sailed them than anyone else alive, for that was his business; he must have waited for something to happen that would turn his adolescent protégé into a proper Master instead of just a boy playing at captains. Strange, that I should have acquired maturity as a sailor through being humbled and hardened by a secret, ineradicable guilt; it would seem that the two things have nothing to do with one another; I certainly had no idea at the time that this was so. But maybe he had. In those years, he certainly knew me better than anyone else alive.

2

The only member of the opposite sex with whom I came in contact occasionally was the refined, still vaguely smelly Miss Crumb in the office of Dutch Shipping. I went there on the rare occasions when I was required to report to London for orders rather than collect them from some agent on the coast. I had not met Mr. Kwel again after our first encounter. Miss Crumb always had "all the details" and proceeded to communicate them to me with the superciliousness of a director's secretary who is no longer subject to air attacks. As London became safer, Miss Crumb became more genteel, to a point where it seemed unimaginable that once upon a time I had ogled her with lechery. Her face was made up as harshly as that of a geisha; her ludicrously long nails looked like the magenta claws of an animal from mythology; but her plaintively refined voice, hoarse from incessant smoking, had the effluvium of a seamen's club late at night. Those clubs were indistinguishable all over England; in every one the pick-up was braying "Boomps-a-Daisy" or "The Lambeth Walk" over a din compounded of the clashes of billiard balls, raucous laughter, the zip and click of shuffleboard disks, the tick-tock of ping-pong and the dull thuds of Missing Links kicking the pinball machine in an effort to get back lost investments.

One day in the early summer of 1942, I was again ordered to report to London for orders. As usual, I entered the outer office prepared to be jocular and continental to Miss Crumb as she briefed me on my next assignment, to which she would react with genteel distaste. But this time, to my surprise, she welcomed me effusively. "Oh, Captain, I'm so glad you are here! Mr. Kwel has been waiting for you all morning. Will you please go straight in? He has no one with him at the moment."

But, as usual, she was overcome by second thoughts. "Wait a moment! Maybe I had better announce you after all," she said, when I was already on my way to the door, and she pushed herself away from the desk where she had sat pecking at the keys of an adding machine with her magenta talons. She got to her feet, pulled down her very tight skirt, minced to the door of the inner office, and lifted a crooked finger to knock; then, overcome by third thoughts, she listened at the crack. "Just a sec, he's on the phone." She went back to her desk and said, with a look of drama on her enameled face, "Isn't it terrible about poor old Captain Loppersum? Or haven't you heard?"

"Don't tell me they sank the *Isabel Kwel?*" I ventured, not unduly harrowed. I had never set eyes on the great Captain Loppersum and had seen little of the flagship over the last two years. The really big ones were out of my class; only occasionally had I caught a fleeting glimpse of them as they ghosted by, furtive and majestic, on the distant horizon, bound for the ocean. I felt no kinship with those famous behemoths; they moved in another world, roaming faraway seas, a different species from "our medium craft," the old, worn packmules like the *Anna*, the *Honesta*, the *Deborah* and the late *Cornelia*, God bless her soul.

"Oh, no, the ship is all right," Miss Crumb said. "It's the Commodore himself. He died last night, here in London. Heart attack."

She got up, put her ear to the door again, whispered, "He's off!" and knocked.

The dry Dutch voice answered, "Come in."

She opened the door. "Captain Harinxma to see you, sir."

"Oh, good for him," the voice said, with surprising enthusiasm. "Show the captain in, will you?"

She smiled at me; I passed close to her as I went in. She smelled better this time; maybe hers was a seasonal affliction.

Mr. Kwel, looking so exactly as I remembered him that it seemed as if he had not been out of that suit for two years, came toward me with both hands outstretched. He grabbed mine, pumped them with bewildering heartiness and said, "Harinxma, I am delighted to see you. Sit down, please, sit down. Cigar?"

I never smoked cigars, but the occasion seemed to call

for something, so I said, "Thank you, sir," and took an expensive-looking cheroot out of the box he proffered. When I did not instantly bite off the tip with my eyetooth but fumbled with it for a moment, he said, "Let me do that for you," took the cigar out of my hand, snipped a V-shaped gap in its tip with a special instrument he produced from his waistcoat, and handed it back to me. Then he snapped a lighter to life and held the flame out to me; as I sucked in the sweet-scented smoke, I tried to figure out what could be up. I felt like a cornered rat faced by a big, purring cat.

"Had a good trip?" the cat asked, affably, when we finally sat facing each other across his empty desk.

"Oh, the usual sort of thing, thank you," I answered. It wasn't a very bright answer, but then, he obviously was not listening. He was looking me over with the swift expert scrutiny of the man-trader. "You have heard about Captain Loppersum?" he asked. "Miss Crumb, I'm sure, has filled you in," and he gave me one of his unexpected, mirthless smiles again.

That smile rang a whole series of alarm bells all over the ship. Whatever the cat might be after, I had to play it as cool and as cagey as I could.

"I understand he passed away last night," I said respectfully.

"He did," he said, and again that smile. "He died the way he would have wanted to, I suppose, if all I have heard about him in the past is correct."

"Ah?" I crossed my legs and tipped the first ashes of my panatella. "How?"

"In a brothel. In full flight, as I understand it." Then, to my alarmed surprise, he winked.

Behind that wink, that locker-room jocularity, lurked a sense of triumph, a cold, consuming hatred. I knew, like everyone else in the tugboat business, that old Bokke Loppersum had made it a habit to go and harass Mr. Kwel in his office every time he came home on shore leave. It had not done him any good, it had not done anybody any good, but it had been a virile ritual of loyalty, like carrying flowers to a dead friend's grave.

Captain Loppersum had been first the sea-father and later the lifelong comrade of a man called Hendrik Hobbema, a tugboat captain who had risen from the ranks during the First World War and started a company of his own. He had made quite a niche for himself, and had even developed into a threat to Kwel's International, when the Depression cut him down; unlike his adversary, he had no relatives or cronies in the banking world to bail him out. He had heroically clung to his small fleet of brand-new tugs, keeping them tied up in port, waiting for a big transport the British Navy was rumored to be preparing, while Kwel scattered his boats on piddling little jobs all over the globe. When the British finally asked for bids on the hauling of a mammoth drydock from the Clyde to Singapore, a job for six prime boats at least, Hobbema was alone in the field. He was sure the job was his, as Kwel simply didn't have the boats available. When he was informed that the British had granted the job to Kwel's International Tugboat Company, the shock literally killed him, for he had signed a mortgage agreement with a bank which included the clause that, should he fail to secure the British job, his boats would be sold by the bank in the open market the next day. Kwel, who had quietly submitted the smaller bid, bought Hobbema's boats for a song, and with them towed the drydock to Singapore. From that day on, Kwel's International had been the sole master of Holland's Glory. The crews of Hobbema's tugs, grumbling and full of hatred, were forced to grovel to keep their jobs; the only one who was famous enough, indifferent enough and huge enough to speak his mind was Bokke Loppersum, Commodore of the fleet. Nobody dared to fire him, not even Mr. Kwel himself; nobody was going to muzzle him either. Practically, there was nothing old Bokke could do; but he could at least make a gesture. Virile loyalty and a Nordic streak of mythic masochism prompted him to go and kick the shins of the man who had killed his friend, each time he found himself in the head office after a long haul. Now he was dead; no wonder Mr. Kwel had offered me a cigar. To him, it must be a joyous occasion; hence the wink and the icy jocularity with which he now could say: "He died in full flight, as I understand it."

"Fancy that," I said, in an effort to sound noncommittal.

It was wasted on him, he simply had not listened. Maybe he never did; maybe all he ever did was look, the way he looked at me now: a probing scrutiny of pale gray eyes as if he were observing my innards on a fluoroscope screen.

Then he said, "Yes," with a sigh, and his eyes lost that clinical look. Whatever it had been he was watching, he had seen enough. "His death comes at an awkward time, for I'm afraid the game is up." He smiled again, this time at me personally, and not at interstellar space. "During her construction, the *Isabel Kwel* was designed to double as a mine layer in case of war; the British have finally dug up this information and claimed her as a subsidiary man-of-war. I have run out of delaying tactics, she is due to sail as a rescue ship with the next convoy to Murmansk. She will be entirely under British control, which is a tragedy, not only for this company, but for the Dutch deep-sea towing business. For the very survival of this company and the future of that business hinge on her. The *Isabel Kwel* is the last tugboat of her class we have left."

It was the first intimation I had of the fate of the behemoths I had seen fleetingly on the horizon, ghosting to their doom. But before I had a chance to comment, he continued, in that flat, whining voice of gentility, "The only thing left for me to do, as a last-ditch effort to protect her as much as possible, is to put someone in command who understands the situation and who can be relied upon to do whatever is in his power to save the ship. I had to come to an immediate decision, and my decision is that you shall be the new Master of the *Isabel Kwel*. She is at present in Holyhead; you are due to sail at dawn the day after tomorrow to Greenock for conversion. So, let's get down to the details."

I had almost dropped my cigar. "You can't be serious!"

"Dead serious." He sounded convincing.

"But, sir . . ."

He brushed it aside. "The fact that you just happened to walk into my office today has nothing to do with it, in case that's what you are thinking. I have had you in mind for this for some time. By appointing you relief captain, I have been grooming you for just this eventuality. The fact that you happen to be in port just now is a welcome coincidence, no more. I would have pulled you off whatever ship you might have been on at this time and sent you to Greenock. Captain Loppersum's mate would have had to take her up there day after tomorrow."

"But why me?" I asked. "Why can't his mate take over command? He's the natural—"

His veneer of bonhomie cracked for a moment. "I'll thank you to let me run my end of the business, Captain," he interjected tartly. "I won't bore you with the considerations which led me to my decision; you'll have to take my word for it that they were valid ones."

"But I am a complete outsider," I insisted. "I have never handled a ship her size in my life. . . ."

"An outsider is what the crew of the *Isabel Kwel* need at this very moment. Someone with enough authority and youth and inner independence to ignore the memory of Captain Loppersum and take them in hand. As to your second consideration: there is no essential difference between the *Isabel* and, say, the *Anna*, only that she is bigger."

"A hell of a lot bigger," I added, disrespectfully. "Seriously, sir: to sail tricycles like the *Anna* or the *Deborah* within constant sight of the coast is one thing; this is an ocean job, on the largest tugboat in the world. I simply don't feel qualified."

"Your feelings, Captain Harinxma," he said calmly, "confirm my opinion. If you were sure of yourself right now, you would not be the man I need. To take over the command of that ship, from that man, at this moment, needs someone who is beset by self-doubt and a sense of inadequacy, yet experienced enough as a craftsman to handle the vessel expertly. The *Isabel Kwel* is our last card; I don't want a hero with panache on her bridge. I want a man who has the sense to be afraid. Would you like me to put that more explicitly?"

"I would like you to forget about it, sir," I said, discarding my cigar in the ashtray. "I appreciate the compliment, but I am not going to mess around with that ship and that crew, not with the ghost of Bokke Loppersum breathing down my neck. To consider me for that post is, if you don't mind my being frank, the brainwave of a man in an office. Every captain in your fleet will tell you that what you need here is another old pro, not an amateur like me. It may have escaped your attention, but I hate the sea, I hate the tugboat business, and I am no fonder of you than I would be of any man who kept me at his mercy with the aid of a corrupt and degrading law for most of my adult life."

It had been no effort, after all these years, to tell him what I thought of him. I enjoyed it and I would not have minded telling him some more. What stopped me was his smile. I didn't like it; it was the smile of a man with a trump card up his sleeve. Then he said, in a conversational tone, "Apart from the compelling reasons for the law, which I'll be happy to explain to you at some future date, I should perhaps tell you that sea days made on board vessels sailing on convoy duty under British charter are exempt. The moment the *Isabel Kwel* becomes a rescue ship, she stops being a tugboat. So, in case you are planning to aim for your Master's Certificate, Merchant Marine, after the war, serving on her will mean totting up a tidy store of valid sea days."

Maybe it is the fate of the rat to think, until the very last moment, that he has outwitted the cat. When he said that, he struck unerringly at my jugular vein. Over the years, the notion of being a galley slave, unable to leave the tugboat service if I wanted to, had become such a basic fact of life to me that it had, without my realizing it, turned from a legitimate gripe into a psychological crutch. I had fallen into the trap that threatens all oppressed minorities: not just my social circumstances, but all my personal faults and weaknesses as well had come to be blamed on the oppressor. Should I go on refusing his offer, I would no longer be turning down the preposterous assignment of Commodore of the fleet and Master of the largest tugboat in the world, I would be turning down the only chance that had ever come my way to shed my bondage without leaving the sea altogether. To refuse now would be to confess that I wanted to be a bondsman, needed to be a slave, that I had turned the law on the sea days into a scapegoat for all the flaws in my personality, from my inferiority complex and incapacity for love to my smoking habits and my intellectual snobbery. It was more than I could face at that moment; had he offered me the supreme command of the Allied Navies, I would have walked out of his office an Admiral. Although I went on protesting for a while, I had no choice but to accept.

He knew it, for he got down to brass tacks at once. His instructions, detailed to an impressive degree, instructed me to refuse all duties that the Navy might try to impose upon the *Isabel Kwel* other than those explicitly agreed upon in her charter as a rescue ship. In particular, all aggressive action that might induce the enemy to single her out for attack should be sternly refused or, if refusal was impossible, evaded by all means my wits could conjure up. I had one supreme duty, and that was to bring her back, as she was the only hope Holland's Glory had for survival and resurrection after the war. "Protect her, Harinxma," he said, as we parted with a handshake that he obviously intended to be meaningful and virile. "The future of the tugboat business now rests on you." I smiled modestly and muttered something humble. I was a big, phony, spineless schmo. Instead of telling him to go to hell with his tugboat and turning away to meet my fate on my own terms like a man, I accepted without a word of protest the role of lackey to a ruthless, greedy capitalist who was bent on protecting his investment from all comers, friend or foe, and the hell with everybody else. Maybe he had won our small and insignificant contest of wills so handily because he was more honest than I. He did not need any illusions about himself to keep operational. He was a selfish bastard without an ounce of compassion, and he knew it, and it did not worry him one bit.

In the anteroom, Miss Crumb sat in wait for me behind her doll's desk with a new expression on her enameled face; she obviously was in the know, and deeply impressed. As I emerged from the holy of holies, she rose to help me struggle into my greatcoat, which was an embarrassing innovation. As she did so, she whispered dramatically, "Commodore! I have something important to tell you, in private. Can we meet after hours?"

"Oh—why, yes," I said, with marked lack of enthusiasm. I wanted to be alone, to think things over; judging by the look on her face, meeting Miss Crumb after hours might well end with her magenta claws fumbling with my collar stud. It was not a pleasing prospect; but I was intrigued, and my curiosity got the better of me. We made a whispered appointment to meet outside Swan and Edgar's, Piccadilly side, at half past six.

It meant that I had to take her out to dinner. I had not been in London often enough to acquire an extensive knowledge of suitable restaurants. I knew only two: a Chinese one in Shaftesbury Avenue and a rather dark, boudoir-like place in a basement nearby, where the members of the world's oldest profession, locally referred to as "Piccadilly Flak," congregated after walking their stints on the edge of Green Park. Thinking it would be the more private of the two, I took her there.

The dinner was a bit of a letdown. After her whispered intimation, I had expected some crucial bit of information, something that would make the whole enigma of my appointment fall into place. As it turned out, she had nothing more momentous to communicate than the report of a letter Mr. Kwel had written to his father that morning and sent by messenger, the moment he heard about Bokke Loppersum's death.

It was the first time I heard that the Mr. Kwel I knew

was not the real bogeyman, but Mr. Kwel Junior. It seemed an anticlimax befitting the day: not only had I conjured up a demon to take the rap for my own shortcomings, I had battled with the wrong one. The whole thing suddenly seemed a comedy of errors: the wrong Commodore telling the wrong owner exactly what he thought of him; two juniors playing at being the Real Thing. There was only one reality left in this bewildering mixture of shadow and substance: every day I served on board the *Isabel Kwel* would be one more valid sea day toward my Master's Certificate, Merchant Marine—one day closer to freedom. I listened to the rest of Miss Crumb's disclosures with dispassionate politeness.

It seemed that the Old Gentleman lived in a villa outside London, that he was nominally retired from the board of directors but could still be "an interfering nuisance, if truth be told." Mr. Kwel Junior had written to his Daddy that, in his opinion, the only Master capable of filling old Loppersum's shoes was young Harinxma, and he proceeded to give his reasons: that I was intelligent, capable, authoritative, and that he had specially groomed me for the job. But there was more than that; there was a supreme reason why he considered me to be ideal; the pity of it was that Miss Crumb, who had been unable to filch the letter from the files without her employer's noticing it with the eyes he had in the back of his head, was forced to quote from memory, and her memory proved to be photographic rather than analytic. She sat there, frowning in the candle-light, her opal nails plucking her violet lips, and tried to conjure up the image of the letter. Somewhere a prisoner of love sat tinkling "St. Louis Woman" on a piano; Cypriot waiters in foul tempers tramped up and down the aisle, shouldering trays, swarthily scowling.

"I think it said that to be a tugboat captain one needs not just experience, but talent," Miss Crumb said, frowning. "He said that it was like composing or painting or writing; what one needed most as a sailor was, er—er, talent, I believe. . . . Or something to that effect," she added lamely with an apologetic little laugh that sent a whiff of her expensive liqueur across the table. She had made it plain that she expected dinner with all the trimmings.

So I had "talent" for being a sailor. It was just the kind of pretentious nonsense you might expect a junior partner with an expensive education to brandish in the face of his millionaire Pa, a kindergarten drop-out. I asked her what the old gentleman's reply had been to his son's homily on talent, or was his reply not in yet? With a sudden recurrence of her genteel manner, Miss Crumb said that, oh yes, the reply was in, but Mr. Kwel Senior replied in Dutch to his son's letters; because she couldn't read Dutch, she couldn't really say what the reply had been, other than that it had made Mr. Kwel say something in Dutch for which he had apologized, needlessly, as she had not understood it. She took another genteel nip of Cointreau, little finger in the air, then she ventured, "But if it's important to you, I suppose I could borrow that letter from the files for an hour or so. . . ." She looked at me with brazen innocence. "What about tonight? We could go by my place and pick up the key to the office."

I realized that, if I played this her way, I could get myself quite an interesting pipeline to the inner office of Kwel's International. Had she made this suggestion a few months earlier, I would have taken her up on it, but after the letter from Sophie's parents, I had entered a period of incuriosity. "I am afraid I have to leave by night train in a couple of hours or so," I said, "so it will have to wait till next time. Anyhow, I can just about imagine what it said. But thanks all the same."

My smile must have been insincere, and she matched it. "Don't mention it," she said, then she looked at her wristwatch and added, "Well, if you have to catch a train, I suppose we might as well move along, don't you think?"

I paid, managing not to scream when I saw the bill; the Cypriot waiter grabbed my money as if it were a payoff to the Mafia. I took her home in a taxi, where we sat in opposite corners with nothing left to say. When the taxi stopped, I got out to see her to the door of her block of flats, despite her protestations that I shouldn't bother. Only after she had fumbled for her key in the blackout and managed to open the door of the dark building did she give away how she felt by saying coldly in the darkness, "Well, good night, Commodore. Thanks for the meal, and good luck on the convoy. From what I understand, you'll need it." Before I had been able to mutter something gallant, she was gone.

"Commodore . . ." It sounded ludicrous, yet she had not said it ironically. Obviously, she accepted my promotion at face value, not as the hoary joke old Mr. Kwel Senior and I knew it to be. I got back into the taxi, gave the driver the address of my hotel and sank back in the corner of the seat. Only then did it occur to me that Mr. Kwel had not mentioned money. Whatever my promotion had been, it had not included a raise. But I did not care. Neither he nor I was in this for the money, whatever he might think. The only piece of information I had received worth the Cointreau was that my Mr. Kwel Junior had an old Bokke Loppersum of his own breathing down his neck. He did not gain my sympathy by it, but it seemed to make him a little more human.

It did not occur to me at the time that this change in my attitude toward him proved him right. Whatever his apoplectic Daddy may have had to say about me, I was now a Commodore.

3

I had been told I would be met by some member of the crew at Holyhead Station; I was not prepared for what I found. I had seen my share of queer fish and egomaniacs during my two years with the medium craft, but this one took the prize. He was so outrageous that I could not bring myself to believe that this must be he, until there was no one else left on the platform.

He was a youngish man, maybe two or three years older than I, in balaklava, surplus RAF flying jacket, white shirt, black tie, green tropical fatigue trousers and tennis shoes. It was a pretty exotic outfit, but it was not his actual get-up that threw me. It was the fact that, as he stood eyeing all uniformed males coming off that train with provocative superciliousness, a puddle of water was growing around his feet. He was dripping wet, from head to toe, and stood there, daring every Merchant Marine officer who came his way to express surprise with as much as a flicker of an eyelid. A few of them did; virtually everyone looked down at the pool of water, and this seemed to give him satisfaction.

He was so wrapped up in his own performance that he did not notice me; maybe he was unprepared for my youth. His defiance indicated that he was the mate, the one who had been passed up for promotion. It seemed obvious that I was going to have a tough time with him, but he did not worry me. As far as I was concerned, he could have stood there stark naked. It was strange; the fact that on board the *Isabel Kwel* I would be collecting sea days that would lead to freedom had liberated me of the last vestige of insecurity. I did not care a damn; the whole thing was crazy. To make me the captain of the biggest ship of his fleet had been an insane thing to do, but that was not my problem, it was Mr. Kwel's. All I was going to worry about, from now on, was how to get through the rest of the war unscathed, so as to enjoy the freedom I was working toward. I walked up to the exhibitionist and said, "You're the mate of the *Isabel Kwel*, I take it? I'm your new captain. The name is Harinxma." I did not as much as glance at the puddle at his feet, I just gave him an insurance agent's smile.

He looked around at me slowly. His eyes were extraordinarily blue, as cold and remote as those of a madman. He had more hostility and frustration piled up inside him than I would care to carry around in the gunpowder room of my subconscious. It must be quite a ship; old Loppersum must have been quite a captain.

"Welcome, Commodore," he said with exaggerated formality. "Kramer, first officer." He followed it with a salute so expansive that its flourish sprayed me with water from his sleeve. "We are so glad to have you with us," he added, while those eyes took me in with icy hatred. "May I take over your load?"

"Thanks," I said and let him take my duffel bag. He swung it onto his shoulder very fast, but I had suspected something and stepped back in time; even so, he nearly knocked my cap off with the thing. He did not express disappointment, he obviously had been conditioned to take his losses in his stride.

"May I conduct you to a hansom, Commodore?"

"Thanks." It must get through to him, despite his preoccupation with his own performance, that he bored me.

"This way, please," he said. "I'm sorry that our effort to organize a barouche for you fell through, Commodore," he continued as we went down the stairs and into the underpass. "The wireless operator and myself had picked one in the High Street that seemed to befit the occasion. An MG, fire-engine red, very dashing. By the time we got it on the road, I realized the WO didn't know how to drive it; he put it in neutral and the thing just started to roll down the hill, backwards. As you can see, we ended up in the drink."

"Fancy that," I said. I didn't want to be too obvious, so I added conversationally, "I trust he's all right."

"Couldn't be better," he replied, with a kind of adolescent smugness. "He's in jail. The MP's insisted that one of us go with them."

"Fancy that," I said.

"It wasn't ours, you see. It belonged to a Polish airman who was sitting in a bar nearby. He must have seen it flash past, down the hill, backwards, and there he was, standing on the quayside, speaking Polish, while we stood on the bonnet of the thing with just our shoulders above water. This way, please."

It was the kind of story one associates with the bright young things who flew the biplanes in the First World War; for two officers of a Dutch tugboat in 1942 it did not work. It was not even embarrassing, just tedious. When we came out of the underpass and emerged into the station square, he bellowed, "Taxi!" A cab drew up, the driver opened the door behind him without getting out.

"After you, sir—I'm sorry: Commodore," the bore said, with another of those salutes.

I stepped forward and got in; before I realized what

he had in mind, I heard the door slam behind me, my duffel bag flew in through the window and I heard him say to the driver, "Take this officer to the Dutch bumboat down at the harbor, opposite the chemist's. You know the one that connects with the Dutch ship?"

The driver muttered something, and while my mate stood preposterously to attention on the curbside, saluting, the taxi kangarooed off, down the steep incline toward the harbor.

I should have been quicker on the ball, I suppose. I was already sitting in a launch with a big Dutch flag and a surprisingly polite crew, on my way across the harbor, when I realized that something must be wrong. This did not look like the kind of workboat one of Kwel's tugs would carry around, not even his flagship. I had boarded her without stepping out of my role of tight-lipped, tough character; normally, I would have asked if this was indeed the boat to the tugboat *Isabel Kwel*, as by nature I am rather spinsterish the moment it comes to buses, trains and aircraft. I looked worriedly ahead and, sure enough, we were heading for a big two-stacked liner flying the Dutch flag. As we approached, I recognized her. It was the *Prins Hendrik*, one of the Harwich-Flushing ferries of the Zeeland Steamship Company.

I did not know quite how to play this hand; I turned to the bosun at the helm and asked, "What's she used for nowadays? Troopship?"

He eyed me with momentary surprise, then he replied politely, "No, she's a prison ship, sir, anchored here permanently. Royal Netherlands Navy."

"Ah," I said. "I see. In that case, I'm afraid I've sent you on a wild-goose chase. Somebody led me to believe that this was the bumboat for the Dutch tug, the *Isabel Kwel*."

"Sorry, sir, it isn't," he said stiffly.

As we were heading for the prison ship at a good clip and he obviously was not about to change course to accommodate me, I said, "All right. As we are on our way, I might as well pay my compliments to the commander. Is the original crew still on board?"

"Yes, sir. We just have a Navy complement, sir."

"All right," I said. "I'll go and see the captain."

So I did. There was some halfhearted piping overhead as I clambered up the gangway, but even though it stopped halfway with a little gurgle of embarrassment, at least they did not take me to be a prisoner. I was welcomed by a quartermaster with the company name on his hat, while in the background a Navy bosun sheepishly tried to hide his bird whistle in his horny hand. I was taken to the captain's quarters at my request and surprised that worthy gentleman half-naked, on his way either into or out of his shower. But he was hospitable enough; he asked what he could do for me, and I told him that a few members of my crew had got into trouble ashore, something to do with a stolen car they had driven into the harbor, and now one of them seemed to be in the clink somewhere. How should I go about getting him released without losing too much time, as I had orders to sail the next day?

He hemmed and hawed and looked important and offered me a cigar. Obviously, this was a welcome diversion; it must be a monotonous existence, anchored out in Holyhead harbor with a bellyful of prisoners and a Navy complement to run his ship. He must feel like a prisoner himself. "Nabbed by British MP's, most likely," he said. "Tell you what. I'm on my way ashore anyhow and I know the characters that run the pen there. I'll see what I can do. Maybe I can have him transferred. Is he Dutch?"

"I suppose so," I said. "I haven't even seen my ship yet. I just heard about this as I was met at the station by my mate."

"Well, he must be," the captain decided, putting on a shirt. "I'll have him switched if I can swing it, and I'll sign his release, at your request, or one of the Navy characters will. Okay?"

"That's very kind of you," I said. "I appreciate that."

"Well, hell," he answered, "if we Merchant Marine people didn't help one another, who would?"

"You're so right," I murmured politely.

"If you'll hold on a second," he continued, "I'll just put on tie and shoes and maybe I can drop you off on my way over."

"That would be a help."

"Fine, let's do that." He rummaged in a drawer among socks and singlets, with a secretive clinking of bottles. He harrumphed, and brought out a black tie. As he stood knotting it in front of his mirror, he asked, "Where are you heading for?"

I told him about the Arctic convoy, and he shook his head, commiseratingly. "Tough luck," he said, "tough luck, boy. God knows I'm sick of being stuck on a reef of kidney beans of my own making in this godforsaken joint, but I wouldn't volunteer for one of those. No, sir. What are you supposed to do in those convoys?"

"Rescue ship."

"Oh, boy! I know about those. If you don't cop it on the swings, you catch it on the roundabout. Well, all I can say is, good luck. All right, let's go."

We went. This time the bosun at the gangway piped with relish, the Navy characters that were about on the promenade deck all stood to attention and the captain strode toward the gangway with his hand at his cap in a

permanent salute, like a prince consort. Obviously, that
kind of thing grew on you. Once in his own launch, he
reverted to being human; there was some more cheerful
chat on his part on the subject of the Arctic convoys, while
the boat churned across the choppy harbor, sneezing
spindrift as it slammed its bow into the waves. Soon, after
rounding a pier with some warehouses, I spotted the
Isabel Kwel.

She was a great deal bigger than I had expected, very
full in the chest, with long, low hindquarters and a stubby
stack. Even at rest, she suggested tremendous power. As
we drew closer, I saw that her paint was scurvy and her
woodwork bare; maybe they hadn't done anything about
that because they were heading for drydock anyhow. But
when I climbed on board, after saying goodbye to my
generous colleague, I saw at a glance that she was a neg-
lected ship. Junk lay about in careless profusion on the vast
expanse of her aft deck. When I climbed the steps to the
boatdeck, I noticed that one of the boat covers was un-
lashed and partially open, and a sack of potatoes bulged
over the edge. Obviously, the cook was using it as his
larder.

It was a strange experience. She was the most typically
Dutch vessel you could imagine, and yet she felt like a
foreign craft. It must have been Captain Loppersum, im-
posing his personality. I saw nobody around, and I didn't
feel like calling "Yoo-hoo" or whatever a Commodore
calls when he arrives on board his ship and finds that
everyone is taking a nap. I didn't particularly care for
being piped on board by a bosun with a bird whistle, but
I didn't care for the other extreme either. But there was
little I could do except let nature take its course. They
were bound to find out sooner or later that they were
blessed with a new captain. I carried my bag past the

boats and the radio cubicle, the engine-room skylight and
the hot, humming stack, to the chartroom entrance. On
the threshold I stopped in my tracks.

Never in my sailing days had I seen such a pigsty. It
looked as if thieves had ransacked it in a hurry, throwing
papers, maps, pencils, rulers, caps, odd shoes, underwear,
flashlights, binoculars, boxes of Band-Aids and empty beer
bottles about them like dogs digging for a bone. On the
table, on top of a chart, stood a mahogany box which
looked like one of those portable bars owned by gentlemen grouse-shooters, but which on closer inspection I
discovered to be an old-fashioned ship's pharmacy. I
smelled a strong, pungent stench that I could not place
at first; all I knew was that it was reminiscent of my
youth and had to do with the aftermath of wild soccer
games played in vacant lots. Then I noticed, beside the
box, a bottle lying open on its side; a sticky brown substance had oozed from it onto the chart, and I recognized
the stench: Peruvian balsam. Obviously, the Master had
cut himself while preparing for his appointment in Samarra and had done some hasty self-doctoring before
making off, struggling into his greatcoat as he went.

The connecting door to the captain's cabin stood ajar;
I pushed it open with my foot. The stench that met me
was powerful. There is nothing quite so pungent as the
lair of a permanently unwashed human male—it acquires
a bouquet all its own, like a buzzard's nest. The room was
in semi-darkness, as the curtains in front of the portholes
were drawn. I stepped inside and looked around. The bed
was unmade, the dresser open, the floor covered with
discarded clothing which my predecessor had obviously
just stepped out of and left for his batman to pick up. I
didn't know who was supposed to pick it up, probably the
cook; whoever it was had either called it a day when he

heard the news, or been paralyzed with grief. In any case, somebody would have to clean out this horse stable before I could even think of moving in. I stepped over the heaps of clothing as over puddles, went to the opposite door and opened it to let in some fresh air. Then I opened the curtains and looked again.

The cabin was roomier than those I had known, but even so it had been too small for the man who lived here. Drawers and wardrobe were bulging; the walls were covered with postcards, framed pictures, a tambourine, a rabbit's foot; over the bunk, on a little shelf in the corner, stood a devotional red light with over it the smoky picture of what at first glance I took to be a saint but what on closer scrutiny turned out to be the faded color photograph of a belly dancer. Other photographs were pinned up in his bunk: three of them, all of the *Isabel Kwel* herself, obviously taken during trials. She looked as if she meant business; but grace was not her foremost characteristic. Whatever dream the great Kwel Senior might have realized with this monster vessel, it was not an esthetic one. At the far end of the cabin, where there should have been a washstand, was another door. I opened it and I found a bathroom, complete with toilet, shower and washbasin; again it was incredibly filthy, as if a number of drunks had used it during a party. Whoever had used it last had forgotten to flush the toilet; there was a grimy ring inside the washbasin; on the little marble shelf underneath the mirror I discovered a glass receptacle with, in it, the ghoulish grin of an extraordinarily large set of dentures. I wondered for a moment how a man could make off for a week end with amorous intentions and forget his teeth; I concluded that he must have had a spare set. Opposite the toilet, yet another photograph of the *Isabel Kwel* was stuck to the wall with surgical tape.

As I stooped to look at the photograph, I heard a sound behind me. I turned and found a small, middle-aged man of grimy appearance with a Bohemian haircut and a towel around his neck, staring at me. His arms were bare and decorated with a profusion of blue snakes; the display on his left arm terminated in what looked like a bracelet but what I later discovered to be a tattooed wristwatch, pointing permanently at five to five. He was unshaven, haggard, and his eyes looked bleary. His motionless presence, framed in the doorway, exuded an odd mixture of hangover and grief.

"And who might you be?" he asked, unpleasantly.

My first impulse was to make a sharp retort, but caution prevailed; I had no desire to become involved with any of these characters. I said, "I'm your new captain."

His eyes narrowed, his mouth went slack, then he said, "You're kidding."

"I'm sorry," I said. "You'll have to get used to the idea. As we are supposed to grow beards for the Arctic, it may get easier as we go along." I stepped out of the bathroom, making him back away, and I added, "Is it you who is supposed to look after this place?"

"I'm not supposed to do anything!" he answered viciously. "Captain Bokke and I have sailed together for over forty years. I've looked after him for thirty, like a mother, because he was a big, wonderful man who couldn't help himself; but that doesn't mean that I have to go down on my knees for any pipsqueak they send down to us with the Old Man not even in his grave! If you want this cabin, Mister, you'll have to look after it yourself! You'll have to clean it yourself, you'll have to keep it clean yourself, and you'll have to change your own diapers!" With that, he turned around and made off.

I should not let him get away with it, not the cook, but

there had been in his insulting tirade something embarrassing and awkward to watch, as if he were not the great
Captain Loppersum's cook of forty years' standing, but his
widow. The suggestion had been so strong that I could not
bring myself to stop him and give him what he deserved.
You make allowances for a widow that you don't make for
anyone else. So I let him go and decided to take him at his
word. I took off my greatcoat and my jacket, rolled up my
sleeves and set about cleaning up the place. I had to live
somewhere. As I stood looking about me, wondering where
to begin, the cook appeared in the doorway once more.

"In port we serve only one table," he said. "Lunch is in
half an hour, dinner at six."

"Okay," I said.

He hung on for a moment, as if he were about to say
something else; his lower lip was trembling, his red-rimmed
eyes had gone moist. I could not make out whether it
was anger, frustration or sorrow, but he looked as if he
had been crying. Whatever it was he had on the tip of his
tongue, he took with him down to the galley.

The moment he was gone, I started to exorcise Captain
Bokke's ghost by carrying out his earthly possessions by
the armful and dumping them on the boatdeck. It was not
a very elegant way of going about it, but I had been overcome by a growing feeling of outrage. I did not want this
to become personal, but I was damned if I was going to
let any one of them push me around just because he did
not like my face, my age or the company. As I started
to take down the pictures in the bunk and blew out the
little red light underneath the mysterious belly dancer in
the corner, I asked myself what I would have done had
I not been a relief captain for two years. For the first
time, I began to understand why Mr. Kwel had picked
me; I certainly could not have received a better training.

But maybe I was just whistling in the dark; if I felt some apprehension, it was not the moment to dwell on it. As I went on carrying out the memory of the great Captain Loppersum, a line from a play by the Belgian writer Maeterlinck kept running through my mind. It was spoken by a medieval crown prince, as he ran his sword through his senile father on the palace steps because the old man tried to block his way. The line was, *"Arrière, cadavre!"* —get out of the way, you corpse. I did not need to be a pupil of the late Siegmund Freud to interpret that one.

But something odd was happening. The more of his stuff I carried out, the more oppressive the feeling of Bokke Loppersum's presence became. I had the eerie feeling that, whereas when I first arrived he had not felt antagonistic toward me, now that I was so ruthlessly uprooting his mementoes he was beginning to get angry. What I was in fact doing was eradicating all remnants of a great sailor's life; the great sailor could not be expected to revel in that activity. If there was such a thing as a man's ghost, his must be aiming powerless kicks at my behind as I bent over the open drawers underneath his bunk, scooping out his possessions. The emptier they became, the more oppressive the atmosphere in the cabin. A bell sounded somewhere in the distance; it was lunchtime, but I did not feel like going down. I stood looking about me with a sense of defiance. I would not rest until I had exorcised his ghost and made this cabin my own.

In the bottom drawer underneath his bunk I found what looked like a large cigar box, with Japanese characters on it. I opened it and saw that it was filled with human hair, glossy and black; a little rubber nipple stuck out among the locks. On the inside of the lid of the box was printed: *Au Secours des Solitaires—Help for the Lonely—Seemanns Hilfe*. The English instructions ran: *Take Niki out of box and blow breath into Niki-toe by mouth, until whole body unroll lifesize. Be full of care not to inflate too much for fear of explosion. In case of need, wash Niki with soft soap and water. If in tropics hair come out, use rubber solution for replacement. If Niki suffer puncture, repair like tire of bicycle. Manufacturered by Imperial Caoutchouc Company, Yokohama, Japan.*

I had occasionally heard rumors about inflatable women, but always taken them to be flowers from the hothouse of some sex-starved stoker's imagination. Here was the real thing. Despite the awareness that I was intruding in another man's private life, I lifted the sinister square parcel out of its box and unfolded it on the bunk. It opened up with a dryish rustle which seemed to indicate it had never been opened before, but maybe I concluded this for reasons of expedience. When it lay unfolded on the bunk, a long flat strip of yellowish material gruesomely reminiscent of parched human skin, I bolted both doors, drew the curtains in front of the portholes, spread my handkerchief over the mouthpiece in a ritual gesture of hygiene and started to blow.

At first nothing seemed to be happening; then, with a ghoulish awakening that revived memories of monster films, the thing on the bed began to move and to sprout limbs. Arms with gruesomely realistic hands fell open and grew at every breath, breasts gradually bulged into obscene protuberances, the face became that of a pop-eyed, cretinous Madame Butterfly, with a pouting little button mouth and cauliflower ears and hair sprouting straight out of her skull as if she had stuck her fingers in an electric socket. There was a gadget in the box to clip onto the toe after inflation, but it had rusted through; it broke when I tried to apply it, and the doll collapsed with a slobbering sigh that smelled, for some reason, of incense. I tried to stuff it back into its box, but there seemed to be more of it now than there had been to start with; in the end, I emptied my belongings into the drawers and stuffed it into my own duffel bag, planning to ditch it as soon as we were at sea.

Disposing of Captain Loppersum's Niki had diminished somewhat the oppressive sense of his presence, but the cabin was by no means decontaminated yet. Apart from all supernatural considerations, it was filthy. What it needed was to be washed down with soap and hot water from top to bottom. Nobody on this ship was going to do it for me, not at this point; that much was clear. To do it myself was the only alternative. I stood for a moment in doubt whether it would undermine my future prestige; on second thoughts, I realized that I didn't care a damn if it did. So it came about that, unknowingly, I performed the most effective rite of exorcism as recommended by parapsychologists; after dragging the mattress out into the sun, I filled the wastebucket from the bathroom with water and, using a singlet I found among the pile on the floor as a rag, I started to wash down the walls.

It was hard work, but I ended up by washing down not only the cabin, but the bathroom and the chartroom as well. I had just ditched the last bucket of rinse water over the edge when the bell sounded again in the distance. I looked at my watch and discovered to my amazement that the time was six o'clock; I had been spring-cleaning for five hours without interruption. When I put my tie back on in front of the bathroom mirror, I discovered that my hands were white and wrinkled. I combed my hair, smarming it down with water, and put on my jacket, making sure it was not bunched up at the shoulders; then I set my face in a scowl of bored indifference and went down to the messroom to meet the staff.

I found the messroom unerringly; even Mr. Kwel Senior's genius had been unable to come up with another location for it than in the dead center of all those fuel tanks that gave his dream ship her formidable action radius. It was no larger than the ones I was familiar with; the long narrow table was ranged along the wall, with an L-shaped leatherette seat behind it; the captain's chair was on the left as I came down. The staff sat ranged on the seat; the moment I reached the bottom of the stairs they rose respectfully to attention, ending up in an awkward position, knees slightly bent.

There were only three of them; an elderly man with a hangdog face and sad pouchy eyes who obviously felt very uncomfortable; a young, innocent-looking chap with big ears and big hands and eyes of such unself-conscious kindness that I could not blame him for not understanding that he was taking part in a gesture of defiance; and next to him my old friend the mate, obviously the leader of the protest, saluting with the same ludicrous flourish as when I had last seen him, standing on the curb outside the railway station. He no longer wore his flying-officer's jerkin, but a uniform jacket; the three rings on its sleeves had been augmented by three more, made of surgical tape. It was all very childish, but the feeling that had inspired it was natural enough, and I decided to ignore it. In his place, I too would have felt hostile toward the interloper appointed over my head.

I sat down in the chair at the head of the table and called, "All right, Cook! Ready when you are!"

It was a shot in the dark, because the cook was nowhere to be seen, but I guessed that he was in on the plot and would be standing at the top of the stairs, waiting to see how it worked out. I was lucky again; after a few seconds of suspense, his unpolished shoes came clonking down the steps, backward, and there he was, carrying a soup tureen. He turned around at the bottom of the stairs and was overcome with indecision when he found the three officers still standing rigidly to attention and me sitting at the head of the table, waiting for his soup.

"All right," I said, "you can serve."

He looked at me with murder in his red-rimmed eyes; then he plonked the tureen on the table, lifted off the lid and took it with him as he clonked back up the stairs, muttering unintelligibly. I considered saying, "All right, gentlemen, you may sit down," but the whole thing was so bloody silly that I could not be bothered. I helped myself to soup and started eating. As far as I was concerned, they could stand there, their knees bent at the edge of the seat in acute discomfort, for as long as they could keep it up, if it made them feel better.

After I had started eating, the older man, obviously the chief engineer, was the first to give up. He sat down awkwardly, unable to hide a grimace of pain; the moment his behind hit the seat, I turned toward him and said, "My name is Harinxma. You are the chief engineer, I take it."

"Pardon?" he asked self-consciously; then he answered himself and said, "Yes," and helped himself to soup.

The young man next to him looked from one to the other in bewilderment; then the older man muttered, "All right, Porks. Pack it up," and he sat down.

"Second engineer?" I asked.

"Yes, Captain, er—yes, Commodore—I mean . . . yes, sir," the young man stammered, smiling innocently. "My name is Alberts. Pieter Rudolf, but everybody calls me Porks." Then he frowned at the soup tureen and cried, "Oh, no! Not potato soup *again*." But he proceeded to help himself to a portion that nearly overflowed his plate.

This left only the mate standing, holding the bag. He

got out of it by saying "Amen" before sitting down. It wasn't a very good joke, but a good try.

Taking pains to sound noncommittal, I said, "Our orders are that we get under way before noon tomorrow, destination Greenock, for conversions." I turned to the chief. "Anything you want done before we sail?"

"What's that?" he asked, awkwardly. "Oh, I see. No, as far as I'm concerned, we're all set."

Then the mate at the far end of the table piped up; his voice was high and strident, like the crowing of a cock. "Ha!" he cried, "but we can't leave! Not until Sparks is out of the clink. We can't sail without a WO, can we now? And God only knows when they'll release him!"

So that was it. He had organized the prank with the Polish airman's car in order to get one of them arrested and thus sabotage our departure. It was a pretty cumbersome way of expressing one's feelings, but the mere execution of the plot must have given him some sense of getting even with whomever it was the head office had preferred to him.

"Oh, that has been taken care of," I said casually. "He should be back some time tonight." The silence that followed was gratifying. They could not know that the whole thing was just another stroke of outrageous luck. If I had not felt such a fool in that launch after falling into their trap, I would not have dreamed of going to see the captain of the prison ship and would have failed to stumble upon the way to get the WO released. In their eyes, it must look like breathtaking astuteness on my part.

The mate could not ask how I had managed it without losing face; so the two engineers and I went on chatting while he sat silently in his corner, his face set. The chief did not say much, but I learned at least that his name was Bout and that he had sailed with Captain Loppersum for

as long as the cook. The boy Porks was a relative new-
comer; he had only sailed with Captain Loppersum since
the beginning of the war.

The meal was pretty bad: leathery lamb chops, waxy
potatoes and the inevitable Brussels sprouts. The dessert
was semolina pudding cast in the mold of a swan, accompanied by a jug of red berry sauce. We had just helped
ourselves to it when a scuffle sounded on the deck and some
angry protestations; then a pair of legs in wrinkly trousers
came stumbling down the steps, backwards. The new
arrival had his hands behind his back; only as the light reflected on metal did I realize that he was wearing handcuffs. He must be the wireless operator. Neatly polished
shoes and knife-edged trousers followed him down; it was
the captain of the *Prins Hendrik*.

When he reached the bottom of the stairs, the prisoner
swung around to face us and cried, belligerently, "Say,
what the hell is this!" Then he caught sight of me, sitting
at the head of the table. His mouth fell open; after a
moment of astonishment, he shrugged his shoulders,
grinned, and said sheepishly, "Oh, well, that explains it.
Greetings, 'Fancy That.' "

"Hello, Sparks," I said, heroically.

It was the wireless operator of the *Anna Kwel*, who
had witnessed the first demonstration of my outrageous
luck when I had picked up South Shields' outer buoy in
the fog, two centuries ago. I was not surprised to see him
here; wireless operators were not employees of Kwel's
but farmed out by Radio Holland, which shuffled them
about according to its own schedule.

What had nearly thrown me was the "Fancy That,"
obviously the nickname by which I was known in the
trade. It was a far cry from "The Professor" or "The

Bookworm" which I had so modestly dreamed up for myself. I had no idea what had prompted it.

"Okay, sir, take 'em off," he said, contritely. "I'll be a good boy now."

The captain of the prison ship did not look happy; obviously Sparks had given him a hard time. "Well, congratulations," he said, with heavy irony. "I don't know what he's like as a wireless operator, but I can assure you that you are not going to have a dull moment on this trip with that joker on board."

"Oh, forget it," Sparks said, obviously eager to call the whole thing off. "How was I to know it was a deal between you and 'Fancy That'? I would have come like a lamb."

The captain looked at me with a frown. "Who is this 'Fancy That'?" he asked. "You?"

"It's a nickname," I said, nonchalantly. Then I gave the wireless operator a look of boredom and added, "But, for the record, I like to be addressed as 'Captain.' All right, let's have the key to these and unlock him, so he can help himself to some semolina pudding before it goes over the edge."

"Well, if you say so," the captain grumbled reluctantly, producing a bunch of keys from the pocket of his greatcoat. "I suppose you know what you are doing." He inserted a key in the handcuffs and started to fumble with them. The procedure was not a demonstration in tenderness; Sparks winced and yelped, "Ouch!" but his jailer was not in a vegetarian mood. Barking "Stand still, you oaf!" he yanked the key out of the handcuffs and tried another one. Sparks, with a grimace of mock submission, winked at me in an effort to turn the thing into a lark. Finally his hands were free and he rubbed his wrists with relief; when he sat down to help himself to semolina pudding, the captain eyed him disapprovingly, put the keys and the handcuffs back in his pocket and said, ungenerously, "Well, he's all yours."

I said, "Let me see you to your launch," and we went up the messroom stairs and out onto the deck.

As we stood at the rail looking down on the boat, the faces of its crew peering up at us like baby swallows from a nest, he said, "You know I had a hell of a time getting that character out of the clink? He made himself obnoxious there. It seems to me there's something more to it than just a drunken gag. Are you sure you want him back?"

"Yes," I said, "he's all right," and I explained the situation to him briefly. "It's all bloody silly and the whole thing fell flat on its face, anyhow, so I'm going to forget about it."

"Well, I suppose you know what you're doing," the captain said, unconvinced. "If you ask me, that character is a sea lawyer born and bred. If he were mine, I'd send him packing and ask the company for a replacement. You can do that, you know."

"Yes, I know, but I'd like to give them all a chance before I start throwing my weight around."

"H'm," he said. "I wouldn't be too eager to please them if I were you. It's none of their business who you are or where you come from; you have been appointed captain of this ship, and if they think that is reason for a demonstration, there is only one answer you can give if you want to stay on top of them: kick 'em in the crotch!"

He said it with passion; the inactivity of his dead ship, turned into a sort of Alcatraz of the Royal Dutch Navy, must have driven him around the bend. For this was nonsense; no sea captain in the twentieth century could seriously maintain that his problems could be solved with the methods of the golden age. We shook hands in the sunset, I thanked him once more for bailing me out, he again wished me luck on those convoys, and so we parted; I felt a surprising twinge of nostalgia when his launch put-putted off into the falling night. It was a pity that in our job you so rarely got the chance to make friends.

When I came back to the messroom, Sparks had obviously filled them in on my reputation. I was not aware that I had any, except the nickname; given the position he found himself in, he must have given me a build-up as a superman, to save face after the ignominious failure of their plot. The chief engineer looked more uncomfortable than ever, obviously yearning to sneak out. The boy Porks gaped at me with round eyes and parted lips. The mate looked bloodied but unbowed. The wireless operator began a long, chatty description of the inside of Holyhead Jail. Cook brought down the coffee, and sat down on the steps to listen. This had not been the custom on any tugboat I had ever sailed on, but then, this was not just a tugboat; this was the flagship of the great Commodore Bokke Loppersum.

The rest of the meal was uneventful. I did not have the impression that they were suddenly filled with love and respect toward me, but they obviously had accepted the inevitable. The chief engineer made off first, then the cook, finally the mate; when I was left with Sparks and the innocent Porks, I bade them good night and went to my cabin.

It smelled clean, looked empty and felt dismal. Rarely in the past had I felt quite so lonely as I felt that night. Because this was my first permanent assignment, I had foolishly hoped for some human contact on board the new ship, something a little warmer and more personal than what I was accustomed to as a relief captain who came and went. I really did not know anybody any more; my last personal relationship had been with my fellow trainees on board old *"Blazes."* Typical of my status since I had left Greenock two years before was that under "next of kin" on the articles for this trip I had put the name of Miss Crumb.

I went to bed. As I lay in the neutral bunk, my only personal touch the small row of books in the corner, I indulged in a moment of self-commiseration. Even if I were accepted as a fact of life after a while, it would have nothing to do with me personally. I had a hunch that the men who had served under Captain Loppersum would only accept me after they had, in some measure, turned me into a worthy replacement for the Grand Old Man. The mate, for instance, could not possibly accept an equal in the post he had coveted; it had to be someone larger than life, either the villain from a Victorian melodrama whom he would love to hate, or another superman, a little more sophisticated and intellectual than the old extrovert had been maybe, but a superman all the same. In my case, it would not be difficult; I was type-cast for the role: shrewd, baby-faced gangster, ruthless and vicious as a rattlesnake, nicknamed "Fancy That." What had that mythological creature to do with me? Not much. But they wanted to set out for the most hazardous convoy duty of the war with the conviction, imposed by self-hypnosis, that they were protected by the legendary "Fancy That" and his proverbial luck. I could hear Sparks creating his Golem now: "Superb sailor, uncanny knowledge of human nature, as cool as they come, mordant wit, brilliant mind. I've sailed with him, I've seen him operate, I've seen him handle men and ships. There's no one I'd rather sail the Murmansk route with. But one thing you should put right out of your mind, fellows: don't expect you'll ever get any human warmth out of him. He's as cold and unsociable as a corpse in the morgue."

I was probably hamming it up a little, lying there alone in the darkness in a dead man's bed; but if I were heading for the Arctic with a brand-new captain aged twelve, that's the kind of character I would concoct to combat the dragon of fear. It was tough luck on my part, but I hoped for all our sakes that they would succeed in drawing enough comfort from some creation of their own making to face death in the Arctic with equanimity.

4

One of them could not face it. I was woken up in the middle of the night by a loud banging on the door of my cabin and a hysterical voice crying, "Captain! Captain! For God's sake, Captain!" I didn't realize that I had locked the door. I leaped out of my bunk, turned the key, and there was the boy Porks, ghost-like in the darkness, his eyes wide with horror, his voice strained as he cried, "Captain, for God's sake, come! Please, come at once! The chief—the chief has killed himself!"

My heart sank. I was overcome by unspeakable apprehension and, at the same time, a cool, collected sureness of mind. I pulled on some clothes and accompanied him to the messroom. Outside the door of a cabin, a small crowd had collected. They made room for me as I came down.

It was a small, sad bachelor's cabin, full of sentimental pictures and spinsterish knickknacks. I saw a cuckoo clock, converted from weights to a spring; a little Swiss weatherhouse; a birdcage; and an orange shade with beads over a bedside lamp. It looked like the cell of a prisoner for life.

He lay on his side on the bunk, as if asleep in the orange light of the bedside lamp. By the side of his bunk stood the cook, his old monkey's face screwed up into a grimace of horror. When he saw me, he cried in a hoarse, high voice, "Now, what would he want to do this for? How could he do such a thing? Look, look, here it is!"

He stretched out his hand and showed me a gun. I took it from him gingerly, by the tip of its barrel, pulled my handkerchief out of my pocket, folded the gun in it and put it on the bedside table. Before bending over the body on the bunk, I turned around and saw the mate in the doorway looking at me with calm detachment. Over his shoulder peered the big-nosed wireless operator. I singled him out and asked, "Are we in contact with any shore station? Locally, I mean?"

"I can raise the harbor office."

"By voice or by key?"

"Either."

"Raise them. Tell them to send a doctor and ask where we are supposed to report this—local police, or what. Hurry."

He said, "Aye, aye," and vanished.

I bent over the body on the bunk. The voice of the cook croaked, "Now, what did he want to do this for? Why? Why? He was such a nice man, we were such good friends, he never had any moods, he was always even-tempered, he never said anything to make us think that he could do something like this. . . ." His voice rose higher, was strangled by a sob, and then he added, crying, "He even killed his little bird!" and burst into hysterical tears.

I turned around, caught the mate's eye and said, "Take care of him, will you?"

The mate did not answer, but I heard him come in behind me and lead the sobbing cook away. I had hoped for a moment that the whole thing might be a mistake; he lay there so peaceably on his side, like a man asleep, and there was nothing about him that suggested death—no wound, not a drop of blood. But when I turned him over, all that changed. He was dead, all right. I remembered thinking, when I had first set eyes on him that night, that he looked like a reliable man, unlikely to bungle any job he tackled. He had not bungled this one.

The police arrived first, very British, very correct, very large in the small cabin with their blue greatcoats and their high pith helmets. They took down all the details, then the doctor came. He was a small man, bad-tempered, obviously angry at being dragged out of bed. However, being English, he might look foul-tempered, but he sounded as if he had been asked in to tea. After a cursory examination of the dead man's head and mouth, he used some Latin words to describe his findings and ended by saying that death had been instantaneous. As I listened to the doctor, I glanced into the birdcage and saw that the cook was right. On the bottom of the cage, which looked very clean and well cared for, with drinking vessel and seed bin carefully filled, lay the little orange powder puff of a dead canary, its head back at an unnatural angle. He must have carefully and quickly broken its neck before putting an end to himself. The police appropriated the gun.

There was some writing by all concerned at the mess-room table. The police wanted the ship to stay in port until further notice, but I told them I was under orders to sail at dawn and that I would appreciate it if they would clear that with their commanding officer. They said politely that they would see what they could do; one of them made the un-British remark that he thought we might have wanted to stay on for the funeral. I could not let him get away with it, not with the others listening in. "Under normal circumstances we would, of course," I answered. "But in wartime one is not entirely one's own master, is one, now?"

The policeman, abashed, said, "Of course, sir. I forgot. Sorry, sir."

There was some commotion on the deck, and a medic came down the steps. "Where's the body?" he asked. "In there? Okay, Joe, hand it down," and he held out his hands to receive a stretcher. He was joined by his colleague, they studied the situation with craftsman-like objectivity, and ended by putting the stretcher on top of the messroom table. Then they went into the cabin to carry the chief out. When they lugged him through the narrow doorway, his arms dangling, his shipmates turned away in embarrassment and misery. Only the mate, his sky-blue eyes cold and remote, went on looking with a scowl on his face, as if, in the distorted reasoning of resentment, all this made sense and one thing was the logical outcome of another. As I stood there, while the medics laid out the chief on the stretcher on the messroom table, I caught myself thinking that I wished it had been the mate who had removed himself from the scene, rather than this decent old man.

They covered the body with a sheet and strapped it down to the frame until it no longer looked like a human being, but like an oblong parcel securely trussed to prevent it from slipping when it was hauled up the stairs to the deck. After they were gone, there was a small pool of blood left on the messroom table that had soaked through the canvas of the stretcher. For some reason, it was the most harrowing sight of all; as no one seemed to do anything about it, I went into the chief's cabin, pulled the top sheet off his bunk and cleaned the table with it.

"Where's the cook?" I asked.

"Passed out," the mate answered. "I gave him a sedative. He'll be all right in the morning."

"Detail somebody to clean out that cabin, will you?"

"Aye, aye."

"Any next of kin that should be notified?"

"Not that I know of. He was a bachelor; I believe he never lived anywhere in his life except on board his ships."

"All right. Let's go and enter this in the journal and make out the forms for the company."

"Who's going to succeed him? Porks?"

It had not registered until then that the second engineer was nowhere to be seen. "Where is he?" I asked.

"In his bunk, most likely."

"Would he be qualified to take over?"

"About as qualified as you were, I would say."

I looked up at him. His cold blue eyes were empty of all feeling, his lips still frozen in that deprecatory scowl. "Listen, friend," I said, "I can understand that you don't care to serve under me. You are welcome to ask for a transfer, but if you don't, let's get one thing clear right here and now: I'm not going to take any more shit from you. You are either going to accept the facts of life or get the hell out. Is that understood?"

His face did not change, his eyes did not waver, yet I sensed somewhere, behind all that armor, a short flicker of panic. I realized that to leave this ship would mean to cut himself adrift on a sea of insecurity.

"I haven't the foggiest idea what you're talking about," he said, brazenly.

But I was sure my intuition had been right. He would not leave, and he was intelligent enough to realize that he could stay only on my terms.

"You're welcome to think it over," I said. "Decide while we're in Greenock. Now go ahead to the chartroom, make out a draft entry for the log. I'll join you there in a minute. First I'll have a word with—what's the boy's name again, apart from 'Porks'?"

"Alberts. Rudolf something."

"Okay."

He turned away and went up the stairs; I realized too late that I had forgotten to ask him which cabin it was, but I didn't want to call him back. I opened two doors at random; the second one was the cook's. He lay sprawled on his bunk in the maraschino light of another of those effeminate little bedside lamps. The first thing that hit me was, again, the overpowering stench of the unwashed human male; the second was the singlemindedness of his decorations. On the walls, over his bunk and beside his washstand mirror, pinned on the door of his wardrobe and even on the drawers underneath his bed, were pictures of cats and kittens. Nothing but cats.

I found the boy's cabin after opening two more doors. He too was lying on his bunk. His eyes were closed, his hands folded on his chest; there was about him the peculiar tidiness of death. For one sick moment, I thought he had committed suicide too, but as I moved over to him, he opened his eyes and rested his shocked, innocent gaze on me.

"I'm sorry about this, Alberts," I said. "You knew him better than I did, but I'm sure he was a good man."

His lips came apart with some difficulty, as if they were stuck together, and he said, "Yes, Captain—Commodore— yes, sir."

Again, as I stood there, his innocence got through to me. It would be like handing the engine room, and with it the fate of us all, to a child. On the other hand, I had a notion that he was an excellent engineer, though be- deviled by a total lack of self-confidence.

"Why do you think he did it?" he asked. "Because of the Old Man? Or because he was deaf? You would not have minded that, would you? Captain Bokke didn't."

So that was it. I should have been quicker on the ball; I remembered how he had acted at the table. Of course: he had been as deaf as a post. Obviously, his old comrades had not given him away, maybe for years. I didn't know what I would have done. Probably I would have sent him packing. I wouldn't knowingly have set out on the Murmansk run with a deaf engineer below. But why kill himself for that? Many men would have jumped at the chance to get off. "I have no idea, Porks," I said. "From what little I know of him, I'd say it was the prospect of sailing without his old friend, certainly on the Arctic route. So, in a sense, it was because of me."

His eyes opened wide, and he gave me a look of shocked incredulity. "Oh, no, sir!" he said. "No, Captain—Commodore—no, sir. We all know about you, we're lucky to have you. It couldn't be that!"

Obviously, the wireless operator had run true to form. The legend had been established, the craving of an orphaned crew for a new father figure stilled. I stood there for a moment, overcome by weariness. The boyish voice said, "I've been thinking. Maybe he had an incurable disease. Do you think he had?"

"That may be," I said, helpfully. "If so, they'll find out in the autopsy."

"Autopsy? You mean—they're going to cut him open?"

His voice sounded so horrified that I answered, "I don't know. I'm not an expert, you know. Sometimes they do."

"Maybe not this time?" He looked at me pleadingly; then it dawned on me that, of course, this crew had never seen action. The boy had never seen a dead man; his sensitive civilian's soul could not even bear the thought that his old chief might be cut open in an autopsy. Mr. Kwel had seen to it that this ship, the apple of his eye, did not run any danger as long as he could help it. They must have been sent all over the globe, to South America and New Zealand, towing like crazy, until finally the war had caught up with them. I had been picked to take this bunch of innocents, as green as grass, straight into the hell of the Arctic convoys. I had not given the future much thought, maybe for understandable reasons. I had better start doing so now.

"Alberts," I said, "I'd like you to have a shot at being chief engineer. You'll be entirely on your own between here and Greenock. What I'd like to do there is to get a new second, not a chief. How do you feel about that?"

He lay staring at me, motionlessly, for so long that I thought he was waiting for me to say more. "Well, what do you say?"

He swallowed, his eyes probed mine in disbelief, then he asked, "You think I could?"

"What do you think yourself?"

His disbelief became panic. "Oh, no," he said, "oh, no, I—I can't say anything about that, I don't know, I want you to tell me. Do *you* think I could?"

It was a pointless question. I barely knew him. But, obviously, it was one of those that rated a serial number. So I answered, promptly, "Yes."

His eyes changed. They seemed to be drained of all uncertainty and apprehension. His face relaxed until, once again, it expressed nothing but innocence and unreasoning trust. "If you think so," he said, "I'll give it a try."

"Good man. We sail as soon as I get clearance from the authorities ashore. Probably soon after nine." But I thought, You infantile bastard, why the hell can't you stand on your own feet? Who do you think I can run to to get rid of the responsibility for my life? But even as I thought it, I realized that I was just jealous.

In the chartroom, the mate sat waiting for me. He seemed a little more human, as if finally something from the outer world had gotten through to him. I read through his draft entry for the log, okayed it and signed the death documents for the company. During all this he sat by my side, subdued, so it seemed, by something that must have happened since I had last seen him; only as I caught him glancing around the chartroom did I realize what had struck him so. I had forgotten that I had cleaned it out; he must have never known it like this. It seemed odd that this should be the thing that got him.

When finally I lay in my bunk once more, dawn was breaking over the harbor. I opened the curtains of the portholes and watched them turn blue with the daybreak. The cabin seemed a little more my own now; the romantic thought occurred to me that Captain Loppersum, whose presence had seemed so oppressive the night before, had been waiting for his old chief and that now the two had wandered off into the night. Yet, there now hung over everything a veil of sadness and tragedy, something melancholy that made me want to turn over and bury my face in my pillow and cry. I did not know what I would be crying for, Bokke Loppersum and his Niki, Chief Bout and his canary, the old cook with his tattooed wristwatch left behind. But maybe my grief wasn't as altruistic as all that. Maybe I only wanted to cry for myself and Sophie. We had started out so innocently and had known so many delightful, carefree hours; what had we done, to find ourselves caught up like this in tragedy and death and slowly encroaching horror? All of a sudden, I was terrified as a vague intimation of what lay ahead of us came over me.

I turned over and buried my head in the pillow.

5

But later that morning, there I was, bright and chipper, on the bridge with my little peaked cap and my duffel coat, ready to play Commodore. Seen from the bridge, the *Isabel Kwel* looked awfully big; I had never maneuvered anything remotely her size—it was like being promoted without transition from a pick-up truck to a locomotive. We were penned in by two large freighters, fore and aft, which did not leave me room to maneuver. I gathered from the telegraphs on the bridge that she was single-screwed, so, theoretically, I could swing her bow out by backing into her aft spring line; but I did not know the slope of this quayside, and, what was more, if she had a single propeller it must be an outsize one. So I went in for some fancy ropework, had her port for'ard spring taken across her bow and belayed to a shore bollard amidships, then I put her rudder over to starboard and pushed the telegraph to Dead Slow Ahead. The boy Porks was on the ball; he responded smoothly and with restraint. Her ungainly stern swung slowly out into the harbor; when it was far enough to allow for its being pulled to either port or starboard by reversing the engine, I backed away from the quay. Her stern pulled to port, so the propeller rotated in the standard direction. It was nice to discover that something was standard on board this monster. I let her find her own way astern; when the swing of her bow accelerated, I told the helmsman to give counter wheel, pushed the telegraph to Half Speed Ahead, and off we went. I still felt small on her bridge, but no longer intimidated. It was a pugnacious smallness: scrappy midget, ready to lick the world.

I had met the rest of the crew before we left; they had not exactly met me with open arms, but there had not seemed to be any spirit of resistance. Most of them were elderly men who must have sailed with both Loppersum and the chief for a long time; they were not in a mood to care much about me, one way or another. Now we were under way, they stood in small, silent groups on the aft deck, gazing morosely at the shore. The cook came up with coffee; he looked as if he had been awake all night, but he was energetic enough, if a man needs energy to be churlish.

As soon as we got clear of the confined water of the harbor, I pushed the engine-room telegraph to Full Speed Ahead and sent the *Isabel Kwel* racing down the channel. She shuddered with the sudden burst of power, but she squatted virtually at once, dragging her stern deep into the water. She now drew a mountainous stern wave and a seething wake, yet her speed did not increase in proportion to her histrionics. Possibly the channel was still so shallow as to create suction, but this did not seem likely. I could only conclude that, considering her power, she was a slow ship that would come into her own only while towing, when she could spend all her thrust on moving the bulk astern rather than her own squat lumbering body. Again I was struck by the odd gracelessness of Mr. Kwel Senior's dream; but then, from a man like him little else could be expected than a bull-necked, barrel-chested behemoth when it came to expressing his personality. Once in the open, she seemed to pick up some speed, but as the vibration of her engine gave the whole ship the shakes, I took down the number of revolutions until she raised her Flemish behind sufficiently to draw a more moderate stern wave. It was good to know we had all that power in reserve, but there was no need at this point to plow the Irish Sea with a vigor that yanked the seaweed out of its bottom at fifteen fathoms.

Even so, coasting along at an easy canter, we made the hundred and fifty miles to the Isle of Bute in the Firth of Clyde in less than ten hours—all of which I spent on the bridge, drinking my fill of the heady draught of power. We arrived in pitch darkness, alongside a sleeping tugboat that I recognized, even at dead of night, as dear old *"Blazes,"* still going strong. The mate hovered on the bridge, unable to hide his nervousness the moment I started to move in; I was not going to let on that I knew the Clyde and that particular mooring like the back of my hand; there was no harm in letting him have a whiff of my supernatural powers now the occasion presented itself. I reduced her speed well in advance, let her brontosaurian bustle slither to starboard until it must seem inevitable to the innocent beholder that she was going to sideswipe old *"Blazes"* with the impact of a ten-car collision; then I put her in reverse, counting on the backwash of her propeller to pull her stern to port for a perfect landing. But this time my luck did not last out. Something went wrong; the propeller churned away, but she did not pull to port. Instead, she did indeed sideswipe old *"Blazes"* with the impact of a ten-car collision.

Whoever lay slumbering on board the old tub rose as one man from their litters, screaming invective. I was badly rattled, but even so it penetrated to me that the invective was English. Innocently, I had expected her to be still manned with Dutch trainees.

Innocently, indeed. When, the next day, I came face to face again with my old friend the British commander, he confessed, after some prodding on my part, that none of my shipmates from the days of dear old *"Blazes"* were still alive. "Yes," he said, with brazen understatement, "OTWA turned out to be somewhat more costly than we had foreseen. But, despite the heavy toll in ships and men, it is performing a sterling service. Those gallant boys from the Netherlands will have us British forever in their debt."

It was a nice little speech, but the first reaction that suggested itself to me was an obscenity.

CHAPTER FOUR

I

I must confess that the crash landing, with which I had delighted the mate and put the cook in ecstasy, bothered me a lot. I could not explain it at all. I was no longer a novice in the handling of tugs; any ship I had ever known would have responded instantly to the backthrust of her reversed propeller and swung her stern to port. This monster had not even begun to respond, even though when I realized what was happening I had revved up the engine to its maximum.

The crew did not seem to be bothered unduly by the gut-shaking collision with which I had moored that night; when I discussed it with the boy Porks, he told me, rather evasively in an obvious effort to minimize the whole thing for my sake, that this had happened once or twice before. When I persisted and inquired if either Captain Loppersum or the old chief had ever done anything about it, he looked at me with puzzlement and asked, "What do you mean?"

"Well," I said, "haven't they ever looked for the cause of her erratic behavior? There must be a reason somewhere, you know."

He shook his head, thinking. "No," he said, "I don't think they did, sir—Cap—er, Commodore. They both just took it to be, well, one of those things. She has a lot of quirks, you know. I love her, but she has a lot of quirks." He said it unself-consciously; to him, as to most sailors, it was as normal to love a ship as it is to love a woman.

I wished I could say the same. Looking back on the tugboats I had known, I realized that I had never loved a single one of them. Maybe it was because so far I had only been a mate or a temporary captain; but, even so, I could not see myself treating a steel contraption as a living being with a personality and a free will. If, at a given moment, the *Isabel Kwel* refused to obey her rudder and the seventy-five-hundred horsepower thrust of her propeller, there must be a cause for it, either in her design or in her engine. Simply to ascribe it to her personality and call it a "quirk" insulted my intelligence.

In any case, whatever the cause of the mystery, I had better get to the bottom of it before leaving for the Arctic. The only way to go about this would be to take her out for a trial run. I would have to put her through her paces, not once but scores of times, repeating that same maneuver over and over again, until I discovered the method in her madness. There must be a simple, mechanical explanation; a ship could not at one moment swing her stern to port when her engine was reversed and to starboard the next, without there being a reason. And I must find that reason in order to prevent its happening again; it was desperately urgent that I do, for on the run to Murmansk I would have enough to worry about as it was, without the knowledge that my ship might go mad at any moment and do the opposite of what I wanted her to do. I was not going to rest until I had ferreted out what it was that had made her sideswipe old *"Blazes"* with such total disregard for my commands and the laws of physics.

I talked Porks into producing a set of builder's plans of the ship that the old chief had kept in a drawer under his bunk; I went over them inch by inch, considering all possibilities, first by myself, then with Porks. I discovered that he was a bright chap; immature as he might be, the moment it came to his job he was excellent. We considered every possibility, from a collapsed manhole cover in the bulkheads in one of the fuel tanks, which could create an adverse wave, to the unlikely chance that the key fixing her propeller to its shaft had been sheared off, which would account for the fact that it happened only in reverse. The friction of the forward thrust might be sufficient to keep axle and wheel securely wedded, while a reverse thrust would push the propeller off the tapered end and make it spin freely in its socket. We spent hours sitting at the messroom table, huddled over the drawings like boys over the building plans of a wireless set; if those sessions did nothing else, they made him stop calling me "Commodore." He settled for "Skipper," and he was the only one. Everyone else, even the huge, uncomplicated buffalo that was the bosun, went stolidly on expressing their loyalty for Captain Loppersum by calling me "sir," traditionally reserved for visitors only.

The next thing was to organize a trial run; fortunately, the British Navy fell in with my plans. We were directed to the Navy dockyard where the *Isabel Kwel* was to be subjected to a complete overhaul under top priority. The first thing they did, once the drydock was raised, was to take off her bronze propeller and replace it with a cast-iron one. I was on hand when they pulled the huge wheel off the axle; it was a monster as tall as a man, with a pitch that must throw as much thrust in reverse as it did ahead; when it finally slid off the tree-sized shaft, three keys were revealed instead of one, and all three of them were in perfect condition. So that was that. A trial run would have to wait until they were through with her in drydock, and that looked as if it were going to take time, for their overhaul amounted to a conversion.

They reinforced her bows, so she could double as an ice breaker. They welded the base for a gun emplacement on the foredeck and for two smaller ones on the bridge, one on each wing. They enlarged the wheelhouse, so it encompassed the whole midsection of the bridge, installed revolving disks in the windows, and armor-plated the roof. Inside, they doubly insulated all pipelines, covered the ceilings with a corklike substance and installed in the engine room an outsize generator to provide the current for heating the wireless cabin, the wheelhouse and all three gun turrets electrically. When they started to install the guns, I became worried. They were not just the basic type of all-purpose banger I knew from some tugs I had sailed; the one on the foredeck was a vicious-looking Oerlikon antiaircraft cannon, the two on the bridge were Bofors guns, obviously meant to respond to surface fire, for which the Oerlikon could not be sufficiently depressed. And this was not all: they then proceeded to erect, astride the two tracks of trolley rails on the aft deck, just forward of the two large rectangular scuppers in the stern coaming that were part of the original mine-laying equipment, an esoteric pair of catapults, looking like large clay-pigeon throwers.

It seemed to me the time had come for a gentlemanly protest. Not only were they turning my tugboat into an auxiliary cruiser, but the location of those catapults was idiotic: by blocking the free swing of the hawser over the aft deck, they ruled out the possibility of towing. Apart from everything else, it seemed nonsense to install armaments far too complicated for a Merchant Marine crew to handle unless they were trained for weeks first. But before I had made my protest, the British sprang their surprise: I was informed that eight professional gunners were to be added to my crew. This was the clincher: blithely to add eight men to a crew that was already housed like sardines in a can demonstrated a total ignorance of living conditions prevailing on oceangoing tugboats.

After insisting for days that I wanted to see the highest-ranking officer responsible for the conversion of my ship, I found myself, to my amazement, face to face with my old friend the commander. He had never hinted that he was in charge of the whole of the Greenock naval establishment, I had always assumed that he was in command of training only; it now turned out that everything to do with auxiliary craft was his bailiwick. He welcomed me so effusively that I knew at once he had a bad conscience; he obviously had been proceeding according to a carefully laid-out plan when he added all those pieces of hardware piecemeal. If I had realized in the beginning what the Navy was up to, I would have stopped the work and called Mr. Kwel in at once. The charter called for a rescue ship, not the *Ark Royal*.

Now, of course, it was too late; everything was welded and riveted into position. Now he could field my protests with debonair detachment, for to block putting on all that junk was one thing, to have it burned and blasted off again was another. The eight characters he was planning to force into my fo'c'sle with a shoehorn were a different thing altogether: here I had caught him in time. I had brought the plans of the *Isabel* with me to show him that the fo'c'sle could not possibly be extended, as it was surrounded by fuel tanks; neither could the officers' quarters, for the same reason. So, unless he wanted to turn our bunks into marital beds by decree, he would have to bestow those eight characters on some other lucky skipper. But he smiled benignly and said, with the nonchalance the British reserve for their most dramatic bits of information, that of course he was aware of this, but the answer was simple: as a rescue ship, we would not be doing any towing on the Arctic route, so I did not need a full complement of able-bodied seamen; eight could be replaced with eight gunners, who would simply move into the vacated bunks.

I tried to match his casualness when I said, "Sir, may I point out to you that I carry only eight AB's in all?"

"Well, now, don't let's get excited over this," he said, with the beginning of a frown. "Let's try and forget about personalities and use our common sense. You won't be doing any towing, so what do you need your AB's for? Lookouts, you'll say. All right, lookouts. Even when you are not under alert, let alone battle stations, you'll have two gunners permanently stationed at the Oerlikon on your foredeck, and two on your bridge. Surely, four lookouts are sufficient?"

"They would be," I said pleasantly. "The only trouble is that your gunners will be supposed to watch the sky for enemy aircraft, while I like my lookouts to keep an eye on the sea. Icebergs and all that, you know?"

He smiled paternally. Any moment now I expected him to wag a finger at me. "Come, come, Captain, don't let's turn this into a pillow fight. Any reasonable person will agree that gunners looking for enemy aircraft will be watching the horizon, because that's where they come from. They don't drop out of the sky like meteors. So: should there be an obstruction to their view, like an iceberg, I trust they could be depended upon to report this to the officer on duty. No, Captain: we simply have to face the fact that you are due to leave Scapa Flow for Iceland exactly one week from today, and you'll need eight gunners more than eight sailors. Those guns are highly sophisticated pieces of equipment, you'll need experts to handle them. And, to quote Billy Brown of London Town, 'I hope you'll pardon my correction: that stuff is there for your protection.' Without wanting to sound dramatic: those guns are all that stands between you and annihilation. So, let's see if we can't work out between the two of us where the hell we are going to put my eight gunners and your, say, four AB's. That will have to be your absolute maximum. What's the rest of your crew? Can you sacrifice anyone else?"

I told him that, despite her size, the *Isabel Kwel* carried only three men more than the ordinary oceangoing tugboat: two AB's and a carpenter. The other eighteen, whom I ticked off for his benefit, were indispensable. I was critically understaffed as it was.

"H'm," he said. "Let's take a dekko at those plans."

I pushed the blueprint over to him; he studied it through narrowed eyes, tapping his teeth with a pencil. "H'm," he said again, after a silence. "It *is* a bit cramped, isn't it? Your designer seems to have had a passion for fuel tanks."

"The designer was the owner, sir," I said evenly.

He gave me a quick, searching look. "I see," he said. "Maybe this war will change all that."

"Would be nice," I said, politely.

"What about scrapping your number-three tank?" he continued. "This one." He pointed it out with his pencil. "That would leave you plenty of bunker capacity, and by putting in a Jacob's ladder rather than steps, we'd get four bunks in there quite easily, I would say."

"In that case I would have to scrap the two aft tanks as well, sir. I'll have to compensate that loss of weight so far forward, or she'll squat even more. As it is, she drags her arse under the moment I push her over seven hundred revs."

"H'm." He studied the plan, biting his pencil. "I see. You have a point there. But even if we were to remove the lot, it would leave you enough fuel to get from Iceland to Murmansk and back, wouldn't it? At present you seem to have enough juice there to circumnavigate the world, without bunkering."

"It isn't that, sir," I said, patiently. "She is already tender enough as it is; if I make her over fifty tons lighter that far below, combined with the added weight of those guns way up, I don't know how she'll handle."

"Tender? This lumbering locomotive? You can't be serious."

I told him about the *Isabel Kwel's* irrational behavior on the night of our arrival, and my conclusion that the explanation seemed to be a critical increase of her metacenter height after she passed a certain degree of fuel consumption. He listened intently, so much so that I began to suspect he liked messing around with boats, like Ratty in *The Wind in the Willows.*

"How absolutely fascinating," he said, when I was through. "You know, the longer I deal with ships, the more I realize that no two of them are alike. This one seems quite a character. You are right, of course; there must be a simple technical explanation why she runs out of control like that, and I do see your point about scrapping those tanks. So, let's postpone our decision until you have had that trial run. When are you planning it?"

"It's up to you, sir. I'm dependent on the yard."

"H'm . . . let me see. . . ." He leafed through some

papers, pulled out a sheet, studied it and said, "Next Wednesday at fourteen hundred. How would that be?"

"If I'm supposed to sail from Scapa Flow next Saturday, that might be leaving it too late," I said, "in case we opt for taking out those tanks. And I think I'll need a full day of trials if I want to do a thorough job. Can't you suspend work on her all day tomorrow? It's Sunday, anyhow. You could have them start work on that new fo'c'sle first thing Monday morning."

He looked at me for a moment, then he said, "All right, schedule your trial run for tomorrow, six hundred. I'll square it with the yard. You don't mind if I come along? Your problem rather intrigues me."

I was not elated at the prospect, but I said, "It will be my pleasure, sir."

"That's settled, then." He rose and held out his hand for one of those foreign shakes. "See you tomorrow, old chap. Ta-ta."

2

The next morning at daybreak, there he was: bundled up in duffel coat and fleece-lined boots, trailed by a rating lugging a picnic basket. He clambered on board, climbed the bridge and said cheerily, "Good morning, Captain. Looks as if it's going to be a glorious day, doesn't it? I didn't know whether you had bothered about vittles for me, so I brought my own. Maybe your bosun can park my man somewhere where he'll be out of the way?"

I called the bosun to tell him he had a visitor, then I asked, correctly, "All right with you if we cast off, sir?"

"Please, please!" he protested. "Don't let me interfere

with the running of your ship, Captain, for heaven's sake! I'm here as a private person today—busman's holiday, you might say."

I cast off aft, swung her stern, backed her out and off we went. I was glad to get moving; they had spent the night emptying those tanks into a series of trucks and had spilled diesel oil all over our deck; the stench had spoiled my breakfast.

I took her out into the Firth. On the Helensburgh side of the Glasgow ship channel was a nice stretch of open water where I could drop a buoy for a reference point and start putting her through her paces.

It was a warm, sunny day and we worked hard. The commander, once he had taken off his fancy boots and forgotten about manners, turned out to be an asset. He obviously knew what he was talking about; he revealed that he had been a tug driver himself, on a Navy W-boat some years back.

We really kept the *Isabel* hopping that day; luckily, our new second engineer had arrived a few days earlier, so Porks did not have to leap like a spider down there, all by himself. I had barely seen the new Second: a heavy, self-conscious man of indeterminate age with ponderous movements; according to his dope sheet, he had spent most of his life on trawlers.

Toward nightfall there was not a single maneuver a ship can make that the *Isabel* had not performed at least twenty times in a row. I backed her, swung her, raced her astern, slammed her ahead, made her spin in circles until crockery started to slither and crash in the galley. I let her run away with the rudder midships and plow back without touching the helm; I finally concentrated on repeating the maneuver that had resulted in her sideswiping old "*Blazes.*" I made her stern swing to starboard while approaching the reference buoy, then slammed her engine into reverse; I tried it again and again, at all angles, all speeds; but whatever I tried, she performed beautifully. Not once did she so much as nudge that buoy; her eager obedience became infuriating after a while; it indeed began to look as if she had a malicious will of her own. For three solid hours I tried all the tricks in the book; she absolutely refused to repeat the malevolent skid that I had been unable to check that night.

At first, the commander had stood aside politely, looking interested; but once I had tried a few times to make her skid, the spirit of the hunt got the better of him and he said, pleasantly, "She just won't oblige, will she?"

"No, she won't," I replied, with an edge of exasperation.

"Maybe emptying those tanks has done the trick? It is conceivable, as you mentioned, that the motion of the fluid created an adverse wave action, adding a critical thrust to her mass."

"I don't think that's the case," I replied. "I know that the bitch will do it again, I feel it in my bones. I don't care a damn *if* she does, you understand—I only want to know *when* she does it, and the hell with why."

"H'm." He rubbed his chin. "When you arrived the other night, it was dark, wasn't it?"

"Yes, sir."

"Pitch dark, I mean. No lights anywhere. All you saw was the vague outline of *Blazer* against the sky."

"Right."

"I needn't tell you that under those circumstances there is a normal distortion. The human eye does misjudge distances the moment darkness is that deep. You may have been closer to *Blazer* than you thought." He added hastily, "Please understand, this is not implied criticism. I know, after today, that you can handle a tug as well as the next man. But there are freakish moments beyond one's control when nature plays a trick on one. Let's assume for a minute that you really were in a position where no man could have judged the actual distance in the darkness exactly. Could your turn have been a little wide to start with? Is it possible that, after you were already committed, you asked for more rudder?"

I remembered that night exactly; I was certain I had not. "I don't think so," I answered, "but if you like, I'll give it a try. I'll start her off in her swing, and then give her more rudder as she skids."

"That's it!" he said. "That might have been it. If it isn't—well, let's try."

We did, and it made no difference: she obeyed demurely. But by then he was in the game heart and soul.

"Do you mind if I give it a bash?" he asked.

I said she was all his, and he went on swinging her around with the same variations in the ratio of rudder, the forward speed, the reverse thrust that I had tried before, again to no avail. She was the meekest, humblest, most docile vessel afloat.

We kept it up till dark, but nothing induced her to give up her secret. The only thing we found out was that those empty tanks did not make her more tender, so my four seamen were out of luck. They would have to bed down in the converted tank underneath the fo'c'sle and breathe whatever fresh air eight gunners and two oilers might leave for them.

On our way back to the yard, on the bridge in the darkening night, he said, "You know, old chap, when I came on board this morning, I was convinced that your crash landing was a result of pilot error. But after today I am sure that there must be one unique set of conditions, one in a million or so, when she will do what she did that night. I've known ships all my life and I have to admit: I wouldn't trust this bitch. You'll just have to stay on your toes, old man. One day you are sure to find out, if you're around long enough."

I didn't quite know what to say to that.

"Yes," he concluded, almost to himself. "This is a wicked ship."

Underneath their mannered boredom, the English are a romantic race.

3

Five days later, we left Greenock for the Orkneys. I had expected to anchor in Scapa Flow, a natural harbor heavily protected by barriers and anti-U-boat nets. After Kapitän Leutnant Prien of the Kriegsmarine had sneaked in there with a submarine and caused havoc, one night early in the war, it had been turned into the safest anchorage on this side of the Atlantic. But although we bristled with guns and our aft deck carried enough depth-charge canisters to blow up a battleship, we were not considered as members of the club. We were directed to moor in Kirkwall, the wide-open civilian basin on the other side of the narrow waist of the island.

When we left, the ship was a mess. The new fo'c'sle underneath the old one had been finished only in the nick of time; it still reeked of paint, which made my seamen sick. The eight British gunners roamed all over the ship and failed to enchant the crew, who were now forced to face the future and whose apprehension showed in irritability, melancholia and lack of respect for their betters. I had been there before: it was the normal mood of transition. But I had never before felt so concerned about it, maybe because this was the first time I sailed with a ship of my own. The whole psychological complex of fear, homesickness and rebellion that afflicted crews leaving for action had always been the mate's headache, not the relief captain's.

But this was *my* crew now, and I worried about them. My mate seemed to be wrapped up in narcissistic contemplation of his own future; the boy Porks was too busy being chief, and the new Second too busy trying to become adjusted; Sparks resided in solitary independence in his wireless cubicle on the boatdeck, fiddling and tootling with his set until he settled for the most irritating sound a loudspeaker can produce—the roars of laughter of an audience in response to an inaudible comedian—interspersing it with shrieks of his own. The bosun was busy sorting out the paint locker, mumbling crankily; the cook seemed wrapped up in his afternoon lassitude, evening blues, midnight spleen or morning snit. I wondered how I would ever manage to pull this bunch of temperamental egomaniacs together into a fighting crew. They had settled back into what must have been their old ways, now the shock of the demise of their Master had worn off, but somehow they seemed to have decided that his absence was only temporary, for they had not accepted me in his stead. They were polite enough, but their behavior gave me to understand, maybe not even intentionally, that I could never fill the shoes of the Old Man. I didn't want to; all I wanted was a relationship a little closer than that between a bus driver and his passengers. But they weren't about to accept me; I might be Commodore of the fleet—in practice I was still a relief captain, sailing another man's ship, whose crew just marked time until his return. It was discouraging, and I felt pretty lonely up there; the only one who betrayed any interest at all in my feelings was the mate. But his interest was not of the kind I had in mind. He watched me with a secret satisfaction, like a rodent exterminator watching a rat helping itself to his poisoned bait.

In Kirkwall basin I moored, stern to the quay, among an untidy, tightly packed crowd of trawlers and coasters of many nations. I had no idea how many of them were fellow rescue ships until the morning after our arrival, when a group of us was rounded up by a naval character and stowed into a bus. When it finally rattled off to cross the three-mile waist of the island, I counted eleven apprehensive men besides myself; they must be the other Masters of rescue ships, and we were obviously on our way to a briefing. They looked a stolid lot, all of them at least ten years my senior: Danish fishermen, Norwegian coaster captains, Belgian trawler skippers. I recognized one Dutchman whom I knew only by sight: the Master of a whale hunter, one from among a litter of harpoon cutters attached to a factory ship. I had overheard the cook telling the bosun that the mother vessel had been torpedoed off Le Havre on her way to the South Atlantic, and that had broken up the set.

We were unloaded near a narrow dock and directed to a Navy launch that proceeded to sport us across the shimmering expanse of Scapa Flow anchorage. It was a lovely day; the horizon was strewn with warships of all shapes and sizes, looking small and harmless like toys in the holiday sun. We found after a while that we were on our way to a bulbous battleship, anchored in the heart of the harbor, looking rather elderly and restless, like a mother duck worrying about her scattered brood. We were piped on board with deference and reacted to this unfamiliar respect by being gallant to one another at the bottom of the gangway, each insisting that the others go first. Once on board, we were guided to a long, low room furnished with what looked like schoolbenches and a lectern at the far end in front of a blackboard. We waited there in silence for a long while, looking away from each other self-consciously, some of us drumming our fingers, some humming, others feigning sleep; each man's private apprehension showed more and more clearly as time ticked slowly by and we were getting more and more uncomfortable, squeezed into those narrow benches. The whole thing had an atmosphere reminiscent of early schooldays, long forgotten. When finally a prim little officer marched in, carrying a briefcase, he was met with the same mute antagonism that used to welcome a new teacher on the first morning after the holidays.

The little officer strode briskly to the lectern and started to take out his notes without giving any evidence that he was aware of our presence. But finally he looked up arrogantly and drank in the spectacle of twelve subdued middle-aged civilians eyeing him morosely from their schoolbenches. He seemed smaller still, standing behind the lectern; the fruit salad of his decorations looked incongruous on him. He gazed at us in silence for so long that we began to feel even more uncomfortable and sheepish; then he said suddenly, in high, clipped tones, "My name is Mashpee, and I represent . . . " Some boor behind me, obviously succumbing to the suggestion of the schoolroom, gave vent to a cretinous guffaw. The teacher, who had been looking the other way, fastened the gaze of his cruel little eyes on me and repeated icily, "MASH-PEE. An old Manx name, for your information. 'Manx': from the Isle of Man."

While he spoke, his eyes never left mine; I felt like a boy singled out unfairly after some traitor behind him has broken wind in class. Although innocent, I instantly felt guilty, and I saw myself sitting there through his eyes: bloody foreign civilian with a bovine face and shifty eyes. I knew, with a sense of fatality, that he would go to his grave with the firm conviction that I had been the one who had sniggered at his name. After a long, motionless stare had duly conveyed that he would get even with me in his own good time, he addressed the class. "So, let's try again: my name is Mashpee, and I represent Rear Admiral Sir Langston Furlow, Royal Navy, Retired, your convoy commander, or, as he'll be referred to in signals, your Comconvoy. I am the commanding officer of your escort, otherwise known as Comescort.

"Anything discussed during this meeting, gentlemen, will be classified top secret," he continued; his bored, *blasé* voice suggested he had made this speech many times before. "I need not explain to you why any information pertaining to the location of our rendezvous with the convoy would be priceless to the enemy. So, the complete frankness with which I will now proceed to give you this information is in itself a token of complete trust in you on the part of His Majesty's Navy." As an afterthought, he added, "We are, of course, honored and privileged to have you gallant allies with us." The whale hunter, in the front row, grunted with a thick Dutch accent, "Hear, hear." It was a bewildering moment of sheer fantasia that seemed to give the little Captain a mysterious satisfaction. He picked up a pointer, turned to the blackboard and pulled down a map in front of it. It showed the Norwegian and Barents Seas from Greenland to Novaya Zemlya; a shaded region to the north indicated the limits of the Polar pack ice. A red line came in from the west, north of Iceland, a green one from the south southeast, east of Iceland; the two converged off Cape Langanes on the northeastern tip of Iceland and continued together to the Kola Peninsula and Murmansk, skirting Jan Mayen and Bear Islands.

"The green represents the convoy which is now on its way from Nova Scotia," the Captain said in his bored, impersonal voice. "The red represents the escort, of which you gentlemen are part. The convoy is made up of forty-eight British and Allied ships carrying airplanes, fuel, munitions and armaments. All these are fast vessels, so the speed of the convoy is going to be fifteen knots. I know you gentlemen will have no difficulty keeping up with this, your vessels have been selected on that very basis. Now, the escort. It consists of six destroyers and fourteen smaller craft, with a mixed Anglo-American cruiser and destroyer squadron in immediate support. There is what we call a shadow covering force, again Anglo-American, which presents a formidable array of capital ships. I cannot, even under this strict security, be more explicit on the subject of that shadow force. You can, however, rest assured that the convoy will receive maximum protection. In case, however, that this should make you feel overly secure, let me warn you gentlemen that you and I are in for a hard time. The enemy is certain to hit at us twenty-four hours a day for the full ten days of our crossing, with everything he can muster. This includes airplanes, Condors, torpedo planes, Stukas, strafers, and what will seem like an inexhaustible supply of U-boats. If the Admiralty has decided to give this convoy maximum protection, it is because the enemy is expected to give us his maximum attention." He turned back to the blackboard, made the map roll back noisily into its container and picked up a piece of chalk. "From Halifax to Langanes, the convoy will be under American escort and proceed in normal formation. As from Langanes, however, the formation will be as follows." He drew two parallel vertical lines on the blackboard and a horizontal arrow pointing away from them. "The convoy will proceed abreast, in two lines of twenty-eight ships each. The reason for moving abreast —and here, gentlemen, you come in—is that in the Arctic the temperature of the water is so low that the human body cannot survive immersion for longer than a few minutes. Therefore, you rescue ships will trail the convoy in this manner." He drew a third vertical line, parallel to the two. "You too will proceed abreast, and each one of you will be responsible for the four vessels directly ahead. Let me show you the pattern of one such unit." He drew four ovals in a square, trailed by one smaller oval. "The convoy will be subdivided into twelve units like this, each made up of four vessels shadowed by a rescue ship. Should any of these four be torpedoed or otherwise destroyed, and the crew find itself in the water, this rescue ship will immediately proceed to pick them up, render first aid, and if you are equipped with a sick bay, you will keep them on board for further treatment. Whenever possible, one of the vessels of the escort will provide coverage while you are working; the moment you have completed your rescue operation you will give four short blasts on your horn or siren—F for Fox—to signify that you are under way to rejoin the convoy. Now, before we go any further, are there any questions at this point?"

It was partly apple-polishing, but I stuck up my hand.

He gave me a withering look and asked tersely, "Yes?"

"About these men we are supposed to fish out of the water. Presumably we'll do that with our boats?"

"Yes," he replied. "There will also be scramble-nets provided. Anything else?"

"Possibly I am in a different position from my colleagues here, but I can't give them any medical treatment worth speaking of. I have no room below decks, my aft deck is a jungle of rails and canisters, I frankly believe that if we were to take on any casualties it would do them more harm than good. Would it be possible for my boats to deliver their casualties to a neighbor who is better equipped?"

He gazed at me expressionlessly, then he asked, "You are the Master of that Dutch tug?"

"That's right, sir."

"I'm sorry, but I can't discuss your case in abstractions. A decision in this matter will have to be left to the officer in command of your vessel; being on the spot, he will be in a better position to evaluate your problem than I." With that, he turned back to the blackboard.

I was suddenly overcome by cold anger. God knew I was not looking for trouble, but I could not let him get away with this, even if he did think that I had thought his name to be the joke of the century. "As it happens," I said, "I am the officer in command of my vessel."

He did not turn to face me. He said, picking up the chalk, "You are not, Captain. You will be replaced by one of His Majesty's officers."

"I'll be relieved of the command of my ship?" I asked, incredulously. Suddenly the classroom was very still.

"You will have a liaison officer on board," he answered, "who will give all orders in connection with convoy duty." He ruffled his notes. "Now, gentlemen, I will discuss what you are supposed to do if, by any chance, you should be left behind by the convoy after being disabled, or have to take to your boats for any other reason. The answer is simple: you shall make for the nearest island downwind. With southwesterlies prevailing, this is likely to be either Jan Mayen or Bear Island. Both islands are patrolled regularly by the Fleet Air Arm. . . . "

I was not listening. I sat in my little bench, tightly pressed against a trawler skipper smelling of fish, trying to regain my composure. My first reaction was a feeling of humiliation; I wanted to get up and shake the little bastard by his neck. Then I realized that, of course, we would need a liaison officer on our bridges, were it only to interpret the visual signals from the escort, as we would be sailing under radio silence. It was just the way he had put it, the vindictiveness of it. Once I had sorted this out, I thought: So what? I had accepted this assignment because Mr. Kwel had offered me the prize of freedom at the end of it; so what if a British officer took over my command? My crew did not care one way or the other, he would obviously be more experienced in convoy duty than I; maybe he would manage to pull that disgruntled, demoralized bunch into a team. Had the great Loppersum still been their skipper, this announcement would have meant trouble; they would have rallied around their father figure with indignation. But my demotion would not mean a thing to them; I was merely an administrative appointee foisted upon them by the head office. I hoped, as I sat there, that the British commander would be a calm, fatherly character, not some little runt like this one with his pissy fruit salad and his mincing voice. Captain Knol of the *Amanda* had warned me against small men: "Watch 'em, boy, for they hate you for every inch you are taller." He had also warned me against stammerers and red-haired women.

Even so, it took me a while to reason myself back into equanimity. When finally I relaxed, Captain Mashpee had reached the end of his discourse. He was now talking about our time of sailing: daybreak the next morning. "There is the possibility of a delay, gentlemen, for, as we all know, convoys do not always run on time. However, you had better be prepared to leave port at six hundred hours. Assemble three abreast and follow the instructions of your Comescort on the cruiser *Intrepid*, who will be me. At Langanes we join the main escort, which enters port only for ammunitioning, as oil and stores are taken on at sea. Gentlemen, as we are not likely to be in such close personal contact again until debriefing at Murmansk, let me take this opportunity to bid you good luck, and good hunting."

He gathered his papers together and marched off into the wings. I was stiff from sitting in that cramped position; as I stood there, stretching, another officer came up to me. He was older, and I saw he was a medical officer of the Royal Navy. He looked refreshingly human. "How do you do?" he said pleasantly. "I am Dr. Hawthorne. About those casualties your boats pick up: all you need do is ask your liaison officer to make a signal to the escort, and they'll send over a launch to take them off your hands. This, by the way, is a common procedure."

"Thank you, Doctor," I said.

He looked at me with knowing gray eyes. "Should there be anything else you feel insecure about in connection with this convoy, don't hesitate to come and see me. I have an office here in town. You are welcome any time."

I again said, "Thank you, Doctor," politely.

"I wouldn't mind Captain Mashpee's manner too much if I were you," he added. "He has been laboring under stress for some time now; this is his fourth convoy to Russia. You'll find that his bark is a great deal worse than his bite."

"Kind of you to say so," I said. "Thanks."

From the way he looked at me I thought he was going to say more. But he smiled, said, "Don't mention it," and wandered off.

On our way back to the bus that stood waiting for us, I felt relaxed and at peace with the world. If truth be told, I welcomed the idea of being relieved of my command. I could not help concluding that the Royal Navy was a better judge of men than Mr. Kwel. When finally I stood washing my hands in my bathroom on board, I decided to ask the cook to help me move my things into the chart-room. I would bed down on the couch there to make room for the new commander of the *Isabel Kwel*. I felt a twinge of regret; the privacy and the comfort of my stateroom had been the only aspect of this assignment that I had enjoyed.

As I stood drying my hands, I heard steps behind me. It was the mate; after our moment of truth in the mess-room, the night the chief died, I had had no more trouble with him. He had not exactly gone out of his way to hide that there was no love lost between us, but as we did not share the same watch, we never met at table except in port. I felt so detached that I did not even begrudge him his imminent satisfaction at the news that I had been relieved of my command. So, I said, nonchalantly, "By the way, I should tell you that we'll sail with an English officer in command."

I don't know what I had expected him to do or say; the fact that he did not say anything took me unawares. I turned around and saw him standing in the doorway, look-ing at me. "*What* did you say?" he asked.

I answered, "You heard me," put away the towel, rolled down my sleeves, muttered, "Excuse me," and pushed my way past him into my cabin. I heard the sharp intake of his breath; then he cried, "Well, I'll be goddammed! This is the bloody limit! You aren't going to take this lying down, are you, Skipper?"

The word "Skipper" came as a surprise. So far, he had

studiously avoided calling me anything. His eyes looked as cold as ever, devoid of any awareness of me as a person, but his indignation seemed sincere. "Why?" I asked. "As far as this Arctic route goes, both you and I are as green as grass. We need all the know-how we can get."

"I don't agree. To sail a tugboat is a specialized job. You've spent your life acquiring this skill. The bloody cheek of those goldfinches, to think they can stick one of their own on the bridge of the largest tugboat in the world and expect him to take over! I think it's time we made it plain to those British that there's a limit to which they can use us for a doormat!"

After two years as a captain of over a dozen different ships, I could not help having acquired some knowledge of men, but he foxed me. I could not get at the truth behind those unemotional eyes; I had no idea whether or not he was on the level. That he liked making mischief was certain; to sabotage the departure of the ship by having Sparks arrested, just for the sake of hazing a new captain, proved that he probably was a past master at it.

"I suppose I could work myself into a state about it," I said, "but I have an unknown ship with an untrained crew and a bunch of gun-toting outsiders on board. I would like to have an expert show me the ropes on one Murmansk convoy at least, before I start thinking about myself as a doormat, and I'd advise you to do the same." I turned away and went into the chartroom.

As far as I was concerned, our conversation was at an end; but I could not put him out of my mind. He had started a new train of thought. I discovered that to be the captain of the *Isabel Kwel* meant something to me, emotionally. I realized that I could be tricked into taking the whole thing as a personal insult again if I was not careful, and that would be suicidal folly. I was certain that we

needed an old hand in command on this trip, with specialized knowledge of the Arctic convoys; he might well
make the difference between life and death to all of us,
and after all those years as a lone wolf I had come to
consider mere survival as the primary objective of my
life.

I heard the door open behind me and a voice asked,
"What the hell is this? Is it true what he says? Are they
giving us a Limey for a skipper?"

It was Porks; as I looked up, I saw loom behind him the
lumbering, pensive bulk of the second engineer.

"No," I said, "a liaison officer, who will give orders in
connection with convoy duty."

Porks gave vent to a staggering obscenity and said, "I
don't know what your attitude is going to be, Skipper, but
I can tell you this much: any Limey who sets foot on this
ship and starts giving orders instead of you will have his
neck wrung by me, with these!" He showed his big, young,
oily hands.

They were oddly moving in their stupid loyalty. I felt
tempted to give in to this sudden wave of friendship and
emotionalism. If I wanted to become the real captain of
the *Isabel Kwel* who commanded the crew's unreasoning
devotion, I could do so now, by exploiting the arrival of
that British officer. It was the oldest trick of all tyrants: if
you want loyalty from your dissatisfied people, find them
an enemy. But I could not bring myself to take Porks' emotion at face value. His reaction was too violent. What was
he afraid of? That the experienced British commander
would find out something about him that he wanted to
hide? Maybe there was indeed something I did not know, a
hidden flaw, a real incompetence, but I shook the thought
off at once. Porks was all right, he was a good engineer.

"Thanks, Porks," I said. "I appreciate it, but I'm afraid

we'll have to postpone our demonstrations until after the first convoy."

"But, Skip!" he cried. "You are the captain of this ship! We don't want anybody else! We know that as long as you are on that bridge, we'll be okay! With a Limey up there, we don't!"

"Well," I said calmly, "you'll have to learn to live with it, that's all I can say. And this, friends, is an order." I turned back to the charts. "Are you ready for bunkering?"

There was a short, unhappy silence; then his voice came, "Ready when you are."

"All right," I said. "The moment the new man comes on, we'll move to the fuel dock. That'll be all for now."

They left dissatisfied, but without protest. I was glad I had nipped this in the bud and that reason had prevailed. But I did not make any more preparations to move out of my stateroom.

4

I sat waiting for him all afternoon. It was a bloody bore, for I had a whole list of things that should be decided upon or done; with six o'clock the next morning for a deadline, there was not much time left. As I sat in my quarters, fretting, doomed to inactivity by his absence, I began to get a mental image of him as the hours crawled by. The fact that he left it so late seemed to indicate that he was indeed an old and experienced hand at the game, but there seemed to be no need to rub it in. He must know that he had me hopping with impatience growing into anxiety, but the rules of the game, which by then I thoroughly detested, demanded that I must never show that by his nonchalant dallying he had turned me into a nervous wreck. Oh, no, I would have to play it the British way, with drawling understatement, eyelids drooping with boredom, lips barely moving. Then the cook, who had been pestering me all afternoon about stores for the voyage, came running up the steps to the boatdeck and hissed, in a stage whisper, "Pst! Here he comes!"

By then, it was five o'clock in the afternoon. I set my jaw and braced myself and fixed a smile on my face. Then he came up the steps, carrying his own duffel bag. That was stupid of the cook—no need to antagonize him at this point. I had already taken a breath for a greeting that would combine politeness with independence when he dumped the bag on the deck, said, "Phew!" and then, on seeing me, with a strong Canadian accent, "Hi, Cap! How's tricks?"

I stood there thunderstruck, incapable of speech or motion. Instead of the grizzled commander of my dreams, I saw a youth in his early twenties, with a chubby face covered with freckles, red eyebrows and a wisp of ginger hair under the peak of a cap that no officer of the British Royal Navy would ever push that far back on his head. On the shoulder tabs of his greatcoat glimmered one half of a wavy stripe. He was the lowest-grade junior officer in the lowest form of human life at sea: a bloody yachtsman.

After a second of perplexity, my mouth went sour with fury. This boy was worse than a joke, he was an insult. What outraged me most was that a commanding officer in the Royal Navy should have stooped to such a slap in the face out of sheer feminine pique. For he was not just getting even with someone who had offended him, he was involving the life of a ship and a crew of twenty-two. This boy looked as if he did not yet know one end of a ship from the other; even if I wanted to, I could not possibly take any orders from him. He must have sensed my hostility; in an obvious effort to break the ice he made things worse by saying, "Well, where's this war I hear so much about?"

I felt such anger at that asinine remark that all I could do, bar kicking him off my ship, was to grunt, open the door of my quarters, step over the threshold and slam the door behind me. There I stood, my face in my hands, and knew a moment of sheer, sickening panic. I had postponed all decisions, all urgent things that had to be done until my all-knowing, serenely calm successor would arrive; now I stood facing the unspeakable chaos of the future alone. I felt a momentary hysterical urge to flee, run blindly ashore, find that doctor, whatever his name was, who had spoken to me that morning and tell him that I could not possibly sail. I couldn't, just couldn't; I was no good, I didn't know my stuff, I was too late with everything, I couldn't possibly face an Arctic convoy with this ship, this crew, this preposterous green brat for a captain. But then the instinct for survival reasserted itself. I took a deep breath, went into the chartroom, peeled off my greatcoat that I had donned for the great welcome and put on my duffel. As I stood there, struggling into it, Cook appeared in the doorway and said, "Table's served."

"The hell with that," I said. "We have to bunker, we have to take on stores, we have to take on water, we'll eat when we're through with all that."

"Hey, listen . . . " he said, angrily.

"Get out of my way!" I pushed him aside, ran up the steps to the bridge, honked the hooter, blew down the tube to the engine room. The bosun came running up the stairs to the wheelhouse; the mate appeared on the foredeck; Porks answered from below.

"Stand by, engines!" I said into the tube. I called to the mate, "Let go fore and aft!" The bosun repeated the order to the aft deck. I saw that there was a space at the fuel dock across the harbor. It might be too small, but I would somehow shoulder my way in there; and I had better be snappy about it, because I heard the throaty "Harrumph!" of the exhaust of a diesel engine being started, a couple of ships away; obviously the whaler had the same idea. My engine roared to life with a thunderous rumble of the exhaust in the stack behind me. I pulled the telegraph on Slow Astern, barked to the helmsman, "Midships!" The mate, luckily, called from below, "All clear for'ard!" The men on the aft deck obviously had a moment of panic when the ship started to back out of her berth with her mooring lines still lashed to our neighbors', but they made it. We backed into the harbor with inconsiderate speed; the whaler had to cut his engine to avoid colliding with our stern. I made it to the fuel dock ahead of him, mooring over the right bow, which was the best side for bunkering. It was more luck than wisdom, but it looked like the latter; I would need a lot of that kind of luck in the next month or so.

The moment we were moored, the hoses for diesel oil and drinking water were lugged across the aft deck; their nozzles started to gurgle and hiss as they squirted their fluid down the feeder pipes. I sent Cook ashore to arrange for our stores to be delivered at once to the loading dock, where, at that moment, ships were still tied up three deep. I might be lucky again; a solitary Danish coaster, moored to the port side of the dock where there was room for only one vessel, looked as if she might be moving out just as we were ready; in that case, I might get served ahead of the two on the starboard side. It was not the civilized British way of queuing up, but I had less respect for the civilized British way that evening than I had had for a long time. Amid all the fuss and the frenzy, I occasionally thought of that bugger Mashpee and how one of these days I'd tell him exactly what I thought of him and his harem mentality.

I was lucky with the loading dock too; the whaler was not on the ball. Even so, it was late and dark by the time we finally were ready to eat. The cook announced that the table was ready, for a second time, with remarkable forbearance. I washed my hands and face and changed into my uniform jacket before going down; the junior officer would be there, and I did not want to look like a slob. I no longer felt any animosity toward him personally; as far as I was concerned, he was welcome to come along for the ride, as long as he did not get underfoot on the bridge. There was no question of his having any say in the command of my ship; he could interpret flag signals and decode messages, that was all. For the rest, I would use my own judgment and trust my luck.

As I came down the messroom stairs, I saw he was not there. But the four other officers were, and I had obviously interrupted something. They were sitting with their heads close together; when they saw me coming, they suddenly leaned back in theatrical poses. Porks, who could not have fooled his own mother, even went so far as to cough behind his hand. Before I had a chance to ask them what was going on, brisk steps came down behind me and the Canadian boy bumped into me so heartily that he nearly knocked my cap off. He said, "Sorry, Cap!" with radiant unconcern. If only he had kept that grin off his face and not behaved quite so much like a popular football player trotting onto the field, he might have fared better. But there he stood, cap on the back of his head, and said breezily to the others, "Hi there! The brass seems to have thrown us together for this trip, so let's make this one happy family, shall we?"

Nobody had a clue as to how to cope with that remark; they just sat there, flabbergasted. I lowered myself into my chair at the head of the table; the boy, with easy self-confidence, sat down on the short seat at the other end. The next moment, Cook came hoofing down the stairs with a plate and a spoon. He slammed these on the table in front of him and said in English, with an atrocious accent, "This ship Dutch ship. Crew no spik English, only me. If you want say something, spik to me, and I spik to them. You feel? Me translate." He pointed at the plate. "You go eat, yum-yum. If you want spik, cry 'Cook' and I come. Happy appetite." Then he turned around and climbed the stairs, virtually wagging his tail.

As I looked from one to the other, they all sat there, their faces innocent and noncommittal, beaming with smugness. It was obvious now what they had been up to: they had agreed to cut him dead by pretending they did not speak English, and they had appointed Cook, who barely spoke an intelligible word, to act as an interpreter. It was a childish thing for grown-up men to do; I should have put an end to it then and there, but at that moment I was not exactly full of charity toward the poor sod, who mumbled, lamely, "I see," and looked at his plate in embarrassed silence. Somehow the sudden collapse of his self-confidence was as irritating as his breeziness had been.

"What is this nonsense?" I asked, in Dutch. "Who dreamed this up?"

Porks replied, "We did, Skipper. All of us. For you." His face radiated such sincerity that he looked like a horse talking.

"Gee, thanks," I said, "but now snap out of it, will you? We can't have any schoolboy pranks like this right now.

Our lives are going to be complicated enough as it is in the Arctic. Soup, please."

Sparks handed me the tureen and I helped myself. Although I did not care a damn, one way or the other, to let them get away with sending the boy to Coventry was something I could not afford at this point. If I really wanted to take control of this ship, I should not become involved by acquiescence in a juvenile plot like this. I was about to tell them to cut it out, but before I had been able to say a word the boy put his foot in it again. He must have made up his mind that the mate was the softest among us, an elementary mistake; he said to him, "You speakee pidgin?"

The mate eyed him like a lynx, savoring a moment of sadistic silence, then bellowed, in Dutch, "Cook! He's talking!"

The words were barely out of his mouth when Cook was already there; he had obviously been waiting at the top of the stairs. He pounced on the boy with relish and said, "You spik, sir? Spik to me! Anysing you want?"

The boy looked at him with amazement and said, in a small voice, "Some salt, please . . . "

It seemed humanly impossible for a man to come up with a clanger every time he opened his mouth, but he had done it again. Every cook has his own idiosyncrasy; this one happened to consider it an offense if anyone suggested he could improve upon his cuisine by adding condiments. Porks had warned me about this in Greenock, so I now waited like everyone else until his back was turned before helping myself to salt and pepper. There sat the first real, speaking enemy Cook could lay hands on after two years of war with distant machines, and he asked for salt. The boy, by his extraordinary series of gaffes, was indeed turning himself into the enemy.

Cook said, in Dutch, "You would have thought that the bugger could have pointed at it, wouldn't you, instead of calling me down all the way from the bleeding galley?" Then he picked up the salt cellar, said, with his horrible accent thicker than ever, "Surrtainly, surr, let me help you, surr," and poured the whole of its contents into the boy's soup.

The boy, barely audible, said, "Thank you. . . . "

This went too far; the moment had come for me to intervene. But before I had been able to do so the cook asked, "By the way, Captain, where do you want the bugger to roost? We haven't got a spare bunk left."

He had never called me "Captain" before, and I remembered the meekness with which he had accepted my information that the meal he had come up to announce was indefinitely postponed. Clearly, the arrival of the boy had tipped the scales in my favor; they might have accepted a grizzled British commander, but at the sight of this amateur, they had all come scrambling to my side of the boat.

"On the couch in the chartroom," I answered, in Dutch, "and after you've taken him there, I'd like a word with you." Then I said to the boy, in English, "This may be a good moment for the cook to show you your quarters. Can I have your name, please?"

He looked up at me with unnerving kindness. It was not the look of an intimidated man I had expected, but rather one of embarrassment. "Tyler, sir," he answered, correctly. "Richard B. Tyler. Royal Canadian Navy Reserve."

"All right, Tyler," I said. "You go to your quarters and sort out your gear. I'll be in to see you later."

"Aye, aye, sir," he said.

I gave the cook a look that I hoped would be interpreted as masterful. "All right," I said, "take him away, but no more monkeyshines, please. We'll have to live with this character, and I don't want him in my hair on top of everything else. Now hop it."

The cook answered, "Very good, Captain," with uncharacteristic obedience. "You follow me, surr," he said to the boy. "I show you nice little place for beddy-byes. You not eat that rot-soup, you come wiz me."

The boy mumbled, "Sure thing," and followed him up the stairs.

When he was gone, I faced the conspirators. "All right, let's have it. What's the big idea?"

"It's simply that we have decided we don't want any part of him," the mate said, coolly, watching me. His pale eyes looked as if they took no part in what the rest of his body might be doing; they led their own life, watching, a lynx. "We were prepared to accept a qualified person, because you had made it obvious that was the way you wanted it, but we are not going to take any orders from a snotnose like that, and we trust you won't either."

"Let's leave me out of this for a moment," I said.

"It's exactly as he says, Skip!" Porks exclaimed with passion. "We all decided that if you said we had to accept a British commander, that would be the way it had to be, you are the captain; but this boy! This pipsqueak! How would you feel down below at the controls if you had somebody like him on the bridge to ring down the orders?" He obviously meant every word he said, but again I had the feeling that behind it all he felt vastly relieved. That morning, when he had first heard that there would be a British skipper, he had been a badly shaken young man.

"All right," I said. "So you don't want him as your captain. Neither do I, so that's settled. But what's the point of sending him to Coventry?"

The second engineer, who had been studying his huge fisherman's hands folded on the table, said, without looking up, "Well, in a sense it's none of my business, and I've sailed with enough blokes to know that you should not judge a man too hastily, but in this case I'd say: a little lesson won't do him any harm." He lifted his head and looked at me earnestly. "I don't believe he knows the difference between a tugboat and a steam roller. But I don't think he realizes that himself yet." He obviously was the sanest of the lot.

"I agree," said Sparks. "I'd say, let's keep it up for a few days, just to make sure he won't get the notion, sometime in the future, that he is in command of this ship."

"That side of it you can leave to me," I said. "As to the rest . . . " I had it on the tip of my tongue to tell them to pack it up and leave the boy alone, but something in the stillness of their waiting told me that I had to watch out. They were prepared to accept me, but not as a junior Captain Loppersum. It would have to be on a different basis, the basis of respect for my proficiency at my job. I should be careful not to start throwing my weight around, because I didn't have any, not yet; all I had for the moment was the good fortune that the little runt with the old Manx name had overplayed his hand. The sudden acceptance I had felt coming my way over the past few hours had been bestowed upon me only by virtue of a comparison with a twenty-year-old novice. So I concluded, "You are all adults; what you want to do to the guy is none of my business, as long as it does not interfere with the running of the ship. And when I think it does, I'll tell you." I paused a moment and looked around; they seemed to accept that the subject was closed. "As this is the last table we all share before we sail tomorrow," I continued, "I'd like to talk a few things over with you." I took out of my pocket the piece of paper with the notes I had been making that afternoon while I was waiting for the commander, expecting to discuss them with him. "We have six days before we rendezvous with the convoy, and we'll need every minute of them if we want to be properly prepared for what's ahead of us. Let's take these points one by one, in no particular order. What I want are your comments, in your area of responsibility. Here goes: scramble-nets. Where are they?"

"On the boatdeck, one on each side," the mate answered.

"What are they like?"

"I haven't had too close a look at them, but they seem fairly straightforward. About as wide as the boatdeck and, judging from the roll, I'd say that, fully extended, they can't reach more than three or four feet below the waterline."

"How do you propose to rig them?"

"Permanently seems to be the best. Not permanently lowered, of course, but stored. I'd thought a simple block-and-tackle rig, so all we have to do when we need them is cast off one line and, when we're through with them, pull them up."

"Are those things going to interfere with our boats, in the event we should need them ourselves?"

He frowned and gave me a look. "You mean, in case the ship should be listing, rolled down they might interfere with the skids?" He knew his stuff all right.

"Yes."

He thought for a while, then he said, "Let me think that over. I may be able to work something out."

"All right. Sparks: radio silence. As I understand it, we'll get our orders from the escort by flag signals that our friend upstairs is going to interpret for us. I assume he has a code; I propose to get it out of him and give it to you to copy."

"I'd appreciate that."

"Any communication from our side with the escort has to be transmitted by Aldis lamp, I take it. I don't want to be dependent on him for that either."

"No problem."

So it went, for the rest of the meal. Again, after he had put the second course on the table, the cook sat down on the stairs to listen in. I didn't care much for the idea that anything we discussed in the messroom would be for sale to the crew half an hour later in the galley, but an interference with this obviously well-established tradition would again look as if I were throwing my weight around. I would have to put up with his sitting there for a while longer.

We went through my list; then each of them had some queries of his own to add. We did a lot of ground work that night; it was past midnight when we finally left the table.

In my cabin, I remembered I had promised the boy I'd look in. I listened at the connecting door; the chartroom was silent. I hesitated as to whether I should go in, but decided against it. I had enough problems for one night; as long as I didn't hear any strangled sobs next door, I felt justified in concluding that he would live till morning. I'd have a word with him then.

5

The next morning I forgot all about him under the pressure of our departure. We left port on the dot; it was a bit of a scuffle. To set a dozen fair-sized ships moving all at once in the confined space of the harbor made for angry honking, spurts ahead, last-minute backings down and split-second wheel work. Engine-room telegraphs went on ringing on all sides, like cash registers in a department store during a sale; but all of us were experienced crafts-men, each knew his own ponderous monster sufficiently to maneuver it like a rowboat, although it packed enough weight to throw a diesel locomotive off the tracks in a collision. Once outside, our ragged bunch hung around in-decisively for a while until, with the effeminate bloops of a siren, a light cruiser came snorting around the mainland with an angry bristle of foam and a wake like the tail of a sheepdog. It was *Intrepid*, about five thousand tons, four hundred and fifty feet long, raked stem, square stern. She seemed armed with all the conventional equipment and a slowly rotating device in her mainmast, like a flat search-light, which I did not recognize. She rounded us up, blink-ing an Aldis lamp, burping with her klaxon, breaking out a fluttering flag signal that the young Canadian translated as TAKE UP FORMATION. Then his lips moved silently as he stood registering the ill-tempered flickerings of the Aldis lamp directed at us; our place in the small convoy turned out to be behind our whaling compatriot and alongside a respectable-looking Danish coaster that seemed reluctant to acknowledge our presence. The moment we were lined up, another flag signal was hoisted on the cruiser: FULL SPEED AHEAD, MAINTAIN YOUR DISTANCE.

Whenever in the past I had set out to sea with a tug, I had felt a slight exhilaration: there we went, small and pugnacious, terrier of the ocean. It was a boyish feeling; I had first felt it when, aged six, I had paddled out into the breathtaking expanse of the lake behind our village in an old canoe; I now discovered that the feeling depended on being alone. When the twelve rescue ships sailed from the Orkneys for Iceland, I felt like one of a flock of sheep. First the cruiser, streaming paravanes, steamed ahead of our small convoy; then, once we were outside the minefield, she began to circle around us at top speed in what seemed to us a frenzy of self-importance. We were all as green as grass; nobody realized that the German U-boats hovered around Scapa Flow summer and winter, day and night, like a pack of hyenas, waiting for a lamb to stray from the flock. Despite our heavy armament, I felt much more vulnerable and helpless than when I had had nothing to fence with except my wits.

Perhaps it was the presence of the Canadian boy on the bridge that irked me. Whatever I may have felt, he obviously felt like a hero. To him, our setting out on the deadly road to Murmansk was a sailing of Vikings; he could not have the faintest idea of what lay ahead. I tried to occupy myself with other things, but I found my eyes wandering back to him. He stood in the corner of the bridge, hands in the pockets of his duffel, hat on the back of his head, his forelock flagging in the wind, like a dreamer trailing clouds of glory. Cook came up with the morning coffee, each finger of both hands hooked through the handle of a mug. He went to the boy first and said with a big yellow grin, "Here you are, surr, nice cuppee coffee."

The boy shook his head with a smile, a dreamer awakened, and answered, "No, thanks, I don't think I will for the moment," then he turned to me and said, guilelessly, "If you want to turn in, sir, I'll hold the fort."

My jaws stiffened, but I realized at once that this was just another of those blunders, which now began to amount to genius. The cook reacted differently. So far, I had known him only as a tiresome but inoffensive little man; now he looked really frightening. He said, "The gentleman suggests that you go back to bed, Captain. He'll sail the convoy alone."

I answered, "I heard him. That'll do."

"Why don't you kick him in the belly?" he asked in a whisper hoarse with rage.

"That'll do!" I said. "Bugger off."

Cook turned to the boy, who had not noticed any of this, and said, "The captain has only just got up, surr. He would like to stay on the bridge for a little bit longer, if you don't mind." He glanced over his shoulder, like a dog about to snatch something out of a trash can, prepared to dart away from the kick he knows is coming; then he added, "If you want to be sick, go to the shithouse—second door to the right, down steps," and scurried away with his mugs.

But the boy had not noticed anything amiss; Cook's accent was such that to speak in a whisper made him unintelligible. Obviously, he had not understood a word; he was still waiting, unsuspectingly, for my answer to his offer to take over.

My first impulse had been to pin his ears back, but there was something about the way he stood there with the sun on his freckled face and his red forelock in the wind, something so young and innocent that I couldn't help remembering my own first sailing as a mate's apprentice on board the old *Cornelia*. Heaven knew how often I had put my foot in my mouth, during those first days of swallowing apprehension alternating with delusions of grandeur. Captain Bosman had been very kind.

"Thank you, Tyler," I said. "I may take you up on that for a few minutes. I must point out, however, that you are not supposed to be burdened with any responsibility for the running of this ship. Yours is a liaison duty, that's all."

"Oh?" he said and his eyebrows rose in surprise. "Captain Mashpee said—"

"Whatever Captain Mashpee may have said," I retorted, trying to sound patient, "I am the Master of this ship; and unless you are an experienced tugboat man, there can be no question of my delegating any of my responsibility to you. Are you?"

He lowered his eyes almost bashfully and said, "No, sir. I have a lot of experience with handling small boats, though."

"I'm sure you have," I said. "Maybe we are overly sensitive on this point, but we do not think of this ship as a small boat. She happens to be the largest tugboat in the world, with as much power in her as a seventeen-thousand-ton freighter. To handle a ship like this is a specialized craft; if you're interested, I'll be glad to tell you more about it when we have a chance. But there can be no question of your taking on any of the responsibility of the Master, nor, I must warn you, that of the mate, the bosun or even the seamen. So let's forget about Captain Mashpee and the British Navy until you are qualified. You are sailing under Dutch flag and under my command, and I'm pleased to have you on board. All right?" I gave him a smile that must have looked hypocritical to him, then concluded, "On that understanding, I'll be happy to leave you the bridge for a few minutes. Call me if there should be any change in conditions."

He muttered, "Aye, aye, sir." I turned away and went down the stairs to the lower bridge, feeling saintly.

In the chartroom I found his bed still unmade; the stool that belonged underneath the chart table stood beside the couch, with on it an alarm clock, an ashtray full of cigarette stubs and a half-eaten bar of chocolate. On the chart of the Orkneys on the table stood a little leather toilet kit; strewn beside it a shaving brush, a bottle of hair lotion, a comb fuzzy with hair, a toothbrush and a mangled tube of toothpaste. When I opened the drawer underneath the table, I found it full of underwear; a large leather wallet lay on top. As I flung it out, it fell open; I saw it contained the photograph of a dark-haired girl in a bathing suit, holding a kitten. It was a startling picture, for the flesh-colored bathing suit was so revealing that she might as well have worn nothing at all. But, despite the impudence of her pose, she conveyed such innocence and respectability that it was obvious she had had no inkling of its effect. She was a beautiful creature, in her early twenties; her very innocence, emphasized by the kitten she was cradling, made me feel like a Peeping Tom. Instead of scooping out the rest of his underwear and flinging it on the couch as I had been about to do, I put the wallet back in the drawer and closed it. Then I lit a cigarette, and went back to the bridge.

I found him pacing up and down, hands clasped behind his back, jaw set in stern determination, Captain Horatio Hornblower pacing the poop deck. When he saw me, he relaxed and grinned self-consciously.

"Tyler," I said, "I've just been to the chartroom and found it looking like a den in a college dormitory. I'll thank you to clear up all traces of your existence each time before you come on watch. Is that understood?"

"Aye, aye, sir," he said, correctly. "Which watch am I to take, sir?"

"You and I will share the same watch; that is, eight to twelve in the morning, four to eight in the evening, and midnight till four."

"But who will take care of communications while I'm off watch, sir? My orders are—"

"Unless your orders are to go without sleep altogether, the radio officer will fill in for you except during battle stations, when you'll both be on duty. So you had better let me have your code to give to him, he'll need to make a copy of it."

Evidently, he didn't like the idea; but he said, "Very good, sir."

"The moment this watch is over, you'll go to the chartroom and clear up your mess. I don't want to see any of it anywhere, certainly not in the drawer underneath the chart table."

"But where am I to put my gear, sir?" he asked, alarmed. "I haven't been able to find any place to put anything. . . . "

"Sorry, Tyler," I said. "That's the way it is on board a tugboat. You'll just have to use your ingenuity."

I left him standing there, looking unhappy. He had reason to: oceangoing tugboats were notoriously devoid of most of the trappings of civilization; this one, embodying Mr. Kwel Senior's concept of society, seemed to be designed for a crew of nudists. The cook's predicament was even more harrowing than the boy's, hence the sack of potatoes I had spied sticking over the edge of number-one lifeboat when I first came on board in Holyhead which, on closer scrutiny, turned out to contain not potatoes but coal. It was a mystery why an oil-fired galley stove needed coal, and stored in an operational lifeboat at that. The *Isabel Kwel* was, like most oceangoing tugboats, fitted out with twice the number of boats required by law, and these were three times the prescribed minimum size. The reason for this uncharacteristic largess on the part of the owners was that the boats were not intended just to save the crew in case of an emergency, but to double as rescue lifeboats in cases where, on a salvage expedition, the crew of a vessel in distress could be inveigled into abandoning ship. They each provided room for sixty people; the forward port boat proved, upon inspection, to be filled with other stores: crates, bottles, casks, cans, boxes, sacks, bags, baskets; on top of these, winter gear, rubber boots, spare oilskins and bundles of extra blankets. There was enough there for a full-fledged safari into the heart of darkest Arctica; I called the cook out.

The moment he saw me standing by the boat, its tar-paulin cover open, he began to protest in a high, keening voice that I had never heard him use before, and he started a bizarre sort of little dance, twirling around on the boat-deck, wailing that he had absolutely no other place to put anything, that Captain Bokke had given him permission to use that boat, that it was always the same damn stinking story on board all damn stinking tugboats: not a cubic inch of storage space for man or beast, nothing, nothing at all. Where did I expect him to put all this? Where, in the name of the Holy Trinity, where?

It had been a fascinating performance and he must, on occasion, have achieved something by it, for after his final pirouette he ended up in front of me self-confidently, arms spread, feet at right angles, as if the curtain were coming down behind him amid thunderous applause. I unfairly pricked the bubble of his theatrical triumph by asking, "What was that you said?"

For a moment he stood there, eyes blazing, jaw muscles twitching, as if his next move would be a ferret's lunge at my throat; then he rose on his toes and squealed, like a soprano attaining the high C, "I said, *where do you want me to put all that stuff!*"

I was sick of his exaggerations, so I gave him a tone-deaf look and said, "In your bunk."

It turned him into a statue. As I walked away, down the boatdeck to the steps, I didn't hear another squeak out of him. Before sinking from sight down to the aft deck, I glanced at him once more. He was still standing there, frozen, as I had left him. Of all the cooks I had known, most of whom had on occasion scaled the heights of emo-tion normally reserved for the other sex, he had the most striking talent for the drama. I wondered what he would come up with next.

On the aft deck, I found the seven gunners and their corporal working out the intricacies of the depth-charge catapults. The deck was sheltered by the midships from the speedwind of the tug; they had taken off the tops of their battledresses and stood clustered around the gaunt contraptions in their singlets; their arms, as white as slugs, made their tanned hands look as if they were wearing gloves. I joined them and looked knowledgeable while the South African corporal described the principle of the catapults; all I could grasp from his dissertation was that the explosive in the canisters was not detonated by concussion or fuse but by immersion in water, which seemed to call for a good watertight cover over them. When I suggested this, he smiled with polite superiority and explained that to douse them with water would not set them off, not even a wave washing over the aft deck, not even a broadside collision, unless they became dislodged and rolled overboard, which was impossible, as the catapults blocked their way. He sounded so reassuring on the subject of the canisters and went to such lengths to pooh-pooh the idea of there being any risk to our carrying such an earth-shattering load of high explosives on our aft deck that I could not help wondering where the catch lay. I asked him what would happen if we were strafed by enemy aircraft or received a direct hit from surface guns; he looked away and replied casually, "The thing to do, of course, is to try and launch them as early as possible in the game. But that, I'm afraid, is up to the Comescort."

I said, "Thank you," and we went on to inspect and discuss the guns we had on board in the same spirit. Listening to him, I was forced to the conclusion that whatever the Navy might put at the disposal of the convoy by way of an escort was a waste of ships and money, for with these guns, the convoy was as safe as any convoy could expect to be, especially when they were manned by gunners like that little fat one over there. You see him? The swarthy one, with the heart tattooed on his left biceps? An absolutely stunning shot, absolutely stunning. I had noticed the stunning shot before, also the heart tattooed on his biceps with, underneath, the legend *I was Born for Love*. I was not convinced on either count.

The corporal went on extolling his guns until he prevailed on me to sit down behind one of them and take aim at the Dane next door, just to get an idea of the accuracy of the telescopic sight. After he had adjusted it for me, I climbed into the saddle, put my eye to the telescope and saw the captain on the bridge of the Danish coaster pick his nose, inspect the result and wipe it off on the seat of his pants; their ship's dog peered at us between the bars of the rail and wagged his tail. The whole thing seemed ludicrous, I simply could not visualize the reality that awaited us all. We made some gentleman's agreements about watches, co-operation between gunners and the officer on the bridge when it came to moving over to let him have a look at the sea; we spiced our conversation with some casual reminiscing about action we had seen, so as to establish that neither of us could prevail over the other on the basis of experience. I dramatized my past perils somewhat for the sake of the cause; he evidently did the same, as some of his experiences sounded like exploits of Baron von Munchhausen, notably one incident where he had been catapulted from his seat behind a Bofors, somersaulted in the air and landed back astride the saddle in time to staple the swine across the navel.

I went back to the bridge in a pensive mood. The more I saw and heard of my own ship and my colleagues in the small convoy, the less I liked the light-hearted innocence with which we were all trotting toward our Armageddon. That half an hour's briefing by Captain Mashpee on board the battleship had not been nearly enough; all he had been able to give us was the merest hint of what we might expect between Iceland and Murmansk. Making the rounds and being shown all those martial toys, rather than instilling me with confidence, gave me a growing feeling of insecurity. It was suicidal folly to let myself be lulled into complacency by the fatuous reassurances of a gunnery corporal, while my crew had never been shot at in earnest, to say nothing of my communications officer, on whose nerve and accuracy under fire our lives depended. I decided to spend my next watch just lying on my back on my bunk, smoking, trying to visualize as many critical situations as I could think of in which we might find ourselves. I should try to identify with U-boat captains and pilots of the Luftwaffe—what would we look like, for instance, in a convoy seen from the air? What impression would a U-boat commandant get from our silhouette through a periscope against the streak of the dawn? Would that double row of depth charges on the aft deck be easily recognizable as such? For some reason too lofty for the normal mind to understand, the British Munitions Office had painted those canisters white with an orange band in the center. Maybe they had been concerned about drunken ratings stumbling on board at dead of night who might be tripped up by a canister painted gray; in broad daylight in the Arctic, which was virtually continuous during the summer, the dazzling drums on my aft deck seemed designed to attract attention. How could I camouflage them without impairing their availability in an emergency? Tarpaulin? Lumber? This called for more thought, and it was only one of scores of similar problems, each one presenting a lethal danger if left unsolved because of overconfidence or mere sloth.

To retire into the privacy of my cabin to think seemed more urgent by the minute; when the mate came to take over the watch on the bridge and Cook called the second table, I told him to bring my meal to the chartroom on a tray, as I had paperwork to do. Entering the chartroom, I saw the boy's junk still lying about; he had obviously gone straight down to the messroom from the bridge. I tramped out of there without tenderness, thundered down the steps, crossed the deck and yelled down the messroom hatch, "Tyler! *Mister* Tyler! I want you in the chartroom, on the double!" I did not wait for his confirmation; I strode back across the deck, climbed the steps, stamped into the chartroom and slammed the door. I knew I was hamming it up, but I did not feel like British understatement at that moment. When he appeared, after a tentative knock and a bark from me that hurt my larynx, he looked apprehensive.

"Mr. Tyler," I said with sonority. "I asked you to clear up behind you. May I please have the explanation for this . . . ?" I indicated with a sweeping gesture the teen-age chaos in the chartroom.

"But, sir . . ." he began.

"I know!" I bellowed. "You were 'holding the fort' on the bridge! But wouldn't you say it was reasonable to expect that you might clear up this—this *rotzooi*, before rushing down to the messroom and putting your feet in the trough?"

He cast down his eyes and stood to attention, all cub officers unfairly dressed down personified. "Aye, aye, sir."

"Pray do so now, Mr. Tyler," I said, and with that I turned around, stepped across the threshold into my cabin and slammed the door. Once in my cabin, I realized my dressing-down had indeed been unfair, as he obviously would not have had a chance to feed at all had he not gone down in time for the second table; but such was life, and the sooner he got used to it, the better. I forgot about him and proceeded to do what I had set out to do: I lay down on my bunk, lit a cigarette and stared at the ceiling.

The sounds of the ship were all around me. The lock of the communicating door rattled softly with the throbbing of the engine; the wardrobe creaked with the rolling of the ship; water sloshed in the cistern over the toilet. Overhead on the bridge the steps of the mate came and went at walking speed; down below, iron clanked in the engine room; somewhere in the ship, a man was singing. It seemed absurd that this world, this vibrant, living reality, was in imminent danger of being annihilated. The *Isabel Kwel* seemed, that sunny afternoon, as immortal in her youth, her joyous life, as I myself. I might lie there and try to conjure up on the ceiling scenes of fire and death and destruction, but they had an unreality about them that made my awareness wander back to the sounds, the smells, the sights of life, to the animal enjoyment of the warmth, the snugness, the sun-drenched somnolence, the carnal contentment of being part of a summer's day. I had never felt quite so relaxed and happy and at home on a ship before; I felt as if I were part of her, as if we formed one body, of which I was the center of awareness; all nerves and tendons and veins and viscera, reaching into the remotest corners, were concentrated in me. As I lay there, eyes closed, I could interpret every sound, trace every tremor to its origin. It was a healthy body, full of strength, with only that one inexplicable flaw of suddenly going haywire once in a blue moon and refusing to obey the command of my will.

I had often thought about that mysterious streak in her, since the day we put her through her paces. It had not worried me much, not even induced any special wariness in me while maneuvering; I had been sure there was an explanation and that sometime I would stumble upon it. Now, lying on my bunk, awakening for the first time in my life to the never known and never suspected physical unison between a captain and his ship, that one unaccountable speck of madness in her seemed harmless, immaterial. I felt the sudden unreasoning conviction that she would never again do this to me. She might do it to others, but not to me. There was no justification for that sudden certainty; I had no idea that I had finally entered into that most ancient, mystical relationship between man and matter: the comradeship between a sailor and his ship. I was at last, in my turn, imbuing a piece of man-made machinery with a personality of its own, linked to it by a bond of loyalty and devotion, an umbilical cord of love. I was no exception; it was common to us all. Even the dourest Master of the largest liner will secretly stroke the rail of his bridge, thinking, "Well done, old girl," after his steel colossus has eased her monstrous flank alongside the precipitous cliff of a quay. Innocently, I put my hand on the wall beside my bunk, for the first time knowingly touching my ship in a gesture of intimacy. I looked at that wall, then at the ceiling, the door, the portholes while, within me, a new and unknown tenderness hesitantly reached out toward them, the intimate details of the sensuous body of the *Isabel Kwel*. I knew, with the high-plumed presumption of the inexperienced young male, that she would never disobey me again, but would repay my devotion with idolatry. From now on, she would be consumed with only one desire: to comply with the slightest of my wishes— slave, comrade, concubine; alter ego of Narcissus, spectral partner in the imaginary dialogue of the Masters after God.

I had, at that moment, no inkling of the insidiousness of the spell I was submitting myself to. I was young and strong and confident, and I had long been alone; the song of the sirens was new to me. I reveled in that new and unknown sense of security which the very touch of her gave me. She was mine, at last; she had shaken the ghost of old Loppersum, who had obviously never understood her. Our relationship was different; it had suddenly become obvious why she could never really have been his: she was, manifestly, a young man's ship.

Somebody dropped something on the bridge; the mate's pacing stopped; through the open porthole came the sound of laughter. I should concentrate on the future now, start doing what I had planned to do—identify with German U-boat commanders and bomber pilots and review every possible eventuality that might be thrown my way. But I could not do that by lying there; I got out of my bunk and stubbed out my cigarette. I was suddenly full of confidence; I need not lie there thinking any longer. I was ready for the next stage: to write it all down and tick off each subject after thinking it through.

I opened the communicating door, intending to sit down at the chart table, a sheet of paper in front of me; but as I came in, there was the bloody boy, sitting where I had planned to sit, doing what I had planned to do. The picture of the naked girl with the kitten was standing in front of him, propped up against the chronometer box; when he heard the door, he snatched it away and slipped it swiftly into the drawer.

Finding him there irritated me beyond reason. "Mr. Tyler," I said with outraged patience, "I'm afraid you are not quite attuned to life on shipboard yet. This is not your private snuggery, this is the *chartroom*, which must be kept at the disposal of the officer of the watch at all times. Junior officers during their off hours are supposed to play elsewhere."

"But listen, Cap!" he protested, momentarily falling out of his role as Midshipman Hornblower. "I haven't got any place else to go! This is where I sleep, where else do you want me to write my letters?"

"On the table in the messroom," I replied, fighting the impulse to kick him off that stool, "and I'll thank you not to call me 'Cap.' I am not conversant with what is customary in the Canadian Royal Naval Reserve, but where I come from, the Master of a vessel is addressed by his junior officers as 'sir.'"

"Yes, sir. I mean: aye, aye, sir," he muttered, apologetically, hastily gathering together his writings. Then he rose, pulled a handkerchief out of his pocket and dusted the top of the stool with it. It seemed to be a genuine, though pointless gesture of contrition. He snapped to attention, said, "Sorry, sir. Thank you, sir," and turned about with the robot-like precision of the rating that went with the commander in Greenock. He stepped stiffly over the threshold to the bridge, turned about again to salute once more, then he closed the door gingerly, as if he were leaving a sickroom.

Once he had left, I sat down at the table, opened the drawer to get paper, and, by God, there she was again: the girl with the kitten gazing at me with what looked like reproach. I picked her up and threw her behind me on the couch, pulled out a wad of paper, put it in front of me, got up, picked her off the couch, flung her back into the drawer and slammed it shut. Something in the way she seemed to look at me had made me realize that by sending him to the messroom to do his writing I had sent him into the arms of the committee that had sent him to Coventry. For a moment, I considered calling him out of there and telling him to sit somewhere else, then I decided that I could not live his life for him; anyhow, I had other problems.

One of them came in without knocking, just as I was about to start. It was the cook, carrying a tray. He was still demonstratively in a huff, but the first things I saw on that tray were a salt cellar and a pepper mill, so obviously this was a lovers' quarrel. I discovered that I was getting used to the impossible little man; when he spread out a napkin on the far corner of the chart table and carefully laid out a place for one, it occurred to me how lonely and bewildered he must have felt after the death of his beloved captain. Their life together had probably consisted of an endless series of rows; yet how helpless the giant must have been in small things, like putting in collar studs, darning socks, even—by golly!—cutting up his sandwiches, for there he went: cutting up a slice of buttered bread into fingers for me and arranging them neatly on a little side plate. He looked like a comedy figure with his accordion trousers, his scraggy neck, his tattooed wristwatch, yet there was something oddly moving about the way he put all his motherly instincts of protection into the laying of that table. The final touch was a paper napkin he pulled from his pocket; he smoothed it out on his knee, folded it carefully into a triangle and put it beside my plate with the knife on top. He surveyed his handiwork with a critical look, then he turned to me, gestured toward the display with disdain, turned away and stalked out, leaving behind the unassailable proof that, as far as he was concerned at least, the *Isabel Kwel* was again blessed with a captain.

After I had finished my meal, I put an empty sheet of paper in front of me and drew what a U-boat commandant would see if his periscope, scanning the convoy on the horizon, singled out a tugboat trailing four merchant ships. I drew the silhouette of the *Isabel Kwel:* stubby, pugnacious, with hump-shouldered power, yet harmless and inconsequential as a prey. No submarine commander would waste a torpedo on a tugboat, unless he spotted these: the Oerlikon, the twin Bofors cannons on the bridge and, most of all, the catapults for the depth charges.

The Oerlikon he would expect and discount, as it did not concern him, only his brothers of the Luftwaffe. Those cannons were a different story, and the catapults represented a direct and deadly threat. One of those canisters, well placed in the vicinity of his submerged hull, could buckle his plates, burst his rivets and send his ship to the bottom with a broken back. My first objective should be to camouflage the catapults and, after that, those two cannons.

It was not going to be easy. The gaunt silhouettes of the catapults were unmistakable, but there must be a way of disguising them. I had no idea how; perhaps by just doodling, I might hit upon an idea that way. I drew a line from the top of one catapult to the midships and suspended from that line a string of laundry: bedsheets, pillowcases, long drawers, socks, BVDs. It looked a little better, but not convincing. It did not change the outline of the catapults one bit, just made them look inactive. Would that be enough? Would the laundry make the U-boat captain, his eyes glued to his periscope, conclude that once upon a time that tug had doubled as a depth-charge thrower, but that now this must be a thing of the past? Not for a second, if it were me. But maybe I was too familiar with them by now; the engineer in Greenock had explained to me that they were experimental, a new invention by the boffins which the Navy was trying out, especially designed for slow vessels like mine. They were intended to hurl the canisters as far astern as possible, so that, in combination with the top speed of a slow vessel, sufficient distance would be put between it and the exploding canister to avoid damaging rudder and propeller with the shock wave of the explosion. If indeed they were a new invention, there could not be too many of them about as yet, so perhaps the U-boat commandant would not recognize them at a glance. But I could not count on that. If German Intelligence was half as good as it was reported to be, they must have a sketch of the things by now, and the first to receive copies of it would be the U-boat captains. What else could I do to disguise those idiotic things that stood out like sore thumbs on my aft deck? Cover them with something? What could I cover them with that would look natural? An outside privy? Duck blind? Ha ha.

I doodled some more, drew farfetched things, and that was exactly what they looked like: farfetched things. If anything, they drew attention to the catapults rather than disguised them. No, I had to come up with something that would draw the attention away from them. Rig the laundry line with girls' bathing suits? Very funny, considering that anybody swimming in the Arctic for longer than three minutes would be dead. And what would girls' bathing suits be doing on a tugboat? Cook, however, might have some among that pile of junk in number-one lifeboat; from what I had seen, there were things there that would make any U-boat captain's mouth fall open. That was the next problem awaiting my attention: what to do with Cook's junk? My advice to put it in his bunk had been made for its dramatic effect only; I would have to help him find some storage space somewhere. And then, suddenly, as my hand doodled a little lifeboat on the paper, the solution came to me: two birds with one stone. If only that would work! If only . . .

I rummaged in the drawer, found the tape measure I had seen there on a previous occasion, and went to the starboard boatdeck. There, behind the two lifeboats, was a beat-up, scruffy little workhorse called the jolly boat. It was the only one on active duty and was used for everything: painting the hull, ferrying crew and stores. It had oars and an outboard engine, even a little sailing rig; in Greenock I had taken it out just for the sport of it, and so had almost everybody else on board, down to the two oilmen. It was a scruffy little thing, nobody treated it with any consideration, although, considering the pleasure and the service it gave, it was worth its weight in gold. I measured the jolly from stem to stern and discovered it was larger than I had thought it to be, twenty feet over all. It came as a disappointment and I doubted if my plan would work; but I went down to the aft deck, stepped over the legs of gunners asleep in the sun and measured the space between the two catapults: twenty-one feet. I let out a boyish whoop of triumph that woke up the gunner nearest to me; he rose on his elbows and gazed in my direction, then lay down again, obviously concluding it could not have been me.

I ran to the fo'c'sle and called out the carpenter and the bosun. Both were old men, so although they had probably been fast asleep when I called, they had reached the stage where they could obey orders and even carry on a simple conversation without actually waking up. The carpenter was an unknown entity, I had seen him around only occasionally, usually on hands and knees, trying to peer underneath things through a pair of steel-rimmed spectacles. I took them to the aft deck, where I explained that I wanted a high scaffolding built for the jolly boat, so high that it would be clearly visible above the rail. I also wanted two fake arms, like gallows, built onto both catapults, simulating a set of davits, complete with tackle and block. The jolly boat should be fixed permanently, so that it would not be washed overboard by any blue water we might take over in bad weather.

The carpenter had a hard time understanding all this; he could not for the life of him grasp why he should build something for a boat that was not supposed to serve any purpose. I tried to explain to him that it would serve the purpose of camouflaging the catapults that turned our otherwise harmless silhouette into a major threat to any U-boat, but I could not get through to him. The bosun tried to explain it in carpenter's language, but he was not equal to the task either; only when I happened to mention that Cook would be using the jolly boat for storage did the carpenter's face relax.

"Ah," he sighed, smiling with relief. "A cool cupboard."

The bosun and I exchanged a look; he said in a whisper, "Don't worry, Captain. He'll do a top job. He always does, as soon as he can give it a name."

"What say?" the carpenter asked, with that frown again.

"Deaf?" I queried.

The bosun nodded and mouthed over the carpenter's shoulder, "As a post."

It seemed to be a ship of the deaf. Maybe old Bokke Loppersum had been deaf too—it would explain a lot of things.

"You might have told me in Greenock," I said, "when I had to let four men go. He shouldn't be at sea, certainly not where we are heading."

The bosun tried a reassuring smile. He had a broad Germanic face, like the peasant who must have sat as a model for all the apostles on the altars of the early Gothic, so his grin came out as a grimace of sorrow. "He's worth five men, Captain," he said.

I realized that they must be friends of long standing; they probably had sailed with Captain Bokke for forty-five years too, like the cook and the late chief. At their age, I probably would put personal loyalty above all other considerations too. "Okay," I said, "I leave it to you, bosun. Keep an eye on what he does, you've got the idea."

"I have, Captain," he said, relieved.

On my way back to the chartroom, I sauntered past the two rows of gaily painted canisters, tightly packed together on their rails. The mere sight of them filled me with apprehension. I happened to know each one of them packed four hundred and fifty pounds of Amatol, enough to blow up a village. But the gunners sprawled on them, basking in the afternoon sun, with the insouciance of the Italian villagers that till the slopes of Vesuvius. To camouflage those canisters would be my next problem. It seemed insurmountable; but then, so had the problem of the catapults.

As I stood at the top of the steps, on the boatdeck, I looked around and surveyed my ship. The joy and the sense of certainty that had come over me as I lay on my bunk had stayed with me. It was impossible; it simply could not be that this ship, this crew, these men were heading for extinction on the Murmansk route. I did not know why, but as I stood there I had a sense of protection, a charm which made the *Isabel Kwel*, alone among the small flock of sheep now trotting obediently to slaughter, the lucky one, invulnerable, immortal.

CHAPTER FIVE

I

Those six days to Langanes were, had I only known it, the last light-hearted, careless days of my youth. The weather was incredibly beautiful, warm and gentle, the light southerly breeze still carried with it, over all those hundreds of miles across the ocean, the faint summery smell of sun-drenched heather on the Scottish moors. They were glorious days of peace and hope, translucent with an unearthly sheen of lingering daylight that stretched imperceptibly longer until dusk and daybreak were separated only by a short, very blue midsummer twilight in which the stars barely broke through the high haze of the sunset, reaching out across the world toward the high first flush of the dawn.

The small convoy plowed docilely onward across the shimmering sparkling sea, with its sheepdog, *Intrepid*, running up and down our sleepy ranks, whooshing around us in nervous circles, or occasionally lying still alongside our course to let us file past; on those occasions I could, from the bridge of the *Isabel Kwel*, hear the distant "ping, ping,

ping" of her Asdic as we trundled by.

Meanwhile, I went on pitting my wits against those of the unknown adversary. After the carpenter and the bosun had rigged up the jolly boat between the two catapults, the deaf old dodderer proceeded to disguise them as davits and did such an astoundingly realistic job that I came to the conclusion that he had missed his vocation. He should have been a stage carpenter instead of wasting his talents on hands and knees on board an oceangoing tugboat. The result was much better than I had dared hope; no U-boat commander, not even the legendary Kapitän Prien himself, could possibly recognize them for what they were.

Nor could a British cruiser captain, for that matter. While the bosun was painting the jolly boat, a signal came from *Intrepid* by lamp. The boy Tyler, after a momentary confusion, woke up from his reverie and penned it down. When he came to present me with the result, he looked, it seemed, a little wary. I read what he had written: COM-ESCORT TO MASTER ISAB: DO NOT REPEAT NOT OBSTRUCT YOUR ARTILLERY SIGNED MASHPEE END.

The boy, standing to attention, asked, hiding behind formality, "Do you wish me to make answer, sir?"

I said, "I do," and scribbled on the back of his message: MASTER ISAB TO COMESCORT: GO TO HELL SIGNED HARINXMA END.

He stared at it with round eyes and stammered, "I d-don't know that I can send this, sir."

"All right," I said, taking the paper from him, "I'll ask my wireless operator to do it. Thanks very much."

But he came running after me as I was on my way to Sparks' cubicle and said breathlessly, "I didn't mean it like that, sir—I mean—it is maybe a little unusual, but of course, if you tell me to do so, I'll send it, sir, right now."

I looked at his eager face, his adolescent eyes full of

problems, and said, "All right, Tyler, go ahead."

He got busy with the Aldis lamp and I forgot about him. Later Sparks asked, "What was all the chitchat about with the escort?"

"Why?"

"I don't know. Every time I happened to look out of my porthole, they seemed to be asking, 'Would you please repeat that message?' "

"Oh, that must have been after my reply to Captain Mashpee, who told me not to obstruct my artillery."

Sparks' nose, which seemed to wake up and listen whenever a saucy bit of gossip came his way, probed eagerly in my direction. "What did you reply?"

I told him. He told the cook. The cook was in the process of telling the whole ship, when *Intrepid* ran up a flag signal: CONVOY REDUCE SPEED TO FIVE KNOTS.

I was busy complying with this order, trying not to pile up on the tail of the man ahead of me, when Tyler came running with another message meant for us personally. It read: COMESCORT TO MASTER ISAB: DROP OUT OF CONVOY AND LAY TO YOU WILL BE BOARDED SIGNED MASHPEE END.

I obediently detached myself from the convoy; *Intrepid* came close alongside, Asdic pinging; a motor launch was lowered and spumed its way toward us across the glassy sea. It was Mashpee himself who climbed on board the *Isabel Kwel*, with the irascibility of a village doctor aroused at dead of night to attend to an acute appendicitis which he knows, sight unseen, will turn out to be gas. As he hoisted himself over the rail, I became conscious of the fact that we had an audience on both ships. At least four pairs of binoculars on board *Intrepid* were trained upon us, and behind and above me I sensed the motionless presence of members of my crew. I realized, with a lucidity that must be familiar to prize fighters just before entering the ring, that it was a ritual occasion, an ultimate test in which I had to prove myself worthy of being the leader of the pack behind me.

I don't think Mashpee had any such highfaluting concept of our encounter; if he had, he hid it well. As he stood facing me, his mean little eyes at the level of my chin, his oak-leaved cap on the back of his head, his fruit salad partially hidden by an incongruous muffler, one thing was clear: he was hopping, flaming mad, but as his was a British fury, it was visible only in his eyes, at very close quarters. His manner was relaxed and nonchalant, his voice drawling to a point of boredom when he said, after a perfunctory salute that I returned in kind, "Good afternoon, Captain. I would like to have a word with you, if I may."

"Certainly," I replied. "Welcome aboard. What gives me the pleasure of your visit?"

"Well," he said, with that voice of a man stretching his legs in front of a fire that is peculiar to the British on condition they are mad enough, "I thought I'd just hop over to reassure myself personally on the subject of your sanity. Could you perhaps elaborate somewhat on your reply to my order not to obstruct your artillery?"

"Certainly," I answered, trying to match his blandness. "It was my reaction to an error on your part."

"Ah?" he said, giving my mouth the loving look that Jack the Ripper must have given his victims'. "And what would that be?"

I leaned back on the rail and said, pleasantly, "Captain, you are at this moment not on British but on Netherlands territory. The Royal Navy may have chartered the *Isabel Kwel*, but she is still flying the Dutch flag and I, as her Master, am ultimately responsible for her safety and for all measures taken to assure that safety."

"Well," he said, "all that is very interesting. However,

Captain, you are sailing in a British convoy, as part of an escort of which I am commanding officer, and I will have to beg of you to observe, in your communications with the escort, the clarity and the courtesy that are customary among civilized people. You see, I'll have to make a report of the contents of your signal. In the normal course of duty, the yeoman's log book, which lists verbatim all signals exchanged between escort and convoy, will find its way to the Admiralty. In this instance, I have no doubt the Admiralty will want to contact the owners of your vessel —whom, I presume, one might consider as your superiors?"

"I hope the Admiralty will do just that," I said. "I am convinced the owners will be delighted that I took this opportunity to clarify the situation. You see, Captain, from the word 'go' in Scapa Flow, you have, it seems to me, labored under the misconception that you, or someone else appointed by you, could usurp my ultimate authority as Master of this vessel. I tried to convey to you in my signal that I was not going to let myself be pushed around by any navy, be it Chinese, Lithuanian, Yemenite or British."

His eyes remained focused on my throat; but a small smile of sensuous satisfaction seemed to curl his thin lips, as if he had finally spotted the exact location of the jugular vein. "How absolutely fascinating," he said in a tone that conveyed the reverse. "This is pretty strong language for a junior tug driver addressing the CO of an escort of the British Royal Navy, wouldn't you say?"

"I would," I replied, leaning against the rail again, "if I were the person you describe. But you see, Captain, you happen to be on board the largest tugboat in the world, the flagship of Kwel's International Tugboat Company, so I, as her Master, am in fact Commodore of the Netherlands oceangoing tugboat fleet. Now, may I invite you for a drink in my quarters?"

"Awfully kind of you, Captain—er—sorry, Commodore," he answered, the venom so rich in his drawling voice that bile was virtually dribbling down his chin, "but I am already exposing my convoy to an undue risk by slowing it to this speed; so, if you don't mind, I'd like to have a look at your depth-charge equipment, which you have subjected to such baroque modifications, and convince myself that its effectiveness is not impaired."

"By all means," I said. "Be my guest."

We strolled languidly to the aft deck, where the bosun was painting the jolly boat a gay, crazy yellow. Mashpee studied the set-up while extracting a pack of Players from his coat pocket. As he lit his cigarette, I saw that his hand was shaking; although he was looking at my contraption, his eyes remained nervously aware of the sea all the time. I remembered what the doctor had said about him that day in Scapa Flow: "He has been laboring under stress for some time now."

"How absolutely captivating," he drawled. "May I ask what the bloody purpose is?"

"To camouflage those catapults from U-boats."

"And why would you want to do so, may I ask?"

"So as to avoid being torpedoed as a munitions carrier. You realize, I trust, that you are at this moment standing among five tons of Amatol?" I indicated the canisters lining the aft deck.

"Quite," he said. "I haven't exactly calculated what I carry on my bucket, but I would say that it's roughly five hundred tons of TNT, so the situation is a familiar one."

"No doubt it is, but you are a little more nimble when it comes to getting out of the way."

He inhaled a deep draft of cigarette smoke, sighed a

plume into the summer air; the swishing of the waves under the *Isabel's* stern was suddenly audible in the silence. "All right," he said. "Why don't we cut the crap? Take that stuff down."

"I'm sorry," I said, "but I must refuse."

"I order you to take it down. I order you as commanding officer of the escort."

"As Master of this vessel, I refuse."

"All right," he said. "I'll have a report drawn up which I'd like you to sign."

"I'm sorry," I said, "but I'm not signing your reports. I'll sign my own."

He looked at me for a moment, and I waited for an explosion. He was obviously consumed with the desire to scream in my face, but a lifetime of British self-discipline made him salute me with icy courtesy; then he asked, "Where can I find my officer? I think I should have a word with him."

"I think you'll find him on the bridge."

"Thank you." He again saluted, I saluted, then he turned on his heel and marched off. He climbed the stairs to the boatdeck with dribbling little steps, like a ballet dancer, strode to the bridge and vanished with Tyler into the chartroom.

I don't know what he said to the boy, but he must have taken out on him all the pent-up fury that he had been astute enough to keep to himself while still in the arena. Young Tyler looked miserable as he followed his superior out of the chartroom, down the steps to the boatdeck, down to the aft deck and over to the rail, where the launch lay waiting. As he saluted Captain Mashpee at his departure, he looked thoroughly shaken, and I sympathized. It is the fate of the apprentice to find himself caught at times between a mass in motion and an immovable object. Mashpee and I exchanged salutes that were perfunctory to the point where we seemed to be chasing mosquitoes; the launch revved up her engine, ratings caught the lines and off she went, blowing bubbles across the summer sea, back to *Intrepid*. I went back to the bridge, gathered speed and took up position in the convoy again; then a flag signal went up: CONVOY RESUME FULL SPEED KEEP YOUR DISTANCE, and the incident was closed.

But it was not closed as far as the spinsterly community of my crew was concerned. A few hours later, Cook stopped me on my way to my cabin from the aft deck, ostensibly to whisper a private message, but he had made sure that there were plenty of people around to hear it.

"Captain!" he whispered, experienced stage villain whose voice carries to the back of the gallery. "Do you know what he's doing, the English officer? He's writing! He's writing a report on us!"

I looked at him with exasperation. The fact that he had meant this for an audience proved that he too was a congenital troublemaker, like the mate. I felt like chewing him out, but thought better of it. "I should hope so," I said, cryptically, and walked on. I would have to keep my eye on the boy; he might be in for more trouble, as the representative of his CO in the eyes of my crew. I should have a word with him to put him on his guard and to tell him that if anyone started any nonsense he should come to see me at once. I wasn't so much concerned about him, but I wanted to nip any hysteria among the crew in the bud. I wouldn't put it beyond the cook to start talking about a Jonah, and a green crew heading for action might be especially vulnerable to that form of mass psychosis, peculiar to the sea.

But again I forgot about him, this time under the pressing preoccupation of that earthquake load of explosives on my aft deck. I finally settled on camouflaging the two rows of canisters by covering them separately with a lumber floor, two narrow counters on which I had the bosun display artistically all the spare coils of rope and throwlines and all the floats he could dig up from storage, as if in readiness to rescue drowning men. This time I had to imagine observing my ship from above, the way a pilot would see it, and I tried to achieve a realistic view by directing his arrangement of the props from the boatdeck. When finally I was satisfied, I gave the carpenter the order to lash and nail all that stuff down so that in the event of an attack it could not get underfoot or be blown off the counters by the wind; it would indeed be a ghastly mess if all those coils uncoiled and became snarled up in the catapults.

The camouflaging of the two cannons on the bridge wings was a different matter. I tried various solutions, but none was entirely satisfactory; in the end, I had the carpenter construct two flimsy shelters which, I hoped, would look convincing when seen from the air, as they were common on some bridges, especially in the Arctic. A U-boat, however, would be less easily fooled; and any wind above force five was sure to send them flying. But they were the best I could come up with and, anyhow, they were another magical item to establish in the minds, if not the souls, of my crew my superiority over the enemy. During all this frantic activity of ours, the other captains of the convoy, more realistic gentlemen, paced up and down their bridges in the sun, whiling the summer hours away like walruses, waiting with equanimity for whatever horrors the future might hurl their way.

2

While I schemed and measured and plotted, living in my own world, the crew became obsessed with the secret report the boy Tyler was writing in the messroom. Nothing happened outside to take their minds off it; the convoy merely plowed ahead, shepherded along by restless *Intrepid*, and the further north we sailed, the shorter the nights became. Perhaps it was a combination of things; they felt for the first time in their lives as if they were being towed themselves, the insistent daylight kept them awake and behind all their thoughts and actions lurked the sickening fear of what lay ahead. As a result, a nervous excitement got hold of them that expressed itself ultimately in a mental stampede.

The boy had indeed been sitting writing in the messroom for most of the day and the night. First Cook spied on him, then others; the fact that he wrote so lengthily convinced even the more sober ones among them that what the interloper must be doing was writing a report on everyone on board. On the night of the fourth day out, during the second table, Cook suddenly came crashing down the messroom steps in a state of high excitement. "The sneak!" he hissed. "The spy! Do you know what he has done with that report he's been writing? He's sealed it up, in an envelope!"

Unaware of the state of hysteria into which the ship had worked itself, I innocently suggested that perhaps this was the natural thing to do.

But then Cook sprang a shattering bit of information. "Do you know who he has addressed that envelope to?"

he asked, with a theatrical gesture of suspense. "MI!"

It would indeed seem that the boy had been writing a report on us. MI were the initials of Military Intelligence, and in the world of legends of the Merchant Marine those initials spelled something akin to secret police. I submitted, still innocent, that a naval officer who had written a secret report was unlikely to address it to Military Intelligence; but obviously the rest of the staff of the *Isabel Kwel* had no mind for such trifles. In no time at all, the news spread over the ship; on my way back to my cabin I saw, everywhere in the green dusk of the Arctic night, groups of men huddled together, talking in whispers. I was about to enter my cabin when, in the distance, a siren sounded the alert. I had never heard it before, it was a frightening sound. I rushed to the bridge.

In the semi-darkness of a thin translucent night, with a bleary moon somewhere half submerged in the sea, I saw, silhouetted against the faint line of the horizon, my neighbor and the ship ahead of me. Then a dark shadow with a phosphorescent bow wave fluttering in the darkness, like the shroud of a running ghost, flashed past us, flickering a signal by Aldis lamp.

I called, "Tyler! Officer Tyler!" but there was no reply. Sparks, who had come out unprepared, caught part of the message; it seemed to have to do with GUNS. It would have been more reasonable to send someone else to fetch him, but I went to look for the boy myself; for only at that moment did the whole picture of the crew's hysteria seem to piece together in my mind, and I was suddenly worried about him. I ran down the boatdeck, down the stairs, down into the messroom, and there he sat, lost to the world, writing.

"Tyler!" I cried. "What the hell are you doing here? Didn't you hear the alert?"

He looked at me with round alarmed eyes, muttered, "Sorry, sir. One moment, sir," and plucked two unappetizing pink wax plugs out of his ears. "Pardon, sir?"

"We're under alert!" I cried. "You're wanted on the bridge! The escort is signaling, so get the hell up there!"

"Yes, sir, aye, aye, sir!" he replied, getting up, but he seemed to tarry, looking for something, frantically.

"What the devil is the matter now?" I asked.

Then all hell seemed to break loose upstairs. As I turned to run up the steps, I caught sight of an envelope lying on the seat; on it were written the letters *M II*, but it did not register at that moment. The din overhead was so colossal that I flashed up those stairs like a monkey. Outside, the first thing I saw was a strong bluish light right overhead, a parachute flare, which set the whole convoy and the cruiser in a harsh theatrical light. Every single ship of the convoy seemed to be firing at it; the sky was festooned with strings of colored tracer bullets, star shells exploded high in the sky; the suggestion of a fireworks display was so strong that I felt foolishly exhilarated. Our own Oerlikon and the two cannons on the bridge wings were pounding away, hell for leather, although the latter could not be elevated sufficiently to hit any aircraft. The three of them together produced a din as if all the molten-down garden gates of England were being hurled at the sky in one colossal, ear-splitting broadside. Never in my life had I heard such noise; its sheer volume seemed to press me against the rail, gasping. Then I saw flashes of gunfire right ahead of us; I recovered, ran to the bridge and heard the mate yell an order at the wheelhouse; he avoided the stern of the whaler ahead of us in the nick of time, by inches.

After the first chaotic few minutes, everything seemed to pull more or less into shape; then the cannonade around us stopped, as abruptly as it had begun. Our own guns followed suit reluctantly; the silence which followed was so intense that it seemed louder than the deafening roar of the guns had been. In the silence, I saw an eerie little light like a glowworm advance on me. It brought my heart to my throat; for one second, I was ready to scream, like a woman seeing a mouse. Then I realized what it was: a recognition mark, painted on a helmet with phosphorescent paint: one half of a wavy stripe.

"Message from the escort, sir," Tyler's voice said, breathlessly. "END OF EXERCISE CEASE FIRE."

That was the moment the dam broke. Everything I had bottled up inside me since our arrival in Kirkwall erupted in an incoherent stream of abuse. I remember yelling, "Take that pisspot off your goddam block before I knock it off!" and this was the least scatological item in my tirade. I went on screaming even after the little stripe had vanished in the darkness; finally I stopped, with a feeling of powerless rage that rapidly changed into shame. The normally stolid Dutch have a propensity for occasional outbursts of shrieking fury, so I suppose I should resign myself to odd bouts of this national affliction, but I never feel worse than after one of them.

When the All Clear had sounded, I went disconsolately down to the messroom for the cup of tea that, on board oceangoing tugboats, traditionally rounds off any physical commotion such as gales or salvage operations. I felt so deflated and morose that I hardly looked around me, just slumped into my chair, threw my cap onto the seat and hid my face in my hands, with my elbows on the table. Then I heard Cook's voice say, "Your tea, Captain."

I looked up, straight into the eyes of the boy Tyler at the opposite end of the table. He sat staring at me, stony-faced. A mug stood steaming in front of him; between us was the sugar bowl. I felt the need for some kind of gesture;

I stretched out my hand, gave the bowl a push in his direction and said, "Sugar?"

Without warning, he leaped to his feet, sprang at the stairs, scrambled up the steps and vanished; the sound of his running feet on the deck faded in the silence.

I looked around me, astounded, to see the others stare at me in the same blank amazement. Then, suddenly, I worried about him again. God only knew how they had hazed him; under stress, I might well find myself with another Chief Bout on my hands. It was this thought that sent me after him. That night we would move within sight of Iceland, tomorrow rendezvous with the convoy at Langanes, day after tomorrow our moment of truth would be upon us; what we would need above all else, more than camouflaged catapults and canisters, was a sense of comradeship that would make us bear the unbearable together, not every man for himself.

I don't know quite how I expected to find him: with his head on his arms slumped at the chart table, or something of the sort. But when I opened the door, he was sitting bolt upright on the little stool, staring into nothing, a position of defiance rather than dejection. I heaved a sigh of relief. "Well?" I asked. "What was all that in aid of?"

He looked at me stonily; for once he had not leaped to his feet as usual at my entrance. He sat there with the mulish, stubborn expression of an adolescent who has decided that he has had enough.

"Well?"

"I'm just trying to work things out for myself, sir," he said, politely enough, yet without the enthusiastic courtesy I had become accustomed to. "I'm not sure how to cope with all this, but I don't mind telling you that I've just about had enough."

"Enough of what?"

He scowled, but his face was still too young, it came out as a pout. "Of—of everybody's crap," he said.

"All right, let's see if we can trace how it all came about. You realize, of course, that a new junior officer is bound to have a hard time on board any ship, a tugboat in particular. A tug's crew is a closely knit, clannish unit anyhow, and in this particular case you happen to be an alien as well, which makes you still more of an outsider. I'll be happy to try and make things easier for you, but these are facts of life which you'll have to face."

"It isn't that," he said, with his new independence that hovered on the brink of insolence. "I was prepared to take any amount of joshing. I know that's what happens to rookies in any trade, especially on board ship. But this has gone too far. Too goddam far. By half."

Obviously, he was working himself into a state of theatrical exaggeration. I shouldn't let him get away with it, but there were condoning circumstances. First the staff had sent him to Coventry, then Mashpee had taken him to the cleaners, then the crew had started a witch hunt because of his report and finally I had bawled him out in the worst Loppersum tradition. He had had more than his share; he was entitled to a moment of self-indulgence.

"It's not even the bloody unfairness of it," he continued, getting into his stride. "It's the—the violence, the—I don't know—the indecency of it. Back home, we don't treat people that way. I didn't think people were treated that way any place else except Germany. I thought that was what this war was all about: to fight for the dignity of the human individual."

"Now, come," I said, "don't let's get carried away. I'm sure that Captain Mashpee didn't mince his words, and I can't say that I'm a member of his fan club myself, but to equate him with a Nazi . . . "

"You don't know what he said!" he replied, fiercely. "I don't. But I know what I said, myself, when I yelled at you tonight. I'm sorry about that, I suppose you call that indecent violence. But then, we aren't any of us paragons of virtue. And as for Captain Mashpee, he has been laboring under stress for months, this is his fourth convoy to Murmansk. Anything he may have said wasn't said to you but, well—to God. You'll soon understand, yourself."

But he didn't buy it. He looked at me with that sullen stubbornness and said, "I don't care what stress he may have been laboring under, sir, and I don't care what your troubles may have been; I can't accept fighting a war with means that betray its cause." It was quite a mouthful, and he looked pleased with himself. He was a nice guy, but he had a lot to learn.

"I wouldn't have too many illusions about the way this war is fought, if I were you," I said. "Nor about its cause, for that matter. You'll have a hard time surviving as it is, without loading the dice against yourself with highfaluting ethics. When it comes to the shooting part of it, the only ethics worth a damn will be to keep an eye on your buddy to see if he's all right, and a lot of patience with people scared out of their wits, or shell-shocked, or crazed with exhaustion."

"I'm sorry," he said, sullenly, "I still maintain that I won't fight a war with means that betray its cause." He obviously liked that phrase so much he wanted to hear it again. I was not so taken with it.

"And what do you propose to do about it?" I asked.

"I don't know," he said. "I just won't."

I was getting tired of this. "All right, Tyler," I said. "Suit yourself. I don't care why you fight it or how you fight it. As a matter of fact, I don't care if you fight it at all; just keep out of the way of people who are busy trying to keep themselves and others alive. A rescue ship—"

"It isn't that I don't *want* to fight!" he cried, misunderstanding me, probably on purpose. He was enjoying this, and so he should, poor sod, for once. The least I could do to make amends was to bat the ball back a few more times.

"Why do you think I volunteered?" he went on. "I *do* want to fight. I think that Hitler and the Nazis are an obscene bunch of gangsters, and I think it is my duty as a citizen of the free world to help round them up before they destroy civilization. I am prepared to do that, I am prepared to give my life for it; but I will *not* become infected by the evil I am supposed to fight by using their methods. I am sorry, I just won't."

"For Pete's sake, Tyler!" I cried. "What the hell nonsense are you talking? Who is using their methods? I? Because I called you a ball-bearing creep, or whatever it was? You should hear the things I have been called in my time."

"It wasn't you," he said, sullenly. "It—it was the Captain."

He seemed to be sorry the moment he said it; it obviously was against his ethics to squeal on the Captain, but he had aroused my curiosity. I wondered what people like Mashpee, so maddeningly moderate whenever I took them on, said when they let it rip over the head of a subordinate.

"Well? What did he say?"

"He talked about—well—about Frogs, and Niggers that begin at Calais, and . . . and Kikes."

"Hell, Tyler! What would you say about a bloody foreigner who pissed on your boots, the way I did to him, and never mind the justification? And he has been sailing three convoys to Murmansk! If I don't mind being considered a Frog or a Kike that begins at Calais—"

"Where I come from, we don't have any 'bloody foreigners,'" he said, self-righteously. "This is the civilization I am prepared to fight for. I have a friend who is a Jew. He is my best friend. I volunteered because I don't want to live in a world where he can be called a Kike with impunity, not even by a Captain in the Royal Navy, however tired he may be."

"Look at me, Tyler," I said, patiently. "Do I look like a Negro? Or a Jew? Can't you see he just used the first words that came to his mind, any words, because he was cross-eyed with fury? I must confess that I had to restrain myself not to call you a ball-bearing *Canadian* creep tonight, for that has a much more gratifying punch to it. When a man is angry, it's a sheer matter of sound and volume, nothing to do with meaning."

"I wasn't aware of any restraint tonight," he said, pointedly—too pointedly for a junior officer having a manly heart-to-heart talk with his captain.

"You aren't aware of a lot of things yet," I said. "But don't worry, you'll catch up. Whereabouts in Canada do you live?"

But the mule was still hunkering down, refusing to be pulled out of the barn into the great outdoors. "I want my boy to grow up in a world where there is no excuse for that kind of foul, evil talk," he said. "If Captain Mashpee thinks about Jews as Kikes, what the hell is he fighting this war for—if it isn't as a mercenary whose profession is killing?"

Brother, here was one really mixed-up character. On the one hand, he loved leaping to attention and saluting and barking "Aye, aye"; on the other, he called a professional officer a murderer because he had used an unfortunate word in a rage. Whatever lay ahead of him, he had a few lessons in realism coming. Then it penetrated to me that he had mentioned having a son. He seemed indecently young to be a father. "How old is he?" I asked.

This time I got through to him. He suddenly whipped out a wallet, and from it he shook a whole accordion of snapshots. "Here," he said, selecting one and holding it up for me, "here he is: three months, two weeks. Two and a half, rather. And that's Mary, holding him."

There she was again, fully dressed this time, against a background of trees. She held the baby in exactly the same way as she had held the kitten in the other photograph; God, they were young—two kids playing at parents. But what a stunning creature! Not for a long time had the mere sight of a woman aroused the sleeping dog in me to this extent. I hastily said, "Cute"; for I do believe that thoughts can transmit themselves if they are strong enough, and I didn't care to have mine transmitted.

"Here's our house." He held up another snapshot; and there she stood, in the wind, one hand on her hair, the other holding down her skirt, outside a bungalow that looked only partially finished. She did not have enough hands to fight the wind; her breasts were boldly outlined under the flimsy blouse, and so on, and so on. Again I said, "Cute"; it was the wrong word, but he didn't seem to mind. As a matter of fact, he didn't seem to be listening.

He set about showing me the rest of his collection of photographs and telling me more about the folks back home. He said he lived in a small town in Ontario, not far from Kinora. Did I know where Kinora was? I did not, so he asked me if I knew where Winnipeg was. I said I knew, although I did not. Well, his hometown was situated on the banks of a lake called Lake of the Woods. It was a lovely lake, and quite a nice town too. He was kind of proud of it, and he was sure I would like it too, once I came to know it. He described his street, his house, his family, their neighbors, the friend who was a Jew, his other friends who weren't. Then he described her family, their house, their neighbors, her friends, their cat. The whole thing began by being pretty boring; I just sat there, nodding vaguely, thinking about girls' breasts in flimsy blouses and slender thighs in wind-blown skirts. But, gradually, I began to forget that I was just allowing him to have a moment of unburdening; his vivid little images of rural life in central Canada seemed to thaw out something buried and forgotten deep inside me, some long-past innocence, some faintly familiar exuberance of schoolboys running, racing one another on bicycles glistening in the sun, with squealing girls in fluttering dresses swaying precariously on their luggage carriers. An old canoe came sliding down the dark tunnel of a narrow river through a summer wood. A farm tractor hummed drowsily in the distance, a rising lark took its jubilant song to a cloud sailing high in the sky, and in the secret, summer-scented nest of a rick of straw the trembling, throbbing softness of a first, depraved kiss. As I listened, with growing nostalgia, I realized that he was describing my own boyhood, a lost paradise, a world of innocence and decency and longing for the future, a world at peace. For a short, poignant moment I seemed to wake up from a bad dream. What was I doing here, how had I got here, what had lured me further and further away from that innocence, that innate decency, that instinctive and unstinting compassion until I found myself here, on my way to the edge of the world, where Englishmen talking about Kikes would fire blindly at Germans who talked about Unser Shakespeare, and where both the boy and I might perish pointlessly, lost children, carelessly gone astray? It was not a trend of thought of any use to a man in command of a ship full of frightened people dependent on his calm self-assurance.

I suppressed it, consciously and without regret. I would think about all that once the convoy was behind us. But I could not shake it off before I heard myself ask, "Why in hell did you have to leave all that, to come and stick your neck out in this war that is none of your business?"

He stared at me, shocked and incredulous. "What's that?"

I was sorry now, but it was too late. I tried to weasel out of it by saying, "I mean: wouldn't it have been a more effective defense of that world of yours if you had stayed to protect it at home?"

"No man is an island," he said gravely. "Never send to know for whom the bell tolls . . . "

I said, "Crap. There wasn't any bell tolling in Kinora, or whatever its name is. There was a lot of blather about patriotism and freedom and how war makes a man out of you, by people who had either never heard a shot fired in anger or were harking back to the happy days of Mademoiselle from Armentières and Gay Paree." It was a shot in the dark, I had nothing to back me up in this other than the books we have all read about the home front and its demagogues in the First World War. There hadn't been too many about this time, at least not in my part of the world. Everybody had been too scared to use that kind of talk, after the sobering experiences of the last war to make the world safe for democracy. But chances were that in central Canada, where patriotic orators could safely bleat without the remotest chance of conjuring up the avenging angels of the Luftwaffe, the same old cant was still being churned out by the same old idiots.

But the shot went wild. He looked at me with an odd kindness, the same expression with which he had looked at me when he first realized that the officers were sending him to Coventry. "No, Captain," he said, "I couldn't stay home and wait until someone would be able to come and call my friend a Kike to his face with impunity."

"But look," I said, in a last effort to make him see reason, to shake him out of the dream that had tricked him with its errant light into the Arctic, where death lay waiting, "you can't seriously believe that the Germans would cross the Atlantic and occupy Canada, even if they were to win this war? Why not leave the fighting to us, who have been chased from our homes by the Nazis, whose wives and girl friends are in danger of being exterminated by that bunch of lunatics? Why stick your neck out and rush at an enemy who was not threatening either you or your friend or anyone else in your part of the world?" I didn't quite understand myself whose case I was pleading, why I insisted that he should have stayed home to play with his son and walk his dog and read books and listen to music and make love to his wife—and, by God, some wife. All I could come up with as a rationalization was: "Someone should protect that world of yours by perpetuating it, not by running to have yourself shot for an abstraction. Who the hell is going to give your son the kind of boyhood you had, if you are going to get yourself killed in the next week or so?"

He looked at me intently. His adolescent features suddenly seemed but a mask. His eyes no longer were a boy's eyes, but a man's. "My friend is not an abstraction," he said calmly. "And I cannot give my son the kind of boyhood I had if I turn my back on evil and pretend it doesn't exist because it happens to be far away. My Dad never pretended things did not exist, once he had become aware of them."

"What was he?"

"A missionary. I was born in China. He died of cholera when I was a baby. My mother came back to our hometown, and that's where she stayed."

I was overcome by a sudden hostility. "No need to be so goddam patient with me," I said. "My Dad died of the plague, on board a pilgrim ship in the Red Sea, when I was a baby. And I do not have a Jewish friend, I have a Jewish fiancée, who, according to the latest information, has been deported to Poland. So there's no point in going sensitive and noble on me. In my opinion you are a damn fool, and nothing you can produce in the way of arguments is going to convince me you aren't. If I had had a wife like yours, in a country at peace, I would have stayed home and—and loved her."

"Then that is, obviously, where we are different," he said, unfazed but kindly. "I am sorry about your fiancée. I wouldn't have shot my big mouth off if I had known."

I felt a twinge of conscience that I had used Sophie merely to win an argument. The thought of what might be happening to her at this very moment made me want to hide. I got up and said, "All right, Tyler, let's leave it at that. I enjoyed talking to you. Take it easy now."

He rose to his feet and said, promptly, "Aye, aye, sir. And thank you."

As I was about to open the door, he asked, "By the way, would you be interested in this?" I looked around and saw he was holding out a book, one of those cheap paperback editions for the forces. "It's quite good," he said. "It'll show you what I mean about how I want to fight this war."

I wanted no more of this, but I did not know how to refuse it without making it a slap in his face. So I said, "Thanks," and took it. I glanced at the title on my way back to the messroom; it was called *Steady as You Go* and was written by a man who called himself Bartimeus. Its subtitle ran, "Stories that Cover as a Blinding Flash of

Illumination Every Phase of the Battle of the Atlantic."
I put it in my pocket.

3

I forgot about it until I undressed for my four hours off, in the middle of the night that was no night but an endless, restless dusk turning imperceptibly into the dawn. In the meantime, I had told the messroom to lay off the boy from now on. I told them that he had received his lesson, that now we should give him a chance to do a proper job, by which we all were bound to benefit during the action just ahead. I told them about his so-called report and the letters I had spotted on the envelope; obviously, he had been writing to his wife, and his wife's name was Mary.

Maybe it was the shadow of the war, touching them as we approached, maybe their madness had whirled itself out; they listened in silence and had the grace to look embarrassed. The mate wasn't there, neither was the cook, but it would catch up with them.

Before going to sleep for what might well be my last undisturbed four hours, I had a look at the book. I opened it at random, and read: *The big Sunderland flying boat climbed out of the swoop that carried her over the spot where the U-boat had crash-dived. The sea was still convulsed with the explosion of the flying boat's anti-submarine bombs, and as she circled round above the yeasty disturbances amongst the waves the wireless operator was tapping out his summons to the hunters.* It went on like that for a couple of pages, during which three destroyers raced to the spot and dropped some more depth charges. *Then the water darkened suddenly. There was a pungent reek of crude petroleum oil. The remorseless explosions continued. Something dark broke the surface an instant and vanished again. A few objects appeared and floated amid a dark scum; a man's head and outflung arms appeared, smothered in oil, and vanished. The navigator bent over the chart, made another pencil dot, and put a tiny cross through it. Overhead the Sunderland's signal lamp was blinking at them. The signal yeoman on the leader's bridge grinned and flicked the trigger of his lamp in reply. He looked round for his captain. "Flying boat's signalled 'Good hunting,' sir." The commander nodded. "Make back 'Thanks. The brush is yours—'" he paused and looked across the desolate sea. "'If you can find it!'"*

I closed the book and lay there, gazing at the ceiling, wondering how this demonstrated "what I mean about how I want to fight this war." I concluded that maybe someone who had never seen a human being drown in a sea covered with oil didn't know what that sight did to you, even if you were not responsible for it. As for human dignity, this attitude was an insult to it, reducing the killing of human beings to a fox hunt. But maybe I was being overly sensitive. Maybe this was what I myself would be like, if I should ever reach the other end of the Murmansk run. I had no real experience of this myself either. I had seen ships go down and people drown, but a few times only and from a distance. You cannot stop a tow in a channel among the minefields; you have to leave those whose ships are shot or torpedoed or mined from under them to God, their own vitality and the Fleet Air Arm. The last had seemed the most reliable; each time, the FAA had been over the scene of the sinking before we had dipped below the horizon.

I opened the book again and read some more. I had stumbled on the worst bit, it seemed, for as I read on my feeling of indignation lessened. It was a well-written book by a man who obviously knew what he was talking about. After two stories I began to feel almost embarrassed about my disgust at the description of the drowning man and the captain's callous answer. After three, I felt that I would have made a fool of myself if I had gone into that chart-room and held forth at him.

I tried to sleep, but the reading had woken me up too thoroughly. I lay for a while tossing and turning, thinking about cornfields undulating in the wind. It was a trick Captain Bosman had taught me, and it usually worked; this time, instead of staying with the cornfield and its soothing billows, my gaze followed the wind until it hit a blouse and a skirt. Then I thought of her naked body in the other photograph. Then I thought of Sophie, naked among hundreds of tightly packed naked female bodies in a gas-chamber. Then I got up.

It was too early for my watch; I went to the galley to fetch a mug of watchman's tea. To my surprise, Cook was there, stirring a pan on the stove. I didn't ask him what he was doing there at dead of night; it was his business. I sat down on the little bench facing the hot stove and felt the warmth of the wall as I leaned against it. I thought of the times I had sat like this while still a mate and a member of the galley club. Of the things I had lost when I was made a captain, it was the galley I missed most; captains were not expected to consider themselves members of the club any more. I thought of the jokes, the gossip, the tall stories, the sense of belonging that went with being a member of a crew. Yet, I had to confess it: I would not like to go back, not even now. Being a captain seemed to have made me whole; together with my ship, I formed a self-contained unit, with an invulnerable core of deep content-ment. I knew now that the whole "slavery" business was nonsense, that if I were to come out of the war alive I would want to stay a tugboat captain; even without pay, without honor, at the mercy of the owners. It was like an addiction: together with my ship, I could move mountains; alone, I couldn't move a mouse without agonizing over it in tortuous indecision. I began to understand those Old Men from my past, those cowards who had knuckled under to the tyrant without a squeak, abjectly, degradingly. How we had denounced them in the galley club! How we had despised the spineless lackeys! Now I began to understand their detachment from our preoccupation with wages and freedom of choice and dignity and protest. Mr. Kwel seemed far away, further than he had ever seemed before. The warmth of the wall on my back was the warmth of the *Isabel Kwel*—my ship, mine, not some distant gentleman's. He was someone a world away, who just paid for her and me to romp on the high seas, a self-contained unit with an invulnerable core of happiness.

"By the way," I said, sipping. "That was not a secret report he has been writing, but a letter to his wife."

"Ah?" Cook said, shiftily.

"He must have known that you can't leave private letters lying around on a ship, so he put them in separate envelopes and numbered them. His wife's name is Mary, so 'MI' means: Mary, Roman number one, and 'M II,' Mary, two. Okay?"

Whatever it was he was stirring on the stove suddenly needed his attention; he started to fish around in the seething pan with a masher and brought out something limp and dripping. I had wondered what he could be cooking at this hour of the night. He was boiling dishcloths.

I did not pursue the subject; he had heard what I said but did not know how to acknowledge it without losing face. I was curious how he would manage to bury the past; I didn't have to wait long for the answer. He did it by raising another red herring. "By the way, Captain," he said, with sudden urgency, "do you know we have rats on board? And not just little ones, real tigers."

I said, "Don't be silly." One thing oceangoing tugboats never have is rats; they need a cargo to feed on, and space to be rats in.

"Well," he said, throwing a steaming dishcloth into the sink, "if it isn't rats, it's a thief. Do you know I have lost at least three pounds of steak and half a dozen codfish from the galley since the day we sailed from Greenock? Maybe only a man could drag that load away."

I should have been understanding and left well enough alone, but I couldn't help saying, "If that should indeed be the case, we may have to write to Military Intelligence yet."

It wasn't a very good joke; but then, it had been quite a day.

CHAPTER SIX

I

The next day, we joined up with the convoy from America. During the whole of the night that had been no night, the dark mystical mass of Iceland had loomed on our portside: the Ultima Thule of antiquity, not quite real, like the set for a movie about one of those lost continents full of papier-maché dinosaurs.

Langanes was a long, low-lying promontory; we hung around there for a few hours, slowly circling, with *Intrepid* racing around us like a sheepdog smelling the scent of wolves.

I used the delay to make the rounds of the ship, for a last check to see if everything was in order and to wish each man luck. I went from fo'c'sle to engine room, from galley to wireless cubicle; I went to see the gunners on their bunks, the oilman in his stokehold, the bosun on the aft deck, the carpenter in his workshop. I had a chat with each one of them, and it turned out to be as much of a help to me as it was to them. We all knew what lay ahead for us, though most had managed not to think about it. Somehow my making the rounds and spending a few minutes in private conversation with each one marked the moment for us all to face it now like men. I came away from my tour with the realization that I had a crew of exceptionally mature and courageous men; I am sure I must have given them the same impression. The only one who seemed to be out of tune was the boy Tyler, maybe because, despite the fact that the men had now accepted him and even felt somewhat guilty about him, he did not really belong. Maybe it was just that he was an alien; facing death is such an elemental, emotional occasion that our personality instinctively draws upon reserves from the basement of our memories. Sailors are not chauvinists; but that morning each one of us was glad to find that the other was a Dutchman too; it made for shared memories and childhood symbols, which seemed to rally around us in these moments. The gunners were aliens too, but they seemed closer to us than the boy Tyler; between us and them, there was, after all, only the Channel and the treacherous North Sea, while we and he were separated by an ocean, half a continent and the unfathomable chasm between a people at war and a people at peace. He even went so far as to wish me "Good hunting," with a sincerity so guileless that it was completely disarming. I came away from my abortive little encounter with him hoping that he might wake up in time to face the reality of war with fortitude and common sense.

I was sorting out the ship's papers and putting them in the emergency briefcase, when the mate called out, "Here's the convoy!" I joined him on the bridge, but by the time I got there, he looked rather put out, for it was not the convoy; it could not have been, really, as it came up from the east. I could understand his mistake, though, for I saw such a formidable formation of capital ships that to the inexperienced eye they could hardly have been anything else. It was our escort, and it gave me a feeling of immense relief, for it seemed as if the whole of the British Home Fleet had gathered here, supplemented by American warships. I was not sure that I got all the silhouettes right, but I recognized two battleships, at least a dozen cruisers of the size of *Intrepid*, scores of destroyers and a mass of smaller craft, among which were seven "Camm" ships: freighters converted into auxiliary aircraft carriers, recognizable by their ungainly, oddly tilted launching decks. I counted more than fifty ships; it seemed an exorbitant armor for just one convoy, until the convoy itself rose majestically in the west.

I had tried to visualize forty-eight ships sailing in formation and had found it difficult; now I realized I had not even included its escort in that image. The armada bearing down on us consisted of a large cruiser with an airplane on its deck, two destroyers and a dozen coastguard cutters that I recognized from visits to the United States; the entire escort was American. It did not seem as impressive a force as the British escort, but then the run between Halifax, Nova Scotia and Iceland was a comparatively safe one. The Germans had concentrated their U-boat packs astride the Murmansk route, and their planes based in Norway could not reach beyond Iceland.

The ships of the convoy itself had not yet taken up their new formation of two lines abreast; they came toward us in the pattern of counters on a checkerboard. As they drew closer, they looked exceptionally large; I had been used to coastal traffic for so long that these eighteen- and twenty-thousand-tonners seemed huge. It was an immensely impressive sight that struck me mostly by its opulence. The sheer wealth represented by those forty-eight ocean giants must have beggared even the most fab-

ulous silver fleet the Spanish sent across from South
America in their heyday with the loot of a plundered
civilization. There were tankers carrying airplane fuel,
loaded so deeply that from a distance their fore and aft
castles looked like two small craft; there were huge
freighters crammed with war equipment, planes with
folded wings like giant bees lined up on their decks. There
were ships of almost every nationality that had by now
joined the Allies: Panamanians, Norwegians, Greeks,
Americans, Danes, Dutchmen; their crews lined the rail
as they passed us, and everybody waved. It was a strangely
solemn occasion; we did not wave at each other like crews
on vessels passing in the solitude of the ocean, but like
gladiators about to enter the arena.

The convoy slowed down, a flag signal fluttered on
a large British freighter, obviously the flagship with the
Comconvoy on board. When the signal was taken down,
there began a reshuffling on a brontosaurian scale that
brought my heart to my mouth as all those vessels fell into
their new positions, two lines abreast. It was done without
mishap, but there were some narrow escapes indeed as
twenty-thousand-ton tankers sniffed the hindquarters of
mammoth freighters that looked almost feminine with their
deckloads of surrealistic birds like extravagant hats. When
finally the Comconvoy had all the monsters lined up to his
satisfaction, he tied up the loose ends by directing us small
fry to our prearranged stations. The *Isabel Kwel* was given
four colossi of her own to shadow: one British and two
American freighters and a tanker flying the Panamanian
flag. From now on, these four ships would be our sole
concern, the reason for our existence. Whatever might happen, into whatever confusion the convoy might be thrown,
we would have to dog the sterns of these four; and if anything happened to one of them, we would be the ones to

come to her assistance, and to save the lives of as many of the crew as possible. It took a long while before fussy Mashpee was satisfied that everyone was in exactly the right position; only then did he begin to distribute the actual escort around us. It turned out to be very much smaller than I had anticipated: six destroyers, ten odd-looking small craft and two Camm ships; the rest of the comforting fleet of warships we had sighted a few hours earlier took off at high speed in various directions. The American ships that had escorted the convoy so far turned around completely and made off for home. The fleet, now vanishing on the horizon, had split into two forces, one a squadron of cruisers and destroyers, the other made up of two battleships, three cruisers and a flotilla of destroyers. Obviously, they would be the "shadow covering force" Mashpee had mentioned during our briefing; their function would be to engage the enemy before he could get to us. So, in a sense, I told myself, they were indeed our escort, and even more effectively so than if they had hovered in our immediate vicinity; but I saw them disappear with dismay. The odd little craft among our escort, so the gunners' corporal told me, were ack-ack vessels that would not circle around us the way the destroyers did, but would be placed in strategic positions among the convoy, where they would remain for the length of the voyage.

At last a signal went up on the flagship: CONVOY PROCEED FULL SPEED KEEP DISTANCE AND FORMATION and off we went, at steadily increasing speed, until we were running at fifteen knots.

That speed was one of the things that worried me. I knew from my test runs that the *Isabel* could not be pushed over seventeen knots. If anything were to happen to one of the four ships ahead of us, we would have to drop out of convoy to pick up survivors; after that, we would be loping behind the pack for hours on end, panting, tongue lolling, gaining only two miles per hour on the zigzagging herd on the horizon. Those hours would be the worst, all alone without escort in a pack of German U-boats, beset by strafing planes. I would have felt much happier had our margin been an excess five or six knots, but obviously the British had not been unduly worried about it, as we had, according to Mashpee, been selected on the basis of our speed. Now I had the uneasy suspicion that maybe Mr. Kwel had, for some reason, exaggerated our speed. Comparing our insignificant bulk and frumpy appearance to the opulent riches of the giants in the convoy, I began to worry that we would be fortunate if someone noticed our absence in time, or at all. It seemed unlikely that any escort commander would slow down a convoy of forty-eight vessels and eighteen supporting warships, just to give a breathless tug, dropped out of formation to have a pee, a chance to catch up. Considering that Mashpee was that commander, the prospect seemed gloomier still.

But as the mighty convoy cumbersomely made its way through that radiant day across the placid blue sea, the sense of security that I had felt before took hold of me again. It seemed impossible for raiding U-boat packs to get past those two massive concentrations of warships ahead of us, and the triple ring of defense of the restlessly circling destroyers, scanning the darkness below the surface with their Asdics, ready to pounce on any U-boats that came within range with depth charges, gunfire or torpedoes. As to the planes, there were all those Camm ships of the shadowing force, studded with catapult planes; there were these ungainly anti-aircraft vessels, one of them quite close to us, almost in our wake. It sported a gaunt, unfinished-looking scaffolding, rather like a billboard under construction; this, the gunnery corporal explained, was a secret weapon that the Russians had provided for the Murmansk convoys only. It was called a "Stalin organ," and was capable of firing whole clusters of rockets that would decimate any formation of approaching planes. Who would dare to challenge the tremendous destructive power of all those forces protecting us? That first afternoon, it seemed unimaginable that anyone would. I almost came to believe that we might sail all the way to Murmansk unchallenged.

The Arctic Circle, which we had crossed just after leaving Langanes, was a completely arbitrary line. There was no sign of winter in the air, not even fall. We sailed through a dazzling, endless summer's day with flocks of birds and schools of porpoises all around us. Toward evening, we spotted a school of white whales, obviously in flight from all those churning propellers of convoy and escort. We counted eleven of them; it seemed a good omen, confirming my mystical sense of security and immortality. That first day on the road to Murmansk was in some way the happiest day of my life, if the philosopher is right who held happiness to be linked with innocence.

Toward evening, six hours after leaving Langanes, we were spotted by an enemy plane. It was a Focke Wulf Condor, four-engined, flying well within the range of our anti-aircraft guns. To my astonishment, nobody opened fire on it, although it was clearly an enemy plane. The gunners' corporal explained, "No, not that one. Nobody shoots at Charlie."

It turned out that, with peculiar British nuttiness, the Royal Navy had become so fond of the spy plane the Germans sent out at the beginning of each trip, to pinpoint the position of the convoy and radio its position back to base, that they christened it "Charlie" and refused to open fire on it. In the early days, it seemed, Charlie used to hang around a convoy from the first day to the last, and there had been a frequent exchange of signals between him and the escort. On one occasion, the gunner related, Charlie had asked the escort where he was and had been given a position near Easter Island in the Pacific. On another occasion, as Charlie went on circling overhead, the commander of the escort sent him the signal: PLEASE FLY THE OTHER WAY ROUND AS YOU ARE MAKING US DIZZY, and Charlie, politely, obliged.

But this evening Charlie did none of his tricks; he circled over us once and then he made off. The first attack came within three hours.

2

The U-boats were very cunning, for they broke through three lines of defense, the last one our own escort, circling around us with a dozen Asdics pinging away. With heart-stopping suddenness, two ships in the convoy exploded almost simultaneously; the first one three patterns away from us to starboard, then the American freighter in our own pattern, right ahead of us. The tanker, following it at two ships' lengths' distance, had to do some hairbreadth maneuvering to avoid the sinking ship. While I summoned the crew to the boats with our foghorn, the air around us shook with explosions and the *Isabel Kwel* began to roll violently; two destroyers of the escort, racing by at full speed in close range, had started throwing depth charges within seconds after the torpedoes struck, and set us rocking with their wash. Our boats were lowered in record time; the bosun set off in the starboard one, the mate in the other. We were by then sailing through lots of wreckage; during occasional lulls in the thunder of the gunfire and the explosions all around us, I heard shrill voices wailing. Although the sea was slimy with oil, our boats still pitched dangerously in the wash of the destroyers that went on circling around us at top speed, throwing their depth charges. I saw both boats haul in bodies; I was surprised by the number of them; from where I stood I could not distinguish any heads among the wreckage. When the first boat was on its way back to us, heavily loaded, I saw a motor launch approach, flying the Royal Ensign. As the mate came alongside on starboard, brisk British sailors from the launch climbed on board over port.

The sailors helped drag the black, slippery bodies over the rail. They were a grisly sight, scarcely human because of the oil that covered their faces. Many were wounded; their screams as they were dragged over the rail were harrowing. I had rehearsed the drill for this kind of emergency with the crew many times until they could do it automatically. Part of the drill had been that all wounded would be given first aid in the messroom. But the launch had been so quick in coming that they were transferred to her directly from our boats; by the time Cook had his first-aid tea ready, the victims were already on their way to other rescue ships that had sick bays and doctors. By then, the explosions had died down around us and the destroyers had left; I spotted them far behind us, on the horizon, still searching for the U-boat.

Now came the moment that I had feared most. The convoy was a good distance ahead of us; now I had to try and catch up with it at an overtaking speed of only two knots. Yet I was less preoccupied with our safety than I had expected; the memory of the dead and the wounded made our own peril of the moment seem unimportant. At the time, I had watched the ghastly scene on our aft deck without emotion. My mind had been clear and alert, my attention with the ship and the maneuvering; now I began to remember what I had seen, and its full impact began to register. The mate and the bosun, through with putting the boats back in place, came to the bridge. They must have rubbed their faces with their hands, for they looked as black as the men they had pulled out of the sea. The bosun's duffel was smeared with blood; when Cook turned up with the mugs of tea, he asked him how he could wash it off. Then I noticed Tyler standing in a corner of the wheelhouse.

The sight of him gave me a shock. His face was green. His eyes stared at me with such horror that I turned around, thinking something behind me made him look like that. But there was nothing to be seen, only the luminous, radiant Arctic sky that refused to darken, and a few small clouds above the horizon. He looked as if he were about to throw up, so I said, "Go aft and lend a hand with cleaning the deck, will you?" I had become so accustomed to giving a man who was about to be seasick something to do that it occurred to me only later that it had been a peremptory order to give to one of His Majesty's officers.

About a quarter of an hour later, the bosun came back to the bridge and said, "I think you had better go and have a look at that English officer, Captain. He doesn't look too good to me."

I asked why; he shrugged his shoulders. "First he puked in a corner; now he's wandering about, aft, sort of crazy-like, getting in the way of my men hosing down the deck."

I walked down the boatdeck; as I arrived at the top of the steps to the aft deck I saw him. He was standing at the rail, looking at something in his hand, a black object that I could not identify. He stood, lost in thought, while water from the hoses washing the blood and the slime off the deck swirled about his feet. The way he stood there, gazing at the object in his hand, was oddly romantic; it reminded me of Hamlet gazing at the skull. I went down the steps toward him; before I had reached him, he dropped what he was holding, turned away and disappeared down the messroom hatch.

It was a man's left shoe. It must have belonged to an administrative officer, like a purser. It was of a type that no seaman or deck officer would wear on duty, and it had a built-in support sole. If I hadn't watched him contemplating it, the connection might not have occurred to me. Now I saw that it somehow summed up the full horror of the impersonal massacre, the soulless efficiency of the machines for destruction that we had created and that now seemed to consume us all, indiscriminately, friend and foe. To a sensitive boy from a land of peace, cherishing romantic concepts of chivalry and self-sacrifice, the past hour must have been a traumatic experience. So much for Mr. Bartimeus of *Steady as You Go*. So much for every political orator who had rhapsodized in the Canadian cornbelt about "honor," "valor" and "heroism." This carnage had nothing to do with any of these; it had been maximum mechanical violence scientifically applied for maximum destruction; the human element had only been evident in the victims, jumping for their lives into the freezing water like terrified mice. It had been more like an atmospheric disturbance on a cosmic scale than something even remotely connected with men and war; as a result, I somehow felt more confident that we might scrape through than I had before, the way Noah must have felt when the waters raged about his wallowing Ark at the worst of the Great Flood. As the captain of a well-built ship, I could cope with all this; for the boy, who had no responsibility and who was an outsider among the crew, this must have been like a glimpse of hell.

As we slowly overtook the convoy, with the mate on the bridge, I made the rounds of the ship again to see how everyone was doing. They all seemed to have stood up well; they appeared to be, if anything, more sure of themselves than they had when I went to see them at Langanes. Maybe they were just more fatalistic, but it seemed to me they were somehow reassured that under my command they would be as safe as could be expected. There was no longer any doubt about it; they had accepted me completely as their new captain. Sparks even went so far as to say, "I'm glad we don't have to sail this tightrope with cranky old Bokke on the bridge"; but he probably said so only to give me a pat on the back. He couldn't have sailed with Captain Loppersum for more than a trip or two.

I found Tyler in the messroom. He sat at the table, staring at a blank sheet of paper in front of him. He did not notice me coming in through the connecting door from the engine room. A mug of tea stood beside the blank sheet of paper. It must be stone cold by now; Cook had made his rounds about an hour ago.

"Tyler," I said, "now we are going to use this room as a sickbay, you had better go back to the chartroom to do your writing."

I don't know what made me say it, he would be unlikely to be writing during enemy action. I simply felt I would like to have him a little closer to the bridge and to my cabin.

"Very good, sir," he said absent-mindedly. He had not risen. "Do you want me to go now? Or may I finish this first?"

"Take your time," I said. "We won't get another attack for some hours, I'd say." I wanted to say more, to make him talk, for that was what he needed; but he sat there, obviously waiting for me to leave so he could start writing.

When I got back to the bridge, the mate asked, "How is he doing?"

I knew whom he meant, but I asked, "Who?"

"Our mascot, baby-boy."

Now that he had washed the oil off his face, he looked pale and tired; but his eyes were unchanged, they looked as coldly watchful as ever.

"He's bearing up," I said. The mate was the only one on board about whom I wasn't sure. He had done a good job, technically I couldn't ask for anyone better. But I still suspected that he was emotionally unstable; if I was right, he might either crack up and become completely catatonic, which I had seen happen before, or start reveling sadistically in the blood and the gore, which I had never experienced among my crews but had heard about. I didn't know which was worse.

"Aren't we all?" he said.

"Pardon?"

"Bearing up."

"Yes," I said. "How did you make out in the boats?"

He answered with an odd smile, "How do you think?" Then he added, "Wait till I get my hands on one of those bastards. Just wait."

Obviously, he was the only one on board the *Isabel Kwel* who had been able to discern a human enemy behind the mechanical monsters that had clashed with our monsters in a holocaust of dispassionate destruction. It seemed another symptom of lunacy; any enemy he might have seen had been in his imagination. But maybe that was the kind of lunacy needed to win a war. "You did a good job," I said. "Now go and get some rest."

He ignored the compliment. "Okay," he said. "If you

need me, call me. I'll probably be awake anyhow."

He left me deep in thought. I wasn't thinking only about him; I thought of each of them in turn, conjuring them up in my mind, trying to remember details in their behavior that might not have registered at the time. I was not concerned about the *Isabel*; she had come through unscathed. The launch had put out fenders before boarding us and the boats had rubber rubbing strakes, so even the paint-work had not suffered. The bosun and his men had spent hours cleaning the decks; they were clear now. I should have a word with the corporal and tell him his crews must in future remove their own discarded shells and junk, or my men wouldn't get a chance to rest at all.

3

We rejoined the convoy toward the end of my watch; when I came down for the second table, the boy Tyler was there. Only as I saw him did it occur to me that he hadn't shown up at all during the previous watch. He still looked a bit under the weather, but so did we all. He did not talk, but Sparks and the Second kept up the conversation. Sparks told stories about a Brazilian trip; the Second, for some reason, reminisced about beautiful graveyards he had known. He was the only one of our watch who had not seen what went on that afternoon, for he had been in the engine room; maybe that was why. I was sure Sparks felt as sick at heart as I, remembering the wounded. But, whatever we might think or feel, we must have been case-hardened already, for what had happened that afternoon did not put us off our food.

Tyler, however, could not eat a thing. Cook, in an

obvious gesture of conciliation, did his best to force on him a piece of cake covered with a thick layer of imitation cream; but the boy merely shook his head. When the Second lit a cigar, he left.

After he had gone, the conversation lagged. We sat there, seemingly at a loss as to what to say, but we weren't; we were listening. I knew that, despite the fact that Sparks and the Second had sounded so bright, they had been listening all the time too. Our bodies remained tense, we could not relax our muscles. We were coiled like springs, ready to leap to our feet at the first tremor of a distant explosion. The sheer concussion of that torpedo, at least five ships' lengths ahead of us, had nearly thrown me off my feet; its impact must have been colossal. Should we ever find ourselves in the way of one of those, we would never know what hit us—not with five tons of Amatol on the aft deck.

Now he had fallen silent, Sparks looked exhausted, with dark rings under his eyes; the Second looked sorrowful, gazing at his cigar as if it were something left to him by a relative he had loved. When Cook came down with the coffee and began to rave about rats, Sparks said quietly, "Shut up, will you?" Cook did, which showed he was not himself either.

On my way to my cabin, I crossed the chartroom. I had expected to find the boy lying on the couch, but he was sitting at the chart table, his head in his hands, a blank sheet of paper in front of him. I hesitated for a second, but I couldn't think of anything to say, so I went past him through the communicating door and closed it behind me.

But I worried about him; when I was ready to turn in, I went back into the chartroom. He was sitting as I had left him, his head in his hands.

I said, "Don't worry, you'll be all right," and patted his shoulder.

He looked up. "Thank you, sir."

I said, "Good night," and went to bed.

4

———

I was woken up, so it seemed, the moment I fell asleep by the mate bursting through the communicating door, crying, "Air attack!" and popping out again. As I stumbled to the deck, I glanced at the clock and realized that it should be dark, or as close to darkness as it would ever get in these latitudes, yet it seemed bright daylight. When I came outside, I understood why.

Scores of flares were floating, smoking, among the few stars in the high blue sky, placing the convoy in a shrill light. The colored strings of tracer bullets, the ack-ack shells bursting overhead with blinding flashes, the whole thing looked unreal, as it had that night of our first alert, but it was no longer like a fireworks display. I saw three planes brought down in flames; one of them sheared so close overhead that I ducked. It hit the water a few hundred yards to our port side and exploded. The third plane, which came down shortly after it had scored a direct hit on a tanker five patterns to our port side, burst into flames when it hit the water; it set fire to the floating fuel that by then covered the sea, and I saw the boats of the rescue ship that had gone in to pick up survivors hurry out of the fire, burning. Every ship of the convoy, including the freighters, was firing its guns; we started to join the hell chorus ourselves with the Oerlikon on the foredeck. I kept our boats swung out during the whole of the attack, ready to be lowered, but none of the ships in our pattern was hit.

When after about three quarters of an hour the planes retired, no ships had been sunk in the convoy, not even the tanker that was damaged. We saw her crew being taken over by launches from the escort as she slowly fell back. She was listing heavily, but seemed to have settled at about thirty-five degrees. I hoped for a moment, boyishly, that we would be called upon to tow her; I had helped bring in worse ones in the past, when on salvage duty with Captain Knol. But once the launches had made off with her crew, one of the destroyers sank her by gunfire. She blew up at the second broadside with an immense writhing mushroom of fire and, a few seconds later, an explosion of such magnitude that it shook the ship; I heard something fall in the galley with a clatter.

During the entire attack, the boy Tyler had been standing in the corner of the wheelhouse where I had spotted him that afternoon. His face bore a calm, determined expression, but it was as if he no longer lived behind it; it looked like the face of a waxworks statue. I didn't like it; fear has many masks, the calm, smiling one is the worst.

"Tea in the messroom in a few minutes," I said. "Join us if you like."

He seemed to wake up out of a deep sleep. His eyes, as he looked at me, were filled with an odd sorrow. He answered, "Thank you." His voice sounded cracked and old.

He did not turn up for tea. The others talked about him in the messroom. I tried to minimize his affliction, but Sparks had seen him and said that if he went on being scared like this at every action, there would be trouble; then he asked me what I thought. I replied, "He'll get over it," but I was not so sure as I sounded. The Second suggested that I should have a talk with him and tell him to stay below decks as long as the guns were firing. It was the first time I heard him make a suggestion off his own bat; it was a good sign. I said that in my opinion it would not do much good, but he disagreed and told the story of a man he had known on board a trawler at the beginning of the war, who had sat down as good as gold on a little stool in the narrow corridor between the fuel tanks behind the engine room each time they were being attacked.

I said, "This has been his first attack; let's give him a chance." Then I finished my tea and went to the chart-room.

I had expected to find him even more deeply in shock than he had been after seeing the wounded the day before, but I found him sitting at the chart table writing furiously. He had already covered several sheets of paper; when I said, "Tyler, I'd like a word with you," he answered, "Yes, sir; just a minute, please." Only the fact that he had not leaped to his feet, but actually kept me waiting, showed that he was not his normal self. I decided not to crowd him, and sat down on the couch.

It took him minutes to finish; evidently he was finishing the letter, not just a sentence. By the time he had, there were six sheets. He folded them neatly, put them in an envelope, licked it shut and wrote on it *M III*. Then he put the letter in the forbidden drawer under the chart table, turned to me and said, "Yes, sir."

I said, "Tyler, I have the impression that you find it difficult to get used to these attacks." It sounded awkward and a little silly, for he looked at me with that odd, adult sorrow that I could not place. Then he said, "I know, sir. You need not say any more. I'm trying to work it out for myself. I'll get over it somehow. So, please, give me time."

I was about to say, "All right, if you like," when I remembered that I had heard those lines before. I could not remember when or where, only I was sure that it had not been in real life, but in a movie, some movie about the Navy. Then it came back to me: a long, narrow, low-ceilinged cinema full of smoke in Harwich, filled to the brim with noisy sailors whistling and cat-calling at the screen as a brave little coward said to his commanding officer, "I know, sir, I promise I'll get over it; please give me time." Later, of course, he saved the ship at the cost of his own life.

Suddenly, I felt angry. Whatever his world of fantasy might be, where this kind of *Boys' Own Paper* dialogue was normal, I had a real ship to run and a real war to fight. I couldn't allow a junior officer to take time out so he might adjust himself to the war at his ease. The convoy would be attacked again, any moment now; there would be signals to interpret, replies to be made; I needed him on the bridge, were it only to spell Sparks, who had been up there every time while this young man stood battling with himself in a corner. "Look, Tyler," I said, "everyone is scared out of his wits during his first attack, and if you feel ashamed because you were sick when you saw bleeding corpses dragged over the rail, then let me tell you that, had you not been sick, it would have meant that you had no heart, no decency, no human feeling in your body."

But I did not get through to him at all. He smiled, the brave young coward who knows he'll make good, and said, "Thanks, Skipper. It's swell of you to put it that way, but I know—"

"Cut it out," I cried angrily. "Wake up, will you? Be your age! This is war, the real thing, and not some stupid patriotic movie! You are not alone on this ship, you're a member of a crew, and, whatever your private feelings may be, you have a job to do on which other people's lives may depend!"

He looked at me gravely. "I know, sir," he said. "Believe me, I am very much aware of—of the consequences. All I ask of you is to let me work this thing out in my own way, just a little while longer; I'm sure I'll get on top of it. I—I promise."

I sat there, staring at him, groping in vain for a thought, a word, the magic word that would break the spell and liberate this pathetic adolescent from his storybook world. I was overcome by a weariness, in which there seemed to be no other solution than to give up and leave him to his fate; I had other things to do, I was supposed to save lives, not souls. "All right, Tyler," I said, "suit yourself. You are not a member of my crew. I am not in a position to discipline you or mess with you in any way; if you don't work out within a day, I'll have to hand you back to the Navy. You are their problem, not mine."

I got up to go; he startled me by leaping to his feet again and standing to attention. "Thank you, Skipper," he said, chin in, chest out. I fled.

On the bridge, I found the Second and the mate. The Second should have been in his bunk, resting up for his next watch; but then, so should I. I spotted Sparks, lighting a cigarette in the corner by the wheelhouse, and went over to him.

"I've had a word with our friend," I said, "and agreed to grant him one more day to straighten himself out sufficiently to function; if he doesn't, I'll send him back to *Intrepid*. That is, unless you want me to call for a replacement now."

"Not for me," Sparks said. "I don't need him. We're under radio silence anyhow, so I've nothing else to do. And I can't see myself sleeping through one of these attacks." Then he added as an afterthought, "And I'd hate to hand him over to that bastard on *Intrepid*. He's a nice kid." It was the first time the thought struck me that, by his very cowardice, he might be good for the morale of the others. Then the Second said, "The thing to do would be to tear up all those letters he's been writing and chuck 'em overboard." I had not seen him join us; it was such an extraordinary remark that I must have looked startled.

"What on earth gave you that idea?" I asked.

He looked away, suddenly self-conscious again; then he answered with a shrug of his shoulders, "I just know."

"After that," said Sparks, "all we can do is go to bed." He stretched, patted the Second on his back, said, "Good night, Doctor," and went to the stairs, yawning.

"Let's you and I turn in too," I said to the Second, "we need every minute of rest we can get." We left the bridge together; when we were out of earshot of the mate I asked, "Why? Do you think his wife is at the back of it?"

He looked at me with his kind, shy eyes. "No, not his wife personally. Just the fact that he writes to her all the time. That's bad."

"Why?"

He thought for a moment and said, "You can't fight a war in the daytime and sleep at home. You go crazy." Then he smiled apologetically. "At least, that's what I think. Sleep well."

I said, "Sleep well," and went to my cabin through the chartroom. It was empty; I already had my hand on the knob of the communicating door when I turned back to the chart table and opened the drawer. The brown leather frame lay on top. When I picked it up, I found a stack of letters underneath. On top lay the one marked *M III*. I took them out and stood with them in my hand, thinking that I only needed to open these to find the answer to his small enigma, when I felt a draft on my neck. I turned around and saw him standing in the doorway, looking at me. I said, "Sit down, Tyler."

He hesitated. For a moment, I thought he was going to react like any man would, under the circumstances. Then he said, "Aye, aye, sir," and meekly sat down, back in the role of the brave coward who knows he will make good one day.

"If I were to tear up these letters and throw them overboard, what would you do?"

He looked at me in astonishment. For a moment I hoped it might turn into anger, then his face broke into a grin, the grin of the popular young football player that had so maddened me the day he came on board. "Aw, shucks, Cap!" he said. "You wouldn't do that!"

I felt such sudden hostility toward him that I turned away without a word, opened the door and went to bed.

I tried to sleep, but I could not relax. My body remained alert, ready to leap out and rush to the bridge; I tried to force my muscles to relax, but all I achieved was that I began to shiver violently. I couldn't understand it, for mentally I was calm and collected. Maybe it was a reaction, maybe the febrility of the midnight sun. Whatever it was, I began to understand what condition a man would find himself in after months of this. When the doctor in Scapa Flow had said that Captain Mashpee was laboring under some stress, it had been a British understatement indeed.

5

Again I seemed to have barely dozed off when the hair-raising howl of the sirens of the escort wakened me. Then the mate banged on the door, stuck his head in and said, calmly, "Okay, here we go again. Air attack."

This time the sky was light, there had been no need for parachute flares. The convoy lay in plain view of the planes; there were a great many of them. Sparks tried to count them as the attack got under way, but they became so mixed up with the dark little clouds of exploding shells that he gave up. I saw sticks of bombs falling in curves; then they dropped strings of big round ones, connected by a chain, that exploded with deep shuddering convulsions lasting for seconds after they hit the water. I knew what those were, their reputation had spread as far south as the English coast. They were "serial mines" or "rattle mines," designed especially for small, slow craft that presented too small a target to pinpoint. For a while we stood there, watching them drop those lethal strings near the ack-ack ships, capsizing one, damaging another, uniquely by the concussion of their sustained explosion, creating a veritable crater in the sea. Then they came for us.

I saw the round things hit the water close by, over starboard, with spurting fans of spume; the seconds that followed seemed endless. Then the ship rose on top of a steep, quivering hill, as in an earthquake; we slithered down its slope under a blinding shower of flailing spray; only then came the sustained, deafening roar of the explosions.

After that, things were very confused. I thought the ship would never right herself; then I thought we were already sinking, as the spray went on falling like a cloudburst, in solid sheets of water. But she righted herself, the cloudburst stopped; the first thing I heard after my eardrums had recovered from the explosions was screams. I tore open the door to the wheelhouse, because it seemed to come from there; but the helmsman, though dazed and shaken, was in one piece. I ran to the bridge rail and looked down on the foredeck, but it was empty. Then I realized that the screams were coming from the sea. The water had stopped falling; but all around us the sea was still boiling, with thousands of big bubbles rising and bursting at the surface. Then it finally registered: the foredeck had been empty. The men at the Oerlikon had been washed overboard.

I pulled the engine-room telegraph to Stop and scanned the sea behind us. I saw them far astern, a few black dots on the surface. I ordered the mate to lower the starboard boat, but we could not slip it, for the ship had still too much speed. I pulled the engine-room telegraph on Half Astern; but the ship did not respond. For a few sick moments, I thought that she was up to her tricks again, that I hadn't mastered her at all; the warning of the commander in Greenock rang in my mind: "I have known ships all my life, and I wouldn't trust this bitch for a second." Only when the mate's voice hollered from the boatdeck "Astern! Astern!" did it occur to me that the engine room had not acknowledged the order. It couldn't be damage to the engine, something must have happened to the men below. I blew down the speaking tube; there was no answer. I was about to call the mate and tell him to take over while I went down to have a look, when I heard a gurgling sound in the tube, a curse, and then the muffled voice of Porks: "Take it easy . . . he's wounded . . ."

I shouted, "Man overboard! Stand by your telegraph! I'll be down as soon as I can; half astern!"

He muttered, "Aye, aye, just a sec. . . . Half astern, Skip. Keep blowing your orders down, telegraph's out of order."

The ship slowed down and stopped; the small bobbing heads had drifted still further away by then; I swung around, doubled back and lowered the boat.

There had been two men at the Oerlikon; the mate found two. When they came closer, however, I saw that one of them was the bosun, hollering, flailing his arms, stamping his feet; the other body lay slumped on one of the benches. When we hauled them back, the bosun went on bellowing one word that he repeated crazily: "Cold!" The carpenter and Sparks took him down to the messroom. The second body turned out to be one of the gunners; the other gunner was missing. Cook and a seaman dragged a steaming pail aft and down the steps. I shouted through the tube, "Full ahead!" and said to the mate, "Head for the convoy. I'll be back in a minute." Then I hurried down to the engine room.

Everything seemed quite normal there, at first. Then I saw Porks on the other side of the engine covering somebody's head with a bandage. Around him lay wads of bloody cotton waste. It was the Second; he sat on a little stool, quite still, his hands on his knees, as if he were having his hair cut. When he saw me, he tried to smile. His face was smeared with blood, he looked very pale.

Porks was angry. "He ruined the telegraph with his coconut!" he said. "Sit still!"

I looked up and saw that the glass in front of the telegraph dial had been smashed, blocking the hand. "Is he all right?" I asked, shouting over the racket of the diesel engine.

"He?" Porks shouted. "You could stove in a barn door with that head."

I hoped he had not got concussion. "Have him put to bed!" I shouted over the engine. "I'll send someone down to help!"

"Aye!" Porks shouted back.

When I opened the communicating door to the messroom, I was hit by the din of a colossal bellowing and the meaty stench of soup. On the table lay the naked body of the surviving gunner, his blue skin covered with bits of seaweed. Cook was washing him down with hot water; Sparks was slapping him hard. In the corner, all by himself, sat the bosun, also stark naked, flailing his arms and stamping his feet, bellowing. As I came in, Sparks shouted at him, "Oh, shut up, will you!" But he went on bellowing, "Cold! Cold!" He would live all right. The man on the table moaned as Sparks went on slapping his legs and his feet; then the carpenter came down the steps with a glass and tried to make him drink. The reek of brandy mingled with the stench of cooking; I realized that what I had taken for seaweed was vegetables, Cook was washing him down with soup. The communicating door opened and Porks tried to usher in the Second, who had a crude white bandage around his head, through which blood was seeping. As there were enough people around as it was, I went back to the bridge.

As I came on deck, I saw that we were gaining on the convoy; a destroyer was drawing a big white circle around us. From her mast fluttered a signal. Sparks was in the messroom, and he had the copy of the code in his pocket; I opened the door to the wheelhouse and asked the mate, "Where's the Canadian?"

He motioned with his head toward a still figure in the corner. It was Tyler, in the same spot where I had found him twice before. He stood there as if he were asleep on his feet, eyes closed, his face calm and serene.

I cried, "We're receiving a signal from a destroyer! Where's the code?"

He did not answer, he did not even open his eyes; his face remained still and serene. I said, "Okay, Tyler, as soon as we are back in convoy, I'll have you taken off." I meant it.

Then he looked at me; a look so full of despair that I felt sorry for him, but the hell with that. "Where is the list of signals?"

He closed his eyes and said, "In the drawer . . . "

"Which drawer? Speak up, man!"

"Of the chart table."

I rushed to the chartroom, yanked open the drawer, found the list after throwing out photographs, letters, socks and junk, and ran out with it. The destroyer was still circling; now her Aldis lamp was flickering too. The flag signal read: DO YOU NEED ASSISTANCE?

I had no one within call to make answer, so I gave the four short blasts on our air-horn, F for Fox, that normally signified "Rescue operation completed," hoping they would understand. They obviously did, for they went away; when I looked again, they were taking in their signal and racing back to the convoy ahead. I decided to pin that code up in the wheelhouse, for general use. I had to count him out altogether.

When I went in there, he was gone. I had no idea where he was, and I didn't care. I was firmly decided that the moment we were back in convoy I would have him taken off. I went out onto the bridge and stood there, shivering for a while, before I realized that I was not wearing my coat. I went to get it from the chartroom. I found the mess on the table, shoveled it back into the drawer and, suddenly, there was the girl in the invisible bathing suit—stark naked, innocent, infuriating. I flung her into the drawer with a curse, slammed it shut and picked up my duffel coat.

I had one arm inside it when he came in. He looked haggard and deathly pale. I put on my coat and my cap and went toward the door. Then I heard him say, "Sir, I think I owe you the truth. It's not fear."

I turned around. He stood there, Hamlet ready for the

great scene. Well, he would have to find himself another audience. I said, "Fancy that," and opened the door.

"Please!" he cried. "Let me explain! It is terribly important!"

I had had enough. "Tyler," I said, "it may be terribly important to you, but to me and the rest of the men on board ship, you are the least of our worries. I don't care a damn if you are afraid or drunk or in love; as long as you are incapable of doing your duty, you are useless. I can't afford any passengers this trip; I'll have you taken off as soon as Sparks is back and we can raise *Intrepid*. Until then, do me a favor and make yourself scarce."

"I don't care!" he cried in a high, tense voice that sounded as if he were about to crack up. "All I want is for you to understand. I am not afraid, I just don't want any part of it any more!"

"Of what?" I asked, hit for the first time by the thought that he might be sick.

"Of this so-called 'war'! This senseless killing, this stupid brutality, this . . . This is not the way to gain moral victory over evil! This is moral suicide, and I won't be part of it. To—to take part, for me, would mean to destroy everything I hold sacred and—and love!"

I must confess he threw me for a moment. My first reaction was the weary thought: All this, and now a conflict of conscience too. I just couldn't be bothered; and, frankly, he scared me. That line of thought was enough to drive anyone around the bend under the circumstances.

"Friend," I said, "let me give you a piece of advice. Whatever you do, keep that kind of talk to yourself. I'm going to forget you said it, for if I were to report this, you'd find yourself in front of a court-martial the moment they got you home, and there is no doubt what the outcome would be: the firing squad."

I thought that would fix him, but it didn't. He said, still in that high, tense voice, "I know! That's what I want! I can't just bottle this up; I—it is as important to me that I speak out now as it was important that I volunteered. It —it has to do with everything, everything that makes life worth living. I cannot take part in this murder without denying everything I stand for. I'm not interested in life any more if I have to pay for it with—with my soul. I want you to write that report."

He obviously was in dead earnest, but the solemnity with which he now wanted to be shot, as a demonstration against the brutality of war, was as adolescent and un-worldly as his original concept of war as a joust between youthful knights. Maybe it was just a way in which utter fear expressed itself: to run into the firing guns because one's terror has become unbearable. It was known to have happened before; but I could not pull the trigger on him. I could just imagine how Mashpee would react to this kind of conshie talk once I sent him back as a deserter. He would make his execution a process to be enjoyed at his ease, like a gourmet sitting down at table. I couldn't do it; and if his abject terror made my men feel calm and courageous by comparison, he had a constructive function after all.

"Tyler," I said, "let's you and I make a pact. The moment we are safely on the other side, we'll talk all this over, for as long as you like. Right now, I haven't the time; even to report you for desertion is one problem too many. So, let's say this: as long as you stay out of—" A blood-curdling scream, somewhere on board ship, interrupted me.

For one moment I stood petrified, then there was another scream, piercing and insane; I yanked open the door, stumbled over the threshold and collided with the mate;

as we tried to regain our balance, Cook came running down the boatdeck, brandishing a meat chopper, shrieking like a madman. What made us gape after him, flabbergasted, was what he was chasing: three little kittens.

The kittens rounded the engine-room hatch and ran back along the boatdeck on the starboard side; then they tumbled down the steps to the aft deck, ran for the jolly boat and, with a breathtaking leap for such tiny creatures, jumped onto the canvas cover. Part of the cover was loose, and they vanished inside.

I said to the mate, "You go and find out what the hell is going on. This ship is turning into a loony bin," and went to the bridge.

Presently, the mate came back, grinning and shaking his head. Cook had caught the three kittens in the act of snatching a piece of meat off the galley sink. When I asked where the devil they came from, he replied, "Cook always has cats and always gets into a state of fury when they have kittens. But it won't last long; soon he'll be drooling over them and so will everyone else." The way he said it made it plain that this did not include himself.

We joined the convoy and took up our position again; then the corporal came to the bridge, correct and businesslike, to ask me if I would have a moment to deal with the terminal papers on Duncan, Ian, Gunner Second Class, Missing In Action. I went down to the chartroom with him and we were matter-of-fact and efficient; it took only minutes to make Duncan, Ian, officially MIA. I expressed my sympathy, the corporal thanked me. There was the matter of the letter to the next of kin, to be written by the CO of the unit to which the decedent had belonged; technically speaking, I should do it, but as I had not known him at all, we agreed it would be more acceptable if the corporal wrote it. I asked him what kind of boy he had been; he said, "One of the best." When I shook my head in commiseration, he added hastily, almost cheerfully, "Oh, well, it's all part of the game." He left, saluting correctly; only the pallor of his face had given him away. I hadn't known the boy Duncan at all, but I thought I remembered who it was—until I saw that one emerge, yawning, from the fo'c'sle. He was my first casualty all the same, for, whether I could place him or not, he had been a member of my crew. Somehow, the ship would never be quite the same again.

Back on the bridge, I was regaled by the cook to a full word picture of the drama of the cats, when he came up to bring me my mid-watch tea. I listened commiseratingly to the long, emotional saga of a Varmint that had betrayed Trust by giving birth to three Hyenas in the jolly boat and rearing them on plunder snatched from her Benefactor's galley; I did not listen to what he was saying, I only listened to his voice, small and preposterous in the vast, shadowless immensity of the Arctic. Somehow, his preoccupation with the character of a thankless cat under these circumstances was soothing and comforting, because my eyes, though staring at the hazy shapes of the three merchantmen ahead, went on roving over the empty ocean beyond our wake, where a Scottish boy remained behind, dazed and bewildered, alone among the porpoises and the white whales. I presume it affects every captain that way the first time. So far, it had only happened to me on other men's ships, involving other men's crews; I had not turned a hair when the German hit-and-run raider had bagged the stoker who sat relieving himself on the poop, though I had known him much better than I knew Duncan, Ian, MIA.

When, after my watch was done, I passed through the chartroom on my way to my bunk, a cat with three kittens was asleep on a balaklava on the couch, and the boy

sat at the table, writing. Only the cat noticed me as I
came past.

6

The first thing I did when I got up after a couple of hours
of vainly trying to sleep was to go and have a look at the
Second. He seemed all right; his temperature was normal,
his pulse regular, his conversation coherent. The only thing
was that when he tried to stand up, he felt so giddy that
he had to support himself and close his eyes. I told him
to stop experimenting and stay in bed until I allowed him
to get up; I arranged for the oldest of the two oilmen to
spell Porks whenever he could, as long as there was no alert.

In the fo'c'sle, the surviving gunner was back on his
feet. Only the bosun, a picture of health, looked gloomy
and went on shaking his head and saying he would never
be his old self again. I told him to come with me to my
cabin, where I would give him something that would pick
him up. He sat on the couch in the chartroom morosely,
shoulders hunched, his cap in his hands, a broken giant,
while I filled a little bottle with castor oil from the medicine chest. As I handed him the bottle, he gazed at it
somberly, shook his head and said, with his deep voice
lower than ever, that somebody ought to have a look at
his urine. I told him that I would send a sample across to
one of the destroyers if this medicine did not make him
feel better by nightfall. He put the bottle in his cap before
putting it back on his head. Only after his bulk had vacated
the couch did I notice that the balaklava in which the
kittens had slept was empty.

They were on the bridge. The sun made a sliding square
of light on the floor near the starboard telegraph and there

the three of them played, chasing each other's tail while the mother lay in the shade, cleaning herself. Tyler sat on his heels, looking at them, his face young and carefree; at last he looked like himself: a boy who loved animals.

The disk of the sun, low on the horizon, became brighter, and I stood facing it with my eyes closed, feeling the warmth. The planes came out of it.

They came so unexpectedly that the sirens were still wailing as the first volleys of their MG fire rattled sharply overhead. By the time the ack-ack guns opened fire, the Stukas were there.

It was a bad attack; the number of planes grew steadily until it sounded as if there were hundreds of them overhead. They threw rattle mines again, and a lot of bombs. One of the British freighters in our port line received two direct hits in rapid succession and burst into flames. She did not explode, however; she just burned, pouring black greasy clouds of smoke from which yellow flames darted. I lowered our boats when I saw the splashes of people jumping overboard; she was the second ship in line and fell rapidly out of convoy. While our boats were picking up survivors, one of the ships of the escort went on circling around us again, banging away at the sky with all her guns; I saw it was *Intrepid* this time.

Our first boat was coming back loaded with survivors, and I bent over the rail of the bridge to shout an order to the man at the davits as a voice yelled out behind me, "Shelter!"

I made a running jump for the open door of the wheelhouse. As I crashed into the wheelstand, the first bullets strafed the bridge. I had barely scrambled to my feet when the second pass came; then I heard a sharp, high, squealing noise outside. I looked out of the window, saw something small and white twitch in a little pool of blood and then the helmsman shouted, "Captain!"

It happened too quickly, and so unexpectedly that I was slow to react. I saw the boy Tyler rush outside, kneel by the kitten, protect it with his body, stretch out one hand at the sky; I heard him shout, "Stop! Stop! In the name of God, Christ, God, stop!" Then the bullets hit the bridge like the lash of a steel whip, and he fell.

As I ran outside, he lay on the deck whimpering, "Mary, Mary . . . " His face was vacant and babyish with fear. He tried to get up, but slumped back. Blood started to run from the right sleeve of his duffel. "Mary . . . Mary!" he whimpered. Then the fourth pass came.

I don't know who pulled me back. I heard the lash of the steel whip cross him, a ghastly gap of silence in the dotted line of splintering wood that streaked from starboard to port. Then a shadow fell over us and a roaring thunder made the whole ship shake. It was *Intrepid;* she had moved alongside to protect us with her guns. She went on firing until the sound became a deafening shriek in my ears. The boy lay quite still now; I had to step over him when I ran to the port side of the bridge because I heard the sound of screaming over the thunder of the guns. It came from our boats; as I jumped down the steps, Cook came running toward the bridge in his apron.

The next quarter-hour was pandemonium. The results of the machine-gunning of our boats were horrendous. We slaved and sweated, hauling in the dead and the dying, laying them out on the aft deck, on the planking that covered the canisters, on the skylight of the engine room, on the boatdeck, in the passages; there were so many of them that the whole ship seemed to be covered with wailing, bleeding bodies. It was a slaughterhouse.

The launches with the brisk, businesslike sailors came quickly, but even their trained efficiency could not disentangle the nightmare on our decks for a long time. It was hours before the last one had gone.

In the meantime, they had taken away the boy Tyler. A calm, courteous officer disembarked from one of the last launches and asked if he could have a word with me. I took him to the chartroom. He said that Lieutenant Tyler's personal belongings would be collected later and dispatched to the next of kin and that it was the custom for the commanding officer of the vessel to write a personal letter to the widow, or to the parents of those who were unmarried, describing the circumstances under which he had been killed and saying something about his comradeship and his character, as favorable, of course, as possible. I said I would do so as soon as I had a chance; he answered, "Oh, there's no rush, Captain, the mailman doesn't come till Murmansk. Write it whenever you have time."

The sun was going down again before I could at last make up the balance sheet. It seemed a miracle that, apart from Tyler, none of my crew had been killed. We did not even have any wounded, he and a kitten were our only casualties.

7

This time, when we sat down for the second table and the cook brought in a plate of sausages, nobody seemed to be hungry. The messroom no longer smelled of soup; it had been used as an emergency sickbay, and the sailors from the launches had cleaned it with disinfectant before they left. I took one bite and left it at that; I felt sick and dazed. The Second banged on the side of his bunk; Sparks went in to see what he wanted. He wanted another sausage, so we gave him what was left of ours. It was a relief when finally the food was cleared away and we sat stirring our coffee. Cook stayed, sitting on the steps, a mug in his hands.

Sparks was the first to mention him. "I wonder what they'll do with him," he said. "Bury him at sea, don't you think?"

I said I thought so. I had an eerie feeling, as if none of this were real.

Cook said, "Bury him at sea? Not those Canadians. They'll stuff him. They do! Then they send them back to be buried at home."

I felt I could not stand any more of this, so I said, "I think I'll turn in, and I advise you men to do the same. Force yourselves to get some sleep, or you'll crack up."

Cook vacated the stairs for me; I climbed out onto the deck. This time, I did not find anything left behind, shoe or otherwise; the bosun had done a thorough job. No one would suspect, seeing our aft deck now, that only a few hours ago it had looked like a scene from Dante's Inferno. As I passed through the chartroom, I noticed his things. I took his clothes off their hangers and folded them and put them on the couch; then I left them there and went to bed. I still had that feeling of not being able to take any of this as reality. It was not insensitivity, or callousness caused by experience; I knew that all that had happened over the past few days and hours had made a deep impression on me, but, as in the case of severe wounds, there was no pain yet; only the knowledge of what had happened, not the awareness. Maybe this was how nature protected the precious spark of humanity when it was threatened with extinction.

As I lay on my bunk, staring at the ceiling, I still felt nothing, only numbness. Tomorrow or the next day, or maybe as late as Murmansk if I ever got there, the defense mechanism now sheltering me from awareness would let up. What effect would awareness have on me? There would be a sense of kinship with the lumps of refuse dragged over my rail, and a sense of mourning for the boy Tyler, for, despite the fact that he had been useless, he had been very important on board the *Isabel Kwel.* But the main question was, would I feel guilty?

Could I have saved him, had I reacted a split second sooner to the helmsman's shout? Could I have saved him if I had tried to identify with him before it was too late? Could I have saved him at the very beginning, by thwarting the mate's vicious plot of sending him to Coventry? I had not done so because I had been preoccupied with my ship and my men. Maybe I would feel guilty, but any judge, hearing the case against me, would throw it out of court. So what the hell.

This time, surprisingly enough, I slept. While I was asleep, Cook packed the boy's belongings into a box with *Keiller's Marmalade* printed on it; I found it when I came out. I lifted his greatcoat, neatly folded on top, and saw that Cook had emptied the drawer too, for there were the letters. I intended to ask him to take the box away, as I didn't want it hanging around the chartroom, but forgot about it.

I expected them to send an officer to replace him, but they didn't. Not that it mattered; we didn't need him. We hadn't needed the boy Tyler either; it was the pointlessness of his dying that seemed the most stupid and cruel. What a waste; he had been a nice guy.

But, to my surprise, I was less harrowed by his death than I had been by the death of the Scottish boy whose face I couldn't remember and whose body had never been found, but who had been the first I lost as Master of the *Isabel Kwel.*

CHAPTER SEVEN

When the convoy finally reached Murmansk, it had been attacked day and night by U-boats and planes, virtually without respite. When we finally anchored upriver, the forty-eight ships with which we had left Langanes had dwindled to twenty-three. None of us had had any sleep worth speaking of until we got to Russia, and even then things were pretty hectic because of constant air attacks on the town and the harbor. But, at least, we no longer felt like sitting ducks, for the ack-ack around the city was terrific and the sky swarmed with Russian Yak fighters the moment an alert sounded.

We had been kept very busy during the rest of the trip, despite the gaps in the pattern ahead of us. Although the convoy had tightened its ranks, we had more work toward the end than we had had in the beginning, for three of the twelve rescue ships were gone, among them our neighbor, the Danish coaster with the walrus-captain given to picking his nose. She was hit by a stray torpedo, obviously meant for the Panamanian tanker in our pattern; the little ship blew up with such violence that there were no survivors—only the dog, whom we fished out of the sea.

After a few hours of shell-shocked paralysis, the dog had perked up; during the rest of the trip, apart from coping with the nightmare around us, my hair would occasionally rise in horror at inhuman shrieks and hissings right outside my cabin door, which seemed to be the favorite place for the frequent confrontations of the animal world on board the *Isabel Kwel*. I told the cook to lock up either the cat and her kittens or the dog, but of course he did not. Nobody did anything except wolf down his food whenever he could, take a nap whenever he could, and man the boats or the guns around the clock. The mate came out of this very well indeed; he remained a calm, collected craftsman throughout, whom nothing could rattle, and he seemed indefatigable. I still thought his eyes looked insane, but I had to admit that in practice he had turned out to be worth his weight in gold. I could not say the same about Porks, who appeared to be very shaky toward the end of the trip; but then, he had virtually manned the engine alone, the Second still had dizzy spells whenever he got to his feet and could not be trusted with the split-second maneuvering that was required when picking up survivors. So, maybe I was too harsh on him; but I was determined not to sail this route again without a third engineer and a second mate; to run a ship the size of the *Isabel Kwel* under these extreme conditions with a peacetime complement of officers was irresponsible. We had been machine-gunned, strafed and shot at so frequently over the past two weeks that it was a miracle we had no casualties other than gunner Duncan, Tyler and the wounded Second.

The Second was seen by a Navy doctor in Murmansk and told to stay in his bunk until he felt better, which, the doctor said, should be in about a week. The Second was broken up about this; he had looked forward to seeing Russia. So had we, but nothing came of it; Murmansk was out of bounds. The night of our arrival, we felt frustrated; surely we had a right to some gaiety after the trip we had had! Within a few hours, we realized that, whatever might be found in Murmansk for a sailor on shore leave, it was not gaiety. The Germans started to raid the town at dusk and went right on until the quasi-dawn, practically without interruption. We stood looking at the sight from the bridge for a while until it got too cold; there were lots of fires and explosions, and the Russian ack-ack thundered away in one continuous rumble, with frequent volleys of whooshing rockets from Stalin organs streaking into the sky at a terrific pace, like comets, in clusters of about a score. I hardly slept at all; whenever the thunder of the ack-ack and the rumble of exploding bombs started again, I thought our turn had come. It seemed illogical that the Germans should have harassed the convoy all the way from Iceland to forget about it as soon as it was anchored; I breathed a sigh of relief when, next day, all rescue ships were directed downriver, away from the convoy, to wait there at anchor until the freighters were unloaded and ready for the return trip.

As he was leaving, I said to the officer who brought our orders, "By the way, I have a parcel with the personal belongings of that liaison chap who was killed off Jan Mayen. I was told it would be collected here, but so far nobody has come for it. Can I give it to you?"

The officer seemed to be alarmed at the suggestion. "No, no!" he said. "That's not my department at all. You hang on to it, Captain, while I find out for you." I never saw or heard from him again. That night, at supper, I mentioned that I had been asked to write a letter to Tyler's next of kin, giving as favorable a picture of him as possible. I mentioned it because I did not quite see what I could write; perhaps they had some ideas. They had nothing to offer, however, but an embarrassed silence. So I said, "All right, I'll think of something. Pass the gravy, will you?"

I tried that night in the chartroom, but tore up one beginning after another. While I sat there, trying to write to his wife, the memory of him sitting in the same spot doing the same thing became so vivid that it cramped my style. Then I remembered the corporal telling me he would write to the parents of that Scots boy who was MIA; I got up and went to see him in the fo'c'sle. He was playing gin rummy with his subordinates and obviously winning, so my interruption cannot have been too welcome at that moment, but he was very correct about it. When he heard my predicament, he looked astonished.

"But didn't they give you one?" he asked. "It's green, with H.M.S.-Something Office on the cover. You should have been given one with the rest of your forms." It turned out he was referring to a booklet for commanding officers, containing form letters to next of kin. He lent me his, a slim little brochure with about a dozen letters in it, complete to the smallest detail: the deceased was referred to in the text as *John Blank*, becoming plain *John* at the end as the emotion mounted. They must have helped a good many CO's out of nettlish situations, but I did not feel like using any of them. The saccharine sentimentality, mixed with quiet grief and masculine firmness, made them sound as if they had all been written by the same spinster in Belgravia; I couldn't bring myself to send the pathetic girl in the bathing suit a piece of bad fiction instead of something that might be clumsy and inarticulate but that at least had been written with her husband in mind, not the Unknown Soldier.

I went back to the chartroom and tried to be clumsy and inarticulate, but I wasn't successful even at that; all I could produce was variations of the form letters, even worse than the originals. My problem was, I finally realized, the last conversation I had had with him. But for that, I could have come up with something kind though rankly dishonest. To write about a man who was paralyzed with fear and make him sound like a hero was an act of compassion; to write about a man who refused to fight because he did not want to become infected with the evil he was supposed to be fighting presented a problem I could not solve. To call him a hero in the conventional sense of the form letters became an act of betrayal rather than of compassion. I hadn't given the substance of our last conversation much thought and I wasn't planning to; I would think about things like that after the war, if I were still around. But I could not feed his widow a version of his death that would be an insult to his integrity, if indeed his uncompromising stand had been an act of courage and not of extreme fear. I couldn't decide what it had been, I rather suspected the latter; but there always was the possibility that he had indeed decided, quite coolly, that any involvement in the activity of war was against his conscience and that he would rather be shot as a deserter than live as a "murderer." I might not sympathize with that attitude, yet I had to take into account that he might have acted courageously according to his own lights. But how could I write all this to his wife, whose last sight of him had been of a *Boys' Own Paper* hero striding off to defend freedom? Even if she were to understand what I was talking about, which seemed unlikely without first-hand knowledge of reality, she would show it to other people— his mother, for instance. As far as I knew widowed mothers, there was a good chance that this would raise the dickens. And although I was Master of my own vessel, I should have reported him to his CO, Mashpee. No, to mention our last conversation would be pointless.

So I went to bed without having produced anything other than the decision to settle for Letter Number 7, the least obnoxious of the lot, headed: *For use in cases where only partial information may be released, for the protection of the memory of the deceased.* In other words: those shot while looting, killed in a brawl in a whorehouse, or cowards. It ended with the words: *I, his commanding officer, and the comrades of his platoon will remember John Blank for a long, long time.* In all other letters in the pamphlet, John Blank was remembered *fondly, proudly* or *with undying gratitude.*

2

When, the next morning, after my first good night's sleep since Kirkwall, I came to the messroom for breakfast, I discovered that I had not been the only one who had been trying to write a letter to Tyler's widow that night. Cook, of all people, told us that he had lain awake all night, trying to think of something to write to that boy's wife, for it was obvious that she could not be told the truth. He had been such a nice, educated boy, with such fine manners and so polite, a real joy to have on board, but we couldn't tell anybody, and certainly not his wife, that he had been killed because of a kitten, could we now? He suggested that we should doll things up a bit to give that girl something nice and worthwhile to remember him by.

When I asked him what he meant, he looked shifty as

he answered, "I don't know, it's none of my business. I just thought it might be a nice thing to do."

"He's got something there, I must say," someone else said, innocuously. It was the mate. I hadn't eaten with him since Kirkwall; I now realized I had not missed his company at table one bit. "It would be nice if we could substitute a human being for the kitten he had himself killed over. Let's tell her he tried to pull somebody back into the wheelhouse during that air attack. He would have, too, if you ask me. Anybody would."

"Dead or alive?" Sparks asked.

"Huh?"

"Should the person he pulls back be dead or alive?"

"If he were alive, what would he be doing out there on the bridge with the bullets whistling around him?"

"He could have gone berserk, or have been wounded in the first pass."

"I like the word berserk," the mate said, smiling. Strange that a man could be an excellent officer, without fear or selfishness in action, and an unmitigated bastard in repose. "Let him go berserk, shake his fists at the planes, cry something like 'Dirty fuckers' or 'Mother fu—' "

"Easy, easy," the Second grumbled, massively. "You are writing to a bereaved young woman, remember?"

"No, seriously," the mate said, unfazed, "I think it's an excellent idea. Let him save somebody else's life by getting killed himself. And if you want to make those peasants really happy, make it a high-ranking officer. The higher the better."

It seemed incredible, but as I looked around the table, all of them were sitting there with grave religious faces. Obviously, to them it was indeed a fine, humanitarian idea.

I met the mate's eyes as he stared at me with that sneering half-smile I knew so well. I should go easy now; this might look like a clear-cut case of mischief-making to me, but the others should come to that conclusion of their own accord. "Listen, friends," I said, "I have no business messing in your private affairs; if you want to write a letter to that man's widow, it is up to you. But I want to make it clear, before you go any further, that I will not be part of any scheme to tell her a bunch of lies, however well intentioned they may be."

"Why not?" It was the mate again. He had asked it casually, but I knew that tone too. If he and Mashpee should ever get together, I would be in real trouble.

"Because that boy and his wife deserve something better," I said. "This would mean ending their married life with a lie."

"Then what do you suggest?" Sparks asked. "That we tell her the truth?"

"Why not?"

"That he was a coward?" said the mate. "That he hid in a corner of the wheelhouse the moment a gun was fired? That during every attack he was paralyzed with fear and ended up by going berserk over a kitten? Well, I for one would rather have my marriage ended by a lie if it should ever come to that."

"He's right, Skipper!" Porks said. "We can't tell his wife the truth unless we tell her all of it. To tell her that he had himself killed over a kitten is easy enough, but to explain to her why, in a way that would not make her feel ashamed of him . . ." He looked aside and asked, "What do you say, Jo?"

The Second took his time before he answered, "I agree."

For a moment I thought the boy had talked to the others the way he had talked to me. "What would the whole truth be?" I asked.

"Well, I don't know," Porks replied, self-consciously all of a sudden. "We rather led him the hard life, sort of drove him to it, didn't we?"

"Come, come," the Second grumbled, "don't let's exaggerate. All we did was teach him a little lesson."

"Maybe the four of us did," Sparks said, "but when we were through with him, Cook and the crew took their turn with that nutty business about the secret report. When you work it out, you'll find that the poor bastard had only one comparatively easy day of it: the day before we got to Langanes. The next day, the shooting started and he took his nose dive. No, I think the least we can do is write that letter and see to it that his family remembers him as a hero."

There was a silence, in which the mate asked, "Well, Captain? How about it?" He smiled innocently as he spoke, but his eyes were bright with malice.

"As I said, I have no business telling you what to do, as long as we make sure that our letters don't contradict one another."

"You are going to write one of your own?"

"Of course. As his CO, I have to."

"I'd say that Mashpee was his CO."

"All right: as the Master of the vessel on which he was killed. I'll be writing in—well, more general terms, it will be an official sort of thing, so the idea that you people send her a more personal one is fine. Only, if there are any high-ranking officers going berserk on my bridge, I'd like to know about it."

"You mean, you object to it being you?" the mate asked, innocently. He didn't wait for my answer. "Okay, fellows, take me. I don't mind, I've often felt like going berserk, I may do so any day."

He had played that one very well; the Second felt called

upon to defend him against his own generosity. "That's unnecessary," he said. "We'll just keep him nameless. Everybody will understand why we can't reveal his identity."

I should have been quicker on the ball, but the mate had been too nimble for me. To keep the officer anonymous would mean to any intelligent reader that he had been the captain—considering that the only other high-ranking officer on the bridge would be signing the letter with them. As it was, I got up and wished them good luck; after all, why should I care? I would never meet her; if it made the mate happy, let him.

As I sat facing a blank sheet in the chartroom once again, my task seemed easier. If they were writing to her in the vein they had planned, I could indeed limit my letter to some general remarks, vague enough to be sincere and yet noncommittal. I abandoned the idea of using letter number seven; instead I wrote a few lines of my own, saying that during the short time he was on board my ship I had come to appreciate Lieutenant Tyler as an honest, courageous man of the highest motivation. His death had come as a shock to us all, and we were still keenly feeling the loss of his company and comradeship. Part of this was mine, other parts were the spinster's from Belgravia; together we managed to come up with something that violated no truth, but sounded rather like a testimonial written by a lady employer about a maid: what was said seemed less important than what was left out. But although I tried, I could not improve on it. I hoped that, with Sparks and the Second around, the mate's letter would make mine seem restrained rather than shifty.

3

I never got to see their letter. They worked on it that whole evening and most of the next day; I gathered from Sparks that the mate had convinced them that I would be embarrassed if they showed it to me, as that would make me an accomplice by acquiescence. It seemed that he managed to keep in the anonymous high-ranking officer going berserk on the bridge, and I managed to feel good about it, as a small expiation of whatever small guilt might be mine. All I had really been guilty of, when all was said and done, was inexperience; everything had stemmed from that. The real culprit was Mr. Kwel, who had prematurely put me in this position.

It had been some time since I last blamed a personal flaw on the bogeyman. At that thought, I angrily dismissed the whole business from my mind. It's surprising how many things a captain can eradicate from his consciousness without giving them a second thought, by convincing himself that it is in the interest of the ship. It was in the interest of the ship that I should stop agonizing over the past and concentrate on the present, before it blew up in my face.

For, suddenly, there seemed to be a lot of tension on board, now that the pressure was off. Porks quarreled with the Second, the gunners quarreled with the seamen, the bosun even had a quarrel with the carpenter, and the cook seemed to have a quarrel with the world, for the food during the rest of our stay in Murmansk was atrocious. When I complained about it, he became hysterical and said he would like to see anyone cook a decent meal under

constant air attacks, with a dog and three cats fighting
between his legs in front of the stove. He did not exaggerate that much; when we finally left Murmansk, it had
been attacked every night for the entire length of our stay.
We pitied the Russians in their cold, lonesome hell and the
crews of the merchantmen higher upriver, waiting for
their cargo to be unloaded. For some of them, this might
take months, in which case they would have to wait for
the next return convoy. When finally we sailed, our convoy consisted of seven freighters escorted by four destroyers, three auxiliaries, two rescue ships and *Intrepid*. We
were back at sea when, looking for my long coat to wear
on the bridge at night, I came upon the marmalade box
with the boy's belongings. Nobody had come to claim
them, I had forgotten about them myself; I would have to
hand them over at the next port of call.

Our return trip was uneventful; we had been spotted by
only one plane, which approached cautiously and fled back
into the sun hell for leather as soon as the guns of the
escort opened up. We had nothing more serious to do all
day than clean the decks, paint the superstructure and keep
the hardware oiled; watches and meals were taken regularly and with soothing monotony; we might have been
sailing in peacetime. Cook relaxed in his galley and started
treating us to Russian experiments like borscht and pi-
roshki, which were failures; even the seagulls did not like
them, after they had been refused by the three cats. The
kittens were getting bigger and started to lose their innocent look; from touching little fluffy things on wobbly legs
they were turning into miniature jackals, fighting not only
with the dog and their mother but even Cook himself. The
dog had wagged and grimaced and drooled its way into
the heart of every single man on board.

Mashpee himself came on board to deliver our sailing

orders, one frosty morning off Reykjanes, a cape so close to Reykjavik that everybody had spruced up in anticipation of a night on the town. I was more understanding of his condition now than I had been when we had set out from Langanes; also, I had never thanked him for coming to our aid that time we were under direct air attack. I started to say something about it, but he brushed it aside. I might be more understanding of his condition, but he had no empathy with mine. When I told him my crew was exhausted and needed a rest, he raised his eyebrows and asked, "Do they really?"—pronouncing it "rahally." I was tempted to match that, but it occurred to me in time that a man who had been sailing the Murmansk run without respite for months on end could hardly be expected to commiserate with the exhaustion of others after one excursion. He informed me that part of the convoy would continue to Halifax, Nova Scotia, that the escort would be reduced and that I was detailed to serve as a rescue ship to all vessels and stand by in case the Comescort might call for depth charges. I still had a full load of canisters on board, so I was a natural for the choice; but when he said this, I thought I saw a flicker of satisfaction in his mean little eyes, and I began to suspect why he had refrained from calling for our depth charges even when, toward the end of the voyage, it had seemed to me that everybody else had run out of them. I had not realized that this made me a natural for extended convoy duty; if I had ever lived under the delusion that a shared experience might bring us closer, I was cured of that now. I went on protesting for a while, although convinced of the futility of it; he finally unbent to the point of saying with un-British bitterness, "You will find, Captain, that the further west you get, the more dangerous the war becomes, for you are sailing toward the chairborne division. It is my duty, conveyed to me in a signal from Canada marked 'Top Secret,' to warn you that a month ago a U-boat was sighted off the coast of Nova Scotia. As a consequence, no convoy will be allowed to sail without a rescue ship until the danger is past."

We parted with some formality; he did not wish me good luck and I did not wish him any good luck either, although he needed it more than I; I understood that after a quick turnaround at Scapa Flow, *Intrepid* was due to escort the next convoy to Murmansk.

So the *Isabel Kwel* trotted along behind a peaceable covey of four of the slowest ships that must ever have sailed the North Atlantic, all the way to Halifax, Nova Scotia. The crew slept virtually all the way after exhausting all possibilities for distraction, down to the tracing of nudes from the bosun's collection of girlie magazines, on pieces of greaseproof paper. At last, the day before the convoy was due in Halifax, the great spruce-up started.

Suddenly, everybody was overcome by a passion for cleanliness; as requests for hot water poured in, the cook flew into a snit. First he refused to cooperate altogether, then he rationed each man to one pannikin. To keep the peace, I had to bribe him by agreeing to three cold meals that day, providing he would furnish hot water for the lot of us.

That night, at the cold supper, we looked and smelled as if we had come straight out of a Turkish bath. I was intrigued by what looked like puffs of smoke coming out of the Second's open shirt each time he moved his arms; when I asked him what it was, he looked at me in surprise, then he tried flapping his arms, and said, "Oh, that's powder."

I don't think anyone could have given a valid reason for these elaborate preparations. Of course, there was the usual talk about women at the messroom table, but out of the lot only the mate was likely to go ashore and just help himself to a woman before going to the cinema. The rest of them, I was sure, were too sentimental not to make a long, whiney session out of it, gabbing confidences in some smoky bar over bad whiskey or cheap champagne until the whole thing ended in a blur. Yet each one believed that this time it was going to be different; this time he would go ashore in a glittering city full of gay, generous girls; within half an hour of his setting foot in town he would meet a breathtakingly beautiful one who would have her own little flat, where he would spend the evening with his shoes off, in shirt sleeves, on his back on a sofa full of pillows and dolls, and tell her everything, everything: about the convoy and the U-boats and the planes and the fires and the little black heads with the gaping red mouths bobbing on the black sea, and the ringing in your ears because of the explosions that went on ringing in the background all the time, all the time. And then, once the lights were out, he would give her an experience such as she had never known before, and she would conclude, in the gray light of the dawn, that she had at last found the man of her life. He would dress silently in the faint light, careful not to wake her, but she would hear his watch drop or the door squeak and jump out of bed and, on her knees in front of him, clutch his legs, imploring "Don't go, don't go, don't go." But he would disengage her gently, bend down and kiss her hair, and softly go out of the door, down the steps, into the cold gray day, back to his ship; and she would understand because, as the motto said over the pilothouse in Rotterdam harbor, *Navigare necesse est.*

As we rounded MacNab's Island at the mouth of Halifax harbor, I caught my first glimpse of the town. It looked dismal, because it was raining; but the pilot said he was sure it would clear up, it was just typical Halifax weather. This was the first sign of peace: each ship had a pilot. Sparks, who stood on the bridge all dressed up and ready to go, gave him a scornful look and said that this weather seemed to be typical of any place he happened to arrive in with a shore leave ahead. He asked if there was a theater in Halifax.

The pilot asked, "One with live people, do you mean?"

"Well, yes," said Sparks. "A theater."

"No," said the pilot, "I don't think so—not with live people. But there are cinemas."

Sparks said, grimly, "I don't like cinemas." He seemed to hold the pilot responsible for the weather, the dismal waterfront, the slag heaps, the cold, the smell of fish and dead water.

"Well," said the pilot, "that sure is a pity, for there are some mighty nice cinemas here, and it's Merchant Navy Week too, so you guys are going to have a ball." Then he turned to the man at the wheel and said, "Steady as you go."

Of course, that reminded me of Tyler and of the parcel in the wardrobe in the chartroom, waiting to be delivered. I would have to send it from Halifax.

4

I was standing in my bathroom in front of the mirror, knotting my tie, an hour after we had moored, when Cook ripped open the door to my cabin in a frenzy of excitement and whispered, "Captain! Captain! Come quick! She's here! She's sitting in the messroom! Coo! Man! Come down quick! She's got our letter! She got it! Oh, boy! It really slugged her, that letter, it really did! Now she wants to see *you!* Come quick!" And he ran off again, in a high state of agitation.

I had never thought of the possibility of meeting her. It had never occurred to me that she might come all the way from central Canada to visit the ship on which her husband had been killed. As I stood there, stunned, I realized that I could have foreseen it. She would, of course, have inquired about her husband's personal effects, and some humane character at Navy Headquarters might, despite security regulations, have whispered that they were on their way to Halifax in the Dutch tugboat on which her husband had served.

I went on knotting my tie, slowly. I was acutely conscious of the fact that, in her eyes, I was the man for whose sake her husband had laid down his life, if the mate's letter had been as adroit as I suspected. I thought for a moment of slipping away; but I did not want to look more guilty than I probably did already. I decided to face her and have done with it, the sooner the better; I was not going to have my shore leave messed up by anybody. I put on my jacket, my cap, my greatcoat; I hesitated, because I thought I looked too impressive with all that gold braid, then I decided that the more impressive I looked, the more of a hero he became: while I was at it, I might as well make a good job of his beatification.

When I came down the messroom stairs, the first person I saw was a woman wearing a hat covered with fruit, sitting on the bench where he had always sat, tightly squeezed between the Second and the mate, both in their number-one uniforms. I thought for a moment that the cook had gone mad; I knew he was not really interested in women, but he could not be disinterested to the point where he mixed up the gorgeous creature from the photograph with

the frowzy female sitting there, sniffing in her handkerchief. Then it occurred to me that, of course, the girl
would not have come alone. The woman must be his
mother, or hers.

As I came down, a lot of people seemed to be talking;
the moment the four gold rings on my sleeve appeared in
the lamplight, the room fell silent. She was sitting at the
other end of the table, in my chair; next to her sat an
elderly civilian. When she looked in my direction, her face
took my breath away. She was even more beautiful in
reality; her face looked so proud in its grief that I knew at
once that she had swallowed their letter completely: there
sat the beautiful young widow of a very brave man.

When she caught sight of my stripes, her face changed.
I heard a strangled sound; the woman with the hat had
covered her mouth with her handkerchief; she sat gazing
at me, her eyes brimming over. A voice said, "There he is!
That's the Commodore! That's him! There he is!" It was
Cook; he had no notion of what was going on; I could have
kicked him. It was obvious that the mate had done a first-
rate job; this was the entrance of the villain. The silence
after his announcement was so oppressive that I said, awkwardly, "Good evening. I am the captain."

Then she said, "So I see."

I gave her a long, hard stare, but she did not look away.
Her dark, self-righteous eyes were cold and hostile. I said
to the cook, "Get the parcel from the wardrobe in the
chartroom and hand it to the lady, will you?"

Cook answered, "Yes, Com—er—Captain"; he seemed
to have registered, at last, that something was wrong.

I said, "I'm sorry about what happened. You know it all
from our letters. He was a brave man, and we are all proud
to have known him." It sounded as insincere as hell and I
felt acutely uncomfortable, but clearly something was ex-

pected of me and this was the best I could come up with.

The sound she made startled me; it was like a snort of derision. "Proud!" she exclaimed, her magnificent eyes flashing with contempt. "Some people might feel *grateful*, especially those whose life he saved!"

I answered, "Quite," then I saluted, turned on my heel and left. As I emerged into the open, it was still raining. I stepped onto the deck, shaky on my legs. I should have foreseen all this when I let them get away with that goddam letter. I felt like slapping her silly face, but then, she was only acting according to her lights: to her I was the Commodore who had hurled himself onto the bridge, screaming like a banshee, when his ship was machine-gunned by enemy aircraft and to save whose life her husband had sacrificed his own. No wonder she hadn't been impressed by my bangles and my windy authority.

I heard steps stumble up the messroom stairs behind me. I speed-walked toward the gangplank; the steps caught up with me on the quayside, in the dim cone of light from an overhead street lamp through which glistening rain was falling. A voice called, "Captain! Captain!" breathlessly, and I turned around.

It was the elderly civilian whom I had barely noticed, an apologetic man with rimless glasses, much out of breath. "I'm her father," he said, panting. "I'm—I'm so sorry—she acted like that—we talked it over at home—and in the train—she understands it all, honest she does—only, she's very young, and his death has been a terrible shock, she's not at all herself yet. You must not blame her, Commodore, you mustn't—she didn't mean it that way, I swear to you she didn't. . . ."

His kind old eyes, behind the glasses mirroring the lamplight, looked at me pleadingly. I felt sorry for him and embarrassed. "It doesn't matter," I muttered. "I understand. He, er—he was a good sport. I mean, er, a fine officer, I—er—I'm sorry about all this." It sounded even less sincere than my speech in the messroom; but he was incomprehensibly moved. He grabbed my hand and his face twitched as he said, "I'm sure glad to have met you, Commodore—if you should ever come to Ontario, Winnipeg, Lake of the Woods, Kinora . . ."

I said, shiftily, "I will, I will! Thank you very much! Goodbye . . ." and made off.

I did not look where I was going, and the quay was badly lit. Twenty yards further I hit my shin on a bollard and yelped. I heard him call after me, "Commodore! Are you all right?" He was still standing in the swinging cone of lamplight, watching me, rain swirling about him. I shouted, "Yes, sir! Thank you! Good night!" cheerfully, to discourage him from running after me; then I limped down the rest of the quay to where a flight of steps led up to the street. I walked with my fists in my pockets, cursing under my breath.

The boulevard at the top of the steps was empty. I looked up and down the long dismal line of swinging arc lights and rain-swept asphalt, feeling like hell. There was not a soul in sight, except a policeman in a glistening cape, and somebody on a bicycle who kept vanishing in the darkness between the swinging lights. Then I heard a soft rattling sound overhead, and a trolley bus with lighted windows came out of a side street, but it drove off in the opposite direction.

The policeman came strolling toward me and asked, "Looking for something, stranger?"

I said, "Yes, could you tell me how to get to the nearest cinema?"

"The nearest cinema, eh? Let me see . . ." He was obviously glad to talk on a rainy night and wanted to make the most of it. "The nearest cinema—well, now. That would be the Emporium. Now, if you follow this road to the side street where the streetcar came from . . ." He gave me so many directions that I wouldn't have been able to memorize them even if I had been listening. In the end he said, "Come to think of it, why don't you take the street-car?"

I said, "Indeed, why not?" and tried to edge away, pretending I knew where to go for the stop, but he didn't let me off that easily. I must have been the first man he had talked to for hours.

"British?" he asked.

"No, Dutch."

"Freighter?"

"Tugboat."

"Tugboat? How come I've never seen you around here before? I know all the tugboat captains in the harbor."

I said: "Not a harbor tug: oceangoing."

"Oceangoing?" He frowned at me from under his wet hat with a hint of suspicion. "One of them little boats? No kidding."

I said: "Yes," which didn't answer anything; I wanted to get away, but somehow it was difficult.

"No kidding," he repeated. He sounded suspicious now, but prepared to let himself be bribed by a long story in the rain.

I didn't feel like a long story in the rain, so I said, "Ask someone to explain it to you someday. I've got to run along now. They're bigger, you know. Specially built for the job. Good night." I walked away, careful not to hurry, expecting to hear his footsteps catching up with me. As I rounded the corner of the side street from which the trolley had come, I glanced over my shoulder. He was still standing where I had left him, at the top of the steps, looking at the *Isabel Kwel,* his wet cape glistening in the lamp-light.

I took a trolley to the center of the town; as the streets became lighter, they seemed attractive and promising through the rain-streaked windows of the trolley. But when I got out on a big empty square, the rain drenched that promise. I felt queer: giddy and a little sick; my legs were still adjusted to the movement of the ship, and the square seemed to heave with a long, slow swell. Its bleak emptiness gave me an odd feeling of insecurity; I decided that what I needed was not a cinema, but a drink.

I found a bar and had a couple of whiskeys, standing up at the counter. Loud radio music blared from the display of bottles; the bartender looked and behaved like a hospital orderly. The whiskey was too young, its acid smell mingled unpleasantly with the humid stench of my rain-soaked coat. Cold drops dripped off the back of my cap down my neck, I felt as if I had a cold coming. Maybe that was why I had felt queer outside. I drank one more whiskey, to knock out the cold; I had wanted to make it a double, but glanced at the price list in time to see that it cost a fortune by English standards.

When I wanted to pay, however, the bartender said, "No, Cap; this is Merchant Navy Week. While it's on, you guys are not allowed to pay in this town. It's on the house, and thank you for sailing the ships." I was too taken aback to be nice about it; my first reaction was regret that I hadn't ordered a double. Then a man beside me asked, "Had a bad crossing?" I answered: "Middling," feeling foolish. He asked: "Any sign of that U-boat?" I wanted to ask which one, but thought better of it. On the wall was a warning poster showing a little man with one monstrous ear and the words *Careful! Hitler Is Listening!* I said, "Sorry, no information," pointed at the poster and finished my whiskey. The man looked as if he were about to make a thing of it, so I added, "Regulations, you know, old chap. No hard feelings, what? Ta-ta for now. Keep your pecker up," and went back into the rain.

Outside, I stood looking around for a while. I still felt a bit queer: restless and anxious, and the drinks hadn't cured my sea legs either. The only thing in sight that looked at all inviting was the neon sign of another bar in the distance; I was surprised they hadn't blacked out the town, what with that terrible U-boat lurking in the night offshore. As I stood there, the rain drumming on my hat, a voice asked, "Can I help you, sir?" I looked around and saw an elderly man with a soggy hat, carrying a torn umbrella. I asked where the nearest cinema was, and he told me. I touched my cap, said, "Thank you," and started to walk away, for I didn't like the look of him. He called after me, "And thank you for sailing the ships!" in the same tone as the bartender. I might have felt pleased if I hadn't suspected that he had picked my pocket, but my wallet was still there.

I found a cinema at last, and hurried inside without looking at the program, because by then the rain was pelting down. The girl behind the ticket window handed me one before I had asked for it; I saw it was a balcony seat, the most expensive, so I said, "Sorry, but I'd rather have a seat downstairs if you don't mind."

She asked, "Why? That's very close to the screen, you know."

"Maybe, but it costs less."

She looked at me in amazement. "But you aren't expected to pay! This is Merchant Navy Week."

I mumbled, "Oh, I see," turned away, and, sure enough, she called after me, "And thank you for sailing the ships!" I wanted to get at the bottom of this, so I went back and asked, "Say, whose idea is this?"

She gave me a very sweet smile, and answered, "The Chamber of Commerce, I suppose."

I mumbled, "Oh, I see," again; the ticket was getting wet in my hand, but I went on. "Who is paying for all this, for Pete's sake?"

She smiled again, still sweeter this time, and answered, "We are, Captain. We like you people in this town."

I felt like asking her to close up shop and come and have a drink with me, but all this gratitude was a barrier between us; I also still felt a bit sick. I was sure, though, that I could have made a date with her if only I had started talking about that U-boat, and how it had chased us into the harbor, blowing like a whale.

I went inside; the moment I entered the warm, dark cave, I felt better, and I settled down happily, prepared to enjoy myself. It seemed to be a film about gardening; a young girl, kneeling by a flowerbed, a gardening basket beside her, was digging holes with a little spade and putting in onions, reverently, as if she were burying robins. But then there were bangs offscreen and the wails of sirens; and she put what I had taken for a gardening basket on her head—it was a camouflaged helmet. She went on burying robins until somebody called from a window, "Annie! Want to get yourself killed?"

The girl looked up with a sad smile under her helmet, and answered calmly, "Don't worry, Mummy. It doesn't matter any more." I knew the rest of the picture then: her lover was in the Forces, she thought he was dead because somebody had brought home his helmet, but he wasn't; she also thought that she was pregnant and was. I turned out to be so right that it frightened me, as if in that warm dark cave full of people smelling of rain I had discovered I was psychic.

After the main feature there were commercials on lantern slides for electric irons, toasters and bicycles. They fascinated me, for there was a man in uniform on every one of them: officers only, covered with ribbons, who looked with masculine delight at girls in aprons ironing their tunics, burning their toast and riding their bicycles. A man at an organ, emerging from a hole in the floor, played "Roll Out the Barrel" and "Doing the Lambeth Walk."

Toward the end of the lantern slides a hand appeared in front of my nose, proffering a toffee. I looked around, startled, and saw a big woman smiling at me. I said, "Thank you," and took it. She watched me fondly, smiling, while I unwrapped the toffee and put it in my mouth; then she asked me if I had had a bad time. I wanted to make good and tell her whatever she wanted to hear, but I got into difficulties with the toffee and had a bad time until the lights were lowered and the newsreel began.

During the whistles, the bangs and the speeches of the news, I became so conscious of her big, breathing body beside me that I felt as if I were suffocating; finally I got up and sneaked out. The cashier was still sitting behind her little window, but she didn't notice me; she was knitting, somebody in the Forces was going to get a balaklava soon. They were very nice, these Canadians, but I began to feel more and more alien; it seemed as if, despite our mutual goodwill, we were totally unable to communicate because we did not have one point of reference in common.

I went to a couple of other bars, drank whiskey, listened to radio music, heard bartenders say, "Thank you for sailing the ships," and suddenly I had had enough. What the hell was I tramping through the rain for, as sick as a cat, getting drunk, when I had a nice warm ship with a nice warm cabin waiting for me? It made eminent sense, and

I instantly felt better at the mere idea, but I wanted to be absolutely sure that she had left before I went back on board. Pretty as she might be, the others were too eager to get ashore themselves to keep her on board any longer than was strictly necessary, certainly with that powerful escort she carried, so she must be long gone by now, but I did not want to take any risks. I went to two more bars; in the second one I was struck, as I stood sipping my free drink, by the sudden suspicion that I had been there before. All those damn bars looked alike, and so did the bartenders, but this one had looked a little surly as I placed my order. I finished my whiskey rather hurriedly, tried to pay, was told that it was Merchant Navy Week, but he did not thank me for sailing the ships, so I had been right. I had been there before. Now thoroughly fed up, I went back to the ship.

In the trolley I daydreamed about putting my feet up in my cosy cabin, sipping hot tea that I had made myself in the nice hot galley, reading a detective story or idly flicking the pages of a magazine full of glossy nudes stapled across the navel, as the gunners' corporal had done to somebody with his Bofors gun. I had not known I was so fond of that corporal; the mere thought of him made me go all gooey and sentimental inside. I must be drunk. As I had nothing to read, I got out of the trolley and spent twenty minutes trying to find a kiosk or a newsstand; I found several, all closed; in the end I had the intelligence to try a hotel lobby. I picked three books with guns and fainting blondes on the covers and two magazines full of bosoms and buttocks and cartoons of people in beds. When the seedy youth behind the reception desk put a form in front of me and said with a buttoned-up mouth, "If you fill this out, no payment will be necessary, as this is Merchant Navy Week," I said, "Sorry, bud, I am from the gas company," put down the money and marched away, leaving him staring after me, mouth unbuttoned.

Outside, in the street, my shopping under my coat to protect it from the rain, I wondered how to get back to the harbor, for I had wandered about without thinking and had completely lost my bearings. I thought of taking a taxi, but there didn't seem to be any about, nothing but sleek private cars swishing slowly past on the wet asphalt. Only when one of them pulled up and the driver asked: "Taxi?" did I realize that they had all been taxis. I said; "Thank you. To the harbor, please, if it's not too far."

"Far? I'll take you to Winnipeg, if you like. Hop in."

As I sank down in the deep, soft seat I wondered why everyone in Halifax seemed to be part of a secret conspiracy to make me think of her by subtle allusions; it had started with the pilot. I decided it was time I got to my cabin, I had never felt so neurotically scared as I did here in what must be about the safest port on the Atlantic. When I leaned back in the cushions, I pressed the moisture in my greatcoat through my clothes onto my skin, so I spent the rest of the drive sitting on the edge of the seat. The driver became chatty when he saw me perch forward in his rear-view mirror; he started to talk about the U-boat. I thought it was time I did something for this town, after what it had done for me, and said, "I wouldn't worry too much about U-boats, you know. Planes are much worse." He let this sink in, in a long silence; when he spoke again, he sounded truculent, as if I had taken something away from him. Perhaps they needed their U-boat, the way I had needed Mr. Kwel. By the time we got to the steps that led down to the waterfront, under the swinging arc light, he was saying that there were lots of things we boys did not understand, because we had handed over the responsibility for our daily livelihood to the Army or the Navy; it wasn't such a bad life, compared with, for instance, that of a taxi driver with wife and kids to feed. Take rations, for instance . . . I had one eye on the meter, the price had jerked up with nervous little jumps to an amount that had become worrying, so I cut him short and asked for the fare.

He said, "For you guys, no tip," which was still very kind, but I was sure I would have had the ride for nothing if only I had kept my big mouth shut about the national U-boat.

As I descended the steps into the rain-swept darkness of the quay, the prospect I had nursed for the last hour or so seemed to lose some of its attraction. It was infernally dark; apart from the solitary swinging cone of light, there was no streetlighting down there. The lower I got, the more pungent the stench of rotting fish and diesel oil became; I definitely was coming down with a cold, for now I felt sick to my stomach and cold sweat was wriggling down my back. I stepped into invisible puddles twice before I finally reached the circle of light. The lamp squeaked and clattered overhead in the wind; rain smoked about me like spindrift. I crossed the circle of light; then I saw, black in the darkness, the silhouette of the *Isabel Kwel*.

The sight of her gave me such an overwhelming feeling of relief and safety and gratitude that I hurried blindly toward her, forgetting about the bollard that had nabbed me before and now nabbed me again. I hopped about on one foot, grabbing my shin, howling like a dog; another dog answered from the darkness: a long mournful howl of loneliness. It was Dane, our ship's dog, so called because that was how Cook had first addressed him when he lay shell-shocked in the galley, only survivor from our Danish neighbor. I called, "Dane! Pst! Dane, where are you?"

He answered with a howl so forlorn and hopeless that

there could be no doubt who was his master; he carried on like Cook himself, the moment he realized he had an audience. One thing was obvious: he was the only one left on board. Everybody else had ratted, chasing a dream.

When I climbed on board, he came to meet me in the darkness and made me jump as his warm, wet tongue licked my cold, wet hand. He was not tied up; like all ships' dogs, he would never hazard ashore by himself. I had never felt close to him, now his exorbitant welcome filled me with a fondness for him that I had never felt for a dog before. To be back on board my ship, to feel her deck underfoot, her rail under my hand, seemed to lift a load off me. Sickness, loneliness, my cold, even the rain seemed to vanish the moment I was back in the comforting, exhilarating freedom of my own world. Never before in my life had I associated a tugboat with freedom; "prison" had been the word we had used in the past, during those revolutionary jam sessions of the galley club. It had all been hogwash, wild nonsense talk from young men who had no notion what life really was about, what it meant to be alive, a captain. As I walked to the galley, my body, every fiber of it, seemed to fuse with every fiber of her with a feeling of waking up from a two-dimensional dream in the fullness of reality. So much for shore leave in a world at peace; I had felt like a ghost, revisiting the living.

The ship was silent. No generator hummed in her innards; the only light on board shone from the galley, and it was the light of an oil lamp. Cook had obviously gone ashore too, leaving this light to create the impression that there was someone left on board; the engineers had stopped the dynamo. Until they came back, there would be no electricity on board the *Isabel Kwel*. Somehow, the prospect of dressing gown, slippers, hot tea and magazines was even more enticing now I knew myself to be alone.

I considered taking off my greatcoat and the rest of my wet clothes in the chartroom before making the tea; but when I spotted a mouse-colored dressing gown with a molting felt collar hanging from a hook behind the door, I decided to undress in the warm galley. Under normal circumstances the idea of putting on any of Cook's clothes would not have occurred to me, but I was so wet and chilled that I stripped in front of the stove, rubbed myself down with a tea towel, hung my clothes over the line and put on the dressing gown. Looking for a smaller kettle, I opened the door of one of the ovens and discovered to my delight, followed by a captain's frown, a pair of old sheepskin slippers that turned out to be pretty smelly. Who was it that had said you should never hang around in the galley to see what Cook was cooking if you ever wanted to enjoy a meal again? Captain Bosman, probably; all my elementary knowledge of life at sea stemmed from that one voyage under him.

I put on the hot slippers, filled the kettle, put it on the stove and sat down on the bench in front of it. I rested my feet on the rail, wrapped the dressing gown around my legs and had a look at the magazines, waiting for the water to boil; Dane, who had followed my every move with a mysterious hope, slumped down with a sigh underneath me. By the time the lid of the kettle started to click and rattle, I had lost the last vestige of the malaise that had bothered me ashore. I wondered, objectively, what it was that made me behave like a mental patient the moment I ventured away from the ship and found myself among normal people in a normal world. It must be the normal world that did it; I had never felt like this in any English harbor, where the war was part of the daily reality. Here, I had felt that we had nothing in common. I wondered whether we ever would again. Even those who were touched by the war, like the girl and her father, seemed to have no concept of its reality. The very way she had sat there, proud and bereft, had expressed a total ignorance of the hell he had died in. Was their world the real one? If so, we, who were thanked for sailing the ships at the instigation of the Chamber of Commerce, might well find ourselves exiled forever if we should live to see the end of the war. Was our world the real one? If so, I would need a lot of time to think before I could begin to understand what life was all about. Not in my own case so much as in the case of the Danish captain, gunner Duncan, the unknown owner of the shoe, or Tyler. The hell with Tyler.

I found a tray, a teapot, tea, a mug; I poured boiling water into the pot, put it with the mug, the magazines and the books on the tray, wrapped the dressing gown around me and set out for my cabin.

It was pitch dark outside, the rain drummed and gurgled on the deck; it would be more sensible to stay where I was until it stopped. But Cook might come back at any moment; I had to think of his imminent return very hard before I could gather enough courage to take a deep breath and jump.

The rain hit me like hail and went straight through the dressing gown at once. I couldn't run, because the slippers kept coming off; I lost one and groped for it with my bare foot, balancing the tray, while the rain made tinkling noises on the tea things and rattled on the magazines. When I found the slipper and put my foot in it, it was already half full of water. Stumbling along, I began to worry how I would open the door of my cabin with that tray in my hands. When I finally reached it, I put my knee up against the wall, put the tray on it precariously and turned the doorknob with my free hand. The door wouldn't open; only then did I remember that I had locked it when I went out and put the key in my pocket. My trousers were in the galley. There I stood, cursing, getting soaked, wondering what to do: stumble back to the galley, or chuck the tray overboard and scream? Then it occurred to me that the door to the chartroom must be open. I could not remember if I had bolted the communicating door before I left, but I decided to risk it. As I staggered around with my tray, I lost the other slipper and wished it luck; when I finally limped to the door, put up my knee against the wall again and groped for the knob, I knew that if I found this one locked too, I would indeed get the fit of rabies the mate must have described so vividly in his letter.

It was open. It swung toward me, the wind caught it and nearly knocked the tray off my knee. I struggled around it, stepped over the threshold with a sigh of relief, went to put the tray on the chart table and saw someone sitting on the couch in the darkness.

I stood stock still, my heart pounding. The figure in the darkness was so still that my first thought was it must be asleep; but something I sensed in its stillness, a tension, an awareness, told me it was not.

I said: "Hello? Who's this?"

A woman's voice answered: "It's me."

For a mad moment I thought it was the cashier from the cinema; then I realized, with deep alarm, who it was.

I felt sober and calm, but I had the same feeling in the back of my knees that I had at the beginning of an attack. I put the tray down on the table, groped for the matches on the shelf, struck one and lit the lamp.

As I turned around and faced her, my heart started pounding. She sat there, crumpled and forlorn; her dark eyes looked at me with such stark despair that I thought she had gone mad. Her face was a ghastly white, her wet hair hung down her forehead, the fur on the collar of her coat was flattened with rain. She stared at me motionlessly, with that mad, dark despair; then she started to shiver.

I said, "What—" but she didn't let me finish. Her eyes held mine as she asked, "Why did you lie to me?" Her voice was hoarse.

I said, "Pardon?" Then she lifted her hand and I stiffened as the thought of a gun flashed through my mind. But the hand pointed at a stack of papers on the table. "There," she said.

I glanced at them and read, *Darling, darling, I must write all this down at once, or I'll do something crazy. I don't know what is going on on board this ship, but I've never been so scared in my life. Within minutes of my arrival I got wise that they were going to cut me dead. . . .* I did not need to read any further. I had forgotten I had put his letters in that parcel. If only I had followed the Second's advice and thrown them overboard. If only . . .

"Why did you do it?" she asked, her voice quavering.

I tried to collect my wits, think of an intelligent answer, but the discovery of how clumsy, how blind I had been numbed me. I remembered looking at his letters in the drawer, thinking: all I need do is open those to know the truth; she knew the truth now, better than I, who had seen him kill himself in front of my eyes. As I stood looking at her, I saw a tear trickle down her cheek, glistening in the lamplight. A sudden feeling of pity overwhelmed me; I was about to say something when I suddenly became conscious of what I looked like: the drenched dressing gown hanging open, the soggy slipper. I turned to shut the door, closing the dressing gown as I did so; when I stood with my back to her, I heard her cry.

I turned around; she had covered her face with her hands, strands of wet hair had fallen over them. I wanted to comfort her, to say something kind and sensible, but the wet dressing gown inhibited me. I tried to open the communicating door to go to my cabin and change; it was bolted from the inside all right. I had to stay where I was, as I was: looking like a fool, catching pneumonia. I began to get very cold; it made me angry. I said, "I'm sorry about this. I should have known it would happen. I—I'm sorry."

She sobbed, her face in her hands, but I was no longer moved. I said, "Come, go back to your hotel or wherever you are staying; I'll come to see you in the morning and explain."

She tried to control her sobs. Her shoulders still heaved, but she no longer made a sound. I stretched out my hand to help her get up. Then I heard her say, "Coward, coward!"

"I know," I said, "I'm sorry."

"*He* was a coward! He! He!"

I said, "You don't know what you are talking about. Get up, go back to your hotel. I'll see you in the morning. Come on." I touched her shoulder; she looked up so brusquely that she startled me. Her dark, mad eyes stared at me through the tangled strands of her wet hair as she asked, "How dare you talk to me like that? Have you no heart? No decency?"

I said, "Don't talk nonsense. I'll come and see you in the morning. I'm sorry to throw you out like this, but I am soaking wet, and so are you. We don't want to catch our death. Come."

She stood up. I thought she was going to stride out, but she took off her coat, flung it at me, and cried, "There! Wrap that around you if you're cold! I am going to stay right here where I am until I know the truth. The *whole* truth."

She stood facing me, eyes flashing, her chest heaving, and I remembered the photograph. I stooped to pick up her coat, to get away from her eyes. When I faced her again, I said, "You know the truth, you have read his letters; if he wrote what I think he did, you should know by now that he was not a coward, or you'll never know."

"Don't lie to me!" she cried, a cry of anguish. "Why did you folks write that letter if you didn't think he was a coward? Why did you try to hide the truth from me if you didn't think he was?"

I knew I ought to hand her back her coat and push her out, quickly, for she was very beautiful in her despair. But I didn't push her out. I said, "That letter was not written by me, but by my staff. And what exactly do you think happened? How do you think he was killed, if you don't believe that letter?"

She said, "That's what I have come to find out. I want you to tell me, *now*."

"I can't tell you the truth, for I don't know it myself."

"Stop lying!" she cried. "Don't torture me any longer! *Please!*"

I dropped her coat on the couch and turned away. Pouring out a mug of tea, I said, "Their letter may have prettied things up a bit, but, from what I know of it, it is essentially true. He was killed the way they told you: by MG fire, on the bridge, after he had jumped out of the shelter of the wheelhouse."

"Why? Why did he do such a thing?"

"Because he heard screaming."

"Who was screaming?"

I dropped a lump of sugar in the tea and stirred it.

"Who? Who was screaming?"

I held out the mug to her, and said, "I was." I was looking at the mug, expecting her to take it from me; but she didn't. She struck it out of my hand. It crashed against the wardrobe, the broken pieces tinkled to the floor.

"Don't lie!" she shouted, her face close to mine.

I said, "What in the world . . ." but I faltered. She looked as if she were going to spit at me.

"Do you expect me to believe that?" she asked. "You aren't the sort of man to lose your head during a battle and run into machine-gun fire and have yourself killed! But he would! He was a coward, I know it! I've always known it, right from the very beginning! When I got that letter telling me he had died a hero, I . . . . "

"You went mad with joy, I suppose?"

"Yes! I'd rather he died as a man than lived as a coward!"

It was a shocking confession to make. Her father had said she was not herself, I could see now he had been right. No woman of her upbringing would rush through the rain and climb on board a deserted tugboat and sit waiting in a strange cabin for a man she did not know, if she were in her right mind. It could all be explained, all be forgiven; she too was a pathetic victim of romantic slogans, patriotic bombast and total ignorance, as he had been; her ideas about war and bravery had been corrupted, like his, from kindergarten onward, and after the war started, the windbags had continued the corruption. Thinking of political orators and men who wrote books like *Steady as You Go*, I flew into a rage. I began to pace up and down in my wet dressing gown, saying, "Goddammit—Goddammit. . . ." I could not think of anything else to express the anger that choked me.

She asked, "Who was it?" But I went on pacing, cursing, I'd be damned if I'd answer that, God damn her and the whole damn lot of stupid, murderous . . .

She grabbed my arm and shook me and shouted, "Who was it that screamed?!"

I felt her breath on my face. Her eyes were so close now that I could see the lunacy in them, the lunacy of war. I felt a sudden sadness sink through my rage, like a stone, and I said, "A kitten."

She looked at me with a horror that I had not expected. She looked as if she saw him killed in my eyes. Then she made a sound, like a laugh, and her head fell on my shoulder, sobbing.

I said, "Don't. You don't understand," but she could not help herself. She went on sobbing, wildly, hysterically, clutching my arms, shaking me.

I said, "Stop it! Listen to me!" But she went on sobbing and shaking me; when she began to scream in wild hysteria, I grabbed her hair and pulled her head back. She bawled like an animal in pain, her eyes upturned, her nose running; then I slapped her.

She fell silent, instantly. Her eyes slowly opened. For a moment she looked at me the way she had done in the messroom, when she first saw me; then her eyes became gentle and grave, her lips parted; she slumped forward in my arms, and we kissed.

5

When it was over, the whole thing suddenly seemed sordid. She lay weeping on the couch, moaning, "What have I done . . . what have I done . . . " As I got up, I saw his letters strewn on the floor, among her stockings, her underwear, her dress.

I couldn't bear to look at them, and her weeping behind my back became unbearable. I went for my cabin, forgetting that damn door was bolted. I put on the wet dressing gown to go to the galley and get the key.

But once outside, in the darkness, I no longer wanted to

go to the galley. As I stood there, listening to the whispering of the rain, I did not seem to be me, myself, Martinus Harinxma, but someone vague and impersonal, while inside, in the yellow lamplight, the real Martinus Harinxma was still making love to Tyler's widow. I felt as if I were floating somewhere, high up, over the chartroom with its lit portholes in the night, over the ship, the dark harbor, the sea, the war. The first emotion that came to me as I floated there, above it all, was a feeling of compassion for the two of us and what we had done; from that far distance I could see how it had come about.

The rain splattered and gurgled on the deck, a rope of the spray shield on the bridge above tapped in the wind. The feeling of compassion concentrated on her; never before had I felt such tenderness. I wanted to go back into the chartroom, to comfort her instead of leaving her to face it alone; but when I looked through the steamed-over porthole, I saw something white move in the lamplight. She was dressing; I could not go in just yet. I went to the galley to put on my clothes.

In the galley, everything was as I had left it. Dane welcomed me ecstatically, furiously wagging his tail; the kettle was still simmering; there was a soft hiss as a drop fell onto the stove from my trousers on the line. What had happened seemed something I had dreamed or read while sitting there on the bench, with my feet up on the rail.

I took off Cook's dressing gown and dropped it on the floor. It fell with a wet sound. I took off his one slipper and began to rub myself down with the tea towel; then I heard high-heeled shoes on the deck, running.

Panic seized me. I had never thought that she would run off like this, without seeing me again, without giving us a chance to talk about it. I ripped open the galley door and called, "Mary! Mary, don't do that! Don't go away! . . .

Mary, stop! Mary! MARY!"

But she did not listen. I saw her fluttering figure rush through the swinging cone of lamplight and vanish in the darkness. I shouted *"Mary!"* once more, with such despair and urgency that tears came to my eyes, but she didn't stop or look around. I saw her run up the steps to the boulevard and emerge in the arc light; then she was gone. Rain blew in through the open door. The arc light above the steps trembled in the wind.

I dressed hurriedly, put my shoes on without socks, grabbed my greatcoat, ran out onto the quay without my cap. I jumped over the bollard in the darkness, ran through puddles, stumbled up the steps, but when I stood panting on the boulevard and looked up and down the glistening lane of asphalt and lights, it was empty.

Back on board, I found the chartroom in chaos. The mattress had slipped off the couch, the floor was littered with his letters, some of them soaked in tea. The lamp was smoking.

I could not make up my mind if she had left those letters behind on purpose or had forgotten them in her panic to get away. In any case, she could not have read them properly, or she would not have reacted like that. I would have to try and get them back to her, were it only for the sake of his memory. Whatever way she might feel about him now, the time would come when she would understand.

6

I tried to reach her for two days. I rang up all the hotels in town, all the people I could find listed under the name *Tyler* in the telephone book. I went to the headquarters of the Naval Reserve to find out her address—we had sent our letters from Murmansk via them. When they had finally traced it, I tried to call her up at home, but she had no telephone or it was not listed. I called the exchange to ask if there were any neighbors with a telephone; they told me they could only transmit my request to her to call me. I gave the number of the bar from which I was telephoning.

I sat there, waiting, listening to radio music, news, comedians, commercials until closing time. When the bartender would not let me pay, because it was Merchant Navy Week, we nearly had a fight, for by then I was desperate and drunk.

The next morning, at dawn, I was roused by a dispatch rider delivering our sailing orders, for which I had to sign.

TOP SECRET CINCNAT TO MASTER DUTCH TUG ISABEL KWEL BEGINNING JOIN CONVOY NAT ONE TWO SEVEN EASTBOUND DEP TWELVE HUNDRED AUG THIRTY STOP ASSEMBLY HAL HARB ELEVEN HUNDRED REPORT COMESCORT US CRUISER ALABAMA STOP RESCUE DUTY THROUGH GIGHA PASSAGE WHENCE PROCEED INDEPENDENTLY TO KIRKWALL FOR ORDERS SIGNED SPARTACUS END.

It was August the thirtieth. We sailed at noon.

CHAPTER EIGHT

I

During the afternoon of our first day out, I tried to write a note to her, to go with the letters that now would have to be sent back from Kirkwall. I found it impossible to put into words what I wanted to say.

Sorry it happened—don't feel too badly about it—let me explain. It was when explaining my part in it that I got stuck. Her part, it seemed, could be explained more easily. For one mad hour at dead of night, I had seemed to her the embodiment of everything her husband had not been; it would not have happened if the mate's idiotic letter had not made her believe for a few weeks that he had been a conventional hero. An explanation of my part in it was essential, if I wanted to convince her that what had happened between us had not been sordid and furtive.

Every day after leaving Halifax, I tried to write that explanation. I began it scores of times; every moment I could spare, I spent sitting at the table in the chartroom, a sheet of paper in front of me, thinking. If I wanted to make her really understand how it had all come about as far as I was concerned, I had to go back further than that day in Scapa Flow when her husband had first come on board. I would have to start by explaining why the crew had sent him to Coventry and why I had done nothing about it. I had to go back at least as far as when Mr. Kwel offered me the post of Commodore, and she would not begin to understand what that was about unless I told her about oceangoing tugboats and my first involvement with them, which took me right back to my youth. Everything turned out to be connected by countless gossamer threads of cause and effect, and all those threads seemed to converge in the chartroom of the *Isabel Kwel* in Halifax, Nova Scotia, that night in August, 1942. Everything: my mother, Naval College, Captain Bosman, Sophie . . . I would have to write to her, however difficult it might be, if I did not want to do the same thing to her that I had done to Sophie. I knew it could all be explained, that I had been young and inexperienced and all that, but I had deserted Sophie, there could be no doubt about it.

It was interesting, in an objective way, that I thought first of her and not of myself. It made me feel good and mature, with, eventually, even a touch of sanctity, until Cook found the photograph.

He found it during the first dogwatch on the fourth day out, after I had told him to turn out the chartroom and my cabin and give them a good cleaning before we became involved in a new assignment, when he could come up with the excuse that he did not have the time. He had set out, moping, on his unpleasant task with a great show of mops and a dramatic clatter of buckets, but he had perked up considerably when he came running onto the bridge within five minutes, showing an earring on the palm of his hand, with the delight of a child who has found a rare

shell on a beach where he had not expected to find anything.

"Hey, Cap!" he cried. "Look at this! I wonder how that
got there? I found it underneath the mattress on the couch
in the chartroom. . . ."

I tried to exorcise him by saying, "I'll thank you not to
come running onto this bridge at the slightest provocation,
and I absolutely forbid you to call me 'Cap'—is that clear?"

Uniquely as a conditioned reflex, he muttered, "Yes,
Captain, you bet. . . . But where did this come from? Who
was she, eh?"

I snatched the trinket off his grimy palm and said, "If
you are not off this bridge by the time I count three, I'll
kick you off! Scram!"

He fled with a squeal, a Victorian girlish noise, reminiscent of flat-footed chases in box-tree mazes, and ran off,
no doubt to dig some more in the mother lode of the chartroom, his hopes now at gold-fever pitch.

If I had had the slightest suspicion as to what else he was
to find, I would have locked both cabin and chartroom and
hung the key around my neck. As it was, all I did was
worry about the earring. I didn't mind his finding it, I felt
no bashfulness about its becoming known on board, as it
now irrevocably would, that I had entertained a female
visitor in my quarters while everybody else was wearing
his heels down in the rain. I worried because she must have
missed it later that night, and it must have added to her
distress. I decided to refer to it casually in my letter and
to send it back to her from Kirkwall, together with her
husband's letters. I had managed to brush those out of my
consciousness after putting them, unread, back in the
drawer of the chart table where he had kept them himself.
They did not quite fit into the picture of a minor saint.

Ten minutes later, Cook gave a scream down below that

made the helmsman look at me with startled anticipation; then he came scrambling up the bridge steps again, brandishing something, crying, "Now look what I've found! Look! Look!" It was the photograph of the girl in the bathing suit, without its frame, a muddy footprint on its back.

"Where did you find that?"

"Underneath the mat under the chart table, Captain," he answered, gleefully.

My first reaction was incredulous amazement. How the devil could it have ended up there? The only explanation there could be was that it had been among his letters when they were scattered about that night. . . . But no, that was impossible! There had been a frame around it, a big leather frame . . .

The archness of his snigger, laced with halitosis, made me want to wring his neck. I ripped the photograph from his hands and then, prompted by that sixth sense of the sea captain, aimed a shot in the dark. My old familiar alter ego, which had whispered in my ear as early as South Shields, made me ask, "What did you do with the frame, you goddam crook?"

It was a wild accusation; all the poor man had done was find a photograph underneath the chart table, the fact that once upon a time it had been encased in a leather travel frame had no connection with that discovery. Or had it? To my surprise, I saw his eyes go shifty, his grin lose its lewdness. He changed in front of my eyes from one of Susanna's Elders into Ananias, when the apostles discovered that he had swindled them out of the proceeds of the sale of his farm.

"Well?" I asked, with divine wrath. "What did you do with it? Speak up!"

"I—I—I didn't think anybody would want it . . ." he

stammered. "I—when I made up that parcel, it was too big for the box, so I just . . . " He started to edge shiftily toward the stairs.

"Don't go away," I said, suddenly suave. "I'd like to hear a little more about this. Why did you do it? And where is it?"

"It—I—honest, Captain," he pleaded, "I honestly couldn't get it into that box, so I just took the picture out of the frame and put it with his letters."

"Where is it?" I roared.

"In—in my cabin . . ." he whispered, a picture of frailty and cringing subjugation.

"Go get it!" I ordered. "Now!"

He whispered, "Yes, Cap . . ." and virtually vanished in a puff of smoke. I did not hear his steps ring out on the stairs, he must have slid down the banister.

He was back within minutes, carrying the leather frame. He handed it to me from as far away as possible. I opened it sternly; when I saw what he had put in it, instead of the picture of the girl, I almost weakened. It was the picture of a kitten in a boot, cut from some magazine: an image so saccharine and nauseating that even a spinster with a cat complex would have rejected it as too corny. If I had any decency left behind my mask of Captain Bligh, I would give it back to him now, for what I was planning to do with that frame was a great deal less innocent. But I found myself incapable of magnanimity; I closed it with a righteous snap, looked at him with distaste and said, in a voice that could afford by then to sound casual, "I'll send this back to Officer Tyler's widow in due course. You had better get on now with whatever you were doing. It will depend on your future behavior whether I make anything out of this or not. Dismiss."

He crooned, "Oh, Captain, thank you, Captain! Yes—

I'll do your cabin now, oh boy, will I do your cabin. . . ." Babbling, he went down the bridge stairs and vanished into the chartroom. I had played this rather well; the gods had been with me. If I had not, by extrasensory perception, stumbled upon his peccadillo, he would have posted the identity of my nightly visitor in Halifax all over the ship. Now, although he could hardly be expected to forget about it, his style might be sufficiently cramped to leave well enough alone, at least for a while.

But it was not the possibility of our encounter being publicized that distressed me; it was the photograph itself. In the privacy of my cabin, after the watch, I looked at it again, and found that it revived with an acuteness almost beyond endurance both her presence and his. It made me remember her eyes, and his. Never had I felt such a burning shame. I had gradually managed to look back upon that night with almost missionary unctuousness, thinking only of her well-being, mental and spiritual; now I discovered that, however convincingly I might beautify my part in it, I would never be able to explain away what I felt right now, looking at that photograph. My life, which before had appeared to be an intricate but logical continuum of cause and effect, was suddenly balled up into a nest of vipers. I could not understand why the realization of my strong physical desire for her should alarm me so, but it did. My past seemed to surge and seethe behind me; when I started to think about what I had done to other people in my life, it became a snake pit from which there was no escape. Of course, I was responsible for Sophie's torture and probable extermination. Of course, I was responsible for Tyler's death; first I had used his degradation to establish myself as the real captain of my ship, then I had used his agony to bolster the morale of my crew, finally I had used his wife. Her body writhing in passion, his body twitching on the bridge, seemed to become one; her orgiastic cries, his "Mary! Mary!" blended into one wail of agony; and I was responsible for that agony, I was entangled beyond unraveling in his sacrificial slaughter which had ended with his body writhing, moaning, at my feet, the way she had writhed and moaned in my embrace.

Objectively, I knew that this morbid self-incrimination made no sense; but to come to an objective conclusion is one thing, to live up to it another. Before the day was over, I was writing to her again, but this time not a note to go with his letters. This time it turned into a litany of loneliness, pages and pages of incoherent self-commiseration, growing into a love letter. I suddenly came to the conclusion that I loved her, loved her more than I had ever loved anyone before. Suddenly she represented everything that was good and pure and innocent and gay and alive and warm and desirable and exciting; I had never realized that I knew so many adjectives in English, yet I felt in need of more. But all I had in the way of a dictionary was the ship's nautical one, which supplied five synonyms for "tender" but did not mention "love."

I sat writing to her for one entire afternoon watch. At a given moment, I discovered at my elbow a tray with a sandwich and a mug of tea; I had not noticed Cook come in, so wrapped up had I been in my ecstatic dream. The letter was a far cry from "I say, thank you very much," with which I had rewarded my partner in the hangar after our brief encounter on the sugar sacks. She became identified with peace, a home, happiness, life itself; the letter became the reiteration of a daydream, based on the boy's monologue in the chartroom when he had described his world during the crossing from Kirkwall to Langanes. When the time for my watch came up, I had only begun to say what I had in mind; but I could not leave the letter lying about.

Cook's tray meant that he had seen me writing; I knew he would not rest until he had unearthed it, now his curiosity had been aroused. The drawer under the chart table was no longer safe, I had to find another hiding place. I put the letter, which already amounted to twenty-three pages of scrawly writing, in an envelope and looked for a spot that even a ship's cook would not think of; I finally hit upon one: the underside of the bottom drawer under my bunk. I rarely used that drawer, it was heavy and jammed full of clothes; it might not be ideal, but it was the best I could come up with at such short notice. I emptied it out, turned it over and discovered, already hidden underneath it, a dog-eared album of photographs of couples in action, the kind that vendors in Marseilles and Le Havre refer to in a whisper as "*scènes vécues.*" I leafed through the collection; the photographs were of staggering obscenity, but the models so solemn in their acrobatic concentration that the cumulative effect was irresistibly hilarious. I need not wonder who had put them there; I had had only one predecessor on the *Isabel Kwel:* the great Bokke Loppersum himself.

As I sat there on the floor, feeling my ecstasy wilt and die, I realized that the ghost of the old man was still haunting me. I was still very young to be a captain; I still thought this life the best life a man could lead; well, I had just discovered what pathetic loneliness, what mental retardation was the price of our glory. I put the album in my duffel bag, where I found his deflated and forgotten Niki. I would throw them overboard late that very night, when I could do so unobserved. Then I put my letter in the hiding place, put the clothes back in the drawer, closed it and went to the bridge for my watch. But what had happened turned out to be irrevocable; I could not resurrect the lover I had been for only four hours. I could not forget those photographs and the purpose for which the great Captain Loppersum must have used them. When it came down to cold facts, her photograph, in all its guileless candor, performed the same function for me.

During that watch, I decided that there was only one way of getting the ghost of old Bokke off my back: by confessing all this to her. I should use those photographs to demonstrate to her what my life would ultimately look like, unless she helped me. On the basis of that decision, I went back to the chartroom after my watch, to continue my letter. The moment I sat facing a blank sheet of paper again, it was as if my pen took wings. I wrote, again, for hours; in the end, I had to give up because of cramp in my hand, even though the letter was not finished. I would have to continue it later. In the meantime, I did not want it lying around where Cook could get his hands on it, so I pulled out the bottom drawer to put it in the secret hiding place. I found my previous letter there and I wanted to keep them in sequence, so I took them to the chart table, remembering that I had the first one in my left hand and the second in my right. I was about to write the numbers "1" and "2" on them, when the memory of Tyler and his numbered letters hit me.

I stood there for a while, motionless, staring at the two letters; then I put them underneath the drawer, shoved it back in place, and went out on deck. I felt as if my cheek had been brushed by a ghost.

2

After my watch, I could not sleep. The image of Tyler writing haunted me, and the eerie notion that I was living through an experience another man had lived through in exactly the same way, with the same woman. The whole thing took on such sinister proportions in the darkness, as I lay tossing and turning, that I decided to take a sleeping pill and found I was out of them. I would have to get a new supply in Kirkwall; I suspected that, during the next month or so, I might be needing them. I went through a few hours of maudlin self-pity; then, toward dawn, I managed to shrug it all off. Enough of this nonsense; I had a ship to sail, full of frightened men like myself—and maybe that was the key. We all knew what "to Kirkwall for orders" meant: another run to Murmansk. To sail another of those convoys seemed something to avoid at all costs except that of life itself, and I had the impression that the crew, after this short rational period of an interlude without danger, was reverting to its instinctive atavistic relationship with me and expected me somehow to mystically protect them again. The new convoy was not mentioned much; if it was, there always followed a shrug of the shoulders and a grin signifying: Oh, well, "Fancy That" will think of something. "Fancy That" thought of a lot of things, none of them realistic. There was, for instance, the hope that the *Isabel Kwel* might be assigned to mine-laying duty, what with those gates they had put in her stern coaming during her construction, but it would mean that the depth charges would have to be removed and mines put in their stead, and I could not see the Royal Navy going in for anything like that. No, I was afraid that, in this instance, my mystical powers would be of no avail against the dragon of bureaucracy. We were for it, and there was nothing I could do to avert our fate.

But the crew went on blithely trusting in my omnipotence. I noticed it in small things: a subtle change in attitude, a hint of adulation that had been healthily absent ever since we had passed Iceland on our way to Halifax.

One of the most eerie emanations of my reinstatement as tribal chieftain had to do with the girl. Cook had, of course, seen to it that the whole ship knew within twenty-four hours that the captain had had a ding-dong with the English officer's widow in the chartroom that night in Halifax. By all civilized moral standards, this would have been, to say the least, an act of questionable taste. Not so to the small lost tribe inexorably herded toward the edge of the world, haunt of dragons and demons, fatherland of death. They reverted to a much older morality in which a woman was a conqueror's prize, a tribute to his magical powers which had defeated mortal men. I knew my staff must all have seen the photograph at one time or another, and all of them must have fallen in love with her at first sight as I had, if falling in love is taken in its most basic sense. The rest of the crew had ogled her sufficiently when she came on board that night to appreciate her desirability as a female. It was disturbing, but I could not shake the impression that, in some tribal, prehistoric way, I had made love to her on behalf of the crew, that she had been the spoils of a victory of one tribe over another. It disturbed me, because once I followed that thought to its logical conclusion, it meant that when I had held her thrashing, moaning body in my arms, twenty other men had shared that experience by proxy. It was not all that farfetched; I need not go back to the Stone Age to find a precedent; the robber barons and their "jus primae noctis" lay only just behind us in history.

In modern times, the most innocuous description of her vestal function during the great ordeal of the *Isabel Kwel* would be to call her, as the Americans would, "Miss Rescue Ship 1942," or "Queen of the Arctic Convoys." The disturbing part of it was that I could not be sure I had been free of that symbolic concept of her myself. For when all was said and done, what did I know of her? What I had held in my arms had not been a person but a symbol; but then, she had been a symbol to the boy, and he had been a symbol to her, and now she wanted him to be a symbol to his son. All of us were in some measure symbols to others; I was, I knew, a symbol to my crew. If I came out of all my self-searching in deepening gloom with any positive thought at all, it was that we should make it our business to help our fellow men cast off the symbols we were carrying on our backs, like crosses, to which some of us would no doubt eventually be nailed.

It was a thought that might have impressed Captain Bosman, but I doubted whether it would impress the Royal Navy. To the Royal Navy, we were a symbol too, if ciphers could be called symbols. *Tugboat, Oceangoing, 704 tons, armaments: Oerlikon 1, three-inch cannon 2, depth-charge catapults 2, storage for 36 canisters.* I could not see them dispatching that on a mine-laying expedition.

3

I was right. Not only did the Royal Navy remember the canisters on my aft deck down to their individual serial numbers, they even remembered that, at some time in the distant past, I had signaled one of His Majesty's officers, in command of the convoy of which I was part, to go to hell. As I was not a member of the Royal Navy but only part of civilian personnel sailing under temporary charter, there was no call, in this instance, for disciplinary measures; however, the Royal Navy would be interested in my version of the incident, as the undersigned could hardly believe the signal read as quoted in the report and was convinced there must be some misinterpretation. So would I please oblige with a full report in quadruplicate of the incident, substantiated with quotations from ship's log if relevant and signal log if extant. The undersigned was illegible, the envelope, in a final shriek of bureaucratic idiocy, marked *Secret and Urgent.*

I was handed this, to use Mashpee's own word, baroque document as the *Isabel Kwel* docked in Kirkwall. Maybe it was the tugboat man's congenital irreverence toward authority that made me regard it as a joke, maybe it was because the letter conjured up the perfect image of the chairborne division and the magnitude of the problems by which it was beset in its wall-to-wall-carpeted bomb-proof office, underneath the Grand Hotel in Glasgow, to which they tried to give a nautical flavor by referring to it as H.M.S. *Spartacus.*

I tossed the thing into the drawer where the boy and I had once kept our letters and her photograph, deciding to forget about it until I should find myself with enough time on my hands and in the appropriate mood to cope with that kind of emergency.

The next morning, I was ferried across once more to the battleship moored to the buoy in the heart of Scapa Flow anchorage, together with six fellow victims, captains of future rescue ships. I discovered, to my dismay, that we were the only ship that was up for a repeat performance. All the others were new to the game. Old Mashpee must have engineered this; I became convinced that the full load of canisters on our aft deck that he had taken such care to leave untouched was one of the reasons for the repeat assignment, and that he must have known this all along. He was a really charming character, a man whom, as it said in the publicity for Erich von Stroheim, "you loved to hate."

And sure enough, there he was again, striding toward his

lectern in the briefing room with brisk little steps, to peer at the suckers with his mean little eyes before saying, "My name is Mashpee, and I represent your Comconvoy, Rear Admiral Sir Langston Furlow, Royal Navy, Retired."

This time nobody laughed, and I kept my face frozen in a mask of rapt attention. Even so, the gaze of his vicious little peepers swung over to me and he gave me the booby prize of a smile. I did not smile back, I just eyed him vacantly, like a goat. Whatever satisfaction he might get out of all this, I was not going to contribute to it gratuitously.

During the rest of the briefing, he tried once more to get a rise out of me. When discussing flag signals and messages by Aldis lamp to be exchanged between escort and rescue ships, he commented with a smile, "I'm sorry that experience has forced me to add a footnote to this matter of signals, which may seem a little baroque to you, gentlemen, but which I assure you is based on precedent. I must impress upon the Masters of all rescue vessels to refrain from four-letter words in signals exchanged with the escort." He pursed his lips in an expression of oddly arch prudery while waiting for the polite laughter to die down that was his reward for the little joke. Then, again, he gave me the benefit of a smile; this time I returned it with glee. He had not heard anything yet; I decided, then and there, that at the first opportunity I would, in my exchange of signals with the escort, really give him something to write home about to H.M.S. *Spartacus* in Glasgow.

There were only a few new items in his speech worthy of note. A new flag signal had been added to the list, TAKE OFF YOUR ICE; he warned us that winter was about to start up north and that the greatest danger for rescue ships on this route was ice. He proceeded to tell a warning story about a rescue ship in a previous convoy; its crew had not chipped the ice off her superstructure as instructed, and one morning she had turned turtle without warning. Then, another item: there would, this time, be a grain ship among the fuel-, munitions- and armament-carrying freighters. Mashpee was oddly scornful about that one grain ship, almost vicious, as if its presence insulted him for some mysterious reason. He referred to it several times, each time scathingly, as "a baker's cart," "the Hovis express," or "and don't let's forget our cake-carrier: *Fröken Bratt*." The third innovation was an omission: I was not given a liaison officer this trip. He did not make a point of it, but I stood out as the sole exception; maybe I was considered an expert now. I looked around for the doctor and spotted him in a corner of the briefing room, watching Mashpee with what seemed to be professional attention. This time, even I could see that the captain was laboring under stress. As the meeting broke up, I went to say hello to the doctor; he was courteous enough, but it was obvious that he did not remember me. I could not blame him, he must have seen at least a thousand men since.

4

As it turned out, I discovered that Mashpee labored under a great deal more stress than even I, familiar with the hell that was his bailiwick, had presumed. Later that same day, I ran into him in a pub on the harbor called The Crown and Anchor, which was almost entirely taken over by naval personnel. A few hardy taciturn natives insisted on playing darts in the corner, although they had so little space that they virtually had to take the darts in their mouths and spit them at the target. In this mashing bunch of sweaty males, all in various stages of intoxication, I suddenly came face to face with Mashpee, closer than I had ever come. The elbowing crowd squashed us together at the counter, which I had finally managed to reach, clutching the zinc like a raft. I had ordered my bitter, tried to get at my wallet, dug my elbow into somebody's stomach who, as a result, gave a ringing belch in my ear. As I turned to apologize, I found myself nose to nose with my favorite Englishman. He sniggered foolishly, emitting a powerful stench of whiskey; his prim little mouth was slack with inebriation, his eyes so bleary and unfocused that I suspected he was held upright only by the pressure of the crowd around him. He chirped, swaying limply as he was jostled, "Well, well, well, look who's heah! Our gallant ally. Cheers." He was so drunk that he did not even notice he had nothing in his hand. His clumsy gesture of drinking was aborted by somebody ramming him in the back, but he did not seem to mind. He tried again to focus his mean little eyes on me, and when he had difficulty doing so, he made a jocular screwing gesture in front of his nose which, by extrasensory perception, I understood to represent the adjusting of binoculars.

"Do you know what 'gallant allies' is in basic English?" he asked. He did not wait for my reaction, but answered, "Bloody foreigners! Ha! Ha! Ha! Cheers, old fruit."

By then he had delighted me long enough, but I had to finish my bitter standing there at the counter, for to try to carry it into that crowd was foolhardy. The place seemed to become more of a bedlam by the minute, I began to feel as if I were caught in a crush in the hold of a cattle ship.

"Shall I tell you something?" he asked and again produced one of those personable belches. " 'Scuse me. I am delighted you're going to be in on this next convoy, good Captain. Delighted. And shall I tell you why?"

I did not encourage him. If ever I had been a symbol, it was at that moment.

"Because you are a nice, fat, succulent, broad-beamed Dutchman." He smiled good-naturedly. "Not my definition, old thing. That's what Baedeker calls you: broad-beamed Dutchmen. Good old Baedeker: smack on the nose. For, let's face it, old cock. Your arse is as vast as your pretension. Have one on me."

I said, "No, thanks."

He frowned, tried to work that one out, but decided to let it pass, and continued, "So, if any bait is going to bring the bugger out, baby, it is thee!" He brought up a hand that did not belong to him and tried to put it on my shoulder, but the owner thwarted his effort. He tried to look around, muttering, " 'Scuse me," but he was buffeted and thrown against the bar like a bumboat against a quay. "You asked me who I mean," he continued, with amazing continuity, considering his condition. "I cannot tell you, as it's top secret, but I can tell you this: she is big. She is bad. And her name starts with a T and ends with a Z. Oh, what the hell are we fucking around for, old fruit? Have one on me."

I knew at once what he meant, and I began to pay attention to what he was saying. Not so much because he was flagrantly disregarding security regulations, as the Germans could be supposed to be conversant with the location of their own capital ships, but because I did not like the idea of being considered a fat succulent bait for what was, without doubt, the major threat to the Arctic convoys. The battleship *Tirpitz*, of a class with the *Bismarck*, was, as everyone knew, stationed in Alta Fjord in northern Norway. The nightmare of every sailor on the Murmansk run was that, sooner or later, the monster would emerge from its cave to start chopping up some convoy. All one could do in the face of that eventuality was to pray, charitably, that it would be somebody else's convoy. The idea that I should be the bait meant to coax the Minotaur out of his hiding place sounded like the invention of a nasty drunk; but in vino veritas. I wanted to hear a little more about this.

"Fancy that," I ventured.

But he was not listening; again his bleary eyes tried to focus on me. He was so drunk that, to all practical purposes, he was blind as well as deaf; but, whatever the booze might have done to his senses, it had left his vindictive mind unimpaired. "You don't rahally think that the Admiralty is concentrating all those capital ships around you just for your bloody protection, do you now, old thing?" he asked. " 'Sfar as the war effort goes, those bloody convoys to Murmansk are just a fart—'scuse me—farth—no, damn it: *farce.* All we are is a political sop to the bloody Russians. Who the hell wants to help the Bolshies? Be serious. Come on. Be serious."

I said, "I'm serious."

He got that one. "Good," he said. "And you'd better be, old fruit. I don't care a hoot about you and grain ships, but those other poor buggers, carrying the explosives—I think it's a damn shame, to use them as a bait. And I bloody well hate to be the cheese in the trap meself." It had been an extraordinarily coherent and sustained discourse for a man who wouldn't have stood there if the crowd hadn't kept him upright. He again made a gesture of lifting his nonexistent glass when, suddenly, it seemed to penetrate to him that this had been pretty loose talk for a staff officer. He was as nutty as a fruitcake, but a streak of sanity must have penetrated the euphoria in which he gamboled, weightless, in a golden haze. "Confidenshully, ol' boy," he said, suddenly slurring his speech again. "Great confidence . . . shipmates and all that. Have one on me."

A new thought occurred to me. He overacted; all non-essential elements in his monologue had been carefully slurred, but when it came to the business part of it, he had been as clear as a bell. He wasn't all that drunk, but just amusing himself in his sadistic fashion; there was no denying that his hint at the convoys being bait in a trap to catch the *Tirpitz* frightened the pants off me. So I handed him my empty glass, said, "Ta-ta, old fruit. See you at sea," and began to fight my way to the door.

It took a veritable boxing match to break out of The Crown and Anchor and tumble out into the fresh air. Strolling along the waterfront, I tried to sort out what exactly was the sinister portent of the poisonous suggestion he had so artfully planted in my brain until right now I felt like going off the deep end, screaming. The whole set-up made eminent sense, considering the mentality of the parties involved. We all knew that the convoys to Russia were political; the trickle of ships that managed to get through delivered so comparatively little in the way of war material that they could not be considered anything else but a token. This must have irked the Admiralty, as Mashpee's own fury at having to escort a symbolic grain ship demonstrated. They had hit upon a scheme that would make the Murmansk convoys and the vast display of naval power they demanded part of a sensible and worthwhile operation. The *Tirpitz* had lain idle in her lair for many months, despite repeated efforts to smoke her out. Now the Admiralty, with a cynicism worthy of the realistic profession of warfare, had hit upon the idea of coaxing her out. If you had to escort convoys to Murmansk, and if you had to seek out, engage and destroy the *Tirpitz*, the two operations could be profitably combined by using the convoys as bait in a trap. It was a logical, promising set-up, satisfying to naval theorists, unnerving only to the men who sailed the convoys. I had been wondering, after our previous rendez-

vous off Langanes, what had been the point of the tremendous display of capital ships that had proceeded to
disappear beyond the horizon in different directions. We
had received precious little protection from our "shadowing force," at least as far as I had been able to see. Now I
understood the purpose of those two fleets: they were the
prongs of the trap, poised to be sprung. The moment the
Tirpitz emerged from Alta Fjord, irresistibly attracted by
the succulent bait of the under-escorted convoy, the shadowing force would converge and pounce. It was very interesting, very enlightening and utterly terrifying.

5

At first, my growing panic showed itself in disguise. I
worried about Captain Mashpee's blurting out top-secret
information in a pub. I wondered if I should seek out the
doctor and tell him what was going on; obviously the man
was no longer fit to remain in the key position he occupied.
It did not occur to me until it was too late that I was
following the classical pattern of all thoroughly terrified
people: if the truth frightens you, silence the voice that
tells it. It occurred to me only when I was already sitting in
the waiting room of Dr. Hawthorne, leafing through a back
number of *The Tatler* in the company of three Petty Officers, all of whom looked pictures of health and sanity.

When he opened the door of his consulting room to let
someone out, he spotted me and gave a demonstration of
democracy by calling me in ahead of the three Petty
Officers. They did not seem to mind; they obviously had
been in the Navy long enough to take this for granted. I
was surprised to find that he remembered me. If he did not,

he was a master of his trade indeed, for he completely convinced me that, ever since our short conversation a month or so ago, there had not been a day in which he had not thought of me, despite the fact that he had patently not recognized me that morning after the briefing. When I told him I was worried about Captain Mashpee, he said, "Sit down, Captain," took a card out of a filing system and unscrewed a gold-capped fountain pen. Then he asked for my name, nationality, service, rank, number, age, marital status, past illnesses, present trouble.

I had adjusted myself to this game of ping-pong, it did not register straight away that to the last question he expected a long answer. I said, "Well, as I told you, I would like to talk about Captain Mashpee. I met him in a bar . . ."

To my discomfort, he smiled indulgently, and asked, "Apart from that, what can I do for you?"

I answered, "Well—er—I would like a prescription for sleeping pills."

"Why?"

"Because I can't sleep."

"Why not?"

I did not know what to answer to that one, so I answered, "Oh, the usual reasons."

He looked at me musingly for a moment, then he said, "Undress, Captain."

I wondered why that was necessary, but I obeyed; after I had stripped, he gave me a brisk once-over. His fingers, tapping, pinching and prodding, were hard and cold, his ear as he listened on my chest was soft and warm. I looked down on his skull and smelled that he used the same hair lotion as the Second. He went on prodding, pinching and hammering under my knees for a while, writing down his findings as he went along, then he said, "You may get dressed."

While I dressed, he sat writing. I was tying my shoelaces when he put down his pen, leaned back in his chair, gave me another of those musing looks and said, "All right. Let's start at the beginning. Why are you in this war?"

"Because it happens to be there," I said. "Would you know of any other reason?"

He gave no sign of impatience at my truculence. I did not understand it myself; I had come here seeking help and now that he was about to give it to me, or at least courteously trying to find out what my problem might be, I felt overcome by a juvenile urge to sabotage my own diagnosis.

"I mean, were you drafted, did you happen to be on board a Merchant Navy vessel when war broke out, or did you volunteer?"

"I suppose you might say I volunteered," I answered, determined to play my part responsibly. I told him about the choice I had faced just before the collapse of Holland, when the crew of my ghost vessel was about to be evacuated to England. I could have faded out then, but I had not.

"Why didn't you?"

I knew why I hadn't—because I had been less afraid of the war than I had been of Sophie—but I didn't tell him that. Instead, I told him that I had felt badly about leaving my comrades. It did not sound convincing to me, and I suspected that it did not sound convincing to him either. But if it didn't, he gave no sign of it. "You are not Jewish, by any chance?" he asked.

I said I was not, but I told him I had a Jewish fiancée; I don't know why, maybe to give him at least part of the truth, as a gesture. He made me uncomfortable by smiling, as if I had given him all of it.

"Is she still?"

"Still what?"

"Your fiancée?"

"I suppose so."

"You intend to marry her when this war is over, provided you're both still available?"

"I suppose so."

"Is she all right?"

"How do you mean?"

"Well, a great number of Jews have been deported by the Germans as so-called forced labor for the eastern territories. Intelligence seems to indicate that some monstrous extermination program is in progress. Surely you've heard of that?"

I said I had, but that I would have to know a few more facts before I personally could come to such a conclusion. I had not heard from my fiancée for some time, at least not directly. I did not tell him about her parents' letter. It did not seem relevant.

Then he asked, "When you take part in physical violence against the enemy, do you feel that relates to your fiancée?"

"Pardon?"

"Do you feel you have a personal stake in this war? Such as, for instance, restraining the murderous lunatics who drag innocent girls off to concentration camps for mass extermination by various means, such as gas, or machine-gun fire on the edge of graves they have had to dig themselves . . ."

"No, sir, I don't!" I said irritably. I had had enough of this, it was not at all why I had come. "I don't want to rush things," I added, "but I would like to remind you that I came to you simply for a prescription for sleeping pills."

"I know," he said pleasantly. "That's why I'm trying to find out why you aren't sleeping. It would be of more help to you, and in the interests of the war effort, if we could determine what keeps you awake rather than push you under forcibly with pills."

"Be that as it may," I replied, uncooperatively, "I prefer

to be pushed under. I suppose I'll be in need of extensive psychiatric treatment once the war is over, like most of us on the Murmansk run, but for the time being . . ."

"All right," he said, "let's cut a few corners. Who was she, what happened, when and where?"

I just looked at him with my mouth open.

"Come on," he said. "I'm a doctor, not a moralist. The state you are in won't be cured by sleeping pills. Out with it. Who was she?"

I asked, "Which one?" jocularly, but he did not buy it.

"The last one," he said. "The one who sent you here."

A nasty, farfetched thought crossed my mind. "You don't mean to say that she's given me a disease, do you?"

He looked at me as blandly as before, but I seemed to discern a flicker of disapproval in his courteous eyes. "Of course she has," he said lightly, "if you call love by its proper name."

"Pardon?"

"And by love I don't mean just a physical infatuation, although a strong physical desire, especially in its initial virulent stage, will impair the sense of proportion, and consequently the sense of humor. I mean the whole complex, the daydreams of settling in a congenial community, starting a family, going about the normal business of living in a land at peace, which, after all, is our normal habitat. War is a bloody, vicious business at any time, even when clearly justified, as this one is. But although you may be involved in this war with a sense of total justification, as a dirty job that has to be done, you still cannot do that job as a daily commuter from an intimate, tender home life in the suburbs of peace to the Arctic convoys. Am I being too obscure?"

He was not. It was unnerving to hear a trained professional psychiatrist use the same image in connection with

my affliction that the second engineer had used in connection with the boy Tyler. What made it even more
disturbing was that the girl who had haunted the boy
and the girl who haunted me were the same person. I
suddenly felt the urge to confess it all, to tell the man
behind the desk the whole sordid story. But the realization
that I would have to go all the way back to Sophie in order
to have it make sense decided me against it. I would like a
long session with a father confessor sometime, but not
today; I had a ship to sail, all I wanted him to do was to take
my fear away. I had been afraid before, but not the way I
was now, after what Mashpee had told me. I now felt a
clammy, paralyzing terror creep over me whenever I
thought of sailing with another convoy on the Murmansk
run, the day after tomorrow.

"I'm afraid that all this takes us too far afield, Doctor,"
I said. "There is no time for the kind of job you and I
would have to do if we really wanted to cope with this
thing from its roots up. I am not entirely ignorant of the
process of psychotherapy and I don't think there is time
even for a superficial job. Considering I have to see twenty-
two men and a seven-hundred-ton ship through purgatory
during the next few weeks, we had better resort to chem-
ical means. I would really appreciate it if you would let
me have a prescription for those sleeping pills. I'm sure they
will make all the difference."

"When are you due to sail?"

"The day after tomorrow."

He nodded musingly, then he said, "Frankly, Captain, I
would advise you to apply for sick leave."

It came so unexpectedly that it took some time before I
managed to say, "On what grounds? Being in love?"

It was a lame joke, but, to my surprise, he took it seriously. "Not only on your being in love," he answered.

"There are other elements which, for the sake of expediency, I'll bundle together under the heading of 'excessive stress,' aggravated by your emotional involvement. If you like, I'll file the application for you. Today."

"But, Doctor," I protested, "You can't be serious. I—"

For the first time he interrupted me. "Do you want to sail your ship into what you call that purgatory?" he asked. "I mean, do you actually want it, or do you just feel that it is your duty?"

"Well, I don't know about duty," I said, "but to take a whole ship, complete with crew, out of circulation just because her captain has to be cured of sleeplessness . . . "

"Don't agonize over it," he said, rising. "Leave the thinking about duty and cowardice and that kind of thing to me, and accept my decision. It is my job to see that, as far as my department is concerned, I can be reasonably sure that our ships have a fair chance of arriving at their destinations. Come back tomorrow at two fifteen."

"You'll have your answer to my application that quickly?" I asked, incredulous.

"Oh, yes. I'm in daily Telex communication with *Spartacus*, and the man in control of these things and I are old friends. We have batted on this wicket before."

He ushered me to the door, opened it and, as I hesitated in the doorway, he said in a hushed voice, "Take it easy, now. Put the whole thing out of your mind. Tell you what, sit down somewhere where you'll be undisturbed and write the girl a letter in which you describe the sexual act, in detail. It may sound strange to you, but it will do you a power of good—and her too, eventually." Then he called loudly, "Next, please."

As I went shamefacedly through the waiting room, I saw a fat Petty Officer rise from among the covey that sat there flicking the pages of the old *Tatlers* and *Queens*.

I wondered, as I found my way to the front door to the street, what the sexual act would look like once he sat down to describe it, and came to the disconcerting conclusion that the difference would be immaterial.

As I stepped out into the street, I spotted Porks. He was walking along somberly, hands behind his back, his cap on the back of his head. I hoped he would not see me, but he did.

"Skipper!" he called, in a voice that startled the seagulls. I stood still.

He caught up with me and asked, "Where did you come from?"

Dr. Hawthorne seemed to have taken my wits away, for instead of giving him an intelligent lie, I mumbled about a doctor and sleeping pills; he nearly gave me heart failure when he said, "Good! I'll go in there myself and have him take a look at my stomach. I lie awake every night howling with heartburn, and those powders don't seem to work any more."

He turned toward the doorway; I stopped him and said hastily, "He's not an ordinary doctor! He's a psychiatrist." It had been a stupid thing to say; now it was too late.

"A what?" he asked.

I began to explain, edging him away from the doorway, but he was a stubborn Dutchman. "If you could get sleeping pills out of him," he said, "I can get a stronger stomach powder. The chemist said—"

I continued to explain what a psychiatrist was, and in doing so gave myself away.

"You mean that guy can cure the funk?" he asked.

I said, "Let me buy you a drink."

We fought our way into The Crown and Anchor and had our drink at the same bar where it had all started an hour or so earlier, when Mashpee had revealed that all we were, with our loves and our hopes and the ships we sailed, was the bait in a trap set for the *Tirpitz*. Porks went on questioning me about this doctor; when in the end he realized he was getting nowhere, he started to tell me the story of his stomach, at the top of his voice to drown out the bellows and the braying laughter of our fellow bait. I suddenly could not stand any more of it. I yelled into his ear that I would see him for supper, tried to slap his shoulder, which was aborted by someone ducking under my arm to get at the bar, then I beat my way back through the crowd to the cold, clear autumn day outside.

I walked through that day for hours, along the narrow streets of Kirkwall, along the waterfront, onto the commons beyond, daydreaming about what I would do with that sick leave should I ever get it. Realistically, I knew what the answer to the doctor's application would be. Rescue-ship captains do not grow on trees; I was sure that H.M.S. *Spartacus* would be less impressed with the seriousness of my affliction than he had been. But there I was, standing in the sun on the moors, eyes closed, on my way back to Halifax, taking the train to Kinora, a bus to her village, booking a room in a hotel, writing her a note saying I had arrived, and if she did not answer, I would wait in the street outside her house until she came out to do her shopping. The sun was warm on my face, and I was suddenly full of hope, and then I remembered that I had been standing exactly like this, eyes closed, warming my face in the early sun, when the planes came out of it that killed him.

I don't know why, but at that moment I realized that I would never take that leave even if I got it. I could not let the others face the music alone, and the idea that my ship would sail under command of the mate turned the whole thing into nonsense. I should be back on board, right now, getting the ship ready for the new voyage. It was the moment that my alter ego took over once more—un-sentimental, quick-witted, leaving the lover to dream on the moors.

The rest of that day, until deep into the night, I worked like a beaver and never gave her or the doctor another thought. There were a thousand practical things that de-manded my attention: bunkering, taking on stores, collect-ing the Arctic gear for everyone on board, writing a report to Mr. Kwel; around midnight I fell asleep at the chart table while trying to formulate a reply to H.M.S. *Spartacus* on the matter of that naughty signal which would be with-ering, witty and final. I woke up, half an hour or so later, with a cramp in my neck and dragged myself to bed with-out really waking up in the process.

6

———————

The next morning early, Cook and the dog came to wake me with tea and the latest report on drunks returned and outstanding; then the mate came in to say that half of the Arctic gear we had collected the day before was incom-plete, and that there was an officer to see me about the depth-throwing gear. The officer turned out to be a somber Scot from the depot who wanted the obstructions removed from the catapults at once. We got into a long argument as to whose property they were and who had final jurisdic-tion; he maintained, dourly at first but with gradually in-creasing rr's, that whether they were fitted on a chartered vessel or on the back of a whale, they remained the property of the Royal Navy and under the jurisdiction of the Armed Guard responsible for their operation. I maintained that I, the Master of the vessel on which they were mounted, had

the last word, as any lawyer would be glad to prove to
him for a nominal fee. He ended, nostrils flaring like a
horse's, by threatening me with arrest and court-martial;
when I reacted to that suggestion with delight, as it would
mean that I would be sojourning in a snug, warm prison
instead of having my balls frozen off on the Murmansk
run, he left, his brow black as thunder, leaving me under
the terrible threat that he would write it all down in a
report and that I would not fail to hear from H.M.S.
Spartacus.

What with one thing and another, I managed to forget
about the doctor until, at the stroke of two, I sat down in
his waiting room and picked up the *Tatler* of the previous
May. He called me in on the dot. I thought I noticed a
difference in the way he received me; I could not make out
what it was. He said, "Sit down, Commodore." The "Commodore" was new. I suspected this meant what I had expected anyhow. Even so, it hit me hard.

He did not sit down behind his desk this time. He went to
the window and looked out at the harbor and the ships, his
hands behind his back. Then he said, with his back to me,
"Human nature is a funny thing. Occasionally, in my profession, one is tempted to think that men run in molds, but
time and again one is brought up short and corrected."

"Did you manage to get that leave for me?" I asked.

He turned around and looked at me. I knew now what
the difference was; whereas yesterday he had looked at me
with professional interest, he now looked at me as at a
human being. "No," he said. "It has been refused. I'm
sorry."

Even a moment ago, when I first suspected it, I had not
foreseen that the confirmation would affect me so deeply.
I felt tears well into my eyes.

"It wasn't so much the fact that they turned it down that

surprised me," he continued, "but the reason why."

"They didn't believe I was in love, I suppose?" I said. My grin must have been quite a sight, for now tears were running down my cheeks. It completely unnerved me, I had not cried since I was a child.

"The reason why they refused it was, they said, that they cannot do without you, Commodore. They said you were the best rescue captain around, and that your not sailing with the next convoy might result in an excessive loss of human lives."

I felt my perplexity turn into anger. He was insulting my intelligence. I said, "Listen, Doc, I came to see you because I thought you were a psychiatrist. If you think you can take me in with that kind of patter, you are not a psychiatrist but a horse's ass, and sorry if I offended you." I reached for my cap.

When I was ready to go, he still stood looking at me with Expression Number Five, "compassion." Then he said, "I suspected this would be your reaction, so I decided to show you their signal. But as it is confidential, you must give me your solemn promise not to divulge a word of it to anyone, or I'll be in trouble."

"What signal?" I asked, stupidly; when he turned to the filing cabinet behind his desk, I surreptitiously wiped my eyes with my sleeve.

He pulled out a drawer, whisked through a file and brought out a Telex sheet. Something was attached to it with a paper clip that he took off before handing me the sheet. It was the card he had been writing on the day before.

"Here you are," he said.

It was a long signal in capital letters, hard to read, as it was made up of Telex abbreviations. It bore the code letters of H.M.S. *Spartacus*, was addressed RECOM TO MEDS-

CAP, marked PRIVATE AND CONFIDENTIAL, and headed, DEAR HAWTH. Its contents turned out to be surprisingly chatty, a leisurely note from one club member to another. I understood from it that, when my application was turned down, the sender had gone to see "the Old Man" himself in a last attempt to get the decision reversed. The Old Man had been "quite human for once" and explained at length how much depended on the initiative and efficiency of the rescue ships; if they "failed to be commanded by officers of outstanding skill, intelligence and emotional maturity" a considerable increase in the loss of life might result. Somebody had told the Old Man that I was "the most outstanding among the Masters of the rescue fleet"; the sender had been unable to find out exactly what I had done to elicit such praise from "that unusual direction"; but I must have done pretty well to warrant it, as Dear Hawth would appreciate. The signal ended with the sender expressing his regret that this time he had been unable to help: the Dutch Commodore would have to sail with the next convoy to Murmansk, for better or for worse, so "let's all hope he will stand up."

I could not believe my eyes. I did not feel pleased, or amazed, I felt nothing but sheer disbelief. I read the whole thing again; when I came to the end of it, I believed it less than before. I looked at the doctor. He stood leaning against the filing cabinet, observing me.

"Well, will that do for a compliment?"

"But this is nonsense! I didn't do anything special during that trip; the other rescue ships did exactly the same!"

He smiled. "I am sure they did," he said. "May I have that back, please?"

I handed him the sheet; he grinned mischievously and said, "Sorry I can't let you keep this to send to that girl. Beg your pardon, I forgot: you are not in love."

I sniggered idiotically.

He put the sheet back in the file after clipping my card to it. "Well," he said, shutting the drawer, "you'd better be off now. I have other people waiting. Send me a post-card when you get to Murmansk to tell me how you feel."

I said, "God, Doc—thank you, I . . . "

He said, "Me? Why me? I haven't done a thing. I only wish this Silent Service of ours would open its bloody mouth a little more often like this. It would make a big difference in the number of my patients."

I said, "You're telling *me!*"

He opened the door and held out his hand. "Good luck, Commodore," he said. "It's been a pleasure meeting you. Come back when you can. Next, please!"

Part of me felt giddily elated, but the message to Dear Hawth could not quite overcome the ingrained suspicion of the experienced lone wolf. Who could have sold the Old Man this cock-and-bull story? Only one person: Mashpee. If anyone were expected to report on the work of the individual rescue ships, it was he. It seemed baroque indeed that he should have singled me out for such extravagant praise; maybe his conscience had bugged him, and this had been his way of easing it. Whatever his reason, he had done me one hell of a service. For, cynically incredulous as part of me might remain toward the whole thing, it had worked a miracle: the sick, clammy fear that had clutched me ever since Mashpee had hinted at the *Tirpitz* set-up had gone. I could breathe again, relax, live again without a cold, malignant spot at the pit of my stomach. Whatever the psychological malaise had been with which I had been afflicted, I was cured.

7

The cure was almost worse than the disease. My first re-action was to go to The Crown and Anchor to see if Mashpee was there and, if so, to stand him a drink and tell him that he should go and see his doctor sometime. I grimly battled my way to the bar, only to find that he wasn't there; but I decided that once I had got this far I might as well have a double Scotch and wait awhile. He might turn up; most people did, sooner or later. Maybe I should not send him to the doctor, but to the Old Man, whoever that was; he obviously didn't need to describe the sexual act in detail so much as he needed the Old Man to tell him, in person, that he was one hell of a little Comescort, the best Comescort of the Home Fleet, and that if he were to stop needling foreign tugboat captains an excessive loss of human life might result. He took a long time turning up; after a series of solitary whiskeys I could no longer hold down my exultation at being miraculously cured, so I stood the two bodies closest to me a drink. In that thrashing pig sty, anybody standing anyone else a drink was drunk, but the candor of my explanation must have convinced whoever they were that I wasn't, for they finally accepted and lifted their glasses to toast me, with the foreseeable result that their drinks ended up in my face. But hell, I didn't mind, I thought it was funny; and not just vacuous, huh-huh funny, but the expression of a deep, sincere feeling of friendship and love. They were wonderful people, wonderful to be alive with, and I loved them to the point where I wouldn't mind laying down my life for them. No kidding: if someone were to come into this pub with a burp gun and say, "One of you has to be shot," I would slam the bar and shout, "Take me!"

I did, and somebody began trying to take me away. It made me angry, because this was important. I had suddenly discovered the essence of Christianity: no committee, no sale of one's goddam conscience to a church or somebody in the sky with a beard, no: Take me! Slam! That's what Jesus had said, and I said it again, for all the world to hear: Take me! Slam! This time, I missed the bar and hit something else instead, and suddenly I found myself thrashing, gasping, in a mass of flesh heaving all around me. As I was dragged out backward, I gave them a last message: we must break with that idiotic tradition of the Silent Service, and open our traps once in a while, like H.M.S. *Spartacus*. Now let me tell you what H.M.S. *Spartacus* said. . . .

Somebody covered my mouth with his hand and I felt arms around me. But I went on talking despite the hand as I was being carried out, for this was important, they should not miss this last message, there was no point in silencing me before I had told them what H.M.S. *Spartacus* had said.

How I got on board and onto my bunk, I do not know. I seem to remember somebody saying "wheelbarrow," but I don't think it came to that, for I remember using my legs—slow, graceful movements, like skating. I remember Sparks and the cook bending over me in my bunk; they looked harassed and I tried to console them, for I loved them, they were wonderful people. As they started tickling me, I got angry despite my shrieks of laughter, and I remember yelling, "Stop that!" several times; they must have been undressing me. But my anger was not directed against them personally; I remember saying, "You lucky buggers," fondly, several times, and as they did not seem to realize how lucky they were, I started to tell them what H.M.S. *Spartacus* had said about their Commodore. Somebody must have put a hand on my face again, this time over my eyes, for suddenly it was dark; but I still could speak, so I went on telling them what H.M.S. *Spartacus* had said about me, until it penetrated to me that there was nobody left to listen; it had not been a hand over my eyes, somebody had turned out the light. I felt hurt and lonely; nobody cared a damn about me, nobody. There I lay, blabbing my head off, and the only one listening to me was old Bokke Loppersum's ghost. I whimpered with loneliness, calling feebly for Cook and a chaplain. I wanted tea, and prayers. The urge to pray became so strong that I got out of my bunk to kneel. The ship collapsed on top of me as I did so; when I came to, I saw the ceiling. I folded my hands with deep sincerity; then Sparks' face floated over me and I heard his voice say, with many echoes, "Now are you going to stay in your bunk or do I have to tie you down?"

I said, "Pooh," for it seemed the only word capable of expressing what I thought of him. It said everything, both "Dear old friend" and "What do you mean, you jerk, addressing me like that?" When he turned away, the idea of being left alone again terrified me. I called, "Sparks!"

He came back and said, still with echoes, "Now what do you want?"

I said, "If you look at me like that, I'm not going to tell you." At least, that's what I wanted to say, but it came out in one piece.

He said, "What?"

I would never be able to tell him, it was too complicated, so I said, "Goodbye, Sparks, dear."

He said, "Jesus Christ, how do you like that? He still asks for beer!"

I said, "No, no! I said, 'Goodbye, dear!' " but he answered, "You're not going to get it. I'd be run in for murder."

I said, "*Dear!* You goddam ass! Dear!"

But he said, his cheek turned toward me, "You'll have to take her out yourself, that's all."

I said, "Are you out of your mind? I may be drunk, but I am still the captain of this ship! You may think it isn't much to be the captain of a muck-spreader like this, but let me give you the name of someone who knows better: the Old Man. You'll wonder who the Old Man is; well, I can't tell you, for I can't break Navy security. But this much I can tell you: his voice is the voice of H.M.S. *Spartacus.*" The name was so beautiful that I said it again, slowly, lovingly, "*Spartacus.* Dear, dear *Spartacus.*"

"Oh, I wouldn't worry," Sparks said, still looking away. "Once you're out in the open, it's easy. You just follow the band."

It made me angry. I asked, "Band? What band? And turn your proboscis toward me, dear."

He did turn around. "Would you believe it?" he said. "He's still asking for beer." Then the light went out again.

I knew that I could not turn it on again myself, ever. I was too weak, too little, too tired; I would have to lie all alone in the darkness, without as much as a photograph to keep me company. Then, as the tears of self-pity started to run down my cheeks, I remembered the boy Tyler, and how lonely he had been. I did not want to think about him; there was no other way out than sleep.

8

When I woke up, we were at sea. I woke up, hollow, weak at the knees, ill, yearning for a convalescent's comforts: a nurse to bring me a cup of weak tea with a biscuit, budding trees outside the window, sparrows on the window-sill. Then it registered, with a vascular contraction: *we were at sea!*

I jumped out of my bunk, stumbled against the ward-robe, the rug slid from under my feet and I landed on the floor. The door to the chartroom opened and the mate looked in; he looked pale and drawn and unshaven. I had forgotten we had been advised at the last briefing to grow a beard.

"Well, well," he said, "Master after God."

"What happened?" I asked. "Who took her out?"

"God," he said, and he went away again, slamming the door.

I became conscious of an acid smell, as in a radio hut after the transmitter has been working. I thought the mate had brought it with him and wondered, weakly, what he and Sparks had been transmitting; then I realized what it was. I looked down at my shirt and closed my eyes. It was the smell of whiskey and stomach acid.

I pulled myself up by the handle of the wardrobe door; it came off in my hand and I fell back. After a lot of effort, I managed to stand up, and I took my shirt off, leaning against the wall. There was a knock on the door and Cook came in with coffee. His conspiratorial smirk made me close my eyes again. He said, "Here you are, Cap. Nice cup of strong coffee. Coo, man, you weren't half—"

I said, "Would you do me the favor of going away, cuisinier?"

When he said, "Wha's dat?" I opened my eyes and bellowed, "GET OUT!"

I had still not regained complete control over my muscles, that scream had been much too loud, it made my throat ache. I decided to gargle, went to my bathroom, and for some reason God made me gargle with after-shave lotion. It brought the mate back, like a bull bursting into an arena. I asked, "What are you supposed to be? A cuckoo clock?" He went away again, hurt.

When I arrived on the bridge, I was dangerous. Feeling small and alone had made me loving, now I felt strong and nasty. When I saw the mate's unshaven cheeks and clinical eyes, I looked away and said, "You may go now. I'll take it from here."

"Why don't you go and have something to eat first?" he asked. "Once I go to bed, I'd like to stay there."

I visualized the messroom and its smells. "Tell Cook to bring me something on a tray on your way past the galley," I said. "You turn in."

He said, "Aye, aye," and went down the stairs.

I called after him, "By the way! Where are we?"

He answered, "Five miles northeast of the channel entrance. The speed is fifteen." Then he disappeared.

When I entered the wheelhouse, the helmsman looked away, shiftily; he had filled the closed-in space with the smell of his natural body oils. I went out again after checking our position and had my breakfast, or whatever it was, sitting on a folding stool in the open, with the tray on another stool in front of me. I thought I was hungry when I saw Cook, but I lost my appetite when I smelled the sausages. I was about to eat the bread when I thought I saw something squirm in it. After scrutinizing the slices closely, I realized it was my eyes. Wherever I looked, I saw squiggles in the center of my field of vision, like clusters of transparent little eels.

It took about an hour before I began to get a clear recollection of what had happened. First I remembered the doctor, then other episodes came back, like pieces of a jigsaw puzzle falling into place. When, at last, I had completed it, the feeling of being cured was still there, although I thought even less of the Telex message from *Spartacus* now than I had yesterday. I knew I had not excelled in any way during that last convoy, so that part of it was baloney; Mashpee must have singled me out for praise just to make sure they would include me on the next one. I watched *Intrepid* as she came wheeling past on her next orbit around the small convoy; I wondered what state he had been in when they got him on board after our encounter in The Crown and Anchor.

It was odd that it should have taken so long before I began to think about her. An instinctive sense of equilibrium must have prevented my doing so before. Everything else was under control again. When I did, the episode in Halifax seemed simple and complete in itself. Now I could write that note to go with his letters without tying myself into knots over it. I knew that, despite Dr. Hawthorne's diagnosis, I was not in love with her. I did not know the first thing about her; it had been merely a brief encounter of symbols: terrified convoy captain and grief-crazed young widow, thrown together in a moment of despair.

I wrote her that very night, and it took me about five minutes. *My dear Mary*, I wrote, *I tried to get hold of you while we were still in Halifax but I did not succeed. During the past weeks, I've tried several times to write to you, but owing to circumstances, I have been unable to find a moment to myself. We are about to rendezvous with an-*

other convoy and as this is the last chance to mail a letter,
I have decided not to keep you waiting any longer for a
word from me, however brief. I promise to write you a
long letter as soon as I possibly can; please do not jump
to any conclusions until you have heard from me again,
which may take some weeks. In the meantime, I am send-
ing you your husband's letters which you left with me.
Yours very sincerely, Martinus Harinxma.

I reread it only once, changed nothing, put it in an
envelope, sealed it and put it with the boy's letters. I made
a parcel of the lot, and put it in the briefcase with the
ship's papers.

I came across the photograph again by accident. It
dropped out of its secret hiding place underneath the
drawer as I pulled it out to get at my winter gear, the day
before rendezvous. I found I could look at it quite objectively now; and, quite objectively, she was an exciting
creature. But that was as far as it went; now I knew for
certain, if I had ever doubted it, that I was not in love.
That feeling had evaporated together with the other ones:
the terror, the fear of death, the small, cold spot in the pit
of my stomach of which I had been so miraculously cured.

I did not quite know what to do with the photograph.
I did not want to break open the package again, and I
doubted whether she would care to have it returned to
her. Until I could come to a decision, I would keep it with
the package and the ship's papers in the briefcase. That
briefcase was back in its emergency position, on the chart
table, by the door, where it could be grabbed in a hurry.
We were back in business.

At mealtimes, on our way to the rendezvous, the new
convoy was not mentioned directly, but it was foremost
in everybody's mind, as was obvious from the studious way
in which the subject was avoided. I tried to be as honest

with myself as I could and came to the conclusion that, of course, I was afraid; but it was a different fear from the dark, bottomless chasm of terror I had felt before, forever present underneath the surface of my consciousness. It was the normal fear of a man who knows that he has a good chance of getting killed in the next two weeks; the kind of fear we all had to put up with. The main thing was not to think about it, and certainly not to bother other people with it. The others obviously felt the same way.

This time, the main topic of our messroom conversation, apart from routine matters to do with the ship, was kangaroo planes. I must have heard that name hundreds of times on the way to Langanes. Sparks had picked up a rumor at the barber's in Kirkwall concerning a new German invention, a bomber that carried a little robot plane underneath its fuselage which it released at a safe distance from its target; the baby plane continued its way alone, without a pilot, to end with a Stuka-like dive, smack in the eye. It sounded like one of those rumors that occasionally captured the imagination of convoy crews; such as the "suction torpedoes" that fastened themselves to a ship under the waterline like leeches and exploded days later; or the "plague capsules," dropped from planes, that exterminated whole crews without a shot being fired; or the German demolition squads disguised as castaways, rescued at sea. The American name for these rumors was "pink elephants," the British called them, somewhat laboriously, "will-o-the-whiskeys," but Sparks was not to be shaken in his firm belief in the kangaroo planes. He said he had set out by taking them as a lark, but then he had met a man in the pub in Kirkwall who was absolutely sober and whose best friend had seen one with his own eyes. His story had been substantiated by an RAF officer at the bar, who had told them that the damn things had been known to the RAF

since last March, so what was everybody in the Merchant
Navy getting excited about, all of a sudden? Like any egg
or fish, it wouldn't bag you unless it had your name on it.
They sounded like nasty contraptions, but they did not
affect my serenity. Ever since leaving the doctor in Kirkwall, I had felt within me that same unassailable core of
calm certainty that had sustained and protected me during
the week before the first convoy. Once again, I felt utterly
confident we would scrape through; again I felt invulnerable, immortal.

The night before rendezvous, when the mystic shore of
Iceland lay on our port side once more, silhouetted against
the glow of the setting sun, I again made the rounds of the
ship to see if everyone was all right and to wish them luck.
I again noticed a change in each one of them after we had
talked for a few minutes; again I seemed to be able to
transfer some of my own serenity and confidence to them.
This time, Porks was the most affected. While we talked,
he sat on the edge of his bunk in his long drawers, his
dogtag glistening in the lamplight among the hair on his
chest; when I was about to leave, he shook my hand with
such fervor that I winced, and he said, "God speed, Skip,
and thanks for what you did for me in Kirkwall."

I said, "Don't be silly." I had no idea what he meant,
but I was ready to accept anything after that handshake.
I opened the door.

"I mean it," he insisted. "But for you, I don't know what
I'd have done. I'd have thrown myself overboard rather
than sail on another of these bloody awful trips if it hadn't
been for what you did."

"What is all this? Go to bed and stop talking nonsense."

"I know I promised him that I'd shut up about it, and
I have, but now that we are about to get another dose, I'll
be damned if I do. So: thanks, Skip. If you hadn't told him

what you thought of me, I . . . well, hell, it made all the difference in the world."

Something urged me to beat it, not to listen, to shut him out. But I asked, "Who are you talking about?"

"Well—that doctor!" he answered, with a beginning of tension. "Now, don't tell me you didn't! If *I* think this is worth breaking a solemn promise for, then the least you can do—"

"All right, Porks," I said, smiling. "I'm sorry. I meant every word of it, so let's leave it at that."

I turned away, I had to get out of there, but he gripped my arm and asked, worriedly, "He didn't put it on, did he? I *am* the best chief you ever sailed with; you *did* mean that?"

"I did," I said.

"You *did* say that you wouldn't sail this convoy without me? You did say that, didn't you?"

"Yes, Porks," I said. "I said that. And I meant it."

He grabbed my hand; I thought he was going to kiss it, but he just grabbed it and held it and said, "I don't care what happens to me, Skip, or to this bloody ship as long as you . . . well, think I'm all right."

I managed to give him a pat on his hand and to say, "Okay, Porks. Good night now. Keep on the ball."

"I will," he cried as I left, as from a window of a departing train, "I promise it won't happen again! I . . ."

It took all the strength and composure I could muster to get to the deck, out into the open, without showing that the stuffing had been knocked out of me. The shattering, gut-wrenching truth was simple. Porks, scared out of his wits like all of us, had gone back to that doctor "who cured the funk"; the doctor had cured it by pulling the same trick on him he had pulled on me: he had forged some exaggerated praise of him as an engineer, pretending he was quoting me, and by doing so had drugged him with euphoric self-confidence in a dose sufficiently large to get him back on board ship and out of the harbor, eager to be the bait in the trap for the *Tirpitz*. The learned doctor was a Judas goat, tricking sheep to their slaughter. His so-called Telex message from H.M.S. *Spartacus* must have been typed out by a rating, who had copied it from a standard form in which only the name and the rank of the sucker had to be filled in.

It was a clever device and virtually foolproof; the professional in me appreciated its ingenuity. I could vouch for its effectiveness too, for it had kept me on top of the world for six days. It might have kept me there for as long as a few minutes before my execution, if dumb, garrulous Porks hadn't blabbed it all out in a moment of bathos. The nonprofessional part of me, the part that felt and hoped and hurt and loved, was shattered. I had the feeling that I had come face to face with ultimate depravity. What an evil thing to do to a human being, a terrified, trusting fellow man under sentence of death, to send him to his death doped and deluded with a shabby lie, a huckster's trick. It seemed to desecrate the very essence of our humanity, and not just Porks' and mine, but his own. Yet it must be common practice; he must have used the same device so often during the past two years that he had become careless and slipped up in our case. Now he had forced me to join him in his dirty game; if I told Porks the truth, he would go to pieces. He felt feeble and insecure enough as it was, in the shadow of the late Chief Bout, his private Captain Loppersum.

When I found myself in the chartroom, alone, I felt like smashing something—hurting myself, getting blind drunk —before the full realization of the truth caught up with me. I sat down at the table, trying to keep that realization

at bay; I covered my face with my hands, and thought:
Keep calm, keep calm, keep calm. I felt the sudden com-
pulsion to rush to the others and tell them the whole story,
the whole sordid story of shabby deceit; I had to tell someone, confront the consequences myself by spelling them
out to someone else. If I had to keep this bottled up inside
me, I'd go crazy.

I took my hands off my face, opened my eyes and found
myself looking at the pen tray. Again I had the eerie feeling of my cheek being brushed by a ghost. I knew, as I sat
staring at that pen tray, a last moment of objectivity. I
was faced with a choice; I could either talk to the others
and destroy Porks' self-confidence, or I could challenge
that ghost by setting foot on the same road the boy had
gone. To destroy Porks at this point would mean to put
the ship in mortal danger; despite my request to Mr. Kwel,
no third engineer had arrived. And if Porks cracked up,
the whole crew would topple, like a row of dominoes,
starting with the engine room. I had no choice; I just
would have to try not to become too deeply involved with
that girl across the ocean, not to let my strength and independence be sapped by the suicidal tenderness she
inspired. I was forewarned, but not forearmed. In this battle there would be no arms, only inner strength; and maybe
even that was an illusion. Maybe all I could trust, once I
entered the magic circle of love, was my luck.

I sat there for a few minutes, contemplating this, calmly
and objectively. Then, suddenly, a terrible weariness, a
sickly fear, rose within me and threatened to overwhelm
me. I grabbed the pen and a sheet of paper and wrote,
*Darling, darling, I must write all this down at once or I'll
do something crazy. I just found out that a doctor in Kirkwall, a psychiatrist to whom I had gone for help* . . .

I wrote on, until my watch came up. When the lookout

of the watch had banged on the door, calling "Captain! Quarter of an hour!" I finished the sentence, put the sheets in an envelope, sealed it and numbered it 3. I went to hide it underneath the bottom drawer in my cabin; seeing the other two numbered envelopes, I felt that this would not do. I either had to back off, if I still could, or throw down the gauntlet to that ghost altogether. It was no use trying to fool myself with subtle variations in an effort to disguise the eerie similarity. I knew I could not back off any more, and I discovered I did not want to either. I felt on top of the world again, I had slain the dragon of fear with the rapture of love.

So I wrote an *M* on each of them, and changed the numbers into Roman ones. I put them back in their hiding place, put on two jerseys, duffel, balaklava, insulated boots, and mittens. I did not put on the silk gloves that went underneath the mittens; it would be a cold night, but not that cold yet.

CHAPTER NINE

I

We made Langanes in late afternoon. During the line-up
of the convoy as the early darkness fell, I noticed how
very much colder it was than last time. I remembered
standing on the bridge in just my duffel coat, watching
those ships maneuver within a hand's breadth of each
other's sterns; this time, I needed all my Arctic gear. The
four ships allotted to us for the coming voyage were three
large American freighters and one old-fashioned pot-
bellied Norse tramp called the *Fröken Bratt*, the grain
ship that Mashpee had taken as a personal insult. She must
be the slowest of the thirty-eight, which meant that the
convoy's speed was geared to hers; when the signal to proceed went up on the flagship, our speed assigned was thirteen knots.

That evening, with the convoy still plainly visible in the
young Arctic night, I heard over the secretive whisper and
hiss of the sea the drone of an approaching plane. I waited
for it to throw out a flare, but it did not do so. It was
Charlie, pinpointing our position, to be transmitted to the

first U-boat pack waiting on our course. I remembered
how last time the corporal had told amusing stories about
the comradely relationship between the escort and that
harbinger of death. This time, the high droning of the
invisible Condor gave me a sense of foreboding that drove
me inside. I was alarmed by the violence of my reaction,
but then, this time I had some idea of what we were heading for.

The next morning, as I was putting on my gear in the
chartroom for the forenoon watch, the first attack came.
I heard the muffled thuds of distant explosions; I could
not make out whether they were bombs or depth charges,
but their effect on me was unexpected. Suddenly, I was
overcome by such abject fear that my first impulse was to
go back into my cabin, bolt the door and hide. I did indeed go back into my cabin; I closed the communicating
door behind me and leaned against it, holding my breath,
listening. The muffled explosions had stopped, but in their
stead there was another noise, slowly getting closer, a soft
thumping, a panting sound. I had never heard that sound
before, and it terrified me; then the answer struck me:
kangaroo planes! This must be the sound the little robot
planes made when, after being released by the mother
plane, they chugged toward their target. I listened, eyes
closed, mouth open, all nerves and muscles taut; then I
had to breathe and realized what it had been: the sound
of my heartbeat in my throat.

The muffled explosions started up again, closer this
time; then a sudden blow slammed me in the back. I gave
an involuntary shout, jumped away. The door swung
open. It was the mate; the shoulders of his coat, his balaklava and his wispy beard were white with hoar frost.
"U-boats," he said, "they're throwing depth charges.
You'd better come up."

I nodded, speechless. I put on the rest of my gear and went to the bridge. The deck seemed slippery; I stumbled as I climbed the stairs. When I arrived on the bridge, I realized that the deck and the stairs had not been slippery. I had stumbled because of the weakness in the back of my knees that I always had in moments of danger, only this time it was worse than I had ever known it to be.

I looked around me. It was a blue, brilliantly clear day. The sun, barely over the horizon, was already blinding. The sea was smooth; I saw our shadow glide over the water, so clearly outlined that I could spot myself standing on the bridge. It was bitterly cold, a cold that seemed to numb my cheeks and that I felt on my eyeballs. My breath came in streams of steam which instantly turned into hoar frost on my shoulders and the front of my coat. Ever since I was a child, this kind of day had filled me with excitement, the elated expectancy of skating and sledding and hot sweet chocolate from booths on the ice. The sudden eruption of a volcano from the forward hatch of a tanker on our starboard side seemed an obscenity. It exploded with clouds of steam and a burst of flame, two patterns away from us; the air was so pure and the light so sharp that I could watch what happened in detail. I had never been able to get accustomed to the destruction of ships, after having been trained for a lifetime to save them; this time, as I watched, the satanic evil of it seemed to be more nakedly revealed than ever before. The escort circled around the convoy, throwing depth charges that set the *Isabel Kwel* trembling with their subterranean convulsions; then another ship went up, one pattern away to our port side, a freighter. She must have been carrying munitions, for she blew up with such violence that bodies and wreckage were still aloft after the ship had already disappeared in clouds of seething steam and black eruptions of oil and refuse. As I stood there, watching the spectacle with revulsion, yet unable to tear myself away, I was overcome by a violent hatred, the insane desire to rush to the port gun on the bridge and start firing, blindly, into the water at those hidden German swine, those surreptitious killer sharks, murdering ships in an orgy of destructive lunacy. Never before had I felt such potential violence boil up inside me; I remembered with a feeling of alarm how, last time, the mate had been the only one on board who responded to the attack by invisible machines with a brainless hatred toward a human enemy. Last time, I had come through unscathed; I had handled my ship and deployed my men with sober judgment, without becoming emotionally involved with the impersonal enemy; now I stood there, shaking with rage, in the mad hope that one day I'd get a chance to throw myself, fangs and claws bared, on one of those bastards, any filthy Hun, and garrote him, break his neck, gouge his eyes out, grind my boot in his slimy mouth. It took an act of will to break away from that hallucination; I turned my back on the odious scene of destruction and went to the wheelhouse.

Inside, it was warm and snug; when I shut the sliding door behind me, it was almost as if I were shutting out the war. Here, in the nerve center of the ship, where all her movements were controlled, I became part of her again and she part of me, an extension of my personality. I was still shaking, but sanity returned. I checked the compass, glanced at the barometer and the electric log, read the mate's last entry in the journal; then I settled in a corner from where I could not see the sea, only the sky. The moment I leaned back against the wall, I relaxed, the shaking subsided and the last vestige of rage ebbed away. But, almost immediately, unobtrusive, insidious fear flowed back in its stead. I couldn't understand it, the danger had passed, there had been no planes, no U-boat would bother about us. They were still throwing depth charges in the distance, but that was mere routine procedure. Yet, as I stood there in my corner, outwardly calm and relaxed, my inner composure was slowly undermined by a pointless, senseless fear spreading slowly through my body, like poison, numbing my nerve ends, pervading my muscles, emasculating my will, a creeping paralysis. It was a strange, deeply alarming sensation, for the fear had nothing to do with me, myself, my mind; it was as if the animal part of me, the instinctive, impersonal part, the six sevenths of the iceberg of my ego that lay below the waterline of my consciousness had taken over control of my body. I wanted to shake myself free, and tried to walk away from that corner, but my muscles refused to obey. I stood there petrified with wordless, incomprehensible fear, like a rabbit paralyzed to a point of self-anesthesia by the mere proximity of a staring, motionless snake. I felt all initiative, all desire to resist slowly drain out of me, and I began to be overcome by a drowsy indolence, a fatalistic resignation, a dreamy feeling of unreality. I seemed to withdraw, slowly, into a small, secret hiding place within myself, a warm, secure, utterly intimate contentment that grew into somnolence as I slowly drifted out of reach of reality and all its threats and horrors. I could be attacked, brutalized, tortured, shot; I knew that as long as I managed to stay hidden in that secret place inside myself, so snug and safe and yet with such feeling of space and solitude about it that it seemed as large as the world, I would feel no pain, no terror, no despair, nothing, just this inexpressible sense of well-being and remoteness, a fleece of cloud in a vast blue sky. I was gazing at the sky beyond the window when I saw, above the spray shield of the bridge, the mast and

stack of *Intrepid* glide by at high speed. The submarine
rumble of exploding depth charges made the ship shiver
and the door of the wheelhouse rattle as in an earthquake.
As I looked at the door I saw the helmsman glance at me
with what seemed to be a furtive look of alarm, and I
remembered that this was the corner where the boy used
to stand. He had stood here each time, frozen in what must
have been the same self-induced retreat from reality.

The realization broke the spell and gave me back the
control over my body. To be haunted by similarities between him and me was one thing; to bring them about
myself, another. I had no business experimenting with this
egocentric preoccupation, I was no lonely outsider driven
into this corner by ostracism and a feeling of uselessness, I
had the responsibility for a ship, a staff, a crew, all of whom
were dependent on my skill and my composure. I was, obviously, more afraid than I had been last time; but so, I
might assume, was everybody else on board. They would
all be watching me, as the helmsman was now watching
my reflection in the window, waiting for a sign, a hint, a
cue. At the first intimation that I was cracking up they
would get flustered; if I abdicated my responsibility by
retreating into that womb of schizophrenic remoteness,
they would panic. So I had better snap out of it and get
the hell out of that corner.

I yawned, stretched, harrumphed, spat, shook my head
as if I were waking up, said, "Boy! I'll fall asleep on my
feet next!", quasi-strolled to the door, like a drunk who
pretends he is sober, and stepped out on the bridge. The
mate was still there, looking like Santa Claus with his white
beard and chest; he badly needed defrosting. I said, "What
about turning in? The worst seems to be over, get some
rest while you can."

He mumbled something, then broke the ice by rubbing

his mouth with his mitten and said, "Aye, aye. Call me if you need me. I won't be asleep anyhow. Not this trip, I won't."

It was quite a confession to make for him, who always played his cards so close to his chest. "I know," I said, "we have all got the same problem. But going without sleep won't improve matters; get yourself some sleeping pills from the pharmacy. If you take one now, you won't be too groggy when your next watch comes up."

"Oh, I don't know," he said, casually, with a great show of superiority. "I haven't reached the point yet where I need drugs."

It was obvious that he could not help cutting off his nose to spite his face, so I said, "Okay, suit yourself," without animosity. I might dislike his personality and be thoroughly fed up with his unrelenting jealousy, but he was a damn good mate. Better to count my blessings than my curses.

The moment he was gone and I found myself alone on the bridge, that idiotic fear came back. It was not as obsessive as it had been when I was standing in the corner of the wheelhouse, but debilitating enough to make me clutch the rail, legs quaking, nervously scanning the sea for periscopes and the horizon for planes. The day was pure and serene, motionless gulls planed overhead, riding the thermals of heat from our stack. There was no longer any immediate danger; I could not understand why my body refused to respond to reason. The midwatch coffee Cook brought up, though tepid by the time it reached the bridge, seemed to ease the quaking of my legs somewhat. It was a damned nuisance, but I would have to learn to live with it.

Only when I thought of her, and fell to daydreaming about our future, did the fear recede.

2

When my watch was over, I went to the chartroom instead of the messroom, for I wanted to note all this down while it was still fresh in my mind.

Dearest, something happened today that seems to settle one thing, if we do indeed accept the possibility that I may be following the same road as he. He was, indeed, afraid; as a matter of fact, I think he was incapacitated by fear. So you were right. It should make me feel sorry for him, but I cannot help feeling selfishly relieved: I need not have agonized over that last conversation he and I had, the day before he was killed. It must have been part of the same pattern, an ultimate paroxysm of fear resulting in panic. Maybe it is still too soon to say, but right now I am convinced that his insistence that he be reported to his CO as a deserter, or a conscientious objector, or whatever it is called at that stage was not an ethical decision, but a blind, suicidal . . .

Cook came to say that the table was waiting. I told him I had a report to finish and asked for my meal to be brought up on a tray. I had intended to write to her only about my experience in the wheelhouse; now I found myself describing everything, beginning with the moment when I had heard those first explosions in the distance and been afraid of the pounding of my own heart. I described my thoughts, my feelings, the way I had evoked her image in my mind when I stood gazing at the gulls planing in the sky. As I sat there, trying to put into words how my thoughts of her had affected me, I suddenly felt prompted to take her photograph out of the briefcase and prop it up against the box of the chronometer; and never mind that he had done the same, it was the only logical spot. As I looked at her, the way she sat there, smiling, alluring, I remembered that night in Halifax, and was surprised to find I felt no physical desire for her. She seemed to conjure up something else, something gentle, tender, infinitely comforting, a glimpse of the future, a hope that grew into certainty. Of course we would meet again, of course we were destined to spend a lot of time together, maybe the rest of our lives; I did not consider the possibility that I might not make the end of the war; the photograph seemed to radiate confidence and reassurance. She was my fixed point in space, by which I could lever myself out of all doubt and despair and fear; she represented all that life stood for, embodied all my secret dreams; I discovered that, despite my intellectual snobbery, my secret dreams had been summed up by the lyrics to many a waltz: a cottage with roses, a little place for two, a fireplace, a dog, laundry on the line, the thin, high cries of a newborn baby.

I wrote it all down. I told her what she personified to me, what gentle joy, what simple decency and kindness, what humanity and compassion she radiated in this hell of man's damnation. When I reached for a new stack of paper, I nearly knocked over a mug full of soup. Cook must have been and gone; the tray with my meal stood beside me. He must have seen the photograph.

It sobered me. I hurriedly put her back in the briefcase, stuffed the unfinished letter in an envelope, hid it with the others under the drawer. There was not much time left before my next watch; no point in undressing. I lay on top of my bunk, staring at the ceiling. My thoughts wandered aimlessly, but the awareness of my senses seemed to be heightened. I noticed sounds I had not consciously listened to since that afternoon between the Orkneys and

Langanes, long ago, when I had lain like this, becoming
aware for the first time of the *Isabel Kwel* as a living
body. I heard the creaking of the wardrobe with the swell,
the sloshing of the water in the cistern above the toilet, the
scraping of iron on iron in the engine room. From the
corner of my eye I noticed things moving, innocent things
which had dumbly moved like this ever since I first took
the *Isabel* out to sea: my military bathrobe from Hope
Brothers, hanging on the wall, jerkily shuffling with the
swell; the buckle on the belt of my greatcoat, flashing as
it swung with the pitching of the ship. Once, these sights
and sounds had been symbols of happiness, of the fullness
of the present, of life itself. Once, the feel of my ship, the
knowledge of my being her center of awareness, had
brought about self-confidence and pride and a feeling of
immortality. What had come over me? What had emascu-
lated me, turned me from that happy, confident man into
this maudlin dreamer, hiding in the skirts of a sentimental
figurine, who had nothing to do with reality? Yes; if I had
the guts to face the truth, I must confess that she had not.
The valentine I had been writing had nothing to do with
the distraught, passionate woman who had clambered on
board a deserted tugboat in the pouring rain at dead of
night, broken into its captain's quarters and jumped him
when he came in with a tea tray. There had not been a
trace of tenderness about her, not a shimmer of simple
decency and kindness, and she had radiated anything but
"infinite comfort." Instead, there had been scorn for the
husband who had died crying her name, because he had
failed to die like a hero. For me, there had been taunting
contempt, eyes flashing in defiance; crockery had crashed
against the wall; she had spat vicious words in my face and
shaken me and worked herself up into hysteria; when
finally I had slapped her face, she had gone limp in my

arms, all soft and sensuous, and pulled me down in a kiss of triumphant surrender. How was it possible that I, normally as wary and cagey as a gambler, had found myself writing about her as if she were a fey, delicate creature, defenseless as a butterfly? I had sat there, in the chartroom, rhapsodizing her innate decency, her gentle compassion, while in reality we had wantoned with naked abandon; at a given moment the mattress had slid off the couch and we had slid off the mattress and onto the floor, among his letters.

Analyzed with kindness, her behavior could be explained, forgiven; but by no stretch of the imagination could it be called tender, compassionate or innately decent. She was none of these things; she was proud and passionate and imperious, obsessed by the primitive concept that masculinity must forever be challenged, taunted into constant reassertion of itself for her own feminine reassurance. I had known the boy Tyler only fleetingly, but enough to suspect that he must have failed to rise to that challenge, bewildered by the apparent contradiction between her imperious behavior and her yearning for subjugation. The last thing she wanted was what he must have turned out to be: a little boy, nestling on his mother's breast, a sentimental baby-talking whelp. "I've always known he was a coward, from the very beginning!" she had cried in her fury; with those words she had bared the secret of their marriage, the reason why, in the bottom of her heart, she despised him. Tyler, earnest and gentle, had been no match for her. She had wanted a lion tamer, not a kitten protector.

I had no idea where and when I had acquired this insight, it was simply what I had sensed in her when she faced me. My reactions had been as instinctive as hers; when I had found myself slapping her face and pulling her head back by her hair, part of me had watched with shocked unbelief. Only when she had dissolved in surrender and had suddenly become soft and vulnerable, and I had found myself responding with an instant protective tenderness that I had never experienced before, had I realized that all was well. This was the way we were meant to be; we had not been hurting one another blindly in blundering violence; we had acted, from the very beginning, in a mysterious harmony. Never before had I made love like this; neither, I was certain, had she.

The truth about us was so much more subtle and intriguing than the fiction I had been concocting in my mawkish letters that I thought of tearing them up and starting anew. But something deterred me: the suspicion that maybe these letters had another function than mere self-articulation, a function I had not been aware of: a form of self-defense against encroaching despair, a last-ditch stand of my most personal individuality against the nihilism of war, against a concept of myself that was being inexorably forced upon me by the reality of the world outside. Amid the massive, impersonal destruction in which I was involved—the annihilation of ships, whole fleets, armies, cities, nations—I, as an individual, with all my love and my hope and thoughts and dreams, was inconsequential, utterly futile, a mere insect. Any moment, tonight, tomorrow, I might be wiped out like an insect, as I saw others being wiped out every day. What was the point of agonizing over right and wrong, trying to probe my motives, my conscience, the secret of my soul, when around me hundreds of men like me were being obliterated by explosions, roasted by fires, crushed by falling spars, or leaped to their deaths in the freezing sea? The moment I became aware of my insignificance, I felt the darkness of total despair close over me. The only defense against that despair was those letters to a girl I had known for one brief hour only, but who had now become my sole concern, my hope, my life.

I got up and went back into the chartroom. I must write to her, at once, and never mind what Cook had seen or what the men might think. Those few moments of awareness had opened a crack in my armor, through which fear was now pouring in. It poisoned the peace of mind in which I had lain there; it filled me with the terror of death; there was only one way out: to scrawl *Dearest, dearest!* on a piece of paper, like a cry for help. After that I sat for a moment at a loss, my mind a blank, the poison pervading my body; then the image of her naked, wide-legged body rose in front of me, like a hallucination, and I began to write.

Never in my life had I written anything like it. Never had her physical presence seemed so real, so bewitching. With the strength of passion, I lifted myself out of the chartroom, the ship, the convoy, the sea; I was back in Halifax once more, once more I had her in my arms; then I heard the door open.

It was the mate. "We're sailing into fog," he said, "you'd better come up. This is going to be interesting."

It took me a moment to recover; then I put on my gear and went to the bridge.

3

We were surrounded by a smoke-like fog, so thick that the flare which the grain ship ahead of us had put on her stern was a mere orange glow, although we were very close to her. The fog seemed to be low-lying; I could not actually see the sky, but it became lighter higher up. Above this low bank the sky must be clear and visibility unlimited.

I knew what would happen. I saw it clearly, as if I were watching from above, a bird's-eye view. I saw the bombers take off from their airfields in Norway. I saw them head out to sea, toward the low bank of fog through which we were sailing. I spotted, with them, the tops of the masts of our thirty-six ships, sailing blindly through the fog; seen from up there, the masts of the convoy, sticking out of the flat white cloud, must look like rows of short black poles, like fences. When the sirens of the escort wailed the alert, I knew what was coming; invisible, unopposed by our guns, they would kill us off like a row of sheep.

They came. A drone of engines drew nearer. Then the crackle of machine guns, the hammering of cannons, high up in the sky. Then the first stick of bombs: a multi-toned whistle, growing to a shriek. Before the explosion shook us, the guns of the convoy opened up, firing blindly at the enemy they could not see.

My mind was clear, I felt no fear or panic; only, I couldn't breathe. I stood there, gasping for air, clutching the port engine-room telegraph; I knew I had to go to the wheelhouse or I'd suffocate. As I groped my way toward it along the rail, I came upon a shape in the fog, someone in a duffel coat. It was the mate; I was in such a hurry to get to the wheelhouse that I did not notice the expression on his face until he barred my way. He looked at me in a way he had never done before; it was a look of sheer, stark horror. For a moment I thought that he was just scared out of his wits, like everybody else; then he cried, "Jesus Christ! Where are you going?" His voice was shrill and querulous.

I found the breath to ask, "Why?" still obsessed by the urge to hide in the wheelhouse.

Then he shouted, "Don't go away! I can't handle it alone! I can't!"

I stared at him in blank amazement for what cannot have been more than a few seconds. But in those seconds it penetrated to me, as in a flash of revelation, what I had done. By living in that world of my own, I had thrown the fear of death into my crew. The helmsman had told them how I had stood paralyzed in the corner of the wheelhouse; the cook had told them about my writing letters with the photograph of that girl in front of me; the mate had found me writing to her again when he came in to call me and it had convinced him that I was indeed about to withdraw from reality entirely, as the boy had done, leaving the command of the ship to him. To confess that he could not handle it was, for him of all people, such an irrevocable, self-destructive thing to do that I felt as if, for a second time, I had witnessed a man commit suicide on my bridge. It brought home to me, at last, how desperate the situation had become while my back was turned. He was the first domino to fall; unless I took control at once, the whole ship would lose its head. I knew what it would mean; to face reality meant to abrogate the dream. I could not live in two worlds at the same time, not fight a war in the daytime and sleep at home; but to give up the dream meant a surrender to the despair she had helped me keep at bay all this time.

I had no choice; this was my ship, these were my men; once I had been proud of that responsibility, now I must pay the price for being Master after God. "Take it easy," I said. "You are not supposed to handle anything, as long as I'm around. But after this attack you'd better take that pill and catch up on your sleep, for without you I can't handle it either." The alter ego had taken over once more.

The fog was now full of the diffused glow of fire, the acrid stench of smoke and cordite. During a lull in the thunder of the gun on our foredeck, I heard cries coming from the sea, "Help! Help!"

I turned to the mate and said, "Lower the boats."

He stared at me, bewildered. "Are you crazy? We'll never find the ship again, not in this fog. Two boat lengths away, and—"

"Put them out with long lines," I said. "Have them steer away from the ship and I'll stream them, like paravanes."

He obeyed; I blew into the engine-room tube and said, "Better be on your toes, we're in for some nifty maneuvering."

Somebody down there muttered, "Aye, aye."

I did not know how I was going to make out; but for the moment I had better try and pick up those survivors crying in the fog, without losing my boats and within the lethal limit of five minutes. By now that water must be really cold.

Pulleys squealed, the boats were lowered, I watched their lines heave and splash after they had disappeared in the fog. I heard the men calling to each other and to the people in the water. The battle around us increased in intensity; but it was no battle, it was a massacre. The din of the guns firing blindly at the sky was so deafening that nobody on board the ships in that fog could hear the sound signals of his neighbor. At a given moment, there sounded a colossal racket of grinding iron and splintering wood close by, over our starboard side; as we floated past, I saw the tangled ghosts of two huge ships, larger than life in that fog, clutching each other in a deathly stranglehold. One must have received a direct hit in the engine room and slowed down, only to be rammed in the stern by the ship behind her. Our boats were hauled back from the fog by their lines; they were full of men. They were barely picked up when there was a wild, huge glow straight ahead, then a light so fierce and distended that it looked as if we were sailing straight into the crater of an erupting volcano. Silhouetted in the inferno, I saw the grain ship ahead of us veer sharply to starboard; I shouted for hard starboard rudder. We heeled as we swung, and sailed into a sea of fire. It must be fuel from the tanker on our port bow, the first in line; she must have broken up as she exploded, and now her burning oil covered the sea. The heat was intense; flames leaped up around us, licked higher than the bridge rail; the spray shield on the port wing started smoking. The tremendous heat of the burning sea dissipated the fog above it; suddenly we were sailing underneath a bright blue sky, and I saw the planes overhead: droves of them, dropping their deadly sticks of bombs, small black coveys, curving down. Then the heat decreased, the light dimmed, I brought the ship back on course. I sighted the stern of the grain ship, then she vanished in the fog once more.

But it seemed to be lifting, and it was. With surprising suddenness, the convoy sailed into the open. From then on, its ack-ack fire became accurate. Falling planes streaked down into the sea and exploded into mushrooms of boiling black smoke. Minutes later, the enemy withdrew.

They left behind a decimated convoy. Of the thirty-eight ships that had set out from Langanes, two days before, twenty-five were left. Three ships were on fire; one of them, in the midst of a heroic effort by her crew to douse the conflagration in her holds, burst asunder with a blinding flash and deafening roar, broke her back and

sank. It was much worse than last time; it was insane to
send men and ships into this hell, sitting ducks for a superior enemy with scores of airfields and U-boat bases all
within striking range, and an unlimited supply of planes
and submarines. It would almost be a humane thing for
the *Tirpitz* to do to come out and put an end to this pointless, gruesome torture.

The wounded were taken away by the launch and ferried to the escort. The bosun and the carpenter washed
the decks; blood ran red out of our scuppers, down our
scorched and blistered flanks. We had come through once
more, but this time it had been closer than ever before.

When Sparks said, as I passed him on the boatdeck on
my way to the chartroom, "Neat work, Skipper, much
obliged," all I could do was touch his arm and remember
that day, long ago, in another world, when he had said
the same to a lucky young captain who had raised South
Shields' outer buoy in the fog.

4

That evening, as the early darkness was falling, I dropped
my own letters and Tyler's, as well as her portrait, into
the duffel bag with Loppersum's Niki and his French photograph album. But as I stood outside in the pale, translucent light of the Arctic dusk, the duffel bag poised on the
rail, listening to the hiss and swish of the bow wave
crossing the swell, I discovered I could not do it.

Tyler's letters were his last, they must contain his final
effort to articulate the meaning of life as he had winnowed
it out of his short existence. I could not just fling them
overboard, to sink slowly with the garbage from the con-

voy's galleys. I felt no such compunction about Loppersum's inflatable woman or his *scènes vécues*, or about my own letters to Mary or even her portrait, but Tyler's letters suddenly seemed a different matter. I had wanted it to be an integral part of a magic rite of exorcism, but now that the decision was made and I was about to do away with the dream, it seemed a small gesture indeed to refrain from destroying a dead man's last confession as well. Although I had never read his letters, I knew from my own that he had not written just to her, but to the future, to life itself.

I took the small package held together with a rubber band out of the bag, then I threw the rest overboard. I waited for the splash of the burial, but I heard nothing, only the swish of the bow wave climbing the silent, swift hill of the swell, and its hiss as it descended into the trough beyond. I stood there, thinking vague thoughts of farewell to Captain Loppersum, last of the great of Holland's Glory, when suddenly, high up in the sky, where the day still lingered in a dark, radiant blue, a slowly waving flag seemed to be unfurled.

First, there was only a hint of faint, delicate tints, like color etherealized, in the zenith of the sky; then it slowly grew, curling and waving, a rainbow unrolling. There was no form to the unearthly light, it curled and twisted restlessly, gradually filling the sky, changing the color of the night. The blue darkness changed to green, then lilac; a violet fringe at its edges descended right down to the horizon. It was as if we had indeed reached the end of the world, the mystical region beyond Ultima Thule. It was aurora borealis, the northern lights, furling and unfurling in restless change, now like a silver shroud, slowly billowing in some cosmic wind, then, over the very zenith, radiating like a world-large star of Bethlehem, shooting silver shafts down to the horizon. In the midst of all that glory, from the silence of the vast, empty sea, there came the drone of insane man in his murderous machine, hunting down his brother to the edge of eternity. The delicate veil of light of aurora borealis was shredded by the explosion of a parachute flare, setting the sea and the convoy in a harsh white light. Then another and another, a whole string of them. The sirens wailed, the guns started firing and there came the evil whistle, growing to a shriek, of falling bombs.

As I stood there, watching, tensely waiting for my own reaction, I felt no fear. The fear never came, but in its stead came something more insidious—disgust. The waste, the destruction, the whole murderous orgy of violence and hatred, of blood and pain suddenly filled me with such unutterable revulsion that I had to turn away and forcibly banish it from my mind. I went to the bridge, decided coolly, acted calmly, handled my ship surely and professionally, but the disgust did not leave me. It was there, pervading everything, until I was moving in a vacuum of indifference.

When the attack had blown itself out, toward dawn, I dragged my weary body back to my bunk and lay down, yearning for sleep, forgetfulness. But I was unable to sleep; I could not shake off this strange disgust, this feeling that I had reached the ultimate point of satiation. I could take no more of this, I no longer wanted to be part of it; and then it occurred to me, as I lay there, that I might not have exorcised the boy Tyler's ghost after all, that I might, unwittingly, still be following the tortuous road he had gone. I remembered his words, during our last conversation, "I don't want to be part of this any more"; maybe he too had lain like this, staring into the darkness, slowly being overcome by irrepressible disgust, until, in the end, he had thrown himself in front of the guns of the enemy, not in a paroxysm of fear, as we had all assumed, but as a last, futile protest of his humanity when an airplane, in a screaming dive, gunned down a kitten.

It was new to me, I who had always held as an axiom that the instinct for survival was man's most basic instinct, because it had been mine. As long as I could remember, I had always wanted to survive, at any price, at any cost, under whatever condition, because my most precious possession, so it had always seemed to me, was life itself.

Now, as I lay there, remembering him, I knew it was not so.

5

After three days and nights of continuous attacks, the men on board the *Isabel Kwel* were so exhausted that all they wanted was to keel over on their bunks for a few precious hours of sleep in the midst of purgatory. As for myself, although I had slept less than the others, I seemed to have lost nothing of my alertness. I observed the world with cool detachment, gradually beginning to wonder, in purely objective curiosity, when and how I would eventually reach the point where I would prefer self-extinction to a further involvement in this frenzy of indiscriminate destruction. It was as if, with my very eyes, I witnessed the total annihilation of reason, mercy, compassion, everything man had painfully acquired after thousands of years of evolution, and now saw the Earth handed back to the mindless brutality of the brontosaurs, battling one another insanely in a sea of blood, slowly sinking under the weight of their own armor.

In the middle of the morning of the fourth day, after

a lull of less than two hours, there were the distant thuds again of submarine explosions, and there came the wails of the sirens, the gunfire of the escort. I did not rush to the deck, none of us did any more, we just went. What would have filled us with apprehension barely three days before now induced only the weary reaction, "There we go again." This time around, it started as a combined attack, routine by now, by U-boats and aircraft. I stood on the bridge, waiting for developments, smoking a cigarette, more apprehensive that it would burn my mitten than that we would be hit by cannon fire or bombs. I was just reflecting, as I watched the faces of the mate and Sparks, that all of us probably felt the same detachment of calm disgust, when suddenly Sparks cried, horrified, "God! Look at Mashpee!"

I had not seen the actual impact as he had; I only saw the debris hurled into the sky after what must have been a tremendous explosion. The impact of its shock wave hit us broadside as the debris came tumbling back into the sea; when we had recovered from its deafening blast, I saw that virtually the whole of the foreship of *Intrepid* seemed to have been blown off. I expected the rest of her to pitch forward and go down, as I had seen happen so many times before, but she did not. She carried on, crazily, half a ship, bowless, gutless, a dismembered wreck, circling around the convoy, shell-shocked sheepdog, mortally hurt, bleeding to death while running on blindly around its flock. Then a signal went up, incredibly, at her remaining mast; a signal I had not seen before. I called to Sparks, "What does he say?"

But already he was looking it up on the code sheet. He pointed at one, at the bottom, under Subsidiary Signals. I read the translation with incredulous awe. It meant: GOOD LUCK.

The death throes of *Intrepid* made every man in the convoy forget for a moment his own danger, the U-boats, the planes, the torpedoes, the bombs. For a minute or so, every sailor seeing *Intrepid* go by, heeling as she went, her headless hull sinking deeper and deeper into the water, stood struck with awe in the face of such bravura, such utter disdain for death. To have hoisted that signal of courtesy at the moment of truth seemed to sum up the essence of Mashpee, of the British Navy, of England herself. Then, with another shattering explosion, what was left of her split asunder midships. Her broken body belched a ball of fire and black smoke; her stacks caved in and tumbled, her stern rose from the sea, four propellers thrashing in the air. Then, swiftly and sleekly, the rest of her slid down under the sea.

As if the enemy had aimed only at this limited objective, the planes, after circling once over the spreading oil slick that was her grave, withdrew and headed for home. A destroyer came racing by, flag signal fluttering.

"That is our new Comescort," Sparks said; then he read from the code: "CONVOY RESUME FORMATION SPEED THIRTEEN KNOTS."

"Next time she comes past," I said, "ask if anyone came off *Intrepid*."

He did; when the destroyer came swooshing past on her next orbit, he clicked with his Aldis lamp. There came a short flickering response before she whisked out of sight.

"The answer is NEGATIVE," he said.

I said, "Thanks."

I felt as if I had lost a friend.

CHAPTER TEN

I

The new Comescort never got the chance to gain the confidence of the convoy. That afternoon, during a merciful lull after the third attack of the day, when everyone was busy clearing his decks of the incredible confusion of empty shells, torn iron plates, splintered wood, glass, ice, shreds of cloth and the ghastly remnants of disintegrated bodies, the destroyer came circling around us at surprisingly slow speed, Aldis lamp flickering. She had to go slowly, for it turned out to be a long and complicated message; she went from ship to ship, repeating it.

"COMESCORT TO CONVOY," Sparks read from his pad. "INSTRUCTIONS FROM ADMIRALTY JUST RECEIVED QUOTE ALL ESCORT VESSELS TO PROCEED SOUTHWARD AT TOP SPEED AS GERMAN BATTLESHIP TIRPITZ HAS LEFT PORT HER COURSE SUGGESTING SHE IS HEADING FOR CONVOY STOP THE ADMIRALTY ADVISES ALL MASTERS TO DISPERSE AND PROCEED TO THEIR DESTINATION INDIVIDUALLY AT THEIR MAXIMUM SPEED STOP MASTERS ARE ADVISED WITH UTMOST URGENCY NOT TO REMAIN TOGETHER BUT TO PUT MAXIMUM DISTANCE

BETWEEN THEMSELVES AND ALL OTHER SHIPS THUS EXTEND-
ING TARGET AREA AND REDUCING NUMBER OF POTENTIAL
CASUALTIES TO A MINIMUM STOP THE ESCORT WILL NOT RE-
JOIN THE CONVOY BUT IMPOSE ITSELF UPON THE ENEMY AS
PART OF THE ATTACKING FORCE UNQUOTE COMESCORT
WISHES YOU GOOD LUCK AND GODSPEED SIGNED HARCOURT
END."

We had barely registered this bewildering turn of events
when Sparks cried, "Hold it! Here comes a message for
us!"

Again the Aldis lamp on board the destroyer flickered
nervously, and Sparks jotted it down. This time the mes-
sage was shorter. COMESCORT TO MASTER ISAB BEGINNING
DISREGARD ORDER TO DISPERSE STOP YOU ARE INSTRUCTED
TO ACT AS ESCORT TO VESSELS HANNA K, SACRAMENTO,
FROKEN BRATT AND TEXAS TRADER WHO WILL REMAIN
JOINED IN CONVOY FOR MUTUAL ASSISTANCE AND PROTEC-
TION STOP TRAWLER LOCH RANNOCH WILL SAIL IN YOUR
SUPPORT STOP YOU ARE AUTHORIZED TO DISPOSE OF DEPTH
CHARGES ON BOARD YOUR VESSEL AT YOUR OWN DISCRETION
STOP GOOD LUCK GOOD HUNTING SIGNED HARCOURT END.

"Any reply?" Sparks asked.

I shook my head. "Just acknowledge," I said, "and thank
him for his good wishes."

While Sparks got busy with his Aldis lamp, the mate
and I gazed at each other, still stunned by this incredible
development. Without the escort, what would be the fate
of all those ships? What would our own fate be, now that
we suddenly found ourselves thrust into the position of
sheepdog to a herd of four defenseless, bumbling, overweight sheep? The *Fröken Bratt* was the grain ship we
had been trailing since Langanes, the other three were
freighters too, all of them old and slow. They obviously
had been joined together into a convoy to give them the

illusion of being protected; their faster sisters might have a chance to elude the enemy with their speeds of twenty knots and up, but not these four, which, churning strenuously at top speed, had barely been able to keep up with the convoy, even at its reduced speed of thirteen knots.

The supporting warships of the escort were lining up in formation; the destroyer flying the commission pennant made one more orbit around the convoy, as if she wanted to count her sheep one more time, futilely, before leaving them to the wolves. Minutes later, they made off at top speed toward the south; freighters and tankers were fanning out toward the northeast, some of them almost as fast as the ships of the escort, others barely faster than the four entrusted to the protection of a tugboat and a tiny trawler. The four huddled miserably together, not quite knowing what to do, trotting along at slow speed on the old course of the vanishing convoy.

As I stood there, indecisively, I felt an unnerving return of that fear beginning to quake in my legs. Then the mate said, "What about calling it a day?"

I looked at him. He stood there, relaxed, smiling. "What was that?" I asked.

"You know and I know that we can't make any difference to these poor bastards one way or another. They are sitting ducks. Why keep up the pretense? Why let ourselves be shoved around any longer by those bloody cowards who left us to rot?"

"What would you suggest?" I asked, watching him.

His eyes avoided mine; otherwise he seemed as cool as a cucumber. If I had not seen him look at me for a moment without a mask that other day, I would have been convinced that he was unshakable. "I suggest we do what the convoy did," he answered, calmly. "Let's hoist the signal 'Good luck and good hunting,' turn around and go home."

"Where's home?"

"Kirkwall."

"Court-martial, you mean."

He snorted derisively. "Balls," he said. "If there's going to be any court-martial over this, it's the Admiralty that will be in the dock, and that crappy new escort commander who left a convoy in the lurch. Could you have seen *Intrepid* doing that? Mashpee would have told those blimps in London to go and screw themselves, rather than leave eighteen ships without protection in the face of what must be the whole of the German U-boat Waffe, lying across our course. You don't kid yourself that we'll come out alive at the other end if we obey that order, do you? Let those four poor sods fend for themselves like the other ships; and let us fend for ourselves. It's every man for himself now. And your first loyalty as a Master, if you'll allow me, is to this ship. Your prime duty, I would say, is to see to it that the *Isabel Kwel* makes it in one piece, if you can." He grinned, quasi-apologetically, but his eyes were not apologetic at all; they were as cold and hard as diamonds, the coldness of utter terror.

Maybe, if it had happened in the previous convoy, I would have given it a second's thought. Now, I did not hesitate at all. To leave those four wallowing manatees to be picked off by the Germans without a rescue ship to take care of their survivors would mean that, although still physically unharmed, I had become a casualty of this epidemic of insanity all the same. If I was concerned about man's humanity, to leave that convoy of four misfits to its fate in order to save my own skin would be moral suicide.

"Sorry," I said. "The answer is negative."

He gave me a look of such hatred that it shook me. "You miserable yellow bastard," he said, his hissing voice low and vicious. "Why don't you get back into your corner in the wheelhouse? Or into your cabin to fuck a dead shipmate's wife?"

"That'll do," I said calmly. "You'd better beat it." Each word we spoke made a little cloud in the icy air. It made the whole thing seem odd and laborious, and somehow harmless.

"Oh! Now we are the Commodore again, are we?" he asked, scathingly. "Well, let me warn you, Commodore: *you* may not care a damn about this ship, but I do! I . . . "

"That'll do! If you don't like my decisions, you can lodge a protest with the owners after this trip." I turned away from him and called, "Sparks!"

"Right here," Sparks said, comforting in his calm.

"We'll have to make a signal for those freighters," I said. "I suppose I am Comescort now."

Sparks grinned. "Seems to me you're First Sea Lord now. Nobody else left to give any orders but us chicken. So, let's get with it."

"All right, make up this signal: COMESCORT TO CONVOY BEGINNING LET US TRY AND MAKE THE BEST OF THIS. VESSELS PLEASE LINE UP ABREAST, LOCH RANNOCH WILL FOLLOW SACRAMENTO AND TRADER, ISAB WILL FOLLOW FROKEN AND HANNA, SPEED THIRTEEN KNOTS. IN CASE OF ATTACK REDUCE TO EIGHT KNOTS TO ENABLE ISAB TO CIRCLE AND PLACE DEPTH CHARGES."

"Attaboy," Sparks said. "You're doing great."

I considered for a moment adding some encouragement, such as "Good luck," or "Godspeed," but decided against it. Every man on board those four ships knew exactly what our chances were; to be British about that would call for an Englishman.

"That's all," I said. "Sign it Harinxma. End of message."

"OK with me, Skipper," Sparks said, smiling. "In for a penny, in for a pound."

The mate, back to his old self, spat on the deck; but it no longer meant anything. He always had shown a remarkable capacity for cutting his losses.

2

———————

As we ponderously started to plow on toward the northeast, after making up convoy, the faster ships had all but disappeared from sight. Soon we heard explosions and the distant rumble of gunfire in the northeast quadrant, and we saw many planes on the horizon, swooping and diving.

Although I could not see what was going on, even through my binoculars, it did not take much imagination to visualize the scene. The Luftwaffe, no longer challenged by the massive and accurate ack-ack of the warships, was taking its time in finishing off, one by one, the defenseless ships now scurrying frantically in all directions, with no hope of shelter in sight. Reason told me that even if we should remain unnoticed for a while, it could not possibly last.

Within the hour we were indeed spotted. Odd planes in twos and threes made passes over our small convoy at various times without going into attack; by the time darkness fell, our position must have been reported to base many times over, we were the only concentration of ships left in the vicinity. But the spotting planes must also have reported our speed; they were concentrating on the fast ones first.

We heard them hunting down isolated fugitives all through the night. We saw the glow of several fires on the horizon and felt rather than heard the quakes of distant explosions. Toward dawn the fighting seemed to die down, they must have sunk all that were within earshot of our crawling convoy.

I was prepared for it, and had been since the day before; yet the attack took me by surprise. Without any warning whatsoever, the *Texas Trader*, largest of the four freighters, blew up with an eardrum-shattering explosion and a column of fire that roared above her masts. She broke up at once, the two halves sinking independently; I saw the little trawler *Loch Rannoch* rush toward her, although there could not be many survivors left; she was showered with debris as she pitched and rolled to their aid.

I don't know how long it took me to recover from the impact of the shock wave and the din of the explosion; it cannot have been more than seconds. The three other ships of the convoy, obviously stampeding, were trying to increase speed rather than slowing down as I had told them to do in my instructions; I told Sparks to run up the signal: SLOW DOWN TO EIGHT KNOTS I WILL CIRCLE. The *Hanna K.* and the *Fröken Bratt* obeyed; the *Sacramento*, larger and obviously faster than the others, went on plowing ahead on her own. I knew that the only hope for these ships was to stay close together so that I could surround them with a pattern of depth charges; the *Sacramento*, by breaking away from the convoy, was running headlong into destruction. I called to the corporal, who was standing by the starboard bridge gun: "Can you give her a warning shot across the bows? If she does not obey my signal, she's done for."

"I doubt it, but I'll have a go," he answered, with the debonair calm the British assume in action. He sat down at the gun, took aim through the telescope sight and fired five rapid shots at the fugitive. I saw the splashes of their impact in the sea behind her; obviously the gun did not carry far enough. Even so, someone on the *Sacramento's* bridge must have got the message; she decreased her speed and allowed the small convoy to catch up with her. I called the corporal again and asked him to stand by with the starboard catapult.

"How many canisters to a pattern, sir?" he asked me.

I had not the foggiest idea, but this was not the moment to tell him. "No limited pattern this time," I answered, brazenly. "I'll circle at full speed, just go on throwing as fast as you can. I don't know how many of them there are down there, but let's shake 'em up."

He saluted, said, "Yes, sir," and left at a run. After he was gone, I remembered that the destroyers, whenever they threw depth charges, had rarely thrown more than six. Maybe that was a pattern and maybe it made sense—certainly for us, as we had only a limited amount of the things on board. If I started to launch them indiscriminately at this first attack, I would soon be defenseless in the face of the next packs we came across. Although it was against one of the elementary rules handed down to me by Captain Bosman for a Master to reverse an order once it had been given, I was about to call him back and tell him to make it six when there was another colossal explosion, very close, followed by a blast so fierce that the ship heeled sharply under its impact. It was the *Hanna K.*, her entire foreship right up to the bridge blown out of existence by what must have been the ignition of two holds full of munitions. For a moment, I considered going to her rescue, as she was our responsibility, but the depth charges seemed more urgent. I ordered the mate and bosun to swing out the boats anyhow; they obeyed with such alacrity that I was coaxed into slowing down for a short half-stop, just enough to allow them to lower and away.

They were on the ball, all right; I pushed the engine-room telegraph back to Full Speed Ahead after mere seconds. The ship shuddered as her huge propeller started to thrash away under her stern; she gathered speed in what, considering her proportions, was a flying start; I signaled to the corporal on the aft deck that he could go ahead. The arm of the catapult leaned back, then he pulled a handle and it snapped back into position, hurling a canister astern. The canister, grotesquely gay with its white and orange paint, tumbled down and hit the water two ships' lengths astern. We were six lengths away before the submarine explosion came, yet it was so convulsive that it lifted the *Isabel*'s stern perceptibly, made her disobey her rudder for a few alarming moments, lurching on her course. But already the second depth charge had been hurled by the corporal; she had no time to recover steerage before the second impact walloped her stern and made her yaw wildly. I yelled to him, "Take it easy! Take it easy!"

He did not hear me, but someone else did and slammed him on the shoulder; he looked back at the bridge, cupped his hands behind his ears. Again I yelled, "Take it easy! Wait for my signal!"

He waved, as a token that he had understood, and spoke to his crew; from then on, he watched the bridge. I signaled him each time the *Isabel* was back under control after an explosion.

What remained of the *Hanna K.* was soon gone; by the time we had sorted out our procedure, all that was left of her was the usual sad flotsam, forlorn and scattered, and a growing oil slick, shimmering like mother-of-pearl in the early sun. I saw our boats and those of the *Loch Rannoch* move among a tangle of wreckage, dragging in bodies; the trawler herself hovered on the periphery of the mess, obviously wary of damaging her propeller, which was too close to the surface for her to venture among the floating debris.

I had nearly completed a full circle, throwing charges as

we went, when suddenly there was another of those sickening convulsions; this time it was the *Fröken Bratt*. A huge plume of dust spotted with debris spurted from her foredeck; there were no flames, and the explosion was much duller than had been the case with the two other ships. The dust remained suspended in the air in a large, slowly swelling cloud; particles rained down from it like a shower, speckling the sea around her, hitting our deck like a squall of hail as I passed at top speed close by her, throwing depth charges in rapid succession. She was going down by the head, but did not seem to be in immediate danger of breaking up; I expected a second explosion, for the U-boat must have realized, as I did, that she was likely to hover unless her bulkheads gave way. I was watching her through my binoculars when suddenly there was a high sharp twang, and another, and another, then something slammed against the starboard flank of the ship. Sparks' voice cried out, "Gunfire! Gunfire astern!"

I swung around and saw, over on our starboard beam, the sleek, whale-like hull of a gray submarine, its decks awash with the confused concentric waves created by the depth charges. On her foredeck I saw men clustered around a gun; as I stood looking, it spat two fierce flashes, there came that twang again, twice, then two sudden spurts of water close by, and a hard, double slam as if I had sideswiped a piling. Obviously, they were not direct hits; what I felt was the concussion of her shells exploding beneath the surface.

I don't know whether every commander under fire reacts that way; to me, at that moment, something unusual happened. It seemed as if my thoughts raced five times as fast as they had ever done before, as if my reactions were so lightning fast that they almost seemed to coincide with the incidents that triggered them. I gave four orders, seemingly all at once: the first to the helmsman, to swing the ship around with her bows headed for the gunfire; the second to the gunners on the bridge, ordering them to open fire on the U-boat; third, I pulled the engine-room telegraph on Half Astern and, fourth, I shouted to the corporal on the aft deck to stop throwing depth charges.

I was not conscious at the time of the juggler's feat I performed by following four observations and their deductions to four separate conclusions simultaneously. The thought of the depth charges on my aft deck and what would happen if the next round of cannon shells were to explode among them made me order the helmsman to swing the ship around. The knowledge that I had to give counterfire in order to make the gun on the foredeck of the U-boat aim at our bridge made me order the gunners to open fire. The consideration that the U-boat's shells must under no circumstances fall wide and strike the aft deck prompted me to reverse the engines. The danger that, in doing so, we might put ourselves above our own exploding depth charges made me order the corporal on the aft deck to stop throwing them. At that instant, I had no thought for the virtuosity of the human brain when faced with mortal danger; even while the ship was swinging around, another salvo came twanging our way and there was a violent explosion on our aft deck.

For a heart-stopping moment, I expected us to blow up; then I saw the crew of the catapult scramble to its feet and I noticed a rectangular gap in our aft rail. By a miracle, the depth charges had escaped even shrapnel damage. Only then did it register that I could see the gap in the stern rail because the jolly boat was no longer hiding it from view.

The two cannons on the bridge started to fire simultaneously the moment the U-boat swung into view. I shouted to the helmsman to head straight for it, to enable both guns to take aim without having to shoot across our bows. He made a mess of it, for I had failed to tell him that I was reversing the engine; so only the starboard one managed to get anywhere near its target. I saw waterspouts squirt up from the turbulent sea close to the U-boat, then again there were flashes, twangs, and before I knew what had happened I was blown clean across the bridge. I managed to scramble to my feet as I heard screams and yells all around me. I thought for a second that I was wounded, but all that had happened to me was that I had been hurled fifteen feet by the explosion. The helmsman lay screaming in the windowless wheelhouse, his hands on his face, blood trickling through his fingers. The portside cannon was pointing crazily at the sky, and I saw that the bridge rail behind it was gone; beside it lay two still forms in a spreading pool of blood. Then I heard a shrill voice cry, "Captain, Captain! Quick, Captain! Sparks . . . " I staggered to the bridge steps to the boatdeck on the port side and saw Cook bent over a mangled mess of flesh and bone and cloth with one boot sticking out of it, back to front.

I don't know what I felt at that moment; as I remember it, I felt nothing. I was not numbed by shock, I was completely alert and objective, but at the sight of those bodies on the bridge and the mangled mess that had been Sparks, I was overwhelmed once more by that disgust. This time, it was so strong that I knew then and there that I had had enough of this massacre. All of me, every fiber of me, the sum total of everything that made up my individuality, now finally rejected the murderous lunacy of it all. I remember standing there looking down on Cook and the remains of old Sparks without sorrow or shock or pity, without even the mere physical reaction of feeling sick. But my mind formulated the clear and articulate decision that if this was what we had all come to, I was no longer interested in being part of the human race. I had reached a borderline that I had not known existed; for the first time in my life, I, in my turn, recoiled from unconditional survival, if this was what it involved. I was through adding my own violence to the slaughter; they could shoot the hell out of me and the *Isabel Kwel*, but I was no longer going to shoot back. I heard the double twang again that was not a shot and was not a whine but sounded as if two strings were plucked on a giant guitar. I waited for the impact, but none came. I saw the horizon whirl past in the wrong direction and realized that we were still running half-speed-astern, in a circle. I went to the engine-room telegraph and pulled it to Stop. One of the gunners at the starboard cannon turned around and cried, "There he goes, Captain! There he goes!"

His colleague at the trigger, after a last burst of gunfire that shook the bridge, climbed out of the saddle. The U-boat was out of range.

"You had better look after your friends over there," I said, "I'm sorry." They stared, aghast, at the other side of the bridge where their dead comrades lay; the pool of blood had reached the stairs to the boatdeck before it froze.

To starboard, I saw the U-boat make off at high speed. I could not understand it. I couldn't understand why her commander had not finished us off while we were reeling under the impact of that direct hit. Then I saw what he was heading for: the stampeding *Sacramento*, running wildly toward the horizon in blind panic, black smoke from overloaded diesel engines boiling from her stack.

It was an uneven race. The U-boat, throwing a bow wave higher than her conning tower, sliced through the waves in pursuit of her prey. She tried to maneuver alongside the *Sacramento;* the hunted vessel swung around in a desperate effort to escape her. Her board guns, meant only for aircraft, were firing at the sky in blind panic. It seemed to take a very long time; the U-boat—stopped, as I no longer saw her bow wave—must have launched one torpedo and missed because of the zigzags of the freighter. The *Sacramento* seemed to have acquired a new and astounding nimbleness, almost impossible for a ship her size, as impossible as the last desperate dashes of a hunted rabbit just before it is downed. I heard wails behind me in the wheelhouse, and I remembered the helmsman.

I hurried in, found him still lying on the floor, cringing, his hands in front of his face, blood running through his fingers, moaning. I bent over him and took his hands down from his face; when I saw it, I felt what I had failed to feel at the sight of Sparks. I turned away and threw up in the corner of the gutted wheelhouse, thinking, "God no, oh God no, God no, no . . . " He must have been hit by flying glass.

"Skipper! Skipper, where are you?"

It was the voice of the mate; I had never heard it like that before. I looked up and I saw him standing in the doorway to the bridge, his face a stark white twisted mask of hatred. He did not look at the helmsman now lying motionless on the floor, he did not look at the damage, he did not even look at me. His eyes seemed to be haunted by an unforgettable vision. "The bastards . . . " he hissed. "The sadistic bastards! Have you seen what they did? Do you know what they did? They gunned the lifeboat, full of people . . . our boat, the bosun's!"

"When?"

"After they were through here! Just before they left! Didn't you hear that one more round they fired? That was the bosun! The bosun and maybe thirty men."

"Any survivors?" I asked, matter-of-factly.

"None," he replied. As if with that reply he had carried out a mission, he suddenly turned away and leaned against the wall of the wheelhouse, overcome by utter weariness. The helmsman on the floor lay quite still now; I no longer was sickened by his face.

"Give me a hand," I said to the mate. "Let's take him down to the aft deck."

"What for?" he asked, without looking. "What good would the aft deck do him?"

"The trawler has a doctor on board," I said. "Let's make a signal asking them to send a boat. Can you make a signal?"

"Why?" he asked, still turned away, leaning against the wall of the wheelhouse. "Where's Sparks?"

"Sparks is dead."

He looked around at me slowly, and his face relaxed as my words sank in, as if they doused his hatred with grief.

"The bastards," he said. "The bastards. Let me lay hands on just one of them . . . "

He had said it softly, almost caressingly; his hatred had not been doused at all; it had become so consuming that he could no longer express it; he stood there, eyes closed, smoothed out by an odd serenity. Then there sounded in the distance once more the sickening, shuddering crunch of a massive explosion. He smiled and said, eyes closed, in a voice that sounded amused, "There goes *Sacramento*. Good luck. Good hunting."

I went out onto the bridge and saw the *Sacramento* go down in the distance. I could not find my binoculars and I did not need them, for I heard the now familiar sound of gunfire; then I saw the *Loch Rannoch* head for the sinking ship. I wanted to call, to warn her with my siren, to do anything to keep her from running to her death. But there she went, dirty little fishing smack from Scotland, red ensign fluttering, rolling heavily with the swell. An unspeakable weariness came over me; for a moment, I felt like lying down on that bridge and closing my eyes and letting whatever fate had in store for us just happen, without feeling, without caring, overwhelmed by that unutterable disgust.

Then, as I looked away because I did not want to see what would happen to that gallant, crazy little trawler on her suicidal errand of mercy, I saw the *Fröken Bratt*, last remaining of our convoy, her head deep down in the water, her propeller churning powerlessly, a dying bird fluttering helplessly in a vain effort to escape encroaching death. And suddenly, as I saw that helpless ship wallowing rudderless amid the refuse of battle, my disgust turned into rebellion. No, goddammit! I was not going to lie down on that bridge and let whatever it was just happen to me! I was not going to put my goddam head under the guillotine, not in a thousand years! If I felt disgusted with the human race, I was not going to step out disgusted with myself. I would show God or Fate or the Life Force, or whatever else the universal heap of cosmic excrement should be called that had created us monsters, how I, Martinus Harinxma, stretcher-bearer of the ocean, would like this goddam universe to be run. It was a bizarre ranting eruption of groggy panache, but suddenly I had only one goal left in life: I was going to tow the *Fröken Bratt* and whatever grain she might have left in her gored belly to the famished suckers in Russia. Had she contained guns or airplanes or tanks or ammunition, I would have let her sink. I might have sunk her myself with the one remaining cannon after taking off her crew, as I had seen that destroyer do during our first convoy, but the fact that her cargo was grain made her a symbol of peace and decency. All she was, as she lay there wallowing, vainly trying to gather speed and steer a course, was a leaking baker's cart, and I was going to see to it that the baker delivered his bread, if I had to sail her backward through hell to do it. And that was exactly what I would have to do; I would have to tow her backward, and I would have to tow her through hell, but I did not care a single damn. I was going to leave this life in a manner appropriate to a human being, not as a raving, panting cannibal, drunk with my brother's blood. I suppose each man goes into shock after his own fashion; this happened to be mine.

The new purpose gave me new strength, and that juggler's virtuosity once more flooded my mind, until I could think and act simultaneously on four different levels. I started by calling to Cook and the Second, whom I saw standing speechlessly on the boatdeck, staring down on the shapeless lump that was now covered with a coat. I told them to come and fetch the helmsman. I called the mate, who stood staring after the little trawler running to her doom, and told him to round up whatever sailors he could find and prepare for towing. I called to the corporal on the aft deck and told him that we were through with depth charges, and asked him to come to the bridge. I blew down the speaking tube to the engine room; when Porks answered, I told him we were preparing to start towing and to stand by at the engine. I heard the mate ask behind me, "Towing? Towing who?"

"The *Fröken Bratt*," I answered, consciously shutting out of my mind the sound of gunfire in the distance, for I did not want to know about it.

I heard the mate's voice, "Are you out of your . . ." but he never finished his sentence. He was interrupted by a loud cheering from the aft deck. It was a sound so incongruous, so obscene amid the dead and dying and the ghastly destruction, that I yelled, "What the hell is going on? Cut that out!"

But then I saw the corporal pointing in the direction of the gunfire, and I heard him shout, "He's got him! He's got him! Old *Loch Rannoch's* got him! Look! Look!"

I looked. There, in the distance, was the little trawler, firing away from her foredeck at the sinking hull of the U-boat. As I looked through the binoculars, I saw the lid of the conning tower close while waterspouts squirted all around it; it did not look to me as if she were actually sinking, but if she were not, it certainly was a crash dive. The only explanation for the fantastic scene of a German U-boat crash-diving to escape a trawler armed with a pop gun was sheer surprise; no U-boat commander in his senses could ever have dreamed of being attacked by such a farcical adversary; it was like a wolf fleeing from an enraged guinea pig. The gun crew on the foredeck of the U-boat must have been taken completely unawares, panicked and run for shelter, back into the conning tower. Once they had started running, their commander had no choice but to dive for shelter himself.

As the conning tower closed, the captain of the trawler backed off, full speed, reversed his engine once more and ran straight for the U-boat, obviously with the insane objective of ramming her as she went down. But by the time the slow little ship reached the spot where the German had crash-dived, she was too late; had she hit him, chances were that she would have gone down herself, rather than the enemy. That Scottish skipper must be hopping mad.

The quixotic dash of the tiny *Loch Rannoch* suddenly made my command to prepare for towing seem reasonable to everyone on board. The Second, who had come to the bridge with Cook to take away the helmsman, seemed to grab hold of the idea of towing as if it were a lifeline by which to haul himself out of this nightmare; his face was chalky white and he was clad only in his overalls, but he did not seem to notice the icy wind.

"How about those two catapults on the aft deck?" he said, his voice calm and reasonable. "Aren't they going to interfere with your hawser, once you start towing?"

"They might," I said, "but what can we do about them?"

"I've got that little cutting rig," he mused, slowly, as if we had no other problem on hand. "You know, that portable oxygen one. They're welded to the deck, I think, on only three stanchions; I could cut those in a jiffy if you want me to, or do you think you'll be needing them again?"

It was, logically speaking, a nonsensical suggestion, as it robbed us of our last defense in the face of a relentless enemy who would, without any doubt, be after us again before the day was over, but I was not concerned with logic any more. I was concerned with values that I still only vaguely discerned but that somehow were infinitely more valid than reason. I felt like saying, "You can take them down, I am through with killing," but instead I said, "Bring it up, and we'll see. If we can't tow with them, we'll tow without."

"All right, will do," he said, and he shambled off, his boiler suit jellying in the breeze.

"You aren't serious, are you?" It was the mate.

"I am. We are going to tow the *Fröken Bratt*, if her captain agrees."

"You're out of your mind," he repeated, quietly. "Where in the name of God would you tow her?"

"Murmansk, I suppose. It's up to her captain."

He looked at me intensely, his cold blue eyes probing mine. I was acutely aware that at that moment I must seem the insane one, yet I knew, more clearly than ever, that he was.

"If you must tow, at least head away from the U-boats,

not toward them," he said.

I knew that this made sense. Everything he said made sense, the way it made sense for a U-boat commander to sink every enemy vessel he could sight, regardless of humane considerations. On that level, the gunning of our lifeboat had made sense too, for the thirty-odd men in it, had they been allowed to reach Allied territory alive, would have turned around and started fighting again. But I was no longer interested in a world where this made sense; I was through with unconditional survival.

"We may make it," I said. "If they spot us, they'll sink us anyhow, never mind which way we're going. Our speed won't be more than three knots at the utmost. If her bulkheads are weak, I may even have to tow her at less than that, but let's leave it up to her captain. He's the one to decide." At that, I turned away and left.

I went for a quick tour of the ship, to check on our casualties and take a look at the damage. I found that, apart from Sparks and the two gunners on the bridge, we had lost the carpenter and a sailor called Heinsius who had been on the foredeck when the shells struck. Wounded were the helmsman, five gunners and an oilman. The damage was much worse than had been apparent from the bridge; the front wall of both my cabin and the chartroom gutted with shrapnel; the first portside lifeboat damaged beyond repair; the bosun's boat lost, the jolly boat on the aft deck reduced to matchwood. The starboard side of the bridge, where the gun emplacement had been, was a shambles; the gun hung precariously from a few bent rafters that had supported the bridge; once the second engineer came up with his cutting gear, he had better start by cutting that gun away before it came crashing down of its own accord and did more damage. When I arrived on the aft deck to look at the remains of the jolly boat, I found Cook collecting the stores that now lay scattered all over the deck, putting them in a laundry basket and carrying them off. It was a constructive activity, yet, at that particular moment, it seemed to be tinged with lunacy. When I saw him stagger past, his laundry basket full of stores, I noticed his eyes and realized that he was in shock. Obviously, every man on board was going through his own reaction.

The exploding shell on the aft deck which had demolished the jolly boat had also twisted and, according to the corporal, irrevocably jammed the starboard catapult, which was the operative one, as the portside rails were empty of canisters; we had spent them all. Looking at the shambles on the aft deck, I realized that our lives had been saved by the jolly boat. It had taken the brunt of the explosion and had shielded the high explosive just behind it from flying shrapnel. As both catapults were now useless, I told the Second when he came trundling by with his cutting gear to go ahead and remove them, but to take it easy with his cutting flame on the starboard side, because of the high explosives. The damage to the stern coaming was superficial in itself; it had been gutted by shrapnel in places; the rectangular hole where the gate had been would have to be boarded up temporarily, but I did not know who could do it, now that we had lost both the bosun and the carpenter.

I could not grasp yet, not quite, that we had lost all those men I had known for so long; their departure did not seem final somehow. Maybe at the bottom of this feeling lay the notion that, in all probability, we would soon be joining them. In the midst of this, a boat from the *Loch Rannoch* came alongside with the doctor and her captain.

The captain was received with a round of applause by those who saw him climb on board, and he reacted with a bashful grin, like an athlete who had won a medal. He had come alongside to ask if I needed any assistance; when I told him that I was planning to tow the *Fröken Bratt* if her captain agreed, he took it entirely as a matter of course. Obviously, he was suffering from shell shock too; we all moved and acted within our own individual cocoons of detachment, with that strange sense of unreality. Not a single word of what we said, not a single act of what we did, made any sense at all, the moment one stopped to consider that the U-boat was likely to surface at any moment and finish us off, the lot of us. It just did not bear thinking about, so we didn't. We behaved as if the war, as far as we were concerned, was over, and as if all that was now left for us to do was to clean up the mess, take care of the wounded and tow the damaged grain ship to Murmansk.

When the wounded were in his boat and he was about to leave, the trawler captain asked if I would be likely to need him; if not, he would prepare to turn around and head for Iceland as soon as he got back on board; he was acting on the advice of the doctor, who said that most of the wounded needed more than the care he could give them. He could be in Seydisfjördur three and a half days from now, if that southwesterly breeze did not freshen too much and if the U-boats and the planes would leave him alone. I told him I did not think I would need him any more, thanked him for his assistance and shook hands, and he waved from the launch as it turned toward his ship, rolling and pitching at a cable length's distance in the steepening swell.

That sou'westerly breeze would present no problem to the *Isabel Kwel* even if it grew into a gale, but it might decide the towing business for us. To start towing a grain ship with water in her holds was tricky enough; the swelling grain would put an awful strain on her bulkheads, rough weather would make it even more hazardous, as she must be floating on her engine-room bulkhead only. I maneuvered alongside her and hailed her bridge via the bullhorn. Her captain answered that he would indeed like to be towed, he was sure we could make it if the weather held out. I asked him where he wanted to be taken, and he replied that he thought we should head for Jan Mayen Island, which at our estimated speed lay about twenty-four hours to the west. There were no repair facilities on Jan Mayen, but in the shelter of the island his crew might be able to patch up the hole in his side with tarpaulin and lumber, so that his pumps could bring the head back up, which meant that he might be able to make Iceland under his own power. It was a complicated and lengthy discussion, full of technicalities yelled through bullhorns from ship to ship. The whole thing became more and more dreamlike, for while we were talking, I expected at any moment to be attacked by the U-boat; but maybe the *Loch Rannoch* had indeed managed to chase it off or damage it sufficiently to send it limping home.

While the captain of the *Fröken Bratt* and I were talking, the Second removed both the catapults from the aft deck and freed it for a hawser; by the time the captain and I had reached agreement, we were ready to start towing. I went to the bridge, sent the mate to the aft deck and maneuvered the stern of the *Isabel Kwel* underneath the overhanging cliff of the freighter's aft castle, rising and falling perilously with the swell. The mate picked up her line; they hauled in our hawser and connected it with a giant shackle to the chain of her stern anchor. There were a few tricky moments when I had to get really close underneath her stern; her propeller and her rudder lay so close to the surface that they presented a hazard in that swell. But the maneuver came off satisfactorily; soon I could push the engine-room telegraph to Dead Slow Ahead, and we started paying out the heavy rope until we were about a ship's length away from the freighter.

Once we started towing, a change seemed to come over the ship. I had the romantic feeling that the *Isabel Kwel* was waking up out of a nightmare when she suddenly found herself back at the kind of work she had been created for. In a sense, this went for all of us; the moment we were sailing a tugboat again and not a rescue ship or a depth-charge thrower or a gunboat, we seemed to wake up, with a sudden poignant nostalgia, out of a nightmare of senseless destruction into a world of peace and decency and creativity. To be towing made us feel like human beings again, individuals trained for a highly skilled profession, contributing their skill to the reconstruction of a ravaged world. Towing the crippled grain ship slowly through the vast emptiness of the Arctic Ocean, it seemed to us as if indeed the war were over.

We had emerged into a clear, frosty day. The wind whistled in the rigging; the hum of the hawser, tautening and slackening, rising and falling with the waves, vibrated through the ship. The mate arranged for the aft deck to be cleaned, then he came up and asked what we were to do with the bodies that the boat of the *Loch Rannoch* had left behind. I asked who they were, and he answered, "Sparks, Heinsius and the carpenter. The English gunners have been taken away."

I told him to prepare them for burial; we would set them over the side as soon as he was ready.

3

Half an hour later, he called me down to the aft deck. He had taken away the planking that had camouflaged the portside canisters, now gone, and used some of the boards as biers on which to put the bodies. The biers were lined up side by side, resting on the rail, their inboard ends held up by members of the crew. The bodies had been put in sleeping bags, weighted down at the feet with I knew not what. They were each covered with a Dutch flag, fluttering in the wind. I had brought along the Book of Common Prayer, and we sang a hymn that was familiar to those of us who had been at sea long enough to have been present at burials before.

> Now the laborous task is o'er,
> Now the battle day is past,
> Now upon the farther shore
> Lands the voyager at last.
> Father, in Thy gracious keeping,
> Leave we now Thy servants sleeping.

The wind blew our ragged song away; at times the swish and gurgle of a passing wave was louder.

> There no more the powers of hell
> Can prevail to mar their peace,
> Christ the Lord shall guard them well,
> He who died for their release.
> Father, in Thy gracious keeping
> Leave we now Thy servants sleeping.

As we started the last verse of the hymn, I thought I heard a sound in the distance, the growing undulating drone of an approaching plane. But no one seemed to notice, no one seemed to care. We sang the last verse slowly and self-consciously, like the others.

> Earth to earth and dust to dust,
> Calmly now the words we say,
> Leaving them to sleep in trust
> Till the resurrection day.
> Father, in Thy gracious keeping
> Leave we now Thy servants sleeping.

It was a plane, all right, and it was heading for us. I felt no panic, no urgency; there was nothing we could do; never before during a burial at sea had I felt so close to those whose bodies now lay waiting to be committed to the deep. It was as if, while we stood there, a small group of men, heads bared, eyes closed, hands folded, waiting for death, we were sharing the same funeral with the dead. I did not know whether it was a spotter plane, or whether the pilot had realized what we were doing and had decided to grant us a short respite in the common reverence for the dead that occasionally unites men for a fleeting moment, even in the midst of battle. While I read the short service, slowly and with a steady voice, none of the men around the biers betrayed by gesture or look that he was aware of the aircraft circling overhead. It was not courage, but detachment, the sensation that it was all happening far away, at a distance that rendered all dangers imaginary. So prisoners must feel when they stand blindfolded, hands tied behind their back, against the wall, during the last moments before their execution.

"Man that is born of woman has but a short time to live that is full of misery; he cometh up and is cut down like a flower. . . ."

When I came to the last part where the planks were to

be lifted at the head to let the bodies slide overboard, the plane was so close that the noise of its engines drowned out the words I was reading.

"*We therefore commit their bodies to the deep to be turned into corruption, looking for the resurrection, when the sea shall give up her dead.*" Then, as I read the Lord's Prayer, the men lifted the planks and the bodies slid into the sea.

We stood there for a moment, motionlessly, with thoughts of farewell, serene and unafraid in that curious isolation, and it was not just a farewell to our dear brothers now departed, but to life itself, which we had loved despite all its ups and downs, all its moments of doubt and loneliness and sorrow. The plane moved away; when we heard it come back in our direction, we knew that it was coming in for the attack. If it had been a spotter plane, it would have left to report our position.

Suddenly, there came the sound of gunfire from the aft deck of the *Fröken Bratt*. It was a pom-pom, firing at the plane as it came swooping down, cannons roaring. I called to the mate, "Swing out the boats!" and rushed to the bridge. I had just set foot on the stairs when there came behind us the shattering sound of a tremendous explosion. I swung around and saw a huge plume of dust and flying debris leap skyward out of her aft hold. The explosion was so massive and final that there could be only one explanation: underneath the innocent grain, the *Fröken Bratt* must have been carrying munitions. It could not be otherwise; no round of cannon fire from an aircraft could have caused this tremendous eruption unless the exploding shells had ignited a load of TNT in her holds. She was going down so fast that I ordered the hawser cut, but already the mate had done so. I saw her crew rush blindly toward the rail, gesturing, beckoning, milling about in panic; as we had difficulty in lowering our boats, I started to swing the ship around to come alongside her so that we could pick the men up from the water when they jumped. I heard the plane coming back, and again I heard the staccato stutter of its board cannons over the whining drone of its engines as it banked, but I paid it no attention. I swung the *Isabel Kwel* around at full speed, headed back for the freighter, aiming to come alongside over my starboard bow. I stood with my hand on the engine-room telegraph, called, "Hard over port!" to the man at the helm; when her long, low stern was well into its swing, I yanked the engine-room telegraph to Full Astern to check her skid and stop her in position. Then it happened.

Despite my putting the engine in reverse, the ship did not respond. She was committed in a full-speed starboard swipe, and although the propeller churned away, it refused to dig in and check that lethal swing toward the heaving hulk of the freighter, now looming overhead. I stood there, helpless, utterly powerless, and watched her seven hundred tons slam broadside into the steel cliff of the freighter. The ships collided with the sound of an explosion and the concussion of a direct hit; there was a deafening, splintering noise as the starboard boat, by now swung out, was crushed against the *Fröken's* hull. Then I heard a shrill voice shriek from the boatdeck, "Skipper!"

It was the mate. He pointed aft. It took me a split second to realize what he meant, then I saw it. Dislodged by the tremendous collision, no longer checked now that the catapults had been removed, the starboard depth charges were rolling down their rails toward the rectangular gap where the mine-laying gate had been torn away.

I knew what would happen. I knew it as I saw one gay orange-and-white canister after another roll toward the stern, with nothing to stop them from rolling overboard at the end of the rails. Then I saw someone on the aft deck leap at them, trying to stop them with a piece of planking. It was the corporal of the gunners, in a last desperate effort to prevent disaster. For one heart-stopping moment, it looked as if he were going to make it, as if he had indeed managed to stop those rolling canisters of death in their tracks, but their momentum was too great. His piece of planking snapped like a match, he lost his balance and, with a shriek of horror, his body, arms flailing, vanished over the stern as the first canister dropped.

The wait between that awful moment and the inevitable sequel seemed endless, timeless. We just stood there, all of us, watching motionlessly, unable to move, suspended in a vacuum of eternity. Then there was a deep, rumbling, shuddering concussion as the depth charge exploded right under our stern. The whole ship was lifted bodily by what looked like a tremendous eruption of boiling milk, a white geyser leaping higher than the aft deck of the freighter. The engine raced crazily as our stern was lifted high; the depth charges on their way down toward the stern came rolling back as the deck tilted. I expected them to explode amidships when they hit the end of the rails, but they did not. The stern sank into a deep trough; the water of the explosion came raining down upon us, a furious cloudburst; the depth charges started to roll toward the stern again, the whole row of them, rumbling down the rails. I slammed the engine-room telegraph on Full Speed Ahead, but the engine raced crazily without any effect; the propeller was gone, torn off by the explosion. The ship was paralyzed forever, this was the end of the line.

I shouted, "Abandon ship! All hands to the portside boat!" and as men started running, I yelled at the heads peering down on us from above, on top of the cliff of the freighter, "Get out of the way! Jump from the other side!

We're blowing up!"

It all happened so fast that the telling takes longer. While the men rushed toward the boat, I saw the depth charges roll toward the gap again. If they were to drop overboard together, they would blow the stern clean off the ship. I saw men in boiler suits come out of the engine-room hatch. One of them was Porks, and I saw he was weeping; then the Second came up, stumbling as he stepped out onto the deck. For a moment, the first depth charge at the end of the row seemed to teeter on the brink, then the sea lifted the stern again and the whole row of them rolled back toward the midships once more.

I cried, "Lower away!" As I ran toward the chartroom to grab the briefcase with the ship's papers, I heard the squealing of pulleys and a voice crying, "Skipper! Come on, Skipper!"

The chartroom was a shambles. The front wall had been blown out; part of the ceiling caved in; the briefcase was gone.

Again the voice cried, "Skipper! Come on!" with desperate urgency.

I came, a running leap. Suddenly I was overcome by a blind panic; I didn't care if I broke my legs.

To my astonishment, I fell on something soft and resilient: a mountain of duffel coats, blankets, sea boots, mufflers—the stores from the jolly, which Cook had put back into the lifeboat. The moment I dropped into the boat, the mate yelled, "Heave away!" and the men at the oars started pulling away from the ship, which was rearing once more, canisters rolling down the rails again toward the water. We must have been no more than five or six boat lengths away when another earthquake came; obviously a second canister had dropped off the stern into the sea. The convulsion it created was so colossal that our boat seemed about to be turned over by a tremendous breaker rolling toward us, lifting us skyward with a hissing crest of foam. I was sure that we would not make it, but the crest passed under us and we slithered down the slope of the wave like a toboggan.

"Heave away!" I yelled, and grabbed an oar myself. We pulled with all our might, and it seemed as if we did not make any headway at all, but then another wave came, lifted our stern and dragged us along. We lay wallowing in its trough when there followed the biggest explosion of all. I don't know how many canisters had rolled overboard this time, but it must have been almost the lot of them, to create such a monstrous eruption. For a few dreamlike, elongated moments, I saw the *Isabel Kwel* lifted bodily out of the water, her stern gone, her foreshortened body capsizing as she rose. I saw the cliff of the flank of the *Fröken Bratt* beside her tilt backward, as if pushed over by a giant hand, and go down in one slow, sloping movement. Then an avalanche of boiling milk came combing toward us, and I knew that this time we could not make it, we just could not. No boat could remain upright on the concave slope of the monstrous, curling wave now towering over us; I hid my face in my hands.

The mountain of water broke over us. For an eternity there was a deafening, hissing sound, so long that I thought: God, please, God, let it be over. Then the hissing gradually drew away; in the silence that followed I heard a thin shrieking voice, like that of a child, crying, "Hilfe! Hilfe! Hilfe!"

I took my hands off my face and looked in the direction of the sound. The boat, swamped, lay wallowing on a smooth black sea; in that sea, close by, the head of a Negro boy was screaming, "Hilfe! Hilfe!" I wondered, groggily, how the *Fröken Bratt* could have had a Negro boy on

board who spoke German; but it was no Negro boy, the
sea was black with oil.

There could only be one explanation for that oil slick:
a submarine had broken up. The boy, crying like a bird in
the oil that smoothed the waves, must be a member of the
crew of a U-boat. It was not the cannon of that plane
that had caused the *Fröken Bratt* to explode with such
violence; she had not had munitions in her hold. She had
been struck by a torpedo from a U-boat lurking close by
while the plane attacked; it must be the same U-boat that
had sunk the others, and now, in a bizarre Wagnerian Göt-
terdämmerung, they had all gone down together, a
writhing nest of vipers of violence, slowly sinking through
the icy water of the Arctic into the deep to which we had
committed the bodies of our brothers now departed.

It took me a few moments to grasp what had happened,
then I ordered the boat over to the drowning boy. I heard
the plane roar overhead, circling; I saw the *Isabel Kwel's*
bows rise out of the sea and slide down backward swiftly,
almost gracefully; then a man leaped up in front of me,
brandishing a boathook. To my incredulous horror, I saw
him start to slam away at the water, jabbing the hook at
the bobbing head black with oil, yelling, "Bastards! Bastards! Sadistic bastards!" at the top of his voice. It was
the mate.

"Grab him!" I called; and many arms were stretched out
toward him, pulling him down. He lost his balance,
dropped the hook, screamed obscene abuse in total hysteria, fighting, kicking, biting, trying to tear himself loose;
in the meantime I bent over the edge and grabbed a slippery, slithering arm.

I thought we would lose him. The oil made him as slick
as an eel; but others helped me, and we managed to drag
him, clumsily, painfully, over the edge of the boat. He

slumped into the sloshing water on hands and knees, shivering, sobbing, vomiting, reeking of crude petroleum; then a deafening roar came streaking past us and again there sounded those odd twangs I had heard before when shells from the U-boat gun had struck close to the ship. I heard the Second cry, "Butchers!" at the sky, then he ducked, hiding his face in the crook of his arm; it was the plane, trying to sink us with its board cannons. It missed, although the boat was rocked by the explosions; then it swooped, swerved, banked and came down for another pass. I watched it coming down out of the sun, then I heard a high-pitched childish voice screaming, in German, "Halt! Halt! I am Heini Rabenschnabel, cook's help second-class, U-237! Don't kill me! Don't kill me! Kamerad! Kamerad! Heil Hitler!" It was the boy, risen to his knees in the fear of death, his oil-blackened face preposterous and comic, his right arm raised in the Nazi salute, staring in incredulous horror at that plane bearing down on him, guns blazing.

I don't know what made me do it. I was through with my life; only a moment ago I had sat there hoping that it would soon be over, yearning to follow Sparks and Mashpee and the carpenter and the others down into the peace of death. But something in the German boy's horror at seeing the plane swoop down on him, to snuff out his pathetic little light in the vastness of the sea, made me want to protect him from the ultimate truth. I pulled him down and threw myself on top of him, the way the boy Tyler had thrown himself in front of the guns of a strafing plane to protect a wounded kitten. I thought: This is what he wanted me to understand, this is why he haunted me, now I know. But now it was too late; this was the end.

I lay on top of the trembling boy for what seemed an eternity. I smelled the reek of the oil on his face, I felt the small warmth of his panting breath on my cheek, I heard his voice whimper close to my ear, "Mutti, Mutti, Mutti." As the plane came screaming down, I put my hand under his head and pressed his face into my shoulder to prevent his seeing the firing squad at the moment of our execution.

As I lay there, pressing his head against me, it was as if, at the very last moment, I had finally touched upon the sense of life, the meaning of it all, the essence of my existence. I had a feeling of such peace, such understanding, such serenity, that it came as an anti-climax, almost as a disappointment, when the world fell silent, the roar of death drew away and I realized that I would have to go on living.

I lifted my head and looked around me, and saw men wake up amidst the chaos of clothing and blankets and stores and bodies and oars. The sea was empty but for some floating debris. All sounds were gone but for the distant drone of the plane, diminishing; far away, beyond the border of the oil slick, sounded the soft swish of waves curling and falling.

"Well, that was a close call," a calm voice said. It was the Second, a placid face close to my shoulder.

Then I heard a sound of weeping, a muffled voice sobbed, "It's my fault, it's my fault—nobody will ever forgive me—nobody can ever forgive me—it's my fault—I did it, I did it—it was me. . . ."

"Don't worry, boy," I heard the Second say, and I saw him stretch out his hand and touch Porks' shoulder. "You couldn't help it. It was a stupid way to build an engine anyhow."

While I sat there with the remnants of that strange, unearthly serenity still about me, I saw the German boy stare at me in terror. With his blackened face, he looked like a child that has suddenly realized it is no longer surrounded

by friends but by alien menacing enemies. I smiled at him
and said in German, "You are a lucky boy, Heini. A very
lucky boy."

He stared at me dazedly; his lower lip began to tremble,
and then he saluted.

I let my eyes roam slowly along the horizon. There was
nothing in sight, not a ship, not a bird, nothing at all, just
the gray empty sea breathing like a sleeper, dotted here
and there with the sparse pathetic flotsam left of the three
ships, friend and foe. I could not recognize any of it as
having belonged to the *Isabel Kwel*, but Cook could. I
heard him cry, "Look, that's ours!" and saw him paddle
vigorously with his oar, swinging the boat around. Then
he bent over the edge and picked up something out of
the water; it was the tray he had so often carried into the
chartroom, whenever I did not want to go down to the
messroom for a meal.

In my state of euphoria, the sight of it triggered the
memory of a poem that I had learned by heart a long time
ago, when I went through a period of wanting to write
poems myself. I had not thought of it for years, and all of
a sudden, there it was, all at once.

> The stately ship is seen no more,
> The fragile skiff attains the shore;
> And so the great and wise decay,
> And all their trophies pass away,
> While some odd thought, some careless rhyme,
> Still floats above the wrecks of time.

Then it occurred to me how baroque this would have
seemed to Captain Mashpee of the British cruiser *Intrepid:*
his favorite Dutch tug driver, lost in the Arctic with a
swamped boat full of junk and bodies, reciting poetry
while gazing soulfully at the horizon. If this fragile skiff

had to attain the shore, I would have to shake the eerie spell of eternity that still kept me completely at peace, utterly serene, totally uninterested in making any moves or plans toward our survival. I would have to shake the be-witching sense of relativity which made me feel that for us to start scrambling toward some distant shore was not only futile but shortsighted to a point of stupidity. The only shore worth attaining was the one we had sung about in our hymn, as the bodies of Sparks, the sailor and the carpenter had rested on the rail of the *Isabel Kwel* waiting to be committed to the deep; that farther shore on which those weary voyagers had landed, and now our ship as well.

Underlying my serene detachment, and my reluctance to start striving for the survival of the flickering candle flames of our lives, was a homesickness, a deep wordless yearning for that world which had gone forever, the *Isabel Kwel*. The thought of her, sinking slowly through the lightless depths toward the bottom of the Arctic Ocean, filled me with such sorrow, such an overwhelming sense of loss, that I took up life again as an escape, saying, "All right, men. Let's sort ourselves out and see where we go from here."

4

Before we had sorted ourselves out, the Second spotted a ship on the horizon. It seemed to be heading straight for us; we waved and shouted, setting the dog barking and prancing excitedly on the mountain of Cook's stores.

It was the *Loch Rannoch;* her captain had seen the plane dive from afar and heard the distant explosions. Being the man he was, he had turned around to go and look for survivors, despite the danger to himself, his crew and the wounded he had taken on earlier.

We were picked up toward nightfall: seven men, a boy and a dog; all that was left of Holland's Glory.

CHAPTER ELEVEN

I

"Yes, I believe he's off the line," Miss Crumb said, gingerly putting down the interoffice phone. "Would you like to go in?"

In the past, she had always had second thoughts at this point; so when she stopped me as I was about to knock, I was overcome by a comforting sense of tradition. "Just a sec!" she said. "Maybe I'd better make sure. . . ."

She teetered to the door. Her skirt seemed still tighter and her heels higher than last time I had seen her; her mere act of walking was about to become a vaudeville act. Otherwise she had not changed and, obviously, neither had I, in her eyes at least. Suddenly, the weight of history, all those climactic moments we had shared, brought about more than a pleasant sense of tradition. Out of the blue, I was struck by the thought that what I really had been looking for during the past three days, roaming the streets of London, hesitating in the porches of churches, was not some wise and patient father confessor, but Miss Crumb. A meal with her in her flatlet, followed by a cup of tea and the *Evening Star* on the couch while she did the washing-up, topped off by the two of us on the couch with the sobbing violins of "Tuesday Serenade" in the background, seemed much more attractive than a session at the confessional. My yearning for a priestly voice saying, "Tell me, my son, tell me all of it," suddenly appeared rather pretentious, pure Bosmania; the truly liberating formula I had been looking for was, "Ah-ah, Commodore! Naughty!" followed by a playful tweak of the commodorial nose. I imagined myself waking up at dawn with her in my arms, sleepily fondling her breasts before drifting off into sleep again; it was such a mirage of peace and sheer relief that I blurted out, in my most British voice, "Miss Crumb, I'd like to have dinner with you tonight. Not in a restaurant this time, if you don't mind, but at home."

Her onyx-clawed finger, ready to knock on her master's door, froze in surprise and seemed to look at me, like the glass eye of a doll. "Home?" she asked, nonplussed.

"At your place. I'm afraid that's the closest thing to home I have, at the moment."

It was a pretty direct approach, to say the least; but it did not seem to shock or even surprise her. She gave me a calm, unrattled look which, for a moment, I mistook for disapproval; then she said, thoughtfully, as if this were the end of a long conversation, "I don't think I have enough of that rabbit left, and it's just about closing time. . . ."

"So, let's hurry! We'll take a taxi to Soho, buy a couple of bottles of South African wine and pick up some fish and chips on the way. Have you got a radio?"

She had not been listening. "Shepherd's pie," she said, with a frown of concentration. "Do you fancy shepherd's pie?" Before I had been able to answer enthusiastically in the affirmative, she pointed at the door and asked, "What about *him?*"

"He can wait," I said, grandly. "I'll see him in the morning."

Her eyes opened wide and suddenly she looked the way she should have looked to start with: coy and genteelly outraged. "Christmas!" she said. "Aren't you the impetuous one! And what if it's urgent?"

"It can't be urgent," I said, suddenly feeling the sheer physical longing to lie in her arms. "I sank his last ship, so he and I have plenty of time for talk."

"I'm afraid you haven't," she said. "He just bought another one, almost as big as the *Isabel*."

"You're joking. . . ."

"A Japanese oceangoing tugboat, confiscated by the Navy."

"Japanese?!"

The door opened. "Miss Crumb . . . " Then he saw me. "Ah, Harinxma! Come in."

I suddenly did not want this conversation. I did not want to talk about it, not yet. I was on the point of telling him that I would see him tomorrow, when she caught my eye and smiled, as if she were soothing an obstreperous child. Somehow, she managed to condense a long, complicated signal into that fleeting smile: Don't! I know you're strong and brave, but there's no need to prove it to me at this point by being rude to him. We have time enough to go to Soho, and anyway I have a couple of things to finish here first, so why don't you go and have a chat with him? Come on, go in.

I said, "Thank you, sir," and went in.

He closed the door behind me. I expected him to go to his desk, as usual; but this time he did not. He stopped beside me; then, rather shyly, he put a hand on my shoulder. I looked at him, startled and wary; but for the first time his impersonal face seemed almost human, as if at last it had been touched by tragedy. "Well, we did our best," he said. "I'm happy that you were spared. It isn't the ships that matter, but the men who sail them." After that, he hurried for shelter behind his desk. Once safely in his chair, he opened his cigar box and proffered it to me. I wanted to show that I had appreciated his moment of sincerity, and I said, "It will be a long time before we get another one like her." It was all I could think of on the spur of the moment.

He smiled. "Most likely, never; but there will be others. Sit down. Have a cigar." He was his old self again, but I did not mind. I shot quite a line myself; to be comfortable, a man needs clothes to cover his nakedness. I took a cigar and he brought out his lighter.

"Where did you leave your—er—crew, in Reykjavik?" he asked with a short hesitation before the word "crew" as if he were talking about someone who had died and did not know whether to refer to him by name or just as "the body."

I said, "Thank you," and leaned back with my cigar lit. "I put them up with the Americans. They have a billet for transient pilots, a compound of Nissen huts near the airport. They were quite happy to take them in." For a moment, I saw in my mind's eye the curved ceiling of a Nissen hut, a bar with an array of bottles, the jocular notice: *Colonels below the age of 21 will not be served unless accompanied by parent or guardian,* and a grinning Negro corporal with one flashing gold tooth, expert at handling shell-shocked crews who came wandering in dazed and on the brink of tears, after a flight in which some of their buddies had been killed.

"Why the Americans?"

"Since the escort left us in the lurch, the men felt some resentment against the British."

"Unjustified, but understandable."

There was a silence, in which I puffed at my cigar. "You heard how many vessels of the convoy made it to Murmansk?" I asked.

"Two, I gather."

"One. The other one was beached on the Rybachi Peninsula."

"Yes," he said, "it's a shame. You know about the *Tirpitz*, I suppose?"

"Yes, sir," I said dryly. It had been all over Iceland. At first, I had thought the rumor must be a product of American wishful thinking; it was obvious there was no love lost between them and the British. But in the ferry plane, on the way to Prestwick, I had sat next to a commander of the Royal Navy who had confirmed it, poker-faced, but with obvious embarrassment. The *Tirpitz* had left Alta Fjord just long enough to trick the Navy into withdrawing its escort from the convoy; the moment that had been achieved, the battleship had turned about and high-tailed it back to base before the British had been able to spring their trap. Obviously, the whole plan had been known from the very beginning to the German High Command, who had turned it to suit their own ends. Criticism of the Royal Navy had been pretty vociferous in the bars of Reykjavik; I myself would have joined in with relish, had it not been for Mashpee. Whenever I was tempted to feel self-righteous about it, there was *Intrepid*, her four propellers thrashing in the air, flying her signal of defiance, diving to her death.

"Well," he said, "I suppose we'd better get down to a full report. On the telephone, you gave me only the barest outline."

It was the moment I had been waiting for with apprehension. I had known that, sooner or later, I would have to take a deep breath and go through it all over again, move by move, minute by minute. When I had stood on the poop deck of the *Loch Rannoch*, watching the white speck of our lifeboat vanish in the grayness of the Arctic sea, I had felt such overwhelming sadness, such despair, that I had turned away and decided to put the whole thing out of my mind, forcibly, until such time as I would feel ready to face it without the danger of being over-whelmed by emotion. A week had gone by; gradually, I had come to feel more secure, but it was still too early for me to discuss it dispassionately. First, I had to get rid of all that pent-up emotion by letting myself go, blurting it out to someone who would not mind my coming apart at the seams. The idea of the father confessor had seemed a good one, until I had seen Miss Crumb. I might tell it all to her tonight; I was not going to fool around with it here, cigar or no cigar.

"What about tomorrow, sir?" I asked. "It's likely to be a long session and I don't think we should be pressed for time."

He gave me a bland look and said, "Oh, but we have plenty of time as far as I'm concerned. What about joining me for dinner?"

"Thank you, I'd like to, but I'm afraid I have already made other plans, sir."

To my surprise, he said, "Oh, I'm sorry," as if he really meant it. It had never occurred to me that he might be a lonely man.

"We can start as early as you like, tomorrow morning," I ventured, prompted by a vague sense of guilt. "If I had known . . . "

But he did not want me to get any ideas. "Thank you, Harinxma, that won't be necessary," he said coolly, and he rose. "Let's make it tomorrow morning, ten thirty. You obviously need some rest."

I rose too, and said, "Thank you, sir," relieved that we were back in our familiar roles again.

He went to the door. "You had better keep the whole of tomorrow free. After you and I are through with the report, I want you to come with me to see my father and it will take us a while to get there. He's anxious to meet you. The ship was built to his own design, you know. He has taken this rather hard."

I said, "Is that so?" He and I might have found some basis for communication, but I was not about to commiserate with his Daddy. His own design, indeed! Sardine tins for cabins, not an inch of space for stores, and too stingy to replace a right-hand engine-room telegraph that had been mounted on a left-hand engine. I had at last found out, during a session with a sobbing Porks and a paternal Second in the messroom of the *Loch Rannoch*, how the collision with the *Fröken Bratt* had come about. Hepped-up Porks had, for the second time in his life, slammed the engine full ahead in response to the signal Full Astern from the bridge. The first time this had happened had been in Greenock, when I had sideswiped old *"Blazes"* in a similar maneuver. But although he had actually committed the error, Porks could not be held responsible; the responsibility rested with Mr. Kwel Senior. He had refused to replace the engine-room telegraph on the *Isabel Kwel* when she was still under construction, despite the dire warning by Chief Bout that unless it was replaced, there was going to be an accident, sooner or later. Both Porks and the Second had explained it to me, with drawings; what it amounted to was that the *Isabel Kwel* had not harbored a secret flaw, as I had assumed in Greenock. Her erratic behavior, that had seemed so malignant and mysterious when she refused to obey her rudder and slammed into old

"*Blazes*," had been caused by human error after all. But the error had been committed by the old skinflint who had ordered the yard to use as much as possible of the hardware that was being ripped out of the old *Honesta Kwel,* dying under the wreckers' hammers while her granddaughter *Isabel* was being born on the stocks. After that, I was not prepared to commiserate with the devil of my early manhood now that his sins were catching up with him. I hoped, uncharitably, that he would have plenty of time to ruminate upon them before he, in his turn, fell under the wrecker's hammer. "I'm sorry to hear it," I said.

But he did not seem to notice my lack of sincerity; maybe he had inherited from his old man the gift of not noticing what he did not want to notice. He opened the door and said, "Well, good night, Captain. Glad to have you back. See you in the morning." He went back into his office, but left the door open; Miss Crumb, after another motherly smile, mouthed, "Swan and Edgar, same time."

I did not understand why it had to be kept a secret from him; if I wanted to take his secretary out for a night on the town, it was none of his business. But as she had to live with him, I decided to play it her way.

2

We met in the same place, in front of the department store. After I had been pacing up and down for a while with growing embarrassment, she came out of the Underground station, against the tide of the after-office crowd. She tripped toward me on her teetering heels and almost shattered my composure by placing a demure kiss on my mouth, after which she tucked her arm into mine and said,

"All right, Marty, shall we go and shop first?"

For a split second I balked, idiotically; then I put my cap back on at a roguish angle and stepped boldly into the dream by saying, "All right. Let's go."

While we stood waiting to cross over to Shaftesbury Avenue, I said, "By the way, to go on calling you Miss Crumb seems a little out of date. What do I call you?"

She smiled up at me, completely at ease, dependent on my strong male arm. "My real name is Mabel," she said, "but my friends call me Cookie."

The ineradicable snob in me winced, the way he had winced at "Marty"; then the lights changed to green, the crowd moved massively across to Soho, and Marty and Cookie, arm in arm, moved with it.

From that moment on, reality began to conform so completely to my daydream that it seemed as if, during those moments of fantasy, I had been granted a glimpse of the future. We had a jolly time shopping, emerging in the end with an armful of exotic titbits such as Russian meat rolls, melon chutney and matzos. I hailed a taxi and gave the address of her flat; halfway there, I spotted a fish-and-chips shop and told the driver to stop. In its window, the shop carried a crude handwritten notice saying: *Now Frying God.*

By the time I opened the door to her flat with the key I had clumsily fished out of her handbag, I had, for the first time, managed to shake off the ghosts that had haunted me so remorselessly. Her flat, once the heat and the lights were turned on, promised to live up to expectations. It was a roomy bed-sitter with kitchenette, exuding warmth and coziness. It had a comfortable-looking divan, a dining table with two chairs, and one of those chintzy chaises-longues, found only in English bedrooms, that look strait-laced but turn out to be debauched. She dumped her part of the loot on the drainboard, turned on a standard lamp with a foxhunt on its shade and a radio in the corner of the room. While she sorted out the shopping and I laid the table, the radio was splitting its sides, all by itself, at the jokes in a weekly comedy series called ITMA.

ITMA and its cast of comics went on caterwauling, whistling, banging and ululating all through the meal; when it was time for the washing-up, she forced me to prostrate myself on the chaise-longue and put my feet up, exactly as I had dreamed in my moment of clairvoyance. I sensuously stretched, gazed at the foxhunt, closed my eyes and was about to doze off when, to the accompaniment of another explosion of inane laughter from the ITMA audience, a new character entered the invisible stage, welcomed by a wacky voice crying, "Hello there! If it isn't good old Sparks!"

I got up and whirled the knob, looking for another station; Miss Crumb's—Cookie's—voice called from the kitchenette, "Three fifty, darling, That's the Americans."

On three fifty, another crowd was bellowing with laughter at the jokes of Jimmy Durante. I went back to the chair, stretched out again, listened and realized that Jimmy Durante and his stooge were groping their way through an underground passage in an English castle. Suddenly, there was a blood-curdling scream from Durante, the stooge asked, "What was that?" and he answered, "I saw a ghost!" Then another blood-curdling scream, this time in the far distance; the stooge asked, "What was *that?*" and Durante answered, "The ghost saw *me.*" For some reason, it got me. I lay there laughing like a drain, tears running down my face, until, amid whistles, catcalls and cheers, a voice announced, "And here, at last, the number-one favorite of our Stage Door Canteen: Miss Dinah Shore!" The tumult died, an orchestra struck a single

note and there came her voice, simple and straight, singing
"Auld Lang Syne." Something in that voice, that song,
crumbled my defenses. I was totally unprepared for it,
there was nothing I could do; suddenly the whole pretense
of coziness and phoney domesticity collapsed and I just sat
there, my face in my hands, bawling my head off.

I don't know how long I sat there like that, but it was
long enough to make a mess of the whole thing. Good old
Miss Crumb, who had so far performed with such splendid
aplomb, was caught off balance; she stood staring at me,
aghast, totally unnerved, paralyzed by indecision. When I
finally managed to look up at her, crazily hoping that she
would take me in her arms, shelter me, comfort me, help
me, I saw she was as white as a sheet and so obviously
shaken that the mere sight of her distress helped me to get
a hold on myself. I made an effort at pretending that the
whole thing had been hysterical laughter, carried over
from the Durante show, by hitching up a grin that must
have made me look even more terrifying. But although we
managed, after a while, to extricate ourselves from the
outward symptoms of embarrassment, Marty and Cookie
had taken flight forever. We saw the rest of the evening
through with commendable concern for each other's discomfort; if only I had been able to explain to her what
was the matter with me, to give her an inkling of how a
man felt after a shipwreck or a plane crash, she might
have recovered sufficiently to carry it off; she must have
gone in for the whole thing only because she had sensed
that there was more to my bluff proposition in the office
than a sailor looking for a lay. And if the Negro corporal
with the gold tooth in Reykjavik could handle men in
shock, she certainly would have been able to, if only she
had been told what it was all about.

When at last I thought the moment had come to make

my getaway, she suddenly threw her arms around my neck and kissed me, fiercely, passionately, and with overwhelming sincerity. Just as, a few hours before, she had been able to transmit a complicated signal in a smile, she now conveyed in a kiss that she was sorry she had failed me, that she wanted desperately to help me, that she begged me to stay, to give her a chance to show how she felt. But by then it was too late; all I wanted at that moment was to flee.

When I was walking the streets once more, thinking about her, I reflected that the next sailor or pilot who appealed to her for help after a shipwreck or a crash was sure to fare better than I had done. Next time, she would be all a man could hope for after running for days, trying to find someone to stop his running. All she had lacked, in my case, had been the experience she now possessed.

3

The next morning, I was prepared for it. Whatever happened, I was not going to give the same lamentable show in front of Mr. Kwel that I had given in front of his secretary.

When I came in, she was as genteel and supercilious as she had always been, but the smile she gave me was one of concern. Mr. Kwel received me pleasantly, be it without the warm welcome I had been treated to the day before. When we were settled in his office, cigars and all, he suggested that I tell him in sequence what had happened, from the day we left Kirkwall. He would make notes as I spoke; afterward he would dictate a condensed English version of my report to Miss Crumb on the basis of his notes. I did not mind, he was welcome to do with my story whatever he liked; my problem was the telling of it.

But I need not have worried. After a few moments of apprehension, I relaxed and calmly started to tell the story, puffing at my cigar, without batting an eyelid. He listened attentively, without comment, even without questions; only occasionally he jotted down a note. But, despite his attentiveness and his obvious concern as owner of the lost vessel, I gradually became aware of a wall of incomprehension on his part. Not that he appeared to be critical or suspicious; he was obviously eager to listen with understanding and sympathy, but it became more and more apparent that he did not really know what I was talking about. He knew about ships, he knew about men; what he knew nothing about was the emotional relationship between the two. Not that this was important for my report; all he wanted was the facts; human emotions were pertinent only as far as they had influenced the course of events. So I related the facts, without mention of my visits to Dr. Hawthorne and the like, although it was clear to me that there the process of emotional escalation had started which had culminated in Porks' fatal error.

Leaving out the human element meant leaving out Porks' mistake; I did so without flinching, as it had not really mattered. Even had I been able to moor alongside the sinking *Fröken Bratt* more decorously, it would have made no material difference to the outcome. But even as I was presenting this case, I realized it was a high-handed presumption on my part. It might be unlikely, but there was, theoretically at least, the possibility that, had the canisters not been dislodged, I might have taken on more members of the crew of the *Fröken Bratt* and even made off before she sank. In that case, I would certainly have been attacked by the plane that had tried to sink the lifeboat; it would probably have scored a direct hit among the canisters, which would have had the same effect as the collision. But I could not be sure of that; theoretically, there was a chance we might have been able to make it, damaged but afloat, back to Iceland the way the *Loch Rannoch* had; for if the plane had failed to sink us, the U-boat's gun would have finished us off. So a case could be made that Porks was responsible for the loss of the *Isabel Kwel*, and I should mention his mistake. But this was not a court of inquiry; this was a preliminary report to the owner, who wanted to know the circumstances under which his vessel had been lost, but who would automatically be compensated, even if it were not until after the war, from enemy sources. He himself would not be keen to stress the possibility that the loss might have been due not to enemy action but to a mistake made by one of the crew. Whichever way it worked out, if I mentioned him, Porks would be the victim. Disciplinary action was unlikely, but his future as an engineer and as a human being would look bleak. He was a good engineer; given a chance, he would soon acquire the self-confidence to which his technical knowledge entitled him. I did not want him to take the rap for Old Man Kwel's original sin.

Calmly smoking my cigar, I went into great detail: the number of direct hits, the deaths of the carpenter, the gunners, Sparks, the attack on the bosun's lifeboat. I again mentioned the withdrawal of the escort and my crew's reaction to it; I did so to prepare a case in which I could tell the truth without blaming Porks directly. Looking at the man behind the desk, I knew that, despite his keen interest and his intelligent appraisal, I could bring it off; he did not know enough of ships, the sea and sailors to smell a rat. I covered the crucial episode of the collision in the same tone of objective detachment, choosing my words as carefully and painstakingly as before; when it came to the point, I said, "We approached the *Fröken Bratt* at a fairly high speed, I reversed the engine to line up alongside her, but the damage from the direct hits must have involved the controls from the bridge to the engine room, and the *Fröken Bratt* herself was moving to a degree that was difficult to judge at that point. So I came alongside her more forcefully than I would normally have done; although in itself inconsequential and even routine, as I had moored just as forcefully on other occasions, the impact this time must have tripped a critical balance of forces. It dislodged a row of depth-charge canisters on the starboard side of the aft deck, which then started to roll toward the gap in our stern that I mentioned before, where the minelaying hatch had been blown off."

There it was; I had passed the finish line without change of voice or of pace, and Mr. Kwel suspected nothing. I had never given the reason for our trial run in the Firth of Clyde; my mention of the presence of the Commanding Officer, Towing Operations, of the Royal Navy made it tacitly understood that the trials had to do with our conversion for Arctic duty.

Once I had passed that point, the rest was easy. I completed my story with the mention of the rescue of the German cook's help, Heini Rabenschnabel, and this was where Mr. Kwel put his first question.

"A German prisoner? Where is he? What did you do with him?"

"I handed him over to the authorities."

"Which authorities? Where?"

"The British Provost Marshal in Reykjavik."

"What on earth did you do that for?!"

I could not understand his sudden agitation; for over an hour I had been telling him about the destruction of the last of his capital ships and he had not put a single question; now, at the mention of the pathetic child who had lain crying in my arms, he became irritated. "Because it seemed the logical thing to do, sir, under the circumstances," I replied.

"I wish you had consulted me!" he cried testily, throwing down his pencil. "This is unfortunate, Captain, very unfortunate indeed."

"What would you have liked me to do, sir?"

"Why, take him along, of course! Keep him! You should have reported his capture to me, and I would have told you what to do with him."

Suddenly, it occurred to me that he might be a better man than I had suspected. Would he have kept Heini Rabenschnabel out of prison camp somehow, maybe by putting him to work on one of our medium craft? It was a short-lived illusion.

"The Dutch government has made it plain to me on several occasions that any prisoners of war taken by my vessels should be handed over to the Dutch authorities, so that they could present them to the British. It is very important for our national image that these things are handled through the proper channels."

"I am sorry if I have damaged our national image, sir," I said, gravely.

But he must have sensed my contempt, and he made things worse by chickening out. "Oh, well, there's no man overboard. It's a pity, that's all. Next time, please remember that in cases like this your first responsibility is to your owners."

"I see. I apologize, sir."

"That's quite all right." There was a short, strained silence in which something seemed to be decided, then he said, "All right," and proffered his box of cigars once more. "Let's call in Miss Crumb, and put all this into a report. I'll dictate it, but I'd like you to be there; should I go off the rails or omit something essential, please correct me."

Miss Crumb was called in and he started his dictation. He did not go off the rails once; his memory was faultless and his sense of organization impressive. It was a lucid, coherent and factually correct rendition of the sinking of the tugboat *Isabel Kwel* and the events that led up to it. The odd thing was, however, that, although factual, it sounded like a complete fabrication. Neither he nor Miss Crumb seemed to have any notion of the reality of the war as it was known to those who took the brunt of it. I sat there, listening, with a growing sense of loneliness; it was Halifax, Nova Scotia, all over again. Maybe what had brought this about was the business of Heini Raben-schnabel, the repulsive reduction of his individuality to that of a dead duck after a shoot, a unit in a body count. Heini had been very distressed when I had handed him over to the British; ever since that moment of truth in the lifeboat, he had clung to me as if I were his only friend in a hostile world. The reason was probably that I spoke German.

"All right," Mr. Kwel said. "That seems to be it, for the moment. Anything to add at this point, Captain?"

"No, sir, I can't think of anything."

"All right, Miss Crumb. The Commodore and I will now go and have lunch; if at all possible, I would like to pick this up in, say, a couple of hours' time, to take along to my father. I'm sorry that you may have to sacrifice your lunch hour; you can take the rest of the day off, if you like."

She said, "Very good, sir," and followed us out into the

hall, where she helped him into his coat, respectfully.

We had lunch at Netherlands House, a club for Dutchmen. After he had introduced me to a number of passing dignitaries who stopped to greet him on their way to their tables, he proceeded to tell me about the Japanese prize vessel that he had taken over from the British in partial exchange for the *Isabel Kwel*. It became obvious that he did not care about the *Isabel Kwel* for her own sake, only as part of his fleet—another body count. I gathered it was a fairly new vessel in good condition, not quite as large as the *Isabel* but of a formidable size even so, captured by the British the day after Pearl Harbor. He and I would decide whom to appoint as a skeleton crew, after which I was to fly out to Gibraltar and bring her home for survey and conversion. I listened noncommittally; I would not be available for the assignment, but I was not going to tell him so at this point.

My decision, after the massacre on board the *Isabel Kwel*, not to take part in the war any more, not to fire another shot nor become in any way involved in the death of another human being, had been arrived at under the pressure of extreme circumstances. I don't think I would have stuck to it had it not been for those few unearthly moments in the lifeboat when I lay waiting for death, sheltering the German boy from the terror of his execution. I had been unable to recapture the serenity and the peace I had felt during those moments; but something had happened all the same. The idea of sailing again in command of a ship that, although officially on an errand of mercy, would be armed to the teeth and geared for battle remained repulsive to me, to a point where I felt I could not do it. I had as yet no idea what the alternative would be; to give it any thought would have meant facing the memory that I had so forcibly suppressed. Now that I had brought it all into the open in those measured terms of detachment, I was ready to start thinking about the consequences. During our luncheon, as he sat there chatting about the company and his post-war plans, I began to consider the possible alternatives.

What I really felt like doing was to leave the sea and start work as a medic or something. Despite our differences of age, experience and character, I had arrived at the same conclusion as the boy Tyler: I was determined to kill no more. But this was not enough. I had decided to stop killing well before my experience in the lifeboat. A non-aggressive attitude was not enough; by working as a medic, I would continue to serve whatever it was Tyler's wounded kitten and my terrified German boy had represented in our moment of truth. I had no idea how to go about it, or even with whom to discuss it at this point; he had suggested we meet again in a few days' time to discuss the transport of the Japanese vessel, and that would have to be the showdown. But the future, even the immediate one, seemed abstract and remote. I was obsessed by a new awareness of the fullness of the present, the reality of the now, the total irreality of past and future.

"Well, Captain, shall we go?"

I gazed at him for a moment before the part of me that had detached itself was back in my body, alighting in noisy confusion, like a pigeon. "Yes, certainly, of course," I said, with an inane little laugh. "Whatever you say."

He did not seem to notice anything unusual; he got up, said, "All right, let's go and face Papa," and marched out.

I had forgotten all about the old man. I would have much preferred to be left to my own devices at this point, go for a walk in Hyde Park, roam the streets, thinking.

I simply had to find out what exactly I wanted, what the secret sharer wanted, the part of me that refused to let me fall back into the pleasant attitude of "Let's think about this after the war," which had made life so simple and comfortable before that blasted moment in the lifeboat.

But I could not get out of this; I had to follow him to the bedside of his father, even though I had no interest in meeting him, not any more. If anything belonged to the past, it was the bogeyman of my boyhood.

4

The house was a long way from London, two hours by car. By the time we drove through the garden gate it was late afternoon.

It was a large house of red brick, overgrown with ivy; a housekeeper in a white uniform let us in.

"How is he, Miss Bartels?" Mr. Kwel asked, handing her his hat and coat.

"Very well, I believe, Mr. Harry. Sister Klavermans seems pleased with him today."

Sister Klavermans, I concluded as we mounted a stately flight of carpeted stairs to the second floor, must be the buxom nurse who burst briskly from a doorway on the landing, brandishing a bedpan covered with a towel as if it were a weapon.

"Hello, Sister!" Mr. Kwel called, with the ingratiating voice of a man trying to placate a watchdog too soon.

The nurse looked sternly down the well of the stairs; when we climbed into the light she recognized him. "Oh, Mr. Harry. We are doing fairly well today, thank you. We expected you earlier."

"Yes, I'm sorry. We were held up by circumstances beyond our control."

"I'm afraid that rather limits your time, that's all," she said—with satisfaction, it seemed. "And don't let's have any argument when I come in to tell you it's time for our vital signs," she added. Without waiting for his confirmation, she stalked off with the bedpan, her starched skirt rustling, leaving a faint scent of soap.

Mr. Kwel arranged his tie and brushed up his smile before knocking on the door; he must have received an answer, for he opened the door and went in. "Hello, Papa!" I heard him say, brightly. "How are we today? . . . Just a moment, here he is, here he comes. . . . " He turned to me and beckoned imperatively. "Here he is: young Captain Harinxma."

I went in.

The bed that dominated the room was empty. It was high and full of pillows; on the night tables on either side stood an array of thermos flasks, basins, glasses, one of them holding a thermometer. There was a smell of sickness in the air, although French doors to a balcony were open. In front of the doors, in a wheelchair, sat an old man, wrapped in a blanket. He did not turn around when we came in, but went on staring stolidly ahead at the river, the hills and the sunset. His hands, veined and gnarled, gripped the arms of the chair. Mr. Kwel stood looking down on him, ingratiatingly, shiftily, and, it seemed, poised for flight. I joined him, turning my back to the French doors; then I saw, for the first time, the face of the man who had dominated the years of my youth.

He was ancient, and desperately frail. His skull, covered with flossy white hair, looked as fragile as an eggshell; his ears, disproportionately large and red, looked as if they did not belong to him, but had been put on for the occasion by the nurse, together with his little bow tie, debonair and ludicrous on his pajamas. He had indeed a beard, as I had expected, but it was so thin and sparse that his chin and jaw were plainly visible. His nose was pale and waxy, his mouth crooked and wet with spittle; he would have looked pitiful, had it not been for his eyes. They were not the eyes of an old man at all: bright blue, unflinching, commanding, they sized me up with cursory impatience. He looked like a youthful star of the stage, spoiled and famous, in his dressing room before the performance, already made up for the part of King Lear.

"So you are the young bungler who sank my ship," he said. It was not a question, it was a statement. His voice too was that of a youthful actor preparing for his part. The mouth, old and slack and drooling, was the king's, the voice that of the imperious jeune premier.

"Come, come, Papa," I heard Mr. Kwel say beside me, trying to gloss over the insult with an effort at jocundity. "I have with me the report of the, er, occurrence, as dictated this morning by myself on the basis of what the captain told me. I thought you might care to have a look at it." He held out Miss Crumb's neat typescript, which he had folded lengthwise and put in his pocket as we left the office.

But the old bastard was not to be placated. "I don't want any report that the two of you cooked up after the fact," he said with scorn. "Where is your ship's journal, young man?"

"It was lost, sir," I said. I did not mind him; he did not frighten or even intimidate me. If I felt anything for him at that moment, it was an abstract pity. He obviously was old and feeble and helpless, and hated himself for it.

"That sounds damned convenient," he said, with a mirthless grin of his lopsided mouth. "How did you manage that? Drop it overboard?"

I was acutely aware of the embarrassment of the man beside me; he literally squirmed, although it had nothing to do with him. I was completely unmoved by it; for me, the blatant exaggeration of the accusation had a rather roguish appeal. The eyes went on observing me unflinchingly; the intemperate words seemed part of his disguise. "The log disappeared with the briefcase when the front of the chartroom was blown out by the first direct hit," I replied calmly.

For a moment, the eyes that had been submitting me to such intensive scrutiny seemed to look through me. His face, despite the beard and the old man's make-up, suddenly looked haggard, as if he saw it happen with his own eyes. I remembered that she had been his favorite ship; it began to dawn on me why his outrageous words and behavior failed to impress me. I realized, with a sudden return of that feeling of insecurity in the face of my own emotions, that he understood it all. With the son, I had had the growing impression that he did not know what I was talking about; the father knew, and could not be fooled.

"All right," he said to his son, "let's hear that report."

"You don't want to read it yourself? Shall I get your glasses?"

"No, you read it! But not in English. Translate it as you go along. Go ahead."

"But I don't know if I'll be able to do that, Papa. I mean . . . "

"Read it, please! Go ahead." His tone had been icily imperious, but the knuckles of his gnarled hands had turned white again as they gripped the arms of his chair. He must have been hard to cope with, in his time. No wonder Bokke Loppersum, a giant himself, had been the only one who had stood up to him. The confrontations of those two must have been something to see; it occurred to me that old Bokke might not have been the only one to enjoy them.

Mr. Kwel Junior obediently started to improvise a translation of the report he had dictated to Miss Crumb. At first, I could not understand why the old man had not asked me to speak for myself; but while the voice beside me continued to recite in awkward, halting words an outline of what had happened, the old man's eyes never left me; he looked as if he were watching it all take place in my face. I do not know why, but when I heard it all described again in those unemotional, abstract terms, apparently so unevocative, I felt for the first time as if the wound were uncovered, raw, bleeding, throbbing with pain. It was the old man who did it. He looked at me with infinite sadness; although there was no mention of them, not by so much as a word, he seemed to see and understand all about Sparks, the carpenter, the burial, the ghastly destruction of the ship, the way she had reared as if in pain before she went down, Cook crying, "Hey! That's ours!" and holding up a dripping tray. Toward the end, I could barely hold back my tears. If I had known it was going to be like this, I would never have come. It was as if my heart broke all over again, I was overwhelmed once more by that awful feeling of bereavement, ending in utter wretchedness.

After the voice had stopped reading, there was a silence. Then the old man said, hoarsely, without taking his eyes off me, "Leave us alone."

"Pardon, Papa?"

"Leave us alone," he said, calmly, but with an authority that brooked no argument. "I want to talk to him. When I need you, I'll call."

I felt that the man beside me was about to say something; but he thought better of it. He folded the typescript, put it back in his pocket, and walked quietly away.

I did not see him leave the room; I looked at the old man and he looked at me. I heard the door close; then he said, "So I was right: you *are* the young bungler who sank her. What happened?"

"Pardon?"

"What do you take me for? I designed that ship myself; I have forgotten more about how to handle a tugboat than you will ever know; don't treat me as if I were an accountant, like my son. What happened?"

"Honestly, sir, I don't know. . . . " It was childish, I did not know why I held out like this; I just could not believe that he had spotted the truth, so carefully hidden in my own report that in Mr. Kwel's it had completely vanished from sight.

But he did not relent. His eyes never wavered, his voice remained the same as it had been all along, harsh and disdainful, but dispassionately so. "You cannot 'jolt' depth-charge canisters into rolling down the deck," he said. "Only a collision could have done that. You must have slammed her into that other ship full-speed. Why?"

"The engine room was late responding to my order, sir."

"What order?"

"Full Speed Astern."

"What was your speed when you gave that order?"

"Half Speed Ahead, sir."

"What was the position of your rudder?"

"Hard over port."

"Then your engine room was not just 'late responding.' Your engine room must have reversed the order. Isn't that so?"

"In a sense . . . "

"Stop it! Can't you see that you cannot fool me? I know that ship; to slam her broadside into that wreck with an impact that made a row of depth charges jump the rails, you must have been going full speed ahead. Isn't that so?"

"Yes, sir," I said, at last.

He betrayed no emotion; he was not interested in my feelings, or in anything else about me. All he was interested in was the truth. I was overcome by dejection; I had hoped for a moment that here at last was a man who understood. But he could not be bothered; he wanted to know what had happened to his ship, and the hell with me.

"What did you mean when you said that this had happened before?" he asked.

"Pardon?"

"Your report said that the rough landing could be considered routine, because it had happened before. When? Where?"

It was obviously pointless to go on struggling; I told him, as succinctly as I knew how, about our sideswiping old "*Blazes*" and how I had tried for days to determine what had been the cause.

"It never occurred to you at the time that your engineer might simply have reversed the order?" he asked.

"No, sir."

"Why did you not put in your report that that was the case this time?"

There it was. "I did not think it was material, sir," I replied, staunchly.

"Not material? A ship is sunk as a result of a collision,

and you consider it 'not material' to mention the cause of the collision?"

"I thought, considering the circumstances, that it might be best not to mention it, at this point."

"You mean, you wanted to protect your engineer?"

"I wanted to protect *you*." I said it calmly, deliberately, expecting him to react with anger, indignation, guilt, anything. I should have been prepared for what he did: he did nothing. He went on looking at me with those remorseless eyes, unflinchingly; his voice, as he continued his interrogation, had not changed. It was impossible to provoke him to anger or any other emotion. He could not be provoked; he was as singleminded, invulnerable and merciless as a tank.

"In what sense were you protecting me?"

"Because of the engine-room telegraph, sir, that you refused to replace."

"Engine-room telegraph?"

"The right-hand telegraph that was taken out of the old *Honesta* and mounted on the *Isabel's* left-hand engine, sir, the one Chief Bout warned you about when he said that unless you had it replaced at once, there would be accidents."

"Who told you that story, Captain?" His voice was unchanged, but his eyes, for some reason, suddenly seemed to relent.

"My engineer, sir, who had heard it from Chief Bout himself."

"Captain," he said, and now his voice seemed to have relented too, "has it not occurred to you that your engineer may have been lying?"

My heart sank. It had never occurred to me, and I could not accept it. "No, sir. I am sure he did not."

"Why, Captain? He lied to you once before, when he

helped you explore all possibilities for her disobeying her rudder except the truth: that he had reversed the order from the bridge."

"I believe him, sir, because the second engineer, a man I trust implicitly, corroborated his story. He confirmed that the engine-room telegraph was mounted the wrong way around, and that an error in a moment of extreme stress was virtually unavoidable."

He looked at me, almost kindly, with the same harrowed sadness I had noticed when I mentioned the first direct hit on the *Isabel Kwel.* "Captain," he said, "that telegraph was replaced the day Chief Engineer Bout mentioned it to me. The foreman of the yard, who never handled engines himself, had put it there in slavish obedience to my general instructions to utilize the hardware of the *Honesta* wherever possible. I knew, of course, that to mount a right-hand telegraph on a left-hand engine was asking for trouble, so I made sure it was replaced before the trial run; she never sailed a mile with that telegraph. You are a foolish young man, Captain. What on earth made you assume that none of your officers would ever lie to you? That under your command no engineer would shield a colleague by corroborating a cock-and-bull story? Don't tell me you have the illusion that, as a captain, they would ever trust you sufficiently to make you part of an engine-room plot to hide the truth?"

It couldn't be true, it couldn't be—the Second had been a friend. But then I saw in my memory the engine room, the Second on a stool, having his head bandaged, and I heard Porks shout again over the racket of the engine, "He ruined the telegraph with his coconut! Sit still!" I had looked up at the telegraph and seen the broken glass in front of the dial, blocking the hand. The image was still as clear in my memory as if I were looking at reality. It was a normal dial, a left-hand one.

The realization of their duplicity was so shattering that I balked at accepting it. "I don't understand, sir. . . . Why shouldn't they trust me?"

"Suppose they did, Captain? Suppose your young chief engineer had confessed, in Greenock, that he had switched the engine to Full Ahead instead of to Full Astern in response to your order from the bridge, what would your reaction have been? Would you have said, 'Never mind, old boy, next time better,' and forgotten about it? Or would you have asked the head office for a new chief engineer, instead of for a new Second, and never mind the young man's feelings? Well, Captain?"

"I—er—I suppose you're right, sir."

"And suppose that this time your engineers had confessed that the same man had made the same error for the second time, what would your reaction have been? Would you have hushed up the truth, the way you have now? Would you have supported their story that, after working with the same engine for four years, a man was not adjusted to whatever engine-room telegraph he had down there? What would you have done?"

"I would have reported him, sir."

"All right. Go ahead and do so. Tell my son that the report you made is erroneous and ask him to tear it up. Then make a new report and, this time, write it yourself. A full report, Captain, beginning with the episode in Greenock, mentioning the fact that, due to your inexperience as a commanding officer, it did not occur to you at the time that the young man you had promoted to chief engineer might be as inexperienced as you were yourself."

"Just for the record, sir: I did not ask for the job. I was forced into it," I said, patiently.

"Don't you tell me!" he cried, and for the first time, his

voice betrayed real anger. "If I hadn't been tied down to that blasted bed, if I had still been sitting in the office myself, I would have placed you on oceangoing tugboats as a mate, until you knew what you were doing! But if, in my eyes, you are exonerated, it does not mean that you can now worm your way out of telling the truth! You shall tell exactly what happened, and leave it to the head office to take whatever steps they may deem necessary. As matters now stand, all the head office has to go by is a pack of lies, concocted by a couple of schoolboys whose only interest is the skin of their own backsides, and the hell with the company."

I suppose I should have felt crushed or hostile under his tongue-lashing; instead, I seemed to breathe more freely. "All right, sir," I said. "I'll rewrite my report. I hope, however, that it won't mean that my engineer—"

He did not let me finish. "Never mind your engineer! You leave it to me, whose responsibility it is, to decide what shall be done with that unfortunate young man! It is neither your problem nor your business; you are not responsible for his fate. So don't try to play God, or you may end up guilty of the loss of another ship."

The door opened, brisk steps came in, a voice said, "All right, time's up! Young man, pay your respects and leave!"

The old man said calmly, "That'll do, Miss Klavermans. I'll call you when I'm through."

"Oh, no, you won't!" the nurse said with determination. "It's time for our vital signs. Hop, hop! Pop into bed. Time's up!"

Suddenly, frighteningly, he lost his temper. "You stupid female!" he yelled at the top of his voice, and it was so strong that I involuntarily backed away. "Get the hell out of here! Who do you think you are?! Bugger off!"

She gaped at him, mouth open, as if she had been struck

between the eyes by a snowball. She could not believe this was happening to her; she took a breath to say something: a protest, a plea, I would never know.

"GET OUT BEFORE I THROW YOU OUT!" he yelled.

"I will never come back!" she breathed, dramatically.

"Thank God for that! I am not dead yet! It is too soon for you to turn me back into a baby!"

"As you wish!" she said. "You are an evil old man."

Alarmingly, obscenely, he blew her a kiss; she fled, gasping, from the room.

When he looked at me, I saw to my amazement that he was totally unruffled. His eyes were clear and blue; his voice calm and controlled. It seemed as if his illness, the wheelchair, the bed, the bedpan, were all a fake, part of a plot by a tyrant to trick his opposition into showing their hand.

"Don't worry," he said. "We have this conversation every night. If we did not, I would be breast-fed by now. When are you going to pick up that Japanese?"

I don't know what made me say it; maybe it was the violence he had suddenly unleashed in the atmosphere; despite his mischievousness, it had not been a pretty scene. "I'm sorry, sir," I said, "but I think I'm through sailing tugboats."

He looked at me coldly; for the first time, I sensed in him a tremendous hostility. "So you're going over to the Merchant Marine, are you?" he asked.

It should have been an important moment. For years, I had indulged in daydreams of just this situation: standing opposite the slaveholder, telling him I was leaving for the Merchant Marine. It seemed a pity to now waste so many dreams, so many hours of pacing on the bridge underneath the stars, rehearsing dialogue. "No, sir," I said with a feeling of farewell, "I mean I am through sailing ships, at least for the duration."

His face relaxed, but the hostility in his eyes remained. "Why?" he asked.

I hesitated. I had to tell someone, get it off my chest; but he seemed the last person I should choose. He would debunk all those emotional thoughts about good and evil, peace and compassion, deride my sense of revelation during those moments in the lifeboat, sneer at my preposterous notion of working as a medic. Even so, I blurted out, "It's the violence, the killing, the destruction. . . . I can't go along with it any more."

"And what do you suggest you do about it?"

"I thought of applying for a post as medic, sir."

I stood prepared for the onslaught; but it never came. His voice, when he spoke, was gentle; the hostility had gone from his eyes. "How did this come about?" he asked.

And then I told him. I told him all the things he had already glimpsed behind the formal words of the report— about Gunner Duncan and the shoe and the boy Tyler and the wounded kitten, about Sparks and the helmsman and the sinking of the bosun's lifeboat, about the burial and Heini and what I had felt when the plane came for us. I told him everything I had wanted to tell Miss Crumb, and I didn't try to be stoic or British about it; I just told him, all of it, and what it had done to me.

When I was through, he looked away at the sunset. The silence suddenly lay heavy in the room. In the distance, across the river, a locomotive whistled; a bird answered nearby. It seemed for a moment as if it were peacetime; but his face, as he sat looking into the distance, was grim and drawn with grief, a face of war. Then he said, "No one who hasn't gone through it himself knows what it means to lose your ship. You are young, for you there will be other ships. It's not the first one that seals your destiny, it's the last." He suddenly seemed very tired; I had not been aware of how deeply my story had affected him. He no longer looked like a young actor playing an old man. "You had better go and call that nurse," he said.

As I went to the door he added, "There is a French proverb, *Où Dieu vous a sêmé il faut savoir fleurir.* You won't solve anything by running away. God has sown you on the bridge of a tugboat, and that's where you'll have to flower, for better or for worse." He lifted a frail veined hand and smiled, sardonically it seemed. "Good luck," he said. It was like Mashpee's last signal.

5

The nurse was waiting outside; when she saw me, she marched in before I could tell her anything, once more determined and in command.

"Is he all right?" asked Mr. Kwel Junior, who had been waiting with her on the landing.

"I don't know," I answered. "I think he looks very ill."

"I'll be right with you." He went in.

When he came out, a short while later, he said nothing, and I could read nothing in his gray, closed, bank-manager's face.

We drove back to London through the night, in silence. As we waited for the red slit of a blacked-out traffic light to change to green at some highway crossing, he said, "By the way, these came for you some time ago. I forgot about them yesterday; I'm sorry. I hope they are not urgent." He handed me two letters. "Here," he said. "Use the map light," and he switched on a feeble little lamp underneath the dashboard.

One was an official letter, *On His Majesty's Service, Secret and Urgent;* the other was addressed to *Commanding Officer, Dutch tugboat* ISABEL KWEL, *Netherlands Merchant Marine, London, England,* with the words *Private and Personal,* underscored three times. It came from Canada.

Though it bore no sender's name or address, I realized at once who had written it. I opened it with a sudden sense of finality, knowing, all at once, that she loved me, that she could forget me as little as I could forget her, that she could not live without me. As I pulled the letter out of the envelope, I saw it was very short; it had no beginning.

I need not tell you that we must never see each other again. I cannot find the words to express how I feel, so I won't try; the only thing I can say is that I want to forget what happened as quickly and as thoroughly as I can. I am writing to you only because there is something you must promise me. Without it, I won't know what to do or where to turn. Promise me, on your word of honor as an officer, that you will never tell anyone how he died; for now I have only one thing left to live for: that his son may grow up in the belief that his father was a Hero. It was not signed, and dated September first, two days after our encounter.

It was a chilling letter that left the vulnerable, helpless part of me numb with hurt. The other part, the part that had matured during those moments in the lifeboat, knew at once what I should do. This was a personal challenge; this was my own individual confrontation with the birth of a lie that would grow and take root in a growing mind as it had taken root in Tyler's, until, twenty years from now, another decent, innocent young man would set out to fight a war to save the world. I ought to drop everything now and go to see her, stop her from doing this awful, obscene thing to her husband's memory by forcing her to see the truth about him; I should not rest until I had convinced her that he had indeed been a hero, but not, as she intimated, by conforming to the deadly pattern of self-righteousness and violence, but by breaking the spell of the age-old lie that had sent him marching into war. I knew it was for that truth that he had given his life; I knew also that it was now up to me and me alone to give sense to his seemingly senseless death, to interpret it to his son so that he would see the greatness of it and live to match that greatness for the rest of his days.

But as I slowly folded the letter, and put it back into its envelope, common sense prevailed. How could I possibly go to see her? I wasn't my own master, they would never let me; and even if I were to get the chance, could I be sure of my motives? Could I ever be certain that I had set out to give a point to a dead man's life, rather than to court his widow? After a while, the ramifications became so intricate and so confused that I fled by opening the second letter.

It was from H.M.S. *Spartacus*, and referred to their previous communication of August 14, 1942, concerning a visual signal I had exchanged with the Commanding Officer of the Escort at Lat. 62° 8′ N. and Long. 9° 7′ E. (approximate) which had been reported to read: MASTER ISAB TO COMESCORT GO TO HELL SIGNED HARINXMA END. The matter was now of the utmost importance and urgency, and they once again requested my comment, in quadruplicate, by return.

"Nothing serious, I hope?" Mr. Kwel asked.

"No, sir," I said.

But as I folded *Spartacus*' letter and put it in my pocket together with hers, the memory of *Intrepid*'s end, revived with utter poignancy by the very idiocy of that letter, seemed to decide something for me.

I could not leave the sea, however much I might want to. I would have to flower where God had sown me, for better or for worse, because in some mysterious way that I could only vaguely sense, my sailing on would be Mashpee's immortality, and that of the others I had known, lost on the Murmansk run.

CHAPTER TWELVE

> *From the desk of*
> *Commodore M. Harinxma,*
> *o/b Flagship* ARNOLD KWEL,
> *At Sea, 6th July 1966*

My dear Martinus,

I don't know when you are likely to read all this, but I have just finished the accompanying hefty volume and I feel the need to talk to you.

I started to write weeks ago, just after we left the English Channel, and I have been at it daily ever since. As a Commodore (a real one this time), one has time for such luxuries, while future Commodores, more or less graciously according to their dispositions, keep the watches and sail the ship.

The writing itself was quite an experience; I had no idea, when I started, that it would turn into a letter to my own son. As you may remember, I set out to write to Richard B. Tyler, Jr., in response to his request "to fill in the blanks" in the story of his father, as told to him by his mother. It was not until I got to the episode involving her and me, in Halifax, that I realized I could not possibly tell him the truth.

Although, according to his letter, Mary remarried shortly thereafter (it must have been at about the same time I met your mother) and although we all, obviously, have led happy, well-adjusted lives since, I could not tell him the truth about his father without telling him the truth about his mother and myself, and this would have meant causing them both unnecessary anguish.

It was only at this point that I realized my letter had never really been directed at him, but at you. I could have known this earlier, for what decided me to write it at all was not so much his request as the conversation you and I had after I received his letter. Maybe you have forgotten that afternoon by now; it was the day after my return from the South American job when you and Dane came out with me in the rowboat. We were supposed to be fishing, but spent most of that afternoon discussing your future. You said you wanted to be a pilot ("No, no! Not a RIVER *pilot, a flyer!") and you asked me what I thought. Should you be trained by the Air Force or by KLM?*

I said I preferred KLM; but when you asked me why, I realized that to answer that question I would need more than an afternoon's conversation in a rowboat. To have replied "Because I don't think you should have yourself trained in the scientific application of indiscriminate slaughter and wholesale destruction, just because you'd like to fly an airplane" would have sounded pompous and high-handed. I have never preached at you, maybe out of cowardice rather than pedagogic insight. I have always considered it to be most important that you and I should have a relationship that might eventually turn into real friendship, and, in my experience, any statements or pro-

nouncements that sound as if they were handed down from Mount Olympus are meaningful only to the orator himself, as a preening of the tailfeathers. Their educational effect is nil.

Yet I felt desperately aware that the moment was a crucial one. To my mind (and, I suspect, to the mind of most men who took part in either of the two World Wars) the prevention and ultimate abolition of war is the major issue facing us. I would have failed, not as a parent but as a man, if I had meekly let you wander into an innocent-looking trap without at least speaking my piece. I know that no two men are alike, and I am well aware that you and I are very different, despite some superficial similarities in character and the set of our eyes; but I know also that you are not by nature a killer. I doubt whether anybody is; it is an acquired taste, but violence will arouse a brutish appetite that is latently present in everybody. It is, like its counterpart compassion, an elemental attribute of our humanity, with a propensity for self-escalation. I could not let you fool around with the atom bomb, so to speak, without warning you that all war games are preparations for the time when it is no longer a game, and that before you set foot on that road toward violence, you must realize that you are faced with a choice that will crucially affect not only your own life, but the lives of unknown thousands of others as well.

I do not want to make up your mind for you; I want you to be aware of the consequences of your decision, that's all. Partly through luck—mostly through luck, I'm afraid—I was able to get through the war without killing anyone. After our visit to his father, I told young Mr. Kwel that I could not undertake the assignment of collecting the Japanese tugboat in Gibraltar, or any other assignment that would put me in a position where I might be forced to use violence. It wasn't as good as renouncing war altogether and dedicating myself to the care of the sick, but it was the closest I could come to remaining true to my experience in the lifeboat. I did not have the guts or, to be honest, the true inclination to dedicate myself entirely to others; but I could not resume the killing either. The only solution seemed to be to return to the rank of relief captain and go back to running old, unarmed buckets on the Via Dolorosa of the coastal run. Mr. Kwel realized that he had the choice between having me court-martialed and put in jail for insubordination, or keeping me with the company on its old, weary and domestic medium craft. Being a realist, he chose the latter; but I don't think he ever quite grasped the reasons why I chose to be demoted and hand the Commodore's laurels to my mate. When the Japanese tugboat was overdue on her home run and ultimately reported missing, presumed lost, he must have decided that I had refused the assignment because of some supernatural premonition, for until this very day he occasionally refers to "Commodore Harinxma's proverbial second sight," usually after losing an argument with strenuous good grace.

Until the very end, the tugboats on the coastal run remained unarmed, and so—though I was shot at many times and occasionally wished I had some hardware with which to scare them off—I was never put in a position where I could kill in order not to be killed. But although I am acutely conscious of the fact that I owe my innocence to luck rather than fortitude, I would hate the idea that, by the mere circumstance of my being the father of a war pilot, I might become involved in, if not responsible for, the gruesome deaths of untold numbers of future victims of the Sport of Kings. So I cannot sit mutely by while you try on your first Air Force uniform in front of the mirror, blissfully unconscious of the fact that to volunteer for military training is to sign a pact with violence, and to hand the ultimate moral decision—to kill or not to kill— over to a faceless committee of men who, by their very training and indoctrination, consider genocide a legitimate means of settling human disputes.

Knowing all this, must you now become a conscientious objector? I cannot answer that question for you, not in the abstract. Is a man who witnesses a lunatic firing a machine gun into a crowded street responding to the highest demand of his humanity if he confines himself to looking after the victims, or must he help overpower the lunatic, thus meeting violence with violence, and hope that the end will hallow the means? I know that I myself would not; but I am not sure if my answer is morally more valid than its alternative. Honorable men have decided upon the second course, and I would be a pompous fool if I were to condemn them for a decision which must have been the outcome of much honest soul-searching on their part. All I can and may do is make you aware of the choice; this is why I have told you my story. After reading it, I think you'll be hard put to romanticize war as being virile or heroic, or even human.

Maybe it is too late; maybe I have remained silent for too long. In my eagerness to return to normal life, to put the nightmare behind me, I succumbed to the temptation of forgetfulness. After the war, the world seemed so full of hope and promise. There was so much to be done, so much to be repaired and resurrected, and I became engrossed, passionately, in works of peace. To reminisce about the war always made me feel self-conscious and demonstrative; most veterans feel that way. We frown upon those who arouse the memories we have been at such pains to banish; we congratulate ourselves on our reticence and call it modesty.

Is it? Or did we, unwittingly, allow the seed of the next World War to sprout and take root by trying to forget, and thus failing to warn?

I don't know, I honestly don't know. I keep telling myself, "Remember all the war novels, all the pamphlets, the speeches, the rallies, the anti-war demonstrations after the last one—what difference did they make?" But there is still the suspicion that, in some awful, irrevocable way, I am responsible for your abysmal ignorance of the true, horrendous face of war, your lethal innocence, that may result in screaming women fleeing trailing flames, doused with the improved napalm, "an inflammable jelly that will adhere more thoroughly to the flesh." And why? Because you want to keep the world free from communism, fascism, creeping socialism, imperialism? No: because you were lured into it by an adolescent yearning for comradeship, virility, feminine adoration. Because I wasted time, waiting for you to grow into an adult who would be a friend, and by my very silence, combined with the constant absence of the sailor, handed you over to the enemy, ignorance. It is all very well to say that youth will learn only from example —these are times when a man has to speak, or forever hold his peace.

And so I sit here, in my Commodore's cabin on the flagship of the oceangoing tugboat fleet, once again grown into Holland's Glory, and I am faced with the old familiar question that confronted me at other momentous turning-points in my life: in how far is a man responsible for another man's fate? It confronted me in the case of Sophie, it confronted me in the case of Tyler, and now it confronts me in you. In the case of Sophie, there was no answer, only a "*non sequitur.*" I lived throughout the war in the conviction that she was dead; after Holland was liberated I found she was not only still alive, but married to a young man with whom she had spent the war years in hiding. I was acutely aware that her survival did by no means absolve me; all she had been, all we had been, was—again—lucky.

To me, dear Martinus, the deepest mystery in life, maybe aptly so for a man who has so much to be thankful for, is the role sheer luck plays in human destiny. For it is all very well to say "*Où Dieu vous a sêmé, il faut savoir fleurir,*" but how about Sparks, Tyler, Mashpee, gunner Duncan, the corporal—all those whose young flowers were strewn about the icy wastes of the Arctic Ocean, in the wake of the convoys to Murmansk?

If I could give you the answer to that, son, I would feel that I had left you something of real value. But I'm afraid that all I have to leave you is the question.

And now I really must start thinking about what to write to young Tyler.

Affectionately,
Father

Jan de Hartog

Jan de Hartog was born in Haarlem, Holland, in 1914, and ran off to sea at an early age. In 1940, just after the Germans occupied Holland, his novel HOLLAND'S GLORY *was published, a rollicking story of the Dutch oceangoing tugboats on which he had served. Although it mentioned neither the war nor the Germans, it became a symbol of Dutch defiance and was banned by the Nazis, but not until 300,000 copies had been sold. The author escaped to England, by "the long trail": via Belgium, France and Spain, a journey of six months during which he was imprisoned several times, crashed with a plane and was wounded as he crossed the Spanish border.*

Since then Mr. de Hartog has sailed many miles and has written a goodly number of books. THE LOST SEA, THE DISTANT SHORE *and* A SAILOR'S LIFE *were recently collected under the title* THE CALL OF THE SEA, *and the others are* THE LITTLE ARK, THE SPIRAL ROAD, THE INSPECTOR, WATERS OF THE NEW WORLD, THE ARTIST *and* THE HOSPITAL. THE HOSPITAL *told the true story of a difficult but ultimately successful attempt by the author and a small group of fellow Quakers to change conditions of squalor and neglect in a large American charity hospital.*

Mr. de Hartog's name has also become a familiar one through the great popularity of his plays THE FOURPOSTER *and* SKIPPER NEXT TO GOD. *Three of his novels have also been made into films:* THE DISTANT SHORE *as* THE KEY, THE INSPECTOR *as* LISA, *and* THE SPIRAL ROAD.

Inset map (top left):

MILES
0   100

SHETLAND IS.

ORKNEY IS.

Scapa Flow · KIRKWALL
→ Pentland Firth
→ John o'Groats

HEBRIDES

The Minches

NORTH SEA

SCOTLAND

Gigha Pass

GREENOCK

EDINBURGH

GLASGOW
Firth of Clyde

NEWCASTLE
SOUTH SHIELDS

NORTH CHANNEL
Isle of Man

IRELAND

IRISH SEA

HOLYHEAD

LIVERPOOL

DEN HELDER

AMSTERDAM
NETH.

ENGLAND

HARWICH

LONDON
TILBURY

BELG.

BRISTOL

SOUTHAMPTON
PLYMOUTH

CALAIS

BRUSSELS

English Channel

FRANCE

GUY FLEMING

Main map:

15° W

GREENLAND

JAN MAYEN I.

GREENLAND

DAVIS STRAIT

ARCTIC CIRCLE

DENMARK STRAIT

ISABEL KWEL, CON

C. Langanes
Seydisfjördur

Reykjavik

C. Reykjanes

ICELAND

THE FAEROES

SCAPA FLOW

Limit of Polar Pack ice drift

CONVOY ROUTE, North America to Murmansk

ISABEL KWEL, CONVOY I, RETURN

SCOTLAND

CANADA

IRELAND

ISABEL KWEL, CONVOY NAT 127 EB

GREAT BRITAIN

Long

NEWFOUNDLAND

ENGLISH CH

St. John's

ATLANTIC OCEAN

Halifax, NOVA SCOTIA

SPA